In Her Name
Legend Of The Sword

By
Michael R. Hicks

This is a work of fiction. All of the characters and events portrayed in this novel are products of the author's imagination or are used fictitiously.

IN HER NAME: LEGEND OF THE SWORD
Copyright © 2012 by Imperial Guard Publishing, LLC
ISBN: 978-0984673025

*For all those who stood up for the cause of freedom
during the long, uncertain years of the Cold War..*

FOREWORD

Legend Of The Sword was a much more difficult beast to write than was *First Contact*. Much of the problem I faced when trying to begin the story was that I hadn't the faintest clue of where it was going to go.

As you may know, I don't write from an outline. I can't, or the story comes out like it was extruded from a sausage grinder. Instead, I get flashes in my mind, sort of like snapshots of a movie screen, and then my fingers start to type and words magically appear on the screen. I don't mean to sound silly or mystical about it, but that's really what happens. I don't really think when I write; my brain is just along for the ride, a spectator to the unfolding events.

When I started *Legend*, there were only two things that I knew I wanted to do. I wanted to tell you more about Tesh-Dar, from whom the book gets its title, and I wanted to tell you something about this odd place called Saint Petersburg, which was mentioned in First Contact as the scene of a nasty little war among humankind that had taken place two decades before.

I knew nothing about the planet or its people when I started to write (my fingers keep the details of the story secret), but it unexpectedly evolved into a bit of a Cold War drama, into which the Kreelans plunged with their usual ferocity. I grew up during the Brezhnev years, and I'm sure that helped pull the story in that direction. But I think it's also a cautionary tale that tyranny isn't necessarily just skin deep, and that history can indeed repeat itself if we allow it to happen...

Acknowledgements

Compared to *In Her Name: First Contact*, which seemed to effortlessly take form, it took quite a while for me to come to grips with *Legend Of The Sword*. It was frustrating at times, and I first would like to thank my readers for their support and encouragement when I felt like I was banging my head against the wall trying to get the story off the ground ("Ow! That hurts!").

I also want to thank my editing team, Mindy Schwartz and Stephanie Hansen. They continue to help my writing improve, which – I hope – continues to make a better reading experience for you. It's just hard to believe that such intelligent people would willingly subject themselves to editing the pitiful text of my initial drafts for nothing more than a signed copy of the book, a T-shirt, and some chocolate. When I finally land a big movie deal, I promise you can have all the chocolate you want!

I also want to thank a group of people who seem to be rapidly fading from memory in the post-9/11 world, and in whose honor this book is dedicated: the men and women who fought the Cold War, both in and out of uniform. In particular, I'd like to thank an old friend, Mark Scott, and the others with whom I had the incredibly good fortune to serve in the years before the Wall came down. It was truly the best of times and the worst of times, and I'm proud to have been a part of it.

Last, but certainly not least, is my family: Jan, Ben, Samuel, and of course, Mom and Dad. I would have never made it anywhere without you!

ONE

Tesh-Dar, high warrior priestess of the Desh-Ka, strode quietly along the paths of the Imperial Garden. Protected by a great crystalline dome that reached far into the airless sky of the Empress Moon, the stones that made up the ages-old walkways had come from every planet touched by the Empire. The paths wove their way in a carefully designed pattern for leagues: had Tesh-Dar been of a mind and had the luxury of time, she could have wandered in contemplative peace for an entire cycle and still not fully explored it all. Cut from lifeless rocks adrift in deep space to planets teeming with the fruits of galactic evolution, each stone was a testament to the glory of the Empire and the power of the Empress. Rutted sandstone to crystalline matrix, each told part of the Empire's long and glorious history.

In Tesh-Dar's mind, each step also brought her people closer to their End of Days.

Like the stones, the flora of the Garden was made up of every species of plant that flowered from across the Empire. From gigantic trees that reached up to the top of the great dome to tiny algae, all were preserved for the pleasure and the glory of the Empress. Even species that were incompatible with the atmosphere natural to Her Children were here, protected by special energy bubbles that preserved them in their native atmosphere and soil, carefully tended by the army of clawless ones whose lives were devoted to this task.

Many of the stones she trod upon were from worlds that had been one-time enemies of the Empire, including the dozen or so species Her Children had fought in past ages since the *Kreela* had attained the stars. Now the stones and flora the gardeners tended here were all that was left of them. Some of those ancient civilizations had fought to the last against the swords of Her Children, and were now remembered with honored reverence. Others, broken and beaten, consigning themselves to defeat, had been obliterated by the will of the Empress, their worlds left as nothing more than molten slag, barren of all life. The last such war had ended thousands of generations before Tesh-Dar was born, and some living now thought the records of them in the Books of Time were only legend. Tesh-Dar, greatest of the living warrior priestesses and elder blood sister to She Who Reigns, knew better. There was much in the Books of Time that she fervently wished was nothing more than legend, but wishing did not make it so.

She strolled to a part of the path that was newly added, made up of stones from the planet the humans had called Keran. The rocks and the flora from that world were no more or less remarkable than the other specimens in the Garden, save that they had been taken in a war whose birth she had witnessed, a war in which she would likely die. Now Keran, too, was part of the Empire. The many humans who had lived there, and many who had come from other worlds to aid them, had died at the hands of Tesh-Dar's warriors, and the builder caste had since reshaped the planet in a way more pleasing to Her Children. The reshaping had been done more out of habit than out of need: the Empire had enough worlds on which to live, for as long as her race had left.

Tesh-Dar paused as she stood upon these tokens of Keran in her sandaled feet. The humans had impressed the great priestess: even at the last – exhausted, desperate, and afraid – they had resisted. And those who had come from across the stars to help them, sailing in primitive vessels and fighting with weapons the Empire had retired tens of thousands of cycles before, had fought tenaciously for a world that was not their own. The Empress, too, had been greatly pleased. Yet it did nothing to ease the worry in Tesh-Dar's heart. As the highest-ranking warrior of her entire race, standing only two steps from the throne, Tesh-Dar bore the greatest responsibility for helping to preserve her people and carry out the will of the Empress. But their greatest enemy was not the humans. It was time.

"Why is your heart troubled so, priestess of the Desh-Ka?" the Empress said quietly from behind her.

Tesh-Dar turned and knelt before her sovereign. She had sensed the Empress approaching, of course. While they were sisters born of the same womb, although many cycles apart, She Who Reigned was Mother to them all. United by the ethereal force that was the Bloodsong, the members of their species were both individuals and part of a greater spiritual whole, of which She was the heart. Their purpose for existence was driven by the will of the living Empress, who contained the souls of every Empress who had lived since the founding of the Empire a hundred thousand cycles before. Her body held all of their souls, save one: the First Empress, the most powerful of all, and the one they sought for their very salvation.

"My Empress," Tesh-Dar said reverently as she saluted, bringing her left fist in its armored gauntlet against her right breast, the smooth black metal of her armor ringing in the quiet of the Garden. She had been in the presence of the Empress many times over her long life, but each time was as the very first. She felt a surge of primal power, as if she were standing close to a spiritual flame, which, in a sense, she was. "The humans have given us hope," she said, "yet I fear that we will not find what we must in the time we have left."

"Walk with me, daughter," said the Empress, holding out her arm. Tesh-Dar gently took it, careful not to mar her sovereign's flawless blue skin with her long black talons, and they walked slowly together along this section of the path that was now a remembrance of their first conquest among the humans.

The two were a study in contrasts. While Tesh-Dar had the smooth cobalt blue skin and felinoid eyes shared by all of her race. she stood more than a head taller than most warriors and was wrapped in powerful muscle that made her the most powerful of her species, equal in raw strength to half a dozen warriors. She was clad in traditional ceremonial armor that was as black as night and yet shone like a mirror, with the rune of her order, the Desh-Ka, emblazoned in cyan on the breastplate. Her hair, black as was the norm for her people, hung in elegant braids, so long now that they were carefully looped around her upper arms. That was the only way any of Her Children wore their hair, for it was more than simply a legacy from some long-forgotten biological ancestor who needed it for warmth and to protect the skin: their hair was the physical manifestation of a complex spiritual bond with the Empress. At her neck she wore the ebony Collar of Honor, a band of living metal that all of Her Children came to wear in their youth, when they were ready to accept the Way. Every child wore at least five pendants of precious metal or gemstones that proclaimed their given name. As the child matured, more pendants were added to display her deeds and accomplishments in glorifying the Empress. Tesh-Dar wore more than any other of her kind save one, with rows of pendants flowing across the upper half of her chest. As with all the high priestesses of the warrior orders that served the Empress, she also wore a special symbol at the front of her collar: an oval of glittering metal in which had been carved the rune of the Desh-Ka, echoing the larger image that blazed from her breastplate.

By comparison, the Empress was was typical in size for a Kreelan female. Her dress was as simple as Her spirit was complex: much like the healer caste, all She wore was a simple white robe with no adornments. Around Her neck, unlike the black collar worn by the others of Her race, was a simple gold colored band band. It, too, was living metal, far more resilient than gold, and was the only surviving relic of the First Empress, their only physical link to Her. Passed from Empress to Empress upon each new Ascension, if there was anything that embodied the spirit of the Empire, it would be this simple object.

The most striking feature of the Empress was that her hair, braided but not as long as Tesh-Dar's, was pure white. It was not a random anomaly or an indicator of age: every Empress since the First Empress, Keel-Tath, had been born with white hair. It was part of their ancestral bloodline from those days of legend. Once every great cycle, roughly seven human years, a female warrior child was born with white hair and ebony talons. Not all would ascend to the throne, but the collar of the Empress could only be worn by a warrior who had those two traits. For the white hair proclaimed them as direct descendants of Keel-Tath, and the ebony talons signified that they were fertile.

"I share your fears," the Empress said simply, as they continued walking along the path. There were no lies told in the Empire, no exaggerations or deceit to misdirect or conceal, no factions battling for control. These things had been left behind long, long ago, cut away from their civilization by the wisdom and sword of the First Empress. "Long have we searched for the One who shall fulfill the ancient prophesies, just as we have searched for the tomb of the First Empress among thousands of stars in the galaxy. Much of interest have we found, but not that which we so desperately need."

The Empress's words chilled Tesh-Dar. She did not need to hear them to know they were true, but it was one thing to believe such a thing on one's own, and quite another to hear them from Her lips so plainly spoken.

"There is no hope, then?" Tesh-Dar asked quietly, the hand not holding the arm of the Empress clenching so hard that her talons pierced the armored gauntlet she wore, and the skin beneath. She did not notice any pain.

Stopping in the middle of the path, the Empress turned to her, lifting up Her hand to caress Tesh-Dar's face. "Do not despair so, Legend of the Sword," She said, using the nickname She had given Tesh-Dar long ago, when she had been a child and under Tesh-Dar's tutelage at the priestess's *kazha*, or school of the Way. It was not merely a token of affection, for Tesh-Dar was the greatest swordmistress the Empire had ever known in all its history. Even before she became the last high priestess of the Desh-Ka and inherited her current physical form and the powers that were the legacy of that ancient sect, she had had no rival in the arena. Among Her Children, Tesh-Dar was indeed a living legend.

She gave the Empress a shy smile, something few of the peers had ever seen, her ivory fangs momentarily revealed through parted dark red lips. While her nickname was well-known throughout the Empire, none of the peers - save one - had ever addressed her as "Legend of the Sword."

"Even with all the powers at My command," the Empress went on, "I cannot see the river of time that flows into the future. Our own time among the stars grows short, yes. Yet we have been blessed with an enemy that may provide us the first key to the prophecies: one born not of our blood, yet whose blood sings."

"And the tomb of the First Empress?" Tesh-Dar asked. The prophecies foretold that their race could only be redeemed, the ancient blood curse undone, if Keel-Tath's soul returned to take its place among the thousands of other souls inhabiting She Who Reigned. The curse left by Keel-Tath had doomed their race to eventual extinction, condemning the clawless ones and the warriors with black talons to mate every great cycle or die. Over time, the Empire's population had become unbalanced, with more males and sterile females being born. If the trend continued, in only a few more generations their species would no longer be able to procreate. "How are we ever to find it?"

"That, My priestess," the Empress said, turning to resume their walk along the path, "even the prophecies do not reveal. Yet, I believe that if we find the One, we are also destined to find Her tomb. The fates of the two are intertwined, inseparable. I must believe that the humans are the key."

"You believe that the One is among them?"

"We must hope, Tesh-Dar," the Empress said heavily. "For if not..." She did not have to finish the sentence. If the One was not found among the humans, the *Kreela* would join the races they had destroyed over the ages in dark oblivion. The chances of them finding another sentient race in what time remained to them was infinitesimal. "The One may not yet have been born," She went on. "We shall give the humans as much time as we may to find him."

Him, Tesh-Dar thought. She found it disquieting that the prophecies foretold that their race would be redeemed by a male. That thought led to another as they strolled along, and Tesh-Dar said, "Thy daughter, Li'ara-Zhurah, is to have her first mating. I have tended to her spirit, yet she remains deeply disturbed over what happened to her at Keran." She paused. "I fear her mating will be difficult."

The Empress looked up at the Homeworld, shining full above the great crystalline dome of the Garden, but her mind's eye was on a far away nursery world where Li'ara-Zhurah waited for her mating time. The Empress knew well of what Tesh-Dar spoke, for while She could sense the feelings of all Her Children through the Bloodsong, She was even more attuned to those born from Her own body, as was Li'ara-Zhurah. From when their spirit first cried out in the womb to beyond death in the Afterlife, She could sense the feelings of all. Their joy, their pride. Their fear, their pain. Their sorrow, their anguish.

"I have no doubt it will be difficult," She whispered. "It always is."

***

Many light years away, Li'ara-Zhurah lay in her temporary quarters on one of the Empire's many nursery worlds. To such worlds were the fertile warriors and clawless ones taken to mate and give birth once every great cycle. For if they did not, they would die in horrible agony that even the healers could not avert.

Any other time she would have found a room such as this a place of unaccustomed comfort. It was not large, but it was certainly more expansive than a warrior's typically spartan quarters on a warship or in one of the many *kazhas*. It was well appointed with a thick pallet of soft skins for a bed, and a low table where she and any companions - should she have them - could kneel as was customary to eat and drink. A window of intricately stained transparency, made of material thinner than a hair's breadth, yet strong as steel, was set into the smooth granite walls, flooding the room with serene light from the artificial sun that warmed this planet.

A construct of the builders, the caste responsible for creating anything the Empress called for, this world had been created from an airless rock drifting in deep space, far from any star. The planet was surrounded by a vast cloud of particles, a derivative of the matrix material that the builders used to create whatever the Empress required. The cloud was the planet's primary defense and also what gave it the necessary light and heat to support life, in measure that was identical to the star of the Homeworld. Although every nursery world was zealously guarded by warships of the Imperial Fleet, should one of the nurseries be threatened, the thick but seemingly insubstantial cloud of wispy white matrix material would form into a shell that was impenetrable by anything short of the energies released by a star gone nova. The Empire's mothers and newborns, valued beyond all measure, would not easily fall prey to an enemy.

Even thought this place was warm and comfortable, her body shook from alternating hot and cold flashes. It had already been her time before the attack on the human world, Keran, but she had refused to go to the nursery world before the campaign had ended. She had fought too many challenges for the right to be there, and was willing to risk death from her rebellious body rather than give up her right to be among the first to do battle with the humans.

She had been wounded, her back burned during an attack on a human ship and her side pierced by shrapnel from an exploding human assault boat, but her true scars were inside, upon her soul. Tesh-Dar had been able to excise much of the anguish and confusion Li'ara-Zhurah had felt in the aftermath of the battle. Yet some wounds still lay open, beyond the reach even of the great priestess and, Li'ara-Zhurah feared, even the Empress herself.

The torment of her body from the growing imbalance in her reproductive hormones, however, was as nothing next to the painful fear of the mating ritual. It was not fear of physical pain, but fear of emotional emptiness. Fear arising from the certain knowledge that the creature she was soon to be joined with, one of the males of her species, was barely self-aware. As part of the curse that was the legacy of the First Empress, the males had been reduced to mindless breeding machines that only functioned a single time before dying in agony.

It had not always been so, Li'ara-Zhurah knew, for the Books of Time spoke of the ages before the Curse, when the males were proud warriors and artisans who lived alongside the females. There had once been a time when they mated with physical love, bonded for life as *tresh* who lived as two individuals, yet were one. In the time since the Curse, her people bonded together in pairs, female to female, a bond that was only broken by death. They often might serve the Empress far apart, but their spirits were always entwined in the Bloodsong. And when one's *tresh* died, it was a soul-wrenching experience. Li'ara-Zhurah's *tresh* had died some years ago, and her soul had never entirely recovered. Even now, she would awaken at night with her *tresh's* name on her lips. She could feel a glimmer of her *tresh's* spirit from the Afterlife, but that was all, and it was not enough to ease the pain.

The room she occupied now had two doors: one that led to the corridor outside and the rest of the complex, and one through which the male would be brought when it was time. She nervously glanced from one door to the other, part of her wanting to get on with the ordeal, while the rest of her shamefully wished she could escape.

A gentle knock at the smaller door startled her, and she gasped in fright.

"Come," she called through the haze of fear that clouded her senses, berating herself for being unable to control her emotions. *You have fought in a true battle*, she told herself, *and proved yourself worthy. Be not afraid!*

Telling herself to not be afraid was one thing, but didn't stop the fear from clutching her heart in a tight and icy grip.

A pair of healers entered, closing the door softly behind them. One was senior, as indicated by the many pendants hanging from her collar, and the other was junior. Like all of their caste, they could heal nearly any injury or disease. The specialty of these healers, however, was in understanding what Li'ara-Zhurah was feeling now and helping her cope with what was to come.

They knelt beside her on the soft skins, and the elder healer opened her arms to Li'ara-Zhurah, offering to hold and comfort her.

With a whimper of despair, Li'ara-Zhurah threw herself into the healer's arms, burying her face in the elder's shoulder. The other healer, the apprentice, wrapped her arms around Li'ara-Zhurah, adding her warmth and empathy, helping to soothe the frightened young warrior through the Bloodsong. Mourning marks, a display of inner pain, turned Li'ara-Zhurah's skin black below her eyes, as she moaned and shivered in the arms of the healers.

"Be still, child," the elder healer whispered as she gently rocked Li'ara-Zhurah. She could feel the young warrior's torment in the Bloodsong, sharp and bitter. "Be not ashamed. What you feel now is what each of us feels the first time. Even the Empress Herself."

Li'ara-Zhurah's only response was to tighten her grip on the elder healer. She did not realize it, but her claws had drawn blood from the healer's sides, staining the pure white robes with streaks of bright crimson.

The healer was accustomed to such pain and ignored it. Her attention was focused solely on her young ward. "When you are ready, we will prepare you," she whispered as she gently stroked Li'ara-Zhurah's hair. "It will be difficult, child, but will not last long. You shall endure."

I do not wish to endure, Li'ara-Zhurah railed silently. *I do not wish for any of this!*

But there was no use putting off the inevitable. She was a warrior who had faced the fires of battle against worthy foes and survived. She could not allow herself to succumb to cowardice and dishonor now.

"Let it be done," she rasped, reluctantly pushing herself from the healer's embrace.

The healers helped her to her feet, then carefully undressed her, peeling away the black undergarment that was worn beneath armor, for the warriors, and the robes of the clawless ones like the healers. Then they removed her sandals. She then stood shivering, wearing nothing but her collar.

"Here, child," the elder healer said, pointing to the center of the bed of skins.

Li'ara-Zhurah knelt down as she was shown, then leaned forward on all fours, placing her elbows on the skins, her head close to the edge near the wall. Before her were a set of soft leather cuffs bound by slender but unbreakable cables that were attached to the floor. Her stomach turned at the sight, for they reminded her of the shackles of the *Kalai-Il*, the place of punishment that was at the center of every *kazha* throughout the Empire. Without thinking, she pushed herself away, back up to her knees.

"It is so you do not accidentally injure the male," the apprentice healer, even younger than Li'ara-Zhurah, explained as she and the elder healer gently pushed her back down onto the skins. "You will...not be yourself for a time."

"It is for the best, child," the elder healer said as she fastened the cuffs around Li'ara-Zhurah's wrists, making sure they were fixed firmly but not overtight. "And I will tell you this, even though I know you will ignore my words: it is best not to look at the male when we lead him in. They, too, are Children of the Empress, but they are different than us in more than just gender."

Li'ara-Zhurah had heard the stories, of course, but she had never seen a male of her race. They were kept only on the nursery worlds such as this, never to be seen elsewhere in the Empire. She knew the healer's words were well-intended, but they left her even more frightened. She shivered uncontrollably.

"Imagine how you would like him to appear," the junior healer advised. "And do not fight against what must be. Your body will understand what to do. Close away your mind and let your body take control."

"Do you understand, child?" the elder healer asked.

"Yes," Li'ara-Zhurah said through gritted teeth. Her hands, bound now by the cuffs, fiercely gripped the skins of the bed, her talons cutting all the way through to scrape against the unyielding stone beneath.

"We shall return momentarily," the junior healer told her before the two of them left through the door through which they had entered.

Li'ara-Zhurah squeezed her eyes shut, burying her face in the warm skins, trying desperately to gain control of her fears. Her breath was coming quickly, too quickly, as if she were still running after the great human war machine that had become her obsession during the battle on Keran.

She heard a sound at the door. Unable to help herself and just as the healer had known would happen, she turned to look. There, standing between the two healers, was a male. It - *he* - was clearly young, judging from the length of his braided hair, for there was no use for males other than breeding, and they were bred as soon as they were of age. And once they bred, they died. She had seen images of the male warriors during the time of the First Empress, from ages-old legend, but aside from the blue skin and black hair typical of her race, there was little in this creature that she could recognize from those ancient scenes. He only stood as tall as the healers' shoulders, was dreadfully thin, and had a body that clearly had never endured the physical rigors of the *kazha*. Standing there without clothes, his maleness was alien to her, for she had never seen such, even in the ancient images.

The real shock was his face and head. While his eyes were bright and looked normal, they were set in a face that betrayed no sign of intelligence, with a forehead that sloped steeply back, part of a small skull that housed an undersized brain. From his lips began a high keening sound, for his body understood what his tiny brain did not: his purpose for existence was now before him.

Then she noticed his hands: the talons had been clipped from his fingertips, no doubt to keep him from injuring her in his witless passion.

She turned away in revulsion, fighting to keep hold of her sanity as the male eagerly moved toward her. The apprentice healer held Li'ara-Zhurah's shoulders, trying as best she could to comfort her, while the senior healer guided the male's efforts.

Li'ara-Zhurah's thoughts faded to blackness as her body responded to the male's pheromones. She cried out at the momentary pain, whimpering in her heart for the love of her Empress, and begging the First Empress - wherever She was - to return and lift this curse from them all.

What came after was blessed darkness.

***

Tesh-Dar stood in her quarters, part of the complex of buildings that made up the *kazha* of which she was headmistress. Having returned to the Homeworld from her audience with the Empress on the Empress Moon, her thoughts remained fixed on Li'ara-Zhurah. She could clearly hear the melody of the young warrior's Bloodsong that carried her fear and pain, and she ground her teeth at the thought that she was powerless to aid her. Tesh-Dar did not even truly understand what the young warrior was going through, for she herself had never mated. Being born sterile was both a blessing and a curse: she was not subject to the need to mate every great cycle to continue living, but she was a bystander in the continuity of her species, standing a world apart from those who could give birth.

She allowed herself a moment of guilt, for she did not feel this way for all of her wards. She cared deeply for all of them, every warrior of every generation she had helped to train here, but for a very few she found that she cared more. Li'ara-Zhurah was among them. It had nothing to do with her being a blood daughter of the Empress, for such things as favoritism had been bred out of her race eons before when the Bloodsong took hold and one's feelings were exposed to all. That had triggered the age of Chaos, when her species was torn apart by countless wars before the First Empress and Unification.

No. She felt strongly for Li'ara-Zhurah because of who she was in her heart and spirit. A part of Tesh-Dar fervently wished that this young warrior would be the one with whom she could share her inheritance from the Desh-Ka order, who could follow in Tesh-Dar's footsteps as high priestess. For Tesh-Dar was the last of her kind: after the death of the First Empress, the warrior priestesses of the ancient orders were only permitted to select a single soul as a replacement, transferring their powers to their acolyte in a ceremony that dated back tens of thousands of cycles before the Empire was founded. If Tesh-Dar died before passing on her knowledge, the powers of the Desh-Ka, the greatest of all the warrior sects in the history of her race, would be lost forever. She was already older by fifty cycles than was normal for her kind, and old age gave little warning before death would take her. There was no gradual descent into infirmity over the course of years for the warriors, no time to make considered choices for an acolyte: when a warrior's body reached the time appointed by Fate, death came in days, weeks at most. Even the healers could not predict when it was time to pass into the Afterlife until a warrior's body began to shut down.

Dying without an heir was one of the few things Tesh-Dar had ever truly feared in her long life. But she could not choose an heir out of fear, for it was a choice she could make only once. After she surrendered her powers to her successor, there was no turning back.

"Do not let your heart be troubled so, great priestess," a voice said softly from behind her.

Tesh-Dar turned to see Pan'ne-Sharakh standing at the open door. Of the many souls Tesh-Dar had known in her life, Pan'ne-Sharakh was unique. The greatest living mistress of the armorer caste, she was among the oldest of their race, far older even than Tesh-Dar. Such were her skills that she had served as the armorer of the reigning Empress and the Empress before Her, eventually retiring from Her personal service as age took its toll. Pan'ne-Sharakh's collar was the only one in all the Empire that bore more pendants than Tesh-Dar's, with rows hanging down nearly to her waist, shimmering against the black of her robes. Tesh-Dar had known her since Tesh-Dar was a child, but much of their lives had been spent on opposite sides of the galaxy. After Tesh-Dar had taken over as headmistress at this *kazha* several dozen cycles ago, Pan'ne-Sharakh had joined her, and since then they had been nearly constant companions whose personalities complemented each other: Tesh-Dar was the embodiment of physical power and ferocity, while Pan'ne-Sharakh represented wisdom and faith.

"Forgive me, mistress," Tesh-Dar told her with a warm but troubled smile, "but much weighs upon my heart."

"As it must in this time of war," Pan'ne-Sharakh replied as she shuffled into the room. "Something to ease your troubles, great priestess," she said with an impish grin as she held up two mugs of the bitter ale that was a favorite drink among their kind.

"You will put the healers to shame," Tesh-Dar told her, gratefully accepting one of the large mugs. After she took a long swallow of the warm, bitter drink, she said, "It is not the war with the humans that troubles me, mistress. It is my own mortality. I do not fear death, but if it comes before I have found a successor..." She shrugged. "Then my life -

and that of all those who came before me - will have been without meaning, without purpose. I believe Li'ara-Zhurah is the one I would choose, but her soul is yet stricken with grief, and anguished all the more by her first mating. She is the closest I have ever found to a worthy successor, yet I am unsure." She paused, staring out the window of her quarters at the Empress Moon. "*I must* be certain. I can make no mistake." She would rather face a *genoth*, a great and deadly dragon native to the Homeworld, with her bare talons than endure the bitter emptiness of failure. She fought to keep the rising tide of trepidation in her soul from gaining a firm hold, for the strength of her Bloodsong carried her emotions to every soul in the Empire like tall waves upon the ocean, and it was irresponsible of her to let her worries so taint the great river of their race's collective soul.

"To my words, you will listen, child," Pan'ne-Sharakh said in an ancient dialect of the Old Tongue that was rarely spoken anymore. She lifted a hand to the center of Tesh-Dar's chest, gently placing her palm on the cyan rune of the Desh-Ka that blazed from her shimmering black armor, and said, "In all the cycles of my long life, never have I known a greater soul than yours, save for the Empress Herself. Upon the second step from the throne do you stand, high priestess of the Desh-Ka, but not merely for your feats of courage and glory. What has made you great is here, in your heart, a heart that is known throughout the Empire. I know not if Li'ara-Zhurah is to be your chosen one. But know it *you* will, when the time is upon you. No doubt, no uncertainty will there be. All that has come to pass in the thousands of generations since the First Empress left us has been for a purpose. The strength and powers you received after the Change, when you became high priestess of the Desh-Ka, was for a purpose." Her eyes blazed as she stared up at Tesh-Dar, radiating an inner strength that Tesh-Dar could feel pulsing through the Bloodsong. "Yes, the End of Days for the First Empire looms. *Yet even this has a purpose.*"

"But what?" Tesh-Dar asked in frustration. "The end of all that we have ever done, all that we have ever created? Leaving behind nothing but dead monuments to half a million cycles of the Way?"

"No, my child," Pan'ne-Sharakh said, a knowing look on her face, as if she had already seen the future. "The death of the First Empire shall herald the birth of the Second."

TWO

The conference room was small and sparsely furnished with a faux wood table and a dozen comfortable but well-worn chairs. Several vidcom units that had seen better days were spread out over the table top. A large wall display, the only device in the room less than ten years old, glowed with brilliant images. The carpet, once a regal blue, had long since faded, with the deep pile worn through to the nap in several places. The odors of caustic cleaners, furniture polish, and air fresheners competed with the reek of stale cigarette smoke for dominance in the room's confines. The air handlers had never worked properly, and there were no windows to air out the smell, for this room was buried a hundred meters below the surface. And it was always either too hot or too cold here.

The room's hand-me-down appearance was ignored by the men and women who sat around the table. Like the room itself, they were shabby and worn. Their eyes, however, reflected hope and determination as they focused their attention on the wall display.

"Turn it up, please," said the man seated at the head of the table. In his mid-fifties, he had the distinguished look of a scholar, with a patrician nose and high cheekbones that set off a pair of blue eyes sparkling with intelligence. His well-trimmed hair had been brown, but was now mostly gray, and had receded little over the years. He had taught English literature at a university on Earth for a number of years before he had been compelled to return to his home planet of Riga, eventually becoming President of his home world's government. It was a grandiose-sounding position that, in reality, left him little more than a figurehead, a lackey to the greater power that controlled his planet and its people. He tried to suppress the hope that the words he was about to hear from a woman he had never met would mean the release of his planet from bondage and tyranny. Although a man who was well acquainted with disappointment, he found that he was unable to hold back a tingle of excitement. His name was Valdis Roze.

A young man with deep circles under his eyes quickly manipulated the controls for the wall display, bringing up the volume, and the recording of what had taken place on Earth three weeks ago began to play. Roze had asked the young man to skip forward past the pomp and ceremony and go straight to the speech. He wanted to see, to hear, the words of the first President of the Confederation of Humanity. He knew she had intended for everyone in the human sphere to hear her words, but not all humans were allowed such privileges. Information access for the citizens of Riga was tightly controlled by their masters on the neighboring planet of Saint Petersburg.

A rarity among the great numbers of stars in the galaxy, the Saint Petersburg system had two habitable worlds. The system had been settled in the first wave of the Diaspora, the great exodus from Earth that occurred after the series of wars that had shattered governments and killed several hundred million people. The colonists had been ethnic Russians, plus many people from Russia's immediate neighbors, including the Baltic states. The colony had done well for half a century until the government, controlled by the Russian majority, turned to tyranny. Most of the non-Russian groups were eventually forced to resettle on the system's other habitable planet, which had been named Riga. But "habitable" did not necessarily mean comfortable, and Riga's bitter winters and devastating storms during the summer months made survival a challenge.

The government on Saint Petersburg retained tight control for the next couple of centuries until a visiting dignitary of the *Alliance Française*, investigating allegations of genocide on Riga, was assassinated by the Saint Petersburg secret police. That had triggered the Saint Petersburg War, with Earth and the *Alliance Française* leading a military coalition that had as its goal the liberation of Riga and the institution of a democracy there. The ruling government had not gone down easily, and it took six years of bloody fighting before they were finally defeated.

The victory left a weak Saint Petersburg government in its wake, and in the years that passed after the weary coalition forces returned home, old habits began to reemerge. Roze thought about how, over the last half dozen years, the Saint Petersburg government had quietly reasserted its hold on its former possession. Their secret police no longer murdered Rigan citizens in the middle of the night, but the oppression was no less real. While Riga still enjoyed diplomatic relations with many worlds, Saint Petersburg controlled all inter-system communications. They also held Riga's economy in an iron grip of outrageous taxation and open corruption, and none of the worlds that had helped Riga before seemed inclined to challenge Saint Petersburg a second time on their behalf.

Now alien invaders had come to the human sphere, apparently bent on little but death and destruction.

Roze thought of his reaction – stark incredulity – at the news that the *Aurora*, a Terran survey vessel, had made first contact with a sentient species that had murdered the ship's crew. Then came the annihilation of the colony on Keran, which threw most of the human sphere into a panicked uproar. The Saint Petersburg government, in typical fashion, had flatly labeled the entire affair a hoax, but in Roze's eyes, that only served to increase the odds of it being true. The video reports of the battle that his agents had smuggled past Saint Petersburg's censors were too surreal to be even a Bollywood production. Saint Petersburg jealously controlled the communications buoys that stored and received information from the courier ships that carried information from star to star. While the Rigans could officially send and receive only what the Saint Petersburg government allowed, a well-established web of spies and informants ensured that the Rigan leadership was well-informed.

"That's fine," President Roze said when the young man brought the volume up. The audio was just as impressive as the image display: Roze felt like he was standing right next to Natalie McKenna, former President of the Terran Planetary Government and now President of the Confederation, as she began to speak.

"Citizens of the Confederation," she began, her strong voice a reflection of the will that had carried the Terran Planetary Government from a state of denial to a fierce determination to survive in the aftermath of the Kreelan invasion and destruction of the human colony on Keran. *"Citizens of the Confederation,"* she repeated. "While there are and have been governments in the human sphere made up of more than one world, for the first time since the Diaspora have we truly begun to look beyond our differences, to unite for a common purpose. That purpose, my fellow citizens – my fellow *humans* – is our survival as a species.

"You have all seen the reports of what happened on Keran," she went on, her voice dropping lower in pitch. "Millions of people – of *our* people – were wiped out, exterminated. The fleet of the *Alliance Française* was nearly destroyed, and Earth's fleet severely mauled. Yet our combined forces were almost enough to stop the invasion. *Almost*. We did not believe then. And there will never again be another *almost*. Never again will we give less than our all to defend our people, to defend humanity itself. If the Kreelan Empire has come looking for a fight, we will give it one. And we will emerge victorious!"

The crowd, several million people lining the streets of old New York City on Earth, roared in support. While it would take months for the recording to reach the farthest human settlements, McKenna's speech would eventually be heard by the twenty billion humans living among the stars.

"Yet the battle fought at Keran showed us the crucial importance of unity. Our fleets and ground forces could not communicate properly. Our weapons and equipment are not standardized. Most important of all, we have had no unified military or political leadership." She shook her head slowly. "My friends," she said, "the Kreelans do not care about our differences. They do not care about our history. They do not care about any of our problems, any more than they care about our dreams and aspirations. They have come for one thing, and one thing only: to kill us. If Keran is an example of what they plan for our species, every man, woman, and child of our race is under a threat of death. Unless we unite, unless we can pull together and form a common defense, *we will not survive*." Drawing herself up to stand even taller, she went on, "In that spirit, and as my first official act as President of the Confederation of Humanity, I extend an open invitation to every world to join the Confederation. There will be commitments necessary for the common defense of human space, but your planetary sovereignty will be respected. The Confederation's purpose, reflected in its charter, is not to subdue or absorb its member worlds, but to defend and protect them. As president, I offer that protection unconditionally to any world that chooses to join us..."

Roze signaled the young man to stop the playback. He had heard enough. Looking around the room, he saw the answer to his unasked question – *Should we risk joining?* – written on every face. For there was much risk, particularly for the men and women in this room. Officially, there were no Saint Petersburg military forces currently on Riga, as that had been banned under the armistice twenty years ago. But everyone around the table knew that this was a hollow truth. "Military advisers" were garrisoned near vital installations, including the bunker they were meeting in. Worse, Saint Petersburg had rearmed in blatant violation of the armistice treaty, building heavy weapons and expanding their "coast guard" into a potent navy that Roze believed could challenge even the new Confederation. They also had enough interplanetary lift capacity to land a large occupation force on Riga or any number of other worlds quickly. Riga, by contrast, had only a token paramilitary force of policemen who also trained as militia, armed with weapons controlled by Red Army detachments from Saint Petersburg.

Roze and the others had no illusions about what the "St. Petes" could – and would – do if sufficiently provoked. Riga petitioning to join the Confederation would certainly be provocative. The only question was how strong their response might be.

On the other hand, if Riga's government did nothing, Roze was sure Riga's lot would only become worse. Political pressure from Earth and the Alliance to keep Saint Petersburg in line had evaporated years ago, long before the threat from the Kreelan Empire loomed. Saint Petersburg would have a free hand to deal with Riga however they chose.

"It is our best chance, Valdis," his interior minister, who also doubled as defense minister, told him. "At worst, we will only accelerate whatever the bastards plan to eventually do with us. At best..." he shrugged.

"At best," Roze finished for him, "we may at last have true independence." He looked across the table at his foreign minister. "Send an envoy to Earth with a petition for Riga to join the Confederation."

As the room filled with discussion of fears and opportunities, Roze silently wondered how long he had before the Saint Petersburg secret police would come for him.

***

President Natalie McKenna hated the new presidential complex, particularly her main office. She appreciated that it was new and intended to support the needs of the leader not of a world, but of a union of worlds larger than any other formed in post-Diaspora history. It was huge, over four times the size of the White House that had been the home of the presidents of the old United States, with dozens of rooms and a staff that numbered in the hundreds. Fitted with every conceivable gadget, all the latest and greatest of everything she could imagine and many that she couldn't, the complex was a marvel of technology and engineering. Everything was so high-tech, in fact, that at first she was afraid of using the vidphones for fear of not being able to figure out how to work them.

No, she decided, the only thing she liked about the new complex was the view. Built on Governor's Island, the ten-story complex provided a grand view of modern New York City, including the hallowed ground of what had once been the twin towers of the World Trade Center and the fully restored Statue of Liberty, which had been badly damaged during the wars before the Diaspora. McKenna had arranged her office so that her desk faced toward the window wall that framed the statue in the distance. The sight of Lady Liberty brought her comfort and gave her strength. Today she needed that more than usual.

"How the *hell* could we have let this happen?" she cursed. "I shouldn't have to find out about a resurgent militant government on Saint Petersburg from a Rigan envoy! We should have known!"

Secretary of State Hamilton Barca, who could easily have been mistaken for a football linebacker who happened to be wearing an expensive suit, frowned. President McKenna only cursed when she was extremely upset. Looking across the coffee table at the woman who had been his friend and boss as they had climbed up the political ladder, he was worried for her. An African-American from the old American state of Georgia, Natalie McKenna had grown up poor, owning nothing more than an unconquerable sense of determination, and eventually rose to the most powerful position on Earth as the president of the Terran Planetary Government. Now, with the formation of the Confederation to rally humanity's colonies to a common defense against the Kreelan menace, she had become the most powerful individual in the entire human sphere. Such power, however, was an unthinkable burden of responsibility for a single human being, and he knew the strain was slowly killing her. She had lost far too much weight in the months since the battle for Keran, and her skin was now tightly stretched over her cheekbones. Her hair – raven black only two years ago – had turned almost completely gray. Her face was lined from worry, and there were dark rings beneath her eyes from a constant sleep deficit. Those intense brown eyes, however, were as clear and sharp as ever. Right now they were looking out at the Statue of Liberty, for which he was grateful. Had she turned them on him, he was half afraid he would ignite from her anger and be burned to a cinder.

"It's not Hamilton's fault, Madam President," Vladimir Penkovsky, former head of the Terran Intelligence Agency and now the director of the new Confederation Intelligence Service, said quietly. "We have been reporting for several years on the rearming of Saint Petersburg and the quiet return to power of people who still hold the ideologies and policies that led to the war twenty years ago. The armistice left a power vacuum in its wake that was filled by a weak government, and over time that government has been suborned by the survivors of the old guard. There can be no doubt. Our sources have been excellent; the information is very detailed and we believe it to be quite reliable."

Penkovsky wished he had intelligence half as good on the other problem areas he faced. Saint Petersburg was a special case: there was a great deal of yearning by many of the ethnic Russians there to have the freedoms that their Terran cousins enjoyed, and many Saint Petersburg citizens had secretly provided information to the TIA.

Like the other major powers of the time before the Diaspora, Russia had been devastated by the wars that had led to a frenzy of interstellar colonization missions as the world teetered on the brink of total annihilation. China, its natural resources guttering out, launched a massive invasion of Russian Siberia to take by force what it needed, with a simultaneous attack against northeastern India to secure that strategic theater. Totally overwhelmed, the Russians fought back the only way they could: they obliterated the invading Chinese armies with nuclear weapons. The Indians, also reeling from China's attack, followed suit. Once the mushroom clouds had dissipated, half the major cities in India and Russia were burning nuclear pyres. In China, no city with a population over a hundred thousand people was left standing.

After the war, the Russians who were left banded together politically with the other major survivors of the wars, notably the United States and India, and the resulting unlikely melting pot had, by and large, been extremely successful. It had been a long road back from the brink, but since then Earth's inheritors had enjoyed a kind of global peace that modern humankind had never before known.

Saint Petersburg, on the other hand, had gone the opposite direction. The colonization mission had been led by a small oligarchy of powerful men and women who had been able to muster the resources to finance the mission. Their vision was to create their ideal of "Mother Russia" on a planetary scale, free of the external influences and threats that Terran Russia had suffered. Paranoid, ruthless, and power-hungry, successive generations fell into tyranny in a variety of guises. At last, a form of neo-Communism arose that fostered atrocities that would have made Josef Stalin proud, and eventually led to war with Earth and the *Alliance Française*. The armistice had ended the ordeal twenty years ago, but old ways often died hard. Sometimes, they didn't die at all.

"If we had that much intelligence information," McKenna growled, "then why didn't we do anything about it. Why the *hell* wasn't I informed?"

"You were, Madam President," Barca told her as gently as he could, deciding to dive with Penkovsky into the vat of boiling oil, figuratively speaking. "We got the reports, and plenty of the information showed up in your daily briefings over the last several years. But none of us, least of all me, was going to make more of an issue out of it than was absolutely necessary."

"My God, Hamilton," McKenna said, turning to face him, her face a mask of shocked anger, "why didn't you?" She turned her glare on Penkovsky. "Why didn't *both* of you?"

"Economics," Barca answered bluntly. "After the war, Saint Petersburg was an economic disaster. But Korolev, the new bastard in charge, managed to turn things around by exporting strategic minerals and other raw materials that are always in critical demand. Everybody lined up for the peace dividend."

"Including us," McKenna said softly, closing her eyes. She had been in the Terran Senate then, and had voted for the trade treaty with Saint Petersburg. It had seemed like such a good idea at the time.

"And the Alliance, as well," another voice sighed. Laurent Navarre looked down at the polished wood surface of the coffee table. The former ambassador from the *Alliance Française* to the Terran Planetary Government, he was now McKenna's vice president. Intelligent, charming, and extremely competent, he was a much-valued addition to McKenna's leadership team. "As you may recall, our economy, and Earth's, was in a very bad state in the years after the war. Korolev's government made such a handsome offer to all of us that it was impossible to refuse." He shrugged. "Without that agreement and access to their resources, it would have been at least another decade before our economies would have recovered."

"We made a deal with the Devil," McKenna grated.

"It was not the first time, Madam President," Navarre told her levelly, "and it will not be the last. It is the nature of what we must do sometimes. You know this."

"Yes, I do," she said tiredly as she sank down into the wing-back chair at the end of the coffee table, facing the others. Barca and Penkovsky had been part of her cabinet since her first administration in the Terran Planetary Government. The other key member she had brought along was Joshua Sabine, the Defense Minister, who was away with the Chief of Naval Staff, Admiral Phillip Tiernan, to review the new ships coming off the ways in the orbital shipyards. Navarre was a recent addition, having been the Alliance ambassador to Earth prior to the Confederation's founding. "So, it seems we have a bit of a quandary," she told them. "Saint Petersburg has rearmed in violation of the armistice: so do we go after them, or ignore them and focus on the Kreelans?" She sighed. "I suppose we could count that on the good side of things, in that it potentially gives us more firepower against the Kreelans."

Penkovsky snorted, shaking his head. "They would defend their own world, Madam President," he told her, "but they would never send forces to the aid of another system. I doubt they would even bother to defend Riga. There would be no tears shed by Korolev if Riga shared Keran's fate."

McKenna frowned. "Which brings us to the next problem: if we accept Riga into the Confederation, how is Saint Petersburg going to react?"

"Saint Petersburg's reaction is almost immaterial," Navarre pointed out, "because we do not really have a choice about accepting Riga. The Confederation charter is explicit: membership is open to every world that is willing to help provide for the common defense of humanity. If Riga is willing to meet the requirements of raising a Territorial Army and provides the designated per capita quota of manpower and resources for combat units and shipbuilding, which their envoy indicated that they can, they must be accepted. The Confederation will then be obligated to help train, arm, and equip them. There are some stipulations to keep out the rogue worlds, but not many: a planet led by anything short of an outright dictatorship can meet the basic political requirements." He shrugged. "Saint Petersburg could join if they wanted, and we would be obligated to give them the same benefits."

"Okay," McKenna conceded, "we don't have any choice about accepting Riga. That still doesn't answer my question: how will Korolev's government react?"

"Despite the armistice conditions that made Riga independent," Barca told her, "Saint Petersburg has never really accepted it. They've made placating noises and done the minimum required to observe Rigan sovereignty, but that's it: they still believe that Riga is nothing more than a breakaway state that will someday be brought to heel." He scowled. "Frankly, I'm surprised Riga was able to get an envoy here. If Korolev had known..."

"There would have been no envoy," Penkovsky finished for him.

"Just how far is Korolev willing to go on this?" McKenna asked. "We can't afford to have a second front, a civil war, going on while we're trying to save ourselves from the Kreelans!" Fortunately, the enemy had made no further major moves against human space in the months since the fall of Keran. There had been unverified reports of Kreelan ships in many sectors, but most of them were thought to be either erroneous or even fabricated. The only attacks on shipping had been from pirates, and none of the colonies had reported anything unusual. In some quarters, this long lull was being called the "phony war," and an increasing amount of the

Confederation government's efforts were being devoted to keeping the Kreelan threat foremost in the mind of a public that was easily distracted. McKenna, however, didn't believe that this lull was going to last much longer: she thought of it more as the calm before the storm.

"If we arm Riga and provide them a guarantee of protection – which applies to *any* external threat, not just the Kreelan Empire – as written in the Confederation charter," Penkovsky said with a look at Barca, "Korolev will simply not allow it."

Barca nodded in agreement.

"He's willing to go to war with the Confederation over this?" she asked Penkovsky.

"I believe so, yes."

"Bloody hell," McKenna breathed.

"There may be worse," Penkovsky ventured, clearly uncomfortable about what he was about to say. "I happened to have a report flagged for my review this morning that we recently received from a new source on Saint Petersburg. I...can barely credit the information, but in light of this discussion I cannot in good conscience not mention it."

"Spit it out, Vlad," McKenna ordered tersely.

"You must keep in mind that we have not yet had time to validate this source or the content of the report," he went on hesitantly. "The source indicates that Saint Petersburg has been secretly building a stockpile of thermonuclear weapons."

There was stunned silence around the room. Terran forces had nuclear weapons, as did the Alliance, but the stockpiles amounted to only a few hundred weapons. None had been used, anywhere, since the last wars on Earth before the Diaspora. After the devastation Earth had suffered, the hundreds of millions who had died, no one had ever wanted to unleash them again. With the threat from the Kreelans, McKenna had very reluctantly given authorization to increase the Confederation's weapons stockpile, but only slowly. If the Kreelans used them first, she would give the Navy all the nukes they wanted. But she would not be the first one to open Pandora's Box in this war.

"I do not believe it," Navarre said carefully. "Saint Petersburg has very little in the way of accessible uranium deposits, and what nuclear material they import for their power industry – virtually all of it from the Alliance in the form of pre-manufactured fusion cores – is carefully tracked by an Alliance regulatory commission. I do not see how Saint Petersburg could be getting the uranium and plutonium they would require without smuggling it in. That would be extremely difficult, if not impossible, with the tight controls over uranium mining and production of fissile materials."

"That is what I thought, too," Penkovsky told him, "until I read this report. Tell me, Laurent," he said, "with a power industry that has been based on fusion, solar, and wind generation for generations, why would they have built a few dozen massive coal-fired power plants in the last seven years? And why put them in out of the way locations that must make getting power to the grid extremely costly and difficult?"

Navarre sat back, thinking. He knew a great deal about the planet, having been stationed there as part of the peacekeeping force after the armistice. "Saint Petersburg has a great deal of coal, formed just as it did on Earth, and with very similar qualities. It is easy, if ecologically devastating, to mine it. But I cannot think of why they would need coal power plants: the fusion plants alone give them a net excess of electrical power. As for why they would put them in odd places, I cannot say."

"I must have missed something," McKenna interjected drily. "I thought we were talking about nuclear weapons here, not fossil fuel for electricity."

"Madam President," Penkovsky said, "a fact that was previously unknown to me is that coal typically contains between one and ten parts per million of a particular element that, theoretically, can be captured from the fly ash, which is a byproduct of burning coal." He looked her in the eyes. "That element is uranium. And of that, just under one percent is uranium-235, which is the key ingredient for making nuclear weapons. They would need to burn a lot of coal to get what they need. But if the source's information is correct, the coal burning facilities they have could produce several metric tons of uranium-235 per year. They would still need to refine it, but based on the enormous quantity of coal these plants are reportedly burning, and assuming they have been producing uranium-235 for at least the last three years, they may already have a stockpile of several hundred weapons." He grimaced before he went on, saying, "My analysts also say that this is a very conservative estimate. The information also suggests they are manufacturing tritium, which is a key ingredient for making fusion weapons, but the source did not know where or how they were doing it."

"Good God," Barca breathed.

"Vlad," McKenna said, careful to keep her voice level, "we simply *cannot* have a nuclear war in the human sphere. I would say that under any circumstances, but especially with the Kreelan Empire stalking us." Penkovsky made to speak, but McKenna silenced him with a raised hand. "I know the information isn't verified. I understand that. But you've got to pin this down. If the Confederation has to defend Riga against Saint Petersburg, I don't want our forces facing nuclear weapons. Nor do I want to give Korolev the chance to use them to terrorize other worlds beyond Riga. Pull out all the stops on this one, Vlad. We have *got* to know if this is true and how far they've gotten. And if it's true, we've got to find a way to stop them in their tracks."

Penkovsky, his face grim, nodded. "Yes, Madam President."

Turning to Navarre, McKenna said, "Get with Defense Minister Sabine and Admiral Tiernan on this right away and put together a contingency deployment plan. If we get hard confirmation that this information is true, I want a Navy task force and Marines ready to go in right away..."

***

Lost in thought as his limousine whisked him from the presidential complex back to the newly constructed Confederation Intelligence Services headquarters building, Penkovsky came to the rapid conclusion that their best chance of finding out what was happening on Saint Petersburg lay with a particular special asset.

Her codename was Scarlet.

THREE

"So, what trouble are you going to get into while I'm gone?" Confederation Navy Commander Ichiro Sato said as he ran a finger down his wife's nude back.

"Who says I'm going to let you go?" Stephanie Sato – Steph to her friends – purred as she arched against her husband's chiseled body, goosebumps breaking out over her skin at his touch. He wrapped his arms around her and pulled her close, her back to his chest, burying his face in her hair. "And I never get into trouble," she said primly.

"Liar," he said, playfully nipping her shoulder.

She laughed, but then settled back against him, quiet. Thoughtful. "I'll miss you," she whispered.

"I'll miss you, too," he breathed.

The two of them were an unlikely pair in some ways, but had been brought together by events that had shattered humanity's view of the universe forever. Ichiro had been a young midshipman aboard the survey ship *Aurora* when Mankind made its first contact with another sentient species: the Kreelans. He was the only survivor of that encounter, and had been sent back in his ship by humanity's new enemy to warn his people of the coming war. A year and a half later, the Kreelans had attacked the human colony on Keran, occupying it after a brief but vicious battle with the human defenders. Ichiro had been there, too, on a destroyer of the Terran fleet in the battle that had raged in space. And there he had again lost most of his shipmates, and again the Kreelans had spared his life when they could easily have taken it. It was something he had managed to come to grips with, but he had never truly decided which troubled him more: having so many others die around him, or the enemy letting him live. He had gone to see several counselors to help him come to grips with all that had happened, but in the end the best therapy had been Steph.

She had been a journalist hungry for the big break she needed to make it into the major leagues. Before she met him, Steph had thought nothing of shamelessly using her body to advance her career as a journalist. When then-Midshipman Sato came back to Earth on a ghost ship with his improbable story of bloodthirsty aliens, she had been at the right place to get an exclusive story from the Navy, and his fame had taken her higher than she had ever imagined. She could have taken terrible advantage of him, but that temptation had fallen away when she first met him as a lonely, guilt-ridden soul. They soon became friends, and just before the battle of Keran, they became lovers. After the nightmare of that battle, which she had experienced first-hand as a journalist embedded with the ground troops, they had returned home to Earth, marrying soon thereafter.

Ichiro was Japanese by descent, born and raised on Nagano. Five centimeters shorter and nearly ten years younger than Steph, he was a handsome young man with a lean muscular body and a mind that had been keen enough to record everything he had learned of the enemy on his long, lonely return to Earth aboard the ill-fated *Aurora*. His knowledge had not saved Keran, but it had given humanity the only edge it had in preparing for the coming war. His body was young, but his eyes might have belonged to someone far, far older.

Prior to the war, he would have been considered absurdly young to hold the rank of commander in the Terran Navy. But his performance under fire and the heavy losses among command qualified officers at Keran had changed the rules, and rapid promotion of promising junior officers had been necessary to fill the many new critical positions opening up as the new Confederation's fleet rapidly expanded. Ichiro had also had the benefit of the sponsorship of the Navy's Chief of Staff, Admiral Phillip Tiernan. Some might have thought that Ichiro's rank had been bestowed by the admiral as an act of favoritism. But the Medal of Honor on Ichiro's uniform told a different story.

Based on his actions at Keran that had earned him "the medal," he had been given command of one of the Navy's newest heavy cruisers, the *Yura*. The ship had finished her shakedown trials and was in the yards where the yard hands were making some last minute adjustments while she took on provisions. Ichiro was scheduled to take *Yura* out on her first war patrol the next morning. It was something most of him looked forward to, hoping he could give the Kreelans some of the death that they had come looking for. The rest of him wanted to stay here, holding close the woman he loved.

Steph, too, would be leaving their home here on Africa Station, one of the massive orbital transit stations for people and cargo traveling to and from Earth. She had accepted a completely unexpected offer by President McKenna to be her press secretary. That had been an incredibly tough decision for Steph: she wanted to go where the big stories were as a journalist. Yet after being around McKenna, she had come to realize that she had an opportunity to become part of something far larger than herself, something that could be vitally important to all of humankind. For her, it was a sacrifice to give up her field work, but after the first few weeks on the job it was a sacrifice she had seen as being a worthy one.

"How long until you have to get ready?" she asked him quietly, kissing one of his hands as she stretched her body slowly, suggestively, against his back.

Ichiro grudgingly eyed the clock display. "An hour," he sighed.

"Then let's not waste it," she told him as she turned over, kissing him hard as she straddled his body in one smooth movement.

Ichiro didn't argue.

***

A few hours later, Commander Ichiro Sato, captain of the *CNS Yura*, stood on his ship's bridge as his crew completed preparations to depart Africa Station. He and Steph had said their goodbyes, swearing they wouldn't cry, then crying, anyway. After they parted and before he stepped through the gangway hatch to board his ship, he paused a moment. Closing his eyes, he took one last look at Steph's image in his mind, then reverently put it away in a mental box that he closed and locked. He would set aside time to think of her – and write her letters, even though they probably wouldn't reach her through the slow inter-system mail system until *Yura* returned home – when he was alone in his quarters. Except for those special moments, he would think only of his ship and her crew, and the perils that might await them. That was the best insurance he could provide that he would return home to the woman he loved.

"All umbilicals and gangways have been cast off, sir," Lieutenant Commander Raymond Villiers, Sato's executive officer (the XO) reported. "Africa Station has given us clearance to maneuver. Engineering is ready to answer all bells."

"Helm," Sato said as he settled back into his combat chair in the center of the bridge, "give me ten seconds on the port-side thrusters."

"Ten seconds, port-side thrusters, aye," Lieutenant Natalya Bogdanova answered instantly. She had served with Sato aboard his previous ship, the TNS *Owen D. McClaren*, which had been destroyed at Keran. They had become good friends while serving together aboard *McClaren*, and he was more than glad to have her aboard.

The *Yura* slowly moved away from her berth in the newly-built docks on Africa Station. Over six hundred meters long, *Yura* was a radical departure from previous heavy cruiser designs. Instead of having a collection of several modules and numerous protrusions and appendages attached to a rigid latticework keel, *Yura's* hull was formed of armor plate that encased her entire internal structure. While she was not aerodynamic (a feat the Kreelans had somehow mastered with their ships), and so could not enter atmosphere, her shape was very streamlined. Her profile reminded Sato of a shark, a likeness that he found intensely satisfying. Like a shark, she had teeth: four triple turrets mounting twelve fifteen-centimeter kinetic guns, another six turrets with single heavy lasers, and enough close-in defense weapons and anti-personnel mortars to cover every approach to the ship, save directly astern because of the drive mountings. To round out her armament, she had ten torpedo tubes and twenty-two torpedoes: large, self-guided and highly maneuverable missiles that had proven effective in the fleet battles at Keran.

Yura and her eleven sister ships had been built in just over three months in the emergency construction program begun by President McKenna after the Keran debacle. It had taken three more months to get her ready for combat, and Sato had done his best to use every minute of it to the fullest to prepare his ship and crew. He had mercilessly drilled the men and women who served under him, but always ensured they understood that their survival and ability to carry out their mission depended on how well they could do their jobs, even under the worst conditions. Following the example of his first commanding officer aboard the old *Aurora*, Captain Owen McClaren, for whom the ship he served on at Keran had been named, he forged his officers into a well-oiled team of leaders that quickly earned the respect of the enlisted ranks. Sato knew that they still had to improve in many areas, but he was intensely proud of his crew. He knew that many of his fellow commanding officers doubted – some quite vocally – that he was fit for command. Yet Sato had no doubts that his ship and crew were ready for battle.

Watching the tactical display, which was toggled to a mode optimized for departure and showed only the local space around Africa Station, he ordered, "All ahead one-quarter. Make your course two-eight-three mark zero-seven-five."

Bogdanova echoed his command as her fingers confidently moved over the controls.

While the inertial dampeners theoretically removed any sensation of motion, Sato certainly felt like he was moving as the ship accelerated away from Earth, the great blue marble of Mankind's home rapidly dwindling behind them.

"Captain," Villiers informed him as they reached their planned jump point well out of Earth's gravity well, "the jump coordinates for the squadron rendezvous are verified, and the hyperdrive engines are green for jump. All hands are at jump stations."

This jump, in addition to being the initial leg of their first combat patrol, was also the final test in the squadron's operational readiness evaluation trials. Each of the six ships of the 8th Heavy Cruiser Squadron had jumped from Earth separately over the last three days, with *Yura* being the last. It was a very complex navigational exercise with the ships leaving at different times, briefly patrolling different sets of star systems, and then making a squadron rendezvous at Lorient during a fifteen minute window in twenty-one days.

Sato smiled to himself. It was an incredibly challenging navigation problem that was typical of his squadron commander, Commodore Margaret Hanson. She was something of an odd bird in the Navy, having crossed over from the Terran Army years before. She was as outgoing as she was outspoken, which Sato knew had cost her more than one promotion in the past. Keran, however, had changed things: she had held the rank of commander before that disastrous battle, and had her commodore's rank pinned on little more than three months later. If there had been any silver lining from the Keran disaster, it was the rapid promotion of competent officers like Hanson.

Sato knew that she had been very skeptical about his command abilities when he took over *Yura*. She had been very frank with him in their first meeting when he had joined the squadron.

"Handing over a brand new heavy cruiser – of a completely new design, at that – to someone with no real command experience doesn't make a lot of sense to me," she had told him bluntly. "Admiral Tiernan passed over a lot of fully qualified officers to give you your ship, Sato. He obviously had his reasons, but I don't need to tell you that you're probably not the most popular officer in the Navy at the moment, at least among the officers who've been waiting in line for a command slot."

Sato knew quite well that Tiernan's decision had caused a huge uproar among the command-rank officers, but he was honest enough with himself to admit that he didn't care what they thought. It wasn't that he felt entitled to the ship after what he'd gone through on the *Aurora* making first contact with the Empire, or after what had happened aboard the *McClaren* during the battle of Keran. He would have been happy and honored to serve on any ship that would take the war to the Kreelans. Yet when Tiernan had given him this unique opportunity, there was no way he would have turned it down. He knew that he could fail and be replaced – Tiernan had made that perfectly clear – but he also knew that he could succeed. It would give him one of humanity's greatest weapons against the aliens that had murdered the crew of his first ship and an entire planet of fellow human beings.

Despite her misgivings, after seeing his ship perform in her squadron's exercises, Hanson decided that maybe Admiral Tiernan hadn't had a screw loose when he put Sato in command of *Yura*.

"Sato," she had told him later, "you're probably the best tactician I've ever seen, and *Yura* beat every other ship in the squadron combat evaluations." That was the good news. The bad news came next. "But your ship's administration, commander, is an outright disaster."

He had no good answer for that, other than he simply had not had the time or the training to learn all the things ship captains had to know. Beyond tactics and ship handling, where he excelled, lay paperwork, policies, procedures and much more: even in war, these things persisted, and a ship could not function without them.

He knew that many officers in Hanson's position would have been happy to see him fail, for no other reason than because he hadn't served his time like his peers before getting a command. That, however, was not the sort of officer Hanson was. She saw in him a highly capable junior officer who had the capability to be an outstanding one, and decided to rescue him before he drowned in paper. Taking him under her wing, she brought him up to speed in the more mundane but necessary skills needed to keep a ship running. Sato smiled, remembering some of the commodore's lessons. Hanson was a tough teacher, and he was a determined student.

When the bridge chronometer being used to log their exercise time counted down to zero, Sato turned to Bogdanova and ordered, "Helm, commence jump."

Thirty seconds later, *Yura* vanished into hyperspace, bound for her first patrol station.

***

Roland Mills was fighting for his life. His regiment had been annihilated in an orgy of hand-to-hand fighting with the aliens, with but a hundred or so survivors left when the huge warrior had chosen him for single combat. It was the ultimate adrenaline rush that might even help save a few of his fellow legionnaires.

He knew from the start that he could never beat her. He had seen what she had done in the trench where they had fought viciously against the other warriors, watched as her sword and claws tore his comrades apart like a killing machine. He had seen her snatch others from the trench with some sort of whip with several barbed tails, and heard the terrified screams of her victims as they were yanked from the trench like fish from a pond.

Of all of the trained killers his regiment had to offer, she had chosen him. Setting aside her weapons, she fought him hand-to-hand. She battered him to the ground time and again, and each time he regained his feet and charged her. He had landed his share of blows, bloodying her face. He knew that it was only because she had let him, but that was enough. He kept charging her until he could no longer stand. Then he crawled until he could no longer lift himself from the mud.

It was enough. She would spare his fellow survivors. She would spare him. She rolled him over and he looked up, offering her a bloody smile, a measure of defiance.

She looked down at him, her blue face bearing an inscrutable expression, her cat's eyes taking in the measure of his soul.

She should have just walked away with the rest of her warriors. That was what was supposed to happen. But she didn't.

Instead, one of her massive clawed hands closed around his neck and she lifted him from the ground. Her dark crimson lips parted in a snarl to reveal long white fangs, and an icy chill threaded its way through his heart, eclipsing the pain of his battered body. He suddenly felt a horrible, tearing pain in his chest. Looking down past the alien hand clamped around his neck, he saw his ribs cracked and broken, the flesh torn and bleeding where she had shoved her other hand into his chest. With a smooth motion, she tore out his still-beating heart, holding it up for the other warriors to see, as she bellowed an alien cry of victorious rage. The other warriors howled their approval, and Mills watched in silent horror as they butchered the surviving legionnaires.

He watched the carnage, knowing that he was dead, must be dead, yet he wasn't. His eyes locked with hers as she turned back to him, and the hand that had been holding his heart – where had it gone? – reached back into his shattered chest. Not for another part of his body, but for his very soul...

"Roland!"

Mills snapped his eyes open. His body was drenched in sweat, his heart – still with him, thank God – hammering in his chest, blood pounding in his ears. He had rolled out of his bunk onto the metal deck, shaking so badly that his teeth chattered. Looking up, he saw Emmanuelle Sabourin kneeling next to him, her eyes wide with concern.

"Roland," she said again, softly this time. She helped him sit up, then wrapped her arms around him, holding him tight. "The dream again?"

"Yes," he shuddered, burying his face in the hollow of her shoulder.

Sabourin stroked his hair with one hand as she continued to hold him with the other. Both of them were veterans of Keran, survivors of close and bloody combat. Mills had been serving in the *Légion étrangère* of the *Alliance Française*, which had fought on the surface, while Sabourin had been an engineering technician on the Alliance fleet's flagship. He had fought a now-legendary hand-to-hand battle with a seemingly unstoppable Kreelan warrior, and Sabourin had fought the Kreelan boarders who had taken her ship, saving the few members of the crew who managed to survive. Both had wound up joining the new Confederation

Marine Corps. The Legion, what little was left of it, had been transferred in its entirety to the newly formed service, and Mills had gone along with it. Sabourin had joined the Corps through an inter-service transfer from the former Alliance Navy. They had wound up here on the *CNS Yura* as part of the cruiser's Marine detachment because Sato had known Mills and made a by-name request for him from the transition team that had been integrating the legionnaires into the new Marine Corps. As for Sabourin, she had been given her choice of assignments as a reward for her performance at Keran. After learning that Sato was commanding a ship with a Marine detachment, she requested to serve under him.

Mills had assumed the post of first sergeant of the ship's company-sized Marine detachment, and Sabourin was the platoon sergeant for one of the detachment's platoons. Being the only two veterans in the detachment who had actually fought the enemy, they had immediately gravitated toward one another, and had become lovers not long afterward. They were as discreet as they could be in the confines of a warship, which meant that everyone knew about their relationship, but pretended not to. They both knew that the detachment commander wasn't happy about their affair, but he had made it clear that as long as they did their jobs and kept their personal lives out of the detachment's business, he would be willing to turn a blind eye.

"I wish I understood why this is happening," he whispered. "I wasn't afraid when I fought her. I wasn't afraid during the entire battle. It was such a *rush*. Then when we got back to Avignon the dreams started. They've become so...so *real*. It's bad enough when she tears my heart out." He tried to laugh, but it came out a strangled sob. "But when she reaches for me again..." He shuddered. "I could understand having nightmares about something that happened to me, but what's in the dream didn't. I just don't understand."

"If you were not such a pig-headed bastard and would see a psychologist, they might be able to do something for you," she chided him. It was an old argument they had gone over many times. She was convinced it was post-traumatic stress. He was convinced it wasn't.

"I won't let them pull me from duty," he said stubbornly.

She held him away just far enough to look into his eyes. "If the dreams keep getting worse, my love, the CO will relieve you, anyway. He would be derelict in his duty if he did not." She kissed him, then said, "Roland, you are exhausted and irritable much of the time. You have been losing weight, and you use far too many stimulants." He started to protest, but she put a finger on his lips. "You can lie to the commander, you can lie to yourself, but you cannot lie to me. Do not even try, because I know you too well. Listen to me, first sergeant: you owe it to our Marines to do something about this. If – when – we again go into combat, you must be ready. If you are not, it is not only your life that is at risk. You risk all our lives. Including mine."

She braced herself for the argument to start getting ugly as it always did, and waited for him to trot out the same tired and illogical reasons that he had used before to avoid treatment.

"I'll see the ship's surgeon next watch," he said quietly, completely surprising her. She saw the stark fear in his eyes as he looked at her. "If the dream gets any more real, it's going to kill me."

***

"How many stim packs a day did you say you are taking?" the ship's surgeon asked, eyebrows raised. "I am not sure I heard you right."

"Twelve," Mills told her sheepishly. He already regretted his decision to come to see her. Commander Irina Nikolaeva was the oldest member of the crew, and from her expression Mills suspected she'd seen it all, including stim addiction. Stims were normally included in combat rations to help troops stay awake during extended periods of combat, and the temptation to pilfer and abuse them was the reason that ration packs were normally kept under the lock and key of a responsible junior officer or senior NCO like Mills.

"Twelve," she repeated in her thick Russian accent, shaking her head. "I am surprised you can stand still. Stims are not normally addictive, but taken in such quantities they can be. There are also other negative side effects." She looked at him pointedly. "Cardiac arrest is among them."

"I know all that, commander," he grated. "I wouldn't be taking the bloody things if I didn't feel I had to."

"The dreams," she said.

Mills nodded. He had tried as best he could to explain his recurring dream to her. It had been an uncomfortable, humiliating experience. He knew it wasn't the surgeon's fault; it was simply that he had never before felt compelled to confide in someone like this. Even telling Sabourin had been extremely difficult for him.

"Normally I would say it was nothing more or less than post-traumatic stress," Commander Nikolaeva told him. She saw Mills roll his eyes and did something others rarely saw: she grinned. "I will not insult your intelligence, Mills," she went on. "You already know this. That is the most likely answer, the one we fall back on when we believe it to be true. Or when we have no other explanation."

That caught his attention.

She nodded. "No one else except the captain" – Commander Sato – "has experienced anything like you did on Keran. I have carefully read his account of first contact with the Kreelans, and I believe the warrior you faced may have been the same one he did."

That came as a surprise to Mills. He had first met Sato on the assault boat that had rescued him and the rest of the survivors of Sato's destroyer at Keran. As the senior NCO of *Yura's* Marine detachment, Mills saw Sato fairly frequently. While they had talked about the events at Keran, neither had made the connection about the huge warrior: Sato had never mentioned her from his own experiences, and the dreams had driven Mills to stop talking about his fight with the warrior long before he'd come to the *Yura's* Marine detachment.

"Does the captain have dreams like this?" Mills asked hopefully. He would have been incredibly relieved if someone else was having a similar experience.

"You know I cannot answer that, Mills," she said as she turned to one of the medicine cabinets lining the walls. She pulled out two packets. "This one you already recognize," handing the first one to him.

Mills looked and was surprised to see that it was a package of stims. He looked back up at her, confused.

"These will keep you from raiding the ration packs," she said sternly. "If you need more, come see me. And I want you to replace the ones you took.."

He nodded, his face flushing with embarrassment. It was an old trick to pilfer stims out of rations, but it left whoever received those ration packs with no stims if they really needed it. Replacing all the ones he'd taken was going to be a bit of work. *Consider yourself lucky, mate*, he told himself. *She could have just as easily turned your arse into the captain on formal charges.*

"And these," she said, handing him the other packet, "are tranquilizers. You will take one – *only* one – before you sleep. These should knock you out for at least six hours and suppress your dreams. If they do not work, do not take more: come back to see me. Unlike the stims, these can be very addictive, and if you take too many at one time, they will kill you."

"How long can I take them?" he asked.

She shrugged as she tapped out something on her console. "I hope you will not need them more than a week. That should give you plenty of time to see if the rest of my prescription works."

"And what is that?" Mills asked, suddenly suspicious.

"A talk with the captain," she replied.

***

Mills had thought Sato would get around to seeing him at some point during the week. He didn't expect to see him immediately after his visit to Nikolaeva.

"I've got some free time right now," Sato had told Nikolaeva when she had commed him. "Send him to my cabin."

A few minutes later, Mills stood nervously at Sato's door. He had talked to the captain any number of times during the normal briefings held for the ship's command staff, which included the commander and senior NCO of the Marine detachment. But he had never been in Sato's quarters or spoken to him alone. It shouldn't have bothered him, he knew, but the nervous apprehension wouldn't go away.

He nodded to the Marine on guard duty outside the captain's door, standing at parade rest. The Marine nodded back and palmed the control to open the door.

"The skipper's expecting you, First Sergeant," was all he said.

Mills stepped through the doorway into the captain's private quarters, not knowing what to expect. At that moment, he was frightened more than anything else of the captain thinking he was a coward. There was no getting out of it, however. Commander Nikolaeva had made sure the captain knew what the topic of conversation would be.

He snapped to attention and saluted, "First Sergeant Mills, reporting, sir!" The *sir* came out sounding more like *sah* from his British accent.

"At ease, Mills," Sato said, returning his salute. "Please, come in." Sato gestured to one of the chairs arrayed around a small table that would have been the perfect size for playing cards, but as far as Mills knew the captain didn't play.

Dropping his salute, Mills said, "Thank you, sir." He sat down, but remained rigid as a post.

"Mills," Sato said as he fished around in a wall locker, "relax. If it helps, that's an order. Ah!" He held up a bottle and a pair of tumblers that he'd pulled from the locker. "Pure contraband, of course, but rank hath its privileges, as the saying goes."

When Sato set down the bottle on the table, Mills saw it was a very expensive brand of rum. He knew the captain didn't drink, and his expression must have given away his surprise.

"I normally only drink tea," Sato said darkly as he opened the bottle and poured the liquor into the tumblers, "but the topic of this conversation calls for something stronger." He handed Mills a glass, then leaned back in his chair, his dark eyes fixing the Marine with an intent gaze. "So. Commander Nikolaeva told me you're having a recurring nightmare about the alien warrior you fought on Keran. Let's hear it."

Managing to get over his embarrassment, Mills told the tale of his battle with the alien warrior, describing her carefully, especially the strange ornament on the collar at her throat. Then he spoke of how his dreams had begun, and had recently worsened.

After he had finished, Sato was silent for a moment, looking into his glass as if the answers to all the questions in the universe could be found swirling in the amber liquid. "A good friend gave me some advice once," he finally said, just above a whisper, "just before he died. He said, 'There is no dishonor in living.'" He looked up at Mills with haunted eyes. "I agree with Nikolaeva: the warrior you fought, the one you dream about, is almost certainly the same one that I encountered when *Aurora* was captured."

Taking a gulp of the rum, barely noticing as it burned its way to his stomach, Mills leaned forward. "Do you have dreams, too, sir? Nightmares like this?" he asked, desperate for company in his misery, in his quest for understanding.

"I have plenty of nightmares, Mills," Sato replied, "but none quite like yours. I dream of what happened to me, of events that actually took place, but not of things that didn't happen, or an attack on my spirit or soul."

"You think I'm going 'round the bend, do you, sir?" Mills asked, anticipating that Sato's next words would be to relieve him of duty.

Sato shook his head slowly. "No, I don't," he said frankly. "Mills..." he struggled for a moment, trying to find the right words. "Mills, a lot of people think the Kreelans are like us, simply because they're humanoid in appearance. In the case of the regular warriors, that might be true. But not *her*. She's something else entirely. Mills, I watched her walk through a wall that must have been a meter thick, and she acted like she'd been pricked with a needle when she let me run my sword through her."

"She *let* you, sir?" Mills asked, incredulous.

"Of course she let me," Sato said disgustedly. He took a tiny sip of the rum, managing to force it down. The burning sensation took his attention away from the memory of the warrior looking down at him as he stood there, his grandfather's *katana* sticking through her side. Then she had simply pulled it out and handed it back to him. "Otherwise I'd have been dead with the rest of my old crew. She could probably kill an entire planet single-handed."

"I don't like to give anyone that much credit, sir," Mills said uneasily, fearing that it might actually be true. "I know bloody well that she let me go after having her fun. But I didn't stick it to her with a sword. And we know they're not immortal. We killed plenty of their warriors at Keran."

Sato shook his head. "The only way she's going to die," he said, "is if she wants to. And I think that's what makes her so different. It's not just her physical abilities. There's something more to her that I've never been able to put my finger on, something that goes beyond our experience."

"That doesn't exactly reassure me, sir, if you know what I mean," Mills said quietly before he finished off his rum.

"I know, and I'm sorry," Sato replied. "But we can't control our fears unless we seek to understand them."

Mills nodded, distinctly unhappy. "So where does that leave me, sir?" he asked. "Are you going to relieve me of duty?"

"Not unless you request it or Commander Nikolaeva recommends it," Sato told him firmly. "I agree with the surgeon's assessment that they're probably not a form of post-traumatic stress."

"If not that, then what?" Mills wondered. "Is it some sort of hocus-pocus psychic link from when she was beating my brains out?" He had meant it as a joke. Sort of.

Sato smiled, but a sudden chill went through him. *What if it was?* he thought, terrified of the possibilities.

FOUR

Tesh-Dar slept. She had no true need of it since the Change that had transformed her body when she became high priestess of the Desh-Ka many cycles ago, but after some time, she had found that she missed dreaming. In dreams she found a curious sense of comfort that eluded her while awake, the Bloodsong within her calming from an irresistible river torrent to the gentle swell of an infinite sea. As time wore on, she found that she could sometimes manipulate her dreams to reveal things in the present that were beyond even the reach of her second sight, and sometimes even give her glimpses into the future. And, of course, there were also dreams that were memories from her past.

Not all such dreams were pleasant.

***

"Someday your sword may even best mine, Tesh-Dar," said Sura-Ni'khan, high priestess of the Desh-Ka and mistress of the *kazha* where Tesh-Dar had grown from a child to a warrior nearly ready to formally begin her service to the Empire. "Yet you shall fall – by my own hand if need be – if you do not learn patience when teaching the young ones. Your talent with a blade, with any weapon you have ever held, is far beyond even most of the senior warriors of the Empire. It is because of your skills that I made you a senior swordmistress here. Your duty is to instruct, to pass on to the *tresh*, the young warriors-in-training, what you know. You may do it as you see fit within the bounds of tradition, but this is a duty you are bound to, daughter. It is not something you may choose to ignore."

Kneeling on the cold stone floor of the priestess's quarters, Tesh-Dar's heart was torn between shame and anger. Shame that the priestess's words were true, and anger that she should be so burdened. The Bloodsong did not simply echo the chorus of her sisters' spirits, it burned and raged when she took a weapon in her hand, when she entered the arena. She should not have to teach others, who could not understand what she was able to do; even she did not know exactly how she mastered weapons so quickly and so well. It simply *was*. Born to a race bound to warrior traditions, she was among the best-adapted for the art of killing. She had never taken a life in the arena, for she had no intention of cutting down her sisters. She had fought several ritual combats outside of the arena, but after the last one her reputation was such that no one would challenge her. That in itself was another source of frustration: the only warriors who could face her were the priestesses, and she knew that it would have been a great dishonor to provoke any of them into a ritual battle. She had no peers worthy of her skills, she thought sullenly, and she had not even completed her final Challenge at the *kazha*, this school of the Kreelan Way, after which she would be declared an adult warrior and be free to serve the Empress as She willed.

It was maddening, but Sura-Ni'khan's word was law, and Tesh-Dar had no choice. She would do as she must, biding her time until she was free to seek out her destiny, expanding the frontiers of the Empire in the name of the Empress.

"Yes, my priestess," she said, trying mightily to inject a note of humility into her voice and calm the fire that raged in her veins. She did not wish to disappoint her mentor, but she felt chained away from her destiny.

"My child," Sura-Ni'khan said quietly. "I believe you have the makings of greatness about you. Someday...someday I believe you may be worthy of wearing one of these."

Tesh-Dar glanced up to see Sura-Ni'khan's fingers touching the dazzling ruby-colored eyestone, taken from a monstrous *genoth* she had killed long ago, in which was carved the rune of the Desh-Ka order. It was affixed to her collar, the rune matching the one on her breastplate that blazed in luminous cyan. Of all the warrior sects their civilization had known, even before the founding of the Empire, the Desh-Ka was the oldest, its priestesses the most powerful. But after the Curse laid upon their race by the First Empress, the great orders were dying out.

"I am the last of my kind, Tesh-Dar," the priestess said sadly, "and my time grows short before I must pass into the Afterlife. But I would rather the order end its existence and take my leave to join the Ancient Ones than surrender my powers to one who was not ready, or unworthy." She paused. "Do not disappoint me, young swordmistress."

"I will obey, priestess," Tesh-Dar told her, tightly clenching her silver-taloned hands.

After brooding over the priestess's words that evening, Tesh-Dar had an epiphany: she would do what the Desh-Ka and the other warrior priestesses did, and take up a single disciple. She would train a promising young warrior to a level of mastery that would see them easily through their next Challenge, when the *tresh* fought amongst themselves for the honor of besting their peers. That would see her through her own final Challenge, after which she could leave this place and be free to seek the glories that lay beyond the confines of the Homeworld.

"Your Bloodsong rejoices," a soft and welcome voice said from behind her.

Quickly getting up from her bed of animal hides, Tesh-Dar knelt and saluted. "Mistress," she said happily. Seeing Pan'ne-Sharakh never failed to lift her heart.

With a sigh, the old armorer slowly knelt down on the young warrior's skins. "The priestess spoke with me about you, young one," she said. Her voice was serious, which was unusual for her. "I am concerned."

Tesh-Dar again felt a wave of burning shame, a sensation that was alien to her. Disappointing the priestess was bad enough. Disappointing this ancient clawless one, who stood so high among the peers and had played a major role in Tesh-Dar's young life, was far worse. "I have a plan, mistress," she said humbly. She explained what she planned to do. "I will choose Nayan-Tiral," she went on. "I believe she has great promise. I shall teach her all that I can."

Pan'ne-Sharakh was silent for a time, considering. Then, she said, "It is not unheard of, to train a *tresh* in such fashion. Yet careful you must be, child," she warned gently. "Teach her, yes, but mind the power of your sword hand, the fire of your Bloodsong. You must stay in the here and now, and not let your spirit merge with your sword, or lost shall you be."

Tesh-Dar nodded in understanding. When the most talented warriors fought, they lost all sense of self beyond their weapon and the battle. It was the ultimate state of mind for combat, but could be deadly in the wrong circumstances. Tesh-Dar fell into such a state almost instantly, using the power of the Bloodsong as a source of strength and speed. It was an ability of which she was exceedingly proud, for few warriors had ever attained this state at any age, let alone as a youth. "I shall not fail, mistress," she promised.

Pan'ne-Sharakh nodded, then offered Tesh-Dar her characteristic mischievous grin. "Then come, child," she said, "it is time for us to eat."

***

With the next dawn, after the morning rituals were complete and training was to begin all around the *kazha*, Tesh-Dar took Nayan-Tiral aside and explained her plan.

"Honored am I," the young warrior, whose next Challenge would be her third, said gratefully as she saluted Tesh-Dar.

"Then let us begin," Tesh-Dar told her, anxious not so much to teach Nayan-Tiral, but to prove to the priestess that she could indeed train the young *tresh*, and do so better than anyone at the *kazha* other than the priestess herself.

As the days passed, Tesh-Dar's talents at teaching were revealed in the dramatic improvements Nayan-Tiral made in her swordcraft. Both the priestess and Pan'ne-Sharakh were impressed: it seemed that the headstrong young swordmistress had found her path to enlightening others. It was not the traditional way of teaching those of Nayan-Tiral's age, but it was certainly not unheard of, and Sura-Ni'khan let the pair be.

Then, just as Pan'ne-Sharakh had originally feared, it happened. With the priestess and many of the *tresh* looking on, as was often the case these days, Tesh-Dar began sparring with Nayan-Tiral, demonstrating a new technique with combat weapons that bore a sharp deadly edge. This in itself was no cause for concern, for *tresh* at Nayan-Tiral's level began to train with such weapons; it had its dangers, but danger was the constant companion for any warrior. While Nayan-Tiral was well below Tesh-Dar's skill level, she had learned much from her young mentor, and her pride and love for Tesh-Dar echoed in her Bloodsong. The two danced a deadly ballet, with the younger warrior pressing her attacks with impressive skill and aggression.

So well did Nayan-Tiral do that Tesh-Dar momentarily forgot where she was and what she was doing, the "here and now" that Pan'ne-Sharakh had once spoken of. It only took a single shard of time for Tesh-Dar to fall into the state of mind that so many of the peers sought, yet failed to achieve, merging her mind perfectly with her weapon. It was not a conscious decision; it was simply a momentary lapse of control and an unforgivable act of negligence by a warrior with her skills.

A heartbeat later, Tesh-Dar found herself staring at the blade of her sword, buried in young Nayan-Tiral's chest, the tip having speared the child's heart. The young *tresh's* bright eyes were wide with shocked disbelief as she slumped to the ground, dead, and Tesh-Dar felt a faint flutter in the chorus of the Bloodsong as Nayan-Tiral's spirit passed from this life to the next. Then Tesh-Dar fell to her knees, cradling the young warrior's body in her arms.

"No," she whispered as mourning marks began to flow down her cheeks, turning her smooth cobalt blue skin pitch black. "*No.*" Shivering with grief and shame, she held the young *tresh*, her soul torn by Nayan-Tiral's dead eyes, still staring up at her mentor. Her killer.

***

Her mind returning to the present, Tesh-Dar opened her eyes, willing the dream away. It did not come to her often now, for many cycles had passed since that dark and horrible day. Part of her mind shied away from what came after, but she seized upon the memory, forcing it upon herself in what had become a ritual act of atonement. The night after she had killed Nayan-Tiral, she had faced punishment on the *Kalai-Il*. It was a massive stone construct at the center of every *kazha* in the Empire that served as a living reminder of the price for failing to walk the Way, for falling from Her grace. Nude, shackled hand and foot, Tesh-Dar had hung above the massive central dais as the warriors and the *tresh* of the *kazha* looked on from the great stones that circled the *Kalai-Il*. Sura-Ni'khan had lashed her with the *grakh'ta*, a seven-tailed barbed whip that was one of the most brutal of all weapons, with all her strength. Eight times the weapon struck Tesh-Dar's back, flaying skin and muscle to expose the bone beneath. She grunted in agony, but never cried out. She had shamed the Empress, her priestess, her peers, and herself with her laxity; she would not further shame them by whimpering during her punishment.

When it was over, she was released from the chains, falling to the dais in a bloody heap. But her punishment was not over until she had staggered down the steps and along the stone walk to reach Sura-Ni'khan, who waited for her across a polished stone threshold. Had Tesh-Dar not reached her by the time the gong of the *Kalai-Il* had sounded twelve times, the priestess would have killed her.

Recovering from her wounds had been worse than being lashed, for the healers were not permitted to assist one who had been punished on the *Kalai-Il*. They could cover the wounds in sterile dressings, but that was all. Tesh-Dar writhed in blinding agony for two days. On the third, she forced herself to her feet, donned her armor, and staggered step by step to the arenas to train. In the days that followed, she nearly died from infection, something that was unheard of among her race in these times. Yet, her body eventually healed itself, and Pan'ne-Sharakh and Sura-Ni'khan had helped as best they could to heal her soul.

With a sigh, her ritual self-punishment now at an end, she pushed aside the thick animal hides of her warm bed and rose like Death's shadow in her night-shrouded room, ignoring the chill of the air around her. She stepped to the window that filled most of one wall of her quarters, staring out at the snow-covered landscape that glimmered from the light of the Empress Moon that hung high above. It was winter now in the Homeworld's northern hemisphere, and the outside temperature was so low that anyone trapped at night without a shelter would almost surely perish.

"Only a few steps," she murmured to herself. It was only a few steps to the door leading to the outside and winter's eager embrace. Such thoughts had come to her often after her punishment so long ago, but they were only fantasy. If she had learned nothing else on the *Kalai-Il*, she had learned the true meaning of duty. As often as Death had called to her, promising to take away her pain, as comforting as was the thought of such release, she could no more kill herself than she could bear children.

That thought brought her to Li'ara-Zhurah. Rather than remain on the nursery world until her child was born, as tradition held, she had requested to return to Tesh-Dar's side as the Empire made its next move against the humans. It was unusual for one to be released at such a stage in the mating process, but not unprecedented, and Tesh-Dar could find no reason to deny the young warrior's request. Tesh-Dar's own First, the warrior who had served as her sword hand to assist in the many things the priestess did each day, had moved up another step toward the throne in the rankings of the peers, and was ready to lead her own *kazha*. Tesh-Dar had decided that Li'ara-Zhurah would make an excellent replacement. When the child was near birth, Tesh-Dar would send her back to the nursery world. In the meantime, Tesh-Dar vowed to herself that she would allow no harm to come to her.

Sighing softly, Tesh-Dar knelt to add more wood to the embers of the fire that kept her quarters from freezing, wishing that it could warm her soul.

***

"We have allowed the humans time to recover from the first blow. Now, it is time to begin the true Challenge," Tesh-Dar said from where she stood at the center of one of the many enormous chambers in the Imperial Palace on the Empress Moon. Like all things built by Kreelan hands, it was in its own way a work of art: the floor was a great mosaic depicting the tragedy of the Curse, while the walls and ceiling were made of clear crystal panels that let the light of the Homeworld shine through. Around her, sitting on thick animal hides, were the last of the Empire's warrior priestesses. In the time of the First Empress, they had numbered in the thousands. Now, there remained only a handful more than a hundred. There had not been a council of war such as this for millennia, and it had shocked Tesh-Dar to the core to see that so few priestesses remained. It was a clear and bitter illustration of the plight of her species.

As the highest among them on the steps to the throne, Tesh-Dar led the council. The Empress was not present, for she was content to leave the details of war in Tesh-Dar's hands. "We have shown them our power in the transformation of the world they called Keran, which we took from them," she went on, "and also have we granted them fair combat by adapting our technology to theirs. We do not know how they have reacted as a species, but we will soon find out."

She closed her eyes and summoned an image in her mind of the systems occupied by the humans. They had taken the navigational charts of the first human ship they had encountered and added to it the knowledge from the wreckage of the human ships left in Keran space. It was a convenience, for now that they knew of the humans' existence, the second sight of the Empress could reach into every corner of their domain.

As Tesh-Dar opened her eyes, the image that had been in her mind shimmered into existence in the air next to her. "Now we will begin to bleed them. Our deeds shall bring great glory to the Empress, but we also search for the One," she explained. "There are two hundred and thirty-seven human-settled worlds. These," a cyan halo appeared around sixteen of the planets, including Earth, "shall not be molested for now. They are critical to the humans for producing ships and weapons, and are the largest population centers. Instead, we will make widespread attacks against shipping and smaller colonies, forcing the humans to give battle while not destroying their ability to wage war."

"Would it perhaps not be wiser, Tesh-Dar," said Mu'ira-Chular of the Alun-Kuresh order, "to do the opposite? To bleed their heart worlds first? Where there are more humans, are we not more likely to find the One? Or should we simply attack all of their systems at once?" It would be a trivial matter for the Empire to do so: the human realm was miniscule against the ten thousand suns of the Empire.

"We strike a precarious balance between fate and time," Tesh-Dar explained. "We do not know if the One has yet been born. The prophecies say that we will know him when his blood sings, but little more." Looking at the images of the worlds suspended above her, she went on, "If we attack all their systems, we may exterminate them before he has taken his first breath. If we prolong the war as long as we are able, the Empress believes there is a greater chance of finding him. And thus may we bring Her more glory across the few remaining generations we have remaining."

Mu'ira-Chular nodded, as it was the will of the Empress to follow this course, but her face betrayed her concerns, not least of which was how close was the Empire's end of days. That their race was dying was not a secret, but few beyond the priestesses who had direct contact with the Empress truly understood how closely extinction loomed.

"My sisters," Tesh-Dar told them, "there is no certainty in what we do. There is only certainty in our fate should we fail to find him. And if we find the One, the Empress believes we are also fated to discover the tomb of the First Empress, Keel-Tath. Then...then may the Curse be lifted and our race redeemed in Her glory."

In chorus, the other priestesses murmured, "In Her name, let it be so."

"What are your commands, my priestess?" one of them asked.

"We shall begin by attacking their ships," Tesh-Dar said as bright cyan lines joined the images of the human worlds. "We do not want to sever their lifeblood, merely bleed them and bring them to battle. I leave detailed planning for this to the Ima'il-Kush," she nodded to one of the priestesses, whose domain was the Imperial Fleet. "Then we will attack these worlds," seven planets were highlighted with cyan halos, "using those warriors of our orders who have earned the privilege by right of Challenge. Unlike Keran, these will be extended campaigns that will take many cycles, giving our warriors many opportunities for combat, and hopefully making the humans even more challenging adversaries. At a time of our choosing, we will expand our attacks against additional human worlds. For now, we will wait and see what comes to pass."

The other priestesses spoke amongst themselves for a time, dividing the human worlds among them in such a way that there would be glory enough for all. Their only disappointment was that so many warriors in the Empire would never get the chance to be properly blooded in battle before the humans were exterminated from the galaxy.

As they discussed their strategies, Tesh-Dar looked at the target worlds. Of the seven, none had any particular features that appealed to her more than any other, so she simply picked one at random that would receive her personal attention.

That one, she thought to herself, looking at a heavily forested world with expansive oceans. It had a sizable human population, far larger than Keran, and a great deal of industry, according to the files extracted from the human computers. Had she cared to ask one of the keepers of the Books of Time who were now the holders of knowledge about things human, she could have learned the planet's human name.

Saint Petersburg.

***

In the armory of Tesh-Dar's *kazha*, Pan'ne-Sharakh sat at a low table, her attention focused on an ornate sword. The blade was so long that the tip would touch the ground if she held the handle at chin height. Gracefully curved so that it could be drawn in an instant from its scabbard, the blade shimmered in the light of the torches that illuminated her work. The crystal handle with inlaid gemstones was large enough for the massive hands that wielded the weapon. It belonged to Tesh-Dar, and was one of the many weapons Pan'ne-Sharakh had fashioned for her in their long acquaintance.

The weapon rested in a carefully padded cradle, the edge facing up toward her. With reverent hands she stroked the gleaming silver metal, fashioning its form as an act of will. Much like the builder caste and the matrix material from which they created anything that was necessary to suit the will of the Empress, the armorers had the gift of working the living metal that made up their edged weapons and the collars that all who walked the Way wore around their necks. It was the hardest, most durable substance in the galaxy, yet was malleable as clay to the gentle touch of a skilled armorer. Kreelan blades were not made with the fires of a forge and the hammer upon the anvil, although their body armor was still made in such a fashion. Pan'ne-Sharakh smiled inwardly at the strength she still possessed, even at her advanced age, to wield a hammer to bend such metal as she would.

They were created from ingots of metal, carefully grown over the span of many years. The ingots were smoothed and shaped by the armorer's vision and touch, their spirits in communion with the metal as they stroked the blade into existence. The handles and the hand guards were generally created by more mundane means, although armorers of Pan'ne-Sharakh's skill – of which there had been few over the ages – could form them as an act of will from virtually any material. The form was always functional first, yet every weapon was also a work of art. The warriors brought glory to the Empress in battle, but Pan'ne-Sharakh and her sisters glorified the Empress through the perfection and beauty of their craft.

She lovingly stroked the sides of the blade with her hands, barely brushing it with her fingertips, as her mind focused on its essence. The metal reacted instantly, the molecular structure realigning as she willed.

This was an old weapon, one she had fashioned for the priestess after the Change, after Tesh-Dar had become the last of the high priestesses of the Desh-Ka order. In Tesh-Dar's hands, the weapon could slice through a brace of enemy warriors. Even if the blade was nicked, it would reform on its own back to a killing edge. In Pan'ne-Sharakh's mind, her fingers not only formed and sharpened the blade, but infused it with her love. While she did not lavish this much attention on every weapon, there were a select few such as this one that always received her gentle touch before and after a challenge. Or a battle.

She absently hummed an ancient hymn to the Empress, a harmony to the Bloodsong that was a soothing warmth in her ancient veins. The clawless ones did not feel the same fire as the warriors, yet in some ways they could read the eddies and currents of their race's spiritual river far better than their taloned sisters.

For Pan'ne-Sharakh, applying her craft always allowed her to see more clearly the things in her mind. She knew that something deeply troubled Li'ara-Zhurah, who had begged to return from the nursery world. It was something more troubling than even the priestess believed, but exactly what was beyond Pan'ne-Sharakh's understanding, and perhaps even that of the Empress. She feared that Li'ara-Zhurah might be one among their race, exceedingly rare, who might choose to depart the Way, to fall from Her grace. It would break the heart of Tesh-Dar, who had pinned such high hopes upon the young warrior. Pan'ne-Sharakh had spoken to Tesh-Dar about her concerns, and while the great priestess listened carefully as she always did, she saw no reason to change what was. If anything, it had made her more insistent that Li'ara-Zhurah accompany her on the new campaign against the humans, in hopes that Tesh-Dar could assist the young warrior through the pain that yet wracked her soul.

Switching to a hymn that was an ancient plea for intercession from the Empress, Pan'ne-Sharakh poured her soul into the metal of Tesh-Dar's sword. It was all she could do to help shield the heart of one she so loved.

***

Li'ara-Zhurah stood by Tesh-Dar's side as her new First, watching hundreds of proud warriors filing past, each one rendering a salute to Tesh-Dar. They moved quickly up the massive ramp of the heavy cruiser that would serve as Tesh-Dar's flagship for this new campaign. They did not march in step, nor was there music or speeches to celebrate the mission of carnage on which they embarked. They needed none of these things, for the Bloodsong echoed in their hearts, and it carried them joyfully to war.

The emotional river of fierce anticipation that flowed through Li'ara-Zhurah's own veins left her strangely unmoved. She yearned for battle, yes, but as a form of release for her soul, and not simply to honor the Empress by slaying Her enemies. Li'ara-Zhurah's spirit had been torn during the first battle with the humans on Keran, and just as it had begun to heal, it again had been torn by her first mating.

She shivered as she brutally shoved the memory aside, not noticing how Tesh-Dar suddenly glanced at her, the great priestess's eyes narrowed with concern. Li'ara-Zhurah had been desperate to leave the nursery world: the thought of having to remain there through the entire half-cycle of a child's gestation had been agonizing. It was not that the nurseries were unpleasant, other than the mating experience itself: indeed, in a race that created beauty in all things with the same passion they applied to personal combat, the nurseries were among the most beautiful worlds of the Empire. The warriors and clawless ones awaiting the birth of their children had no duties, no obligations save the normal daily rituals of dressing, meditating, and preparing for sleep. It was a time of unaccustomed luxury and contemplation, with many of the expectant mothers studying passages from the Books of Time or, particularly popular among the clawless ones, practicing one of the many forms of art known to their civilization.

None of this held any appeal for Li'ara-Zhurah. She was not interested in the Books of Time, and cared not for the arts. Her only desire was to grapple with the humans again, to finally gain the spiritual release that had been denied her on Keran. She had sent an urgent message to Tesh-Dar, praying fervently to the Empress that the priestess would not abandon her to the comfortable prison of the nursery.

Li'ara-Zhurah had been shocked when the priestess summoned her to act as her First. While it was an incredible honor, Li'ara-Zhurah's deepest reaction was relief, not gratitude. She boarded a ship for the Homeworld the same day that Tesh-Dar's response arrived, eager to leave the nightmare of the mating ritual behind her.

Now, waiting to board another ship that would again take her to make war on the humans, her hand, as if by its own accord, strayed to her belly. She thought of the life growing within her, and fervently prayed that it would be a female. A sterile female. The thought of bringing forth one of the misshapen males was unutterably vile, and she would not willingly see the torture of mating inflicted upon any fertile offspring. The child was now nothing more than a small but rapidly growing collection of cells, a tiny nub of tissue inside her womb. There would come a time, soon, when its spirit would awaken. It was then, long before even the healers could determine what the child's gender was to be, that she would know if it was to be male or female. She knew the souls of the males formed part of the Bloodsong; but if the songs of the females formed an ever-churning river of emotion, the songs of the males were little more than tiny pebbles at the bottom of the river over which the water flowed. She would know the birth of a female's spirit from its strength and clarity; from a male, she would sense little but its existence. Yet her apprehension about the nature of her child remained. In her darkest dreams she plunged a dagger into her belly, but to do so would have cast her from the grace and love of the Empress to spend eternity in the infinite Darkness.

She knew such thoughts were tantamount to heresy; thus they remained unspoken, especially to Tesh-Dar. She trusted the great priestess with far more than her life: Tesh-Dar had touched Li'ara-Zhurah's spirit in a way that was rare among her people, a gift possessed by only a few of the great warrior priestesses. That was before Li'ara-Zhurah's mating, during the battle for Keran. She would never willingly allow Tesh-Dar to so openly probe her spirit now. Tesh-Dar had the authority and the power to do so if she wished, but Li'ara-Zhurah hoped that the priestess's respect for her would hold her curiosity at bay should she sense anything amiss.

Li'ara-Zhurah knew that her emotions were transparent to the peers, and particularly to Tesh-Dar, but none of her sisters could fully glean the focus of her fears. They believed her soul to still be grief-stricken over what had happened to her at Keran, and she was content to allow their misperceptions to continue. For herself, deep in her heart, she wished for death before the turn of the next great cycle when she would again have to mate. The war with the humans offered her a convenient solution: there would be many opportunities to die with honor for the glory of the Empress.

FIVE

Dmitri Andreevich Sikorsky sat in a small booth in one of the many
nondescript cafés that were scattered about the city of Saint Petersburg,
the capital of the planet that bore the same name. The founders had tried
to recreate some of the ornate majesty of the original city in Russia on
Earth, but had only succeeded in producing a tawdry imitation of Peter
the Great's vision. The only thing they had duplicated with
uncompromising success was the tyranny and despotism that had
characterized so much of the history of their ancestors' motherland.

In times long past, in a nation on Earth that had once been known as
the Soviet Union, Sikorsky would have been known as a dissident. He was
a member of a quiet underground movement yearning for political change,
but unable to openly express it without suffering severe reprisals. More
active demonstrations of political discontent, such as armed rebellion, were
simply impossible, as the government controlled all the weapons. Even
street rallies were tantamount to suicide. The secret police rarely kicked
down doors in the middle of the night anymore because they did not have
to: most of the real "threats to the state" had long since been imprisoned,
exiled to Riga, or executed. That did not keep them from periodically
terrorizing the populace to remind them of the true power of the state, but
Sikorsky and his underground companions were thankful for what few
blessings came their way.

Unable to confront the power of the state in any other fashion,
Sikorsky had done the only thing he could to fight back: he had become
an agent for the *Alliance Française*. Sikorsky considered himself a patriot,
but after he had experienced first hand the excesses of the government and
the Party that controlled it, he had to do something, no matter the risk.

After the armistice ended the war and he was released from military
service, he managed to get a job as a foreman of a construction firm

(which, like all commercial ventures, was owned by the state). He was involved in the reconstruction of the Alliance Embassy, which had been burned to the ground when the war started, and had made a number of friends on the embassy staff. Over the years, he had been required to maintain and repair a number of the buildings on the compound, which gave him continued opportunities to maintain contact with them.

Years later, when the provisions of the armistice that ended the war expired and the Alliance and Terran inspection teams returned home, the true power behind his own government came out of hiding, and a new cycle of repression began. Sikorsky had looked the other way, trying to ignore the truth, until the secret police came for his son-in-law. Like many citizens of Saint Petersburg, the young couple could not afford their own place to live, so Sikorsky and his wife had taken them in until their fortunes improved. Sikorsky had never viewed this as a bad thing, as he cherished his daughter and loved having her around, and her husband was a good young man who treated her well and was respectful toward her parents.

Then, one night, the secret police came. Sikorsky had never thought it would happen to him. Why should it? He had always been loyal. He had fought in the war. He did his job and kept his mouth shut, and his family did the same. Or so he thought.

Roused from sleep when the apartment's flimsy front door was kicked in, he tried to protest. He shut his mouth quickly when a cold-eyed man wordlessly shoved a gun in his face. Without any explanation, without even a single shout, a dozen members of the secret police swarmed into the apartment, beat his son-in-law unconscious, then dragged him out. Sikorsky's daughter, Natalia, was taken out, too. She was not beaten, but was bound with handcuffs. She had looked at Sikorsky as they paraded her out, while he looked on in wide-eyed shock. Her expression had been calm, even proud. The look in her eyes told him that this had not come as a surprise, and that there was a reason the secret police were here. She and her husband had been members of the underground. Dissidents.

Sikorsky would never know what it was that she and her husband had done, for the government did not bother explaining its actions to the great unwashed of its citizenry. He never saw or heard from her or her husband again.

Two months later, the Alliance Embassy's water supply was having problems, and Sikorsky was sent to direct repairs. Knowing that there would be secret police informants on his repair team, he managed to get a moment alone with an embassy military attaché whom he had met years before as a junior Alliance officer right after the armistice. After a very brief greeting, Sikorsky discreetly passed the man a small envelope when he shook his hand goodbye. On the small piece of paper the officer found inside the envelope was written Sikorsky's contact information and the location of a munitions factory that his company had helped build that was illegal under the long-term provisions of the armistice. He had hoped that the Alliance would come and shut down the factory and hold the government accountable. It would not bring back his daughter, he knew, but it was something. For the first time since his military service, he felt like he was *doing* something.

Unfortunately, the French did nothing about the factory that he had risked his life to show them. The inspection teams had long since left the planet, and the Alliance was far more concerned about the state of their economy than an illegal munitions factory. Sikorsky had been devastated, wondering if he had risked his life for nothing.

Even though the Alliance government decided not to act, their intelligence services were very interested in Sikorsky. The information he had provided was the first evidence they had seen that Saint Petersburg was blatantly violating the long-term provisions of the armistice. After verifying the factory's existence using other sources they already had on the planet, they decided to develop Sikorsky as an agent. As a spy.

That had been ten years ago. Ten years since Sikorsky's daughter had disappeared, most likely raped and then murdered. Ten years of watching his wife go from being in a state of near-catatonic depression to becoming a fanatic member of the Party, Saint Petersburg's ruling elite, in some manifestation of guilt-driven insanity that Sikorsky would never understand. Yet even that, in its own way, had served a purpose, for her rabid support for the Party had led to minor but significant promotions for him that had given him access to more people and information that the Alliance had found useful. His construction work put him in touch with many people who were. The latest was a scientist working on a special project to develop coal as a power source. Sikorsky had no idea why anyone off-world would care about such things as coal power plants, but the information provided by the scientist – one of the many informants Sikorsky had recruited over the years – had clearly gotten the attention of the Alliance.

The Confederation, he corrected himself with an inward smile. He was not sure he believed in the ridiculous tale of aliens attacking human space, but the formation of the Confederation was real, and it was an event that he welcomed. In the last few months, Earth had closed its embassy, consolidating its mission in a newly constructed wing of the Alliance Embassy, that was then officially redesignated as the Confederation Embassy to Saint Petersburg. Then the new ambassador of the Confederation Government, who was the former ambassador of the Alliance, presented his credentials to Chairman Korolev. From what Sikorsky's wife had heard from her Party friends, Korolev had been livid about this new development,but had been powerless to do anything about it.

To Sikorsky, anything that the Party did not like was good for his people and his world.

The Confederation's unexpected interest in these strange coal power plants was why he was sitting here in this café. Sikorsky was a frequent visitor here, often holding informal interviews for people looking for a job, and so his presence would not be unusual in the eyes of any secret police informants. He had received a coded message from his Confederation controller to meet someone here who needed the cover of a job in his company. All he had been told was that he was to meet a woman, and her name was Valentina Tutikova. He was to treat her as he would any candidate, reviewing her credentials and interviewing her as he normally would, hiding the cover aspect of their relationship in plain sight of the secret police.

His controller had never had him meet someone like this before, and it had made him nervous. His nervousness had turned to shock when his wife confided in him that one of her Party friends had told her that the daughter of a well-placed bureaucrat was looking for a job, and Sikorsky had been highly recommended. The girl's name was Valentina Tutikova.

Fortunately, he had been making dinner, and when he spilled hot soup all over his pants in reaction to his wife's revelation, she had thought his shouts of pain and annoyance were only the result of some clumsiness on his part. He had been stunned that the Confederation would go so far and risk so much to establish their agent's credentials. It certainly impressed upon him the importance of the person he was to meet. He only hoped that the Confederation was not pulling the proverbial tiger by the tail: the Party and the secret police might have been fooled for now, but he doubted it would last for long.

In the booth, he sipped his tea and consciously avoided looking at his watch as the appointed time for the meeting arrived, trying instead to focus on the morning edition of the latest Party propaganda displayed on the view screen built into the tabletop.

He only looked up when the bell on the door jingled and a young woman walked in.

***

While the documents that every citizen on Saint Petersburg was required to carry said that her name was Valentina Mikhailovna Tutikova, the young woman's true identity, if one could call it that, was Scarlet.

Born Mindy Anne Black, she had joined the Terran Intelligence Agency, or TIA, at the age of twenty. She was a talented linguist, was superbly fit, extremely intelligent and a fast learner, and had nerves to cope with the most extreme situations. TIA had a very special program for such talented people, and it did not take long for her to come to the attention of the powers-that-be.

Two years later, Mindy Black died in a staged vehicle accident. At least that's what the coroner's report said. Since then, the closest she had to a real name was her codename, Scarlet. She had trained for two more years in the skills she would need to survive in the field as one of a handful of special operations agents. They were only assigned the most difficult missions, ones where the value of their objective was only matched by the difficulty in achieving it. Only five people in the entire Confederation knew who and what she was, and only two of them knew she was on Saint Petersburg. One of them was Director Penkovsky. The other was her controller, a man – or woman – she had never met, but whose coded messages sent her across the human sphere to risk her life.

Her mission now was to follow up on the information the Confederation had received that Saint Petersburg was building nuclear weapons and, if she could, verify if it was true. The Alliance had built an extensive network of informants here, one of whom had turned out to be an innocuous construction manager who had turned dissident, and then had become an asset, an informant. He would help her by providing the information, contacts, and access she required for her mission.

The setup with her contact had been arranged through another set of Alliance-turned-Confederation agents, who also arranged for the proper documentation for her when she arrived. The really hard part had been actually getting planetside: it was virtually impossible for any ship, even a small one, to get to the surface without drawing the attention of the planet's coast guard. Getting through customs was also virtually impossible, as the customs teams were led by secret police informants who pried apart every box and container.

Her only option had been an experimental sub-orbital insertion system being developed by the Confederation Marine Corps, and a merchant ship was hastily fitted with a concealed launcher. The timing of the operation was critical: the ship had to arrive at precisely the right time and place in orbit for one of the periodic meteor showers that lit up the skies over much of Saint Petersburg. It had been a divine coincidence that would help cover her arrival; a single brilliant streak across the sky might have drawn unwanted attention. The ship's crew managed to hit the launch window just right, and she was quietly jettisoned from the ship to join a host of other shooting stars. She had never ridden in a deployment pod, which was a grandiose name for a human-sized can covered with ablative material that both absorbed radar tracking signals and acted as a heat shield. She also hoped to never have to use one again: the ride down had been a roaring, bone-jarring experience, and it had taken all her nerve to remain calm as the pod howled down to an altitude of only three hundred meters before it suddenly disintegrated around her. From there it had been a comparatively unexciting, and very brief, parasail ride to the ground.

After carefully burying her chute and other gear that she would not be taking with her for now, she changed into what passed for casual wear in

Saint Petersburg city, carrying what she needed with her in a rucksack that could quickly be altered to look like a well-used soft-sided travel bag.

She had landed a few kilometers from a town to the north of Saint Petersburg, and quickly made her way to the train station there under cover of darkness. Arriving in early morning, just as the first rust-streaked commuter train pulled into the station, she made a quick stop in the women's rest room. There, carefully tucked behind the broken toilet paper dispenser in one of the stalls, were her documents. A rumpled white envelope contained a passport, work permit, a visa to live in Saint Petersburg city, an inter-city travel permit, money card, a Party membership card, and an electronic ticket showing that she had boarded a train yesterday in Vasilevsky, a town further to the north and her home of record as shown in her papers, before transferring to this commuter train. It would not stand up to intensive scrutiny, but it would get her past any militiaman who happened to check her travel itinerary.

After quickly changing into a poor-fitting dark gray pantsuit that was typical of the other women she had seen, she grabbed her bag and boarded the train like everyone else, blending in with the other drab and morose commuters heading to the worker's paradise of Saint Petersburg.

***

Sikorsky watched as the young woman casually glanced around the café. He was about to get up and hail her when the waiter, whom Sikorsky suspected of being a secret police agent, walked over to her. After a brief exchange of words, he pointed at Sikorsky, and the young woman thanked him and headed back to the booth.

"*Gospodin* Sikorsky," she said with an eager smile, "it's so nice to meet you. I am—"

"Valentina Tutikova," Sikorsky said, standing and offering his hand, "of course. It's very nice to meet you, as well." He shook her hand, and watched her as she settled herself into the booth. With drab brown hair cut in the haphazard style typical of the capital city's women and wearing very little makeup, dressed in clothes that half the other women in the city had in their tiny wardrobes, with ugly black pumps to match, she gave the impression of being just another ordinary citizen looking for a job. Even her eyes were a muddy brown as they looked at him eagerly. She appeared to be in her mid-twenties, but he could not pin down her age: he thought she could easily be older, and perhaps younger. She was not ugly, nor was she particularly attractive. She was outwardly unremarkable by any measure, and would have been invisible in a crowd. Even the waiter, who was infamous for ogling the women who came to the café, did not give her a second glance. She made him think of a creature he had once heard about that was found on Earth: the chameleon, able to change the color of its skin to suit its environment. He wondered what she was really like, but decided that it was probably best not to know.

The only sign he had that she was something other than a daughter of a middling Party bureaucrat had been her handshake: his knuckles had cracked under the pressure of her grip. That was saying something, considering that Sikorsky had worked with his hands in construction all his adult life and his upper body was built like a bear. He took it for the silent signal that it was meant to be, before shoving the fact that she was a Confederation agent aside and getting down to business.

"So, Miss Tutikova, let us go over your background, shall we?" he began as he normally did for such interviews. He asked bland questions about her family and education, her Party standing and participation in Party-sponsored events. She gave equally bland answers that, like her train ticket, would never survive a real investigation, but would be good enough for a casual information scan. Together, they fed the eyes and ears of those who cared to listen with mindless drivel.

Sikorsky realized that Tutikova – or whatever her real name was – answered everything so naturally and played her part so well, that after a while he lost all trace of his own nervousness. "Well," he said as he came to the end of his interview questions, "your background is certainly impressive, young lady. I believe we can get you started right away."

"Thank you, comrade," Tutikova told him earnestly. "That is such good news!" She paused a moment, obviously embarrassed. "Would you happen to know where I might find a hotel?" she asked. "I have a city visa, so I can live here, but of course I have not had time to find an apartment."

Sikorsky smiled. "Do not trouble yourself, dear," he told her. "If you wish, you can stay with my wife and myself until you find something." It was a very typical practice: the Sikorskys had an extra room, where their daughter and her husband had lived, and would frequently put up people just like Tutikova to help make ends meet. It was another bit of fortunate timing that the extra room was currently empty.

Putting on a picture-perfect display of gratitude, Tutikova shook his hand again, slipping him a small wad of money as she did. The move was meant to be seen by prying eyes for what it appeared to be: a gray market deal. In a state where everything was controlled by the government, where citizens were expected to aspire to political perfection, it was a supreme irony that anyone who wasn't making small deals on the side was viewed with deep suspicion. The government wasn't concerned about the gray market economy, which worked far better than the "real" economy run by the government. The Party simply wanted its citizens to be doing something incriminating to make the job of the secret police that much easier.

"Wonderful!" Sikorsky said as he clumsily pocketed the money. Gathering up his papers, he ushered Tutikova out of the café. A block down the street, they got in his battered car and he headed for his apartment, the little electric vehicle humming loudly.

"What do we—" Sikorsky began before she cut him off by putting a finger to her lips.

Tutikova — Scarlet — twisted one of the buttons that was inside her jacket and was rewarded with a green glow. It was a counter-surveillance device that would detect any eavesdropping devices or signals in or aimed at the car. "It's safe to talk," she said.

Sikorsky was shocked at the change in her voice, even in those simple words. She was no longer the eager young Valentina Tutikova, but something else entirely. He just was not sure what. "What are we to do?" he asked quietly. "There is no way I can get you into the coal plants without a full security check. That would take time, and..."

"And my cover would never hold," she finished for him, nodding. "We don't need a security check, because the coal plants aren't what I'm after, Dmitri. I need to know where they're taking the slag and fly ash after the coal is burned. We believe they must be transporting it from the plants to some central facility. That's what I'm interested in. We need to find it and figure out a way to get me inside, but finding it will do." If the government was indeed gathering uranium from the waste byproducts of the massive coal plants, there would have to be a large facility where the uranium-235 was being extracted and processed. She hoped the bombs were built at the same facility, but she would not know that until, or if, she got that far.

Sikorsky frowned. "I don't know where they may be taking the waste," he said, "but I know it is carried away by special trains, at least some of it. It is odd, actually: the basic design of the plants has a very large chemical separation complex to break down the waste products. This was a very expensive and difficult part of the plants to build. Then, of what comes out, the majority is slag that is simply dumped next to the plant in mountainous piles. That is what I would have expected them to do, without bothering with the chemical separation processing. What comes out of that, though...that is hauled away in sealed container cars in much smaller trains." His frown deepened. "I always thought that was odd," he went on, "that they would bother sealing up the waste for transport. They told us that it was for environmental safety. I should have known then that there was something wrong." Protection of the environment, or keeping people safe from environmental hazards, had never been high on the list of the government's priorities. He glanced over at her as he made another turn, drawing out their time in the car where they had some privacy. "What is in those trains, Valentina?"

She momentarily debated whether she should tell him. In most operations, the less one knew, the better. There were some cases, though, where everyone was in so deep it didn't matter. If Sikorsky was caught and interrogated now, he would reveal her interest in the coal plants and where the waste products were being taken. That in itself would be enough to lose the game, so telling him what was really going on wouldn't truly matter. "Believe it or not," she told him, "we believe they're extracting uranium and other fissile materials out of the coal ash. We think Korolev is building an arsenal of nuclear weapons."

A horn suddenly blared and Sikorsky cursed as he steadied the car. He had been so shocked he had nearly run into a car coming the opposite way.

"*Bozhe moi*," he whispered. "My God. Is such a thing possible?" The thought of the rulers of this world in control of even one nuclear weapon was terrifying.

She shrugged. "The scientists – including your contact – seem to think it is, at least in theory. I'm here to find out if it's true. Which brings us around again to our problem: we need to find out where those special trains are going."

"I know someone who might be able to help us find out," he told her. "I have an acquaintance, let us say, who has access to the central train scheduling system. We pay him *na levo*, under the table, to help make sure that the trains we use to transport heavy equipment and materials to construction sites reach their destinations on time, or at least not too late. He is not one of us – not a dissident – but he is not a Party man. He is also a fool for attractive young women." Glancing over at her, he said, "But that can wait for later. You must be exhausted. I should get you home and introduce you to Ludmilla, get some food into you, and let you get some rest."

Tutikova shook her head. "We don't have time for rest, Dmitri," she told him gravely. "I only have six days before I'm extracted. After that..." She trailed off, staring out the passenger-side window.

"After that, what?" he asked.

She turned to look at him, and he was shocked at the glimpse of what she really was behind her disguise. Her eyes were hard, and her voice even more so. "Dmitri, they only send me in where things might get very bad. I can't tell you exactly what's going to happen, because I wasn't told. But if I were you, I would make sure to be on a nice visit to the countryside a long way from here in six days." What she didn't tell him was that she was to be extracted by Confederation Marines. And that was if things went well. If things went badly, she wouldn't be extracted at all. Ever.

Sikorsky felt his stomach clench. *Six days*. Punching a small keypad on the steering wheel, he said, "I'll give him a call right now."

SIX

"All hands, prepare for normal space emergence in two minutes," the XO's voice sounded through the compartments and passageways of the *Yura*.

On the bridge, Sato watched his crew in action as the indicators for the various stations throughout the ship changed from amber to green on the status board, signaling the readiness of the various departments for the jump back into normal space. *Yura* was on the third leg of her patrol route, which would take her to Kronstadt, a rapidly growing Germanic colony that boasted fifteen million people and was on a popular trade route between the Confederation worlds and the Rim colonies.

Kronstadt had a small but efficient coast guard, but no true warships – yet. The colony had long produced merchant ships of every size, and after joining the Confederation had shifted over two thirds of its yard capacity to warship production, while retaining the other third for badly needed transports. On top of that, they had implemented a massive building program to double their shipbuilding capacity in eighteen months. While many in the Kronstadt government had still not accepted that Mankind was under serious threat, especially since the Kreelans had not ventured further into human space beyond Keran, there was universal agreement that if the Confederation wanted to finance a major building program, Kronstadt would be happy to reap the benefits of it. The tradeoff was that the colony had to raise a minimum of one Marine assault regiment per million people, and arrange for the training of Territorial Army forces that included every able-bodied male and non-pregnant female of at least seventeen years of age. The Confederation would pay for their weapons and provide the cadre to train them, but the colony had to provide the bodies. For Kronstadt this was not terribly difficult, for they already had a large and well-trained national guard force.

"All stations report ready for emergence, sir," Lieutenant Commander Villiers, his XO, reported. "I suggest that we—"

Sato silenced him with a slight shake of his head. Glancing over at the life support station, Sato saw Midshipman Michelle Sanchez looking at him. Seeing that he was looking at her, she nervously turned back to her console.

"Did you have something on your mind, midshipman?" he asked her.

"No...no, sir," she said stiffly.

Sato suppressed a smile. Sanchez, a black-haired beauty who could melt half the crew with one glance from her deep brown eyes, was bright and competent. If she had a weakness, it was her lack of self-confidence. She consistently had the right answer in any given situation, but was too afraid of making a mistake, of making herself look foolish, particularly when speaking in front of the captain. As her senior mentor aboard ship, he had been helping her overcome this weakness, and had just set her up for a learning experience. This was the first time she had been on the bridge during a normal space emergence, so technically it was unfair to expect her to know all the various protocols. There was one regulation, however, that was immutable, that every officer and rating on the ship should know.

He waited a few more seconds to see if she would react before saying, "Navigation, begin the transpace sequence," he ordered.

"Excuse me, captain," he heard Sanchez say. Her voice was clear, but obviously forced.

"Yes, Sanchez?" he said casually, turning to her.

"Sir...forgive me for saying so, but aren't we supposed to go to general quarters before normal space emergence?"

He gave her something that he rarely gave to anyone beyond Steph and a few close friends: a wide smile. "Very good, midshipman," he told her. Then, with mock reproof in his voice as he glanced at Villiers, he said, "The XO must've forgotten to tell me."

Villiers threw up his hands in mock surrender, which drew smiles and a few chuckles from around the bridge.

"Well done, midshipman," Sato told Sanchez, his voice serious now. "I expect my officers and crew – each and every one of them – to think and, as necessary, to act in the ship's best interests. Going to general quarters before normal space emergence is one of our most important regulations, and for good reason: the enemy could be waiting for us, and we have to be ready to come out fighting. It's unlikely a captain or XO would ever forget to do it, but unlikely things sometimes happen, and it's up to you to ask questions when you think something might be wrong. I'll never penalize you for thinking. Always remember that."

"Yes, sir," she said, sitting up straighter in her combat chair, obviously proud of herself. "I will, sir."

Sato nodded. "In that case, Sanchez, you get the honors: bring the crew to general quarters. Navigation, start the transpace sequence."

"Aye, aye, sir!" Sanchez replied before hitting the general quarters alarm. "All hands, general quarters!" her voice boomed over the piercing hoot of the alarm. "Man your battle stations!"

Villiers started a timer as he himself dashed off the bridge to reach his own battle station in the auxiliary bridge halfway across the ship. The Marines, who were always in their combat armor for any planned normal space emergence, pounded through the passageways to get to their anti-boarding stations, making sure all the airtight hatches were closed behind them.

The status console now showed the "Christmas tree" for general quarters, with all the departments of the ship reporting their readiness. All of the amber lights quickly changed to green and the general quarters klaxon turned itself off.

"Forty seconds flat, skipper," the XO reported breathlessly from the auxiliary bridge as the last indicator turned green. "Not half bad."

Sato nodded his head, inwardly grinning at the thought that Villiers must have broken a world speed record to get to his position in time. He normally would have been at the auxiliary bridge, anyway, but he had wanted to see how Sanchez did first-hand.

As for the crew's time, forty seconds was a huge improvement. At their first emergence, into the Sandoval system, the crew had taken over ninety. They had done a lot of drills between then and now to help them improve. "Agreed," he said. "But we can do better, XO. I'd like to shave at least five seconds off of that next time."

"Will do, skipper," Villiers said. He did not take Sato's comment as a rebuke, but as a challenge. They had a good crew, and they would only get better over time. Like Sato, he wanted to have the ship combat-ready as quickly as possible, since speed was life.

"Navigation auto-lock engaged," the computer's synthesized female voice interjected over the ship-wide intercom. "Transpace sequence in five...four...three...two...one...Transpace sequence initiated. Sequence complete. Emergence into normal space...now."

The main bridge display suddenly lit up with a visual of the Kronstadt system, with the shining crescent of the planet itself directly ahead.

"Navigation confirmed, Kronstadt system," the navigator announced. "Emergence deviation negligible. We're—"

"*Contact!*" the tactical officer shouted. "Four bogies at three-three-eight mark eight-nine relative. Distance fifty thousand kilometers." Four yellow icons appeared on the tactical display to the left of the ship's current heading. Several dozen other icons, all green, also appeared.

Sato didn't hesitate. "Maintain course, all ahead flank!" If the four unidentified ships were friendly, he would just be giving them a good show of how fast *Yura* could accelerate. And if they weren't friendly ships, *Yura* would have the advantage of surprise. "Communications, get a positive ID on those ships."

"All ahead flank, aye," Lieutenant Bogdanova reported tersely as she smoothly brought the ship's acceleration up to maximum. She could feel the deep thrum of the sublight drives vibrate through the deck beneath her feet as *Yura* leaped forward.

"Forward kinetic batteries and heavy lasers locked on and tracking all bogies, sir," the tactical officer reported. "Recommend closing to ten thousand kilometers to engage."

On the bridge tactical display, the green icons representing known friendly ships were clearly scattering away from the yellow icons like a school of fish fleeing from a predator.

"Sir, I'm picking up multiple mayday signals," the communications officer reported. "Eight ships report they've been hit and are losing air. Three of them are Kronstadt coast guard cutters."

The four yellow icons suddenly changed to red.

"Hostile contacts confirmed," the tactical officer reported. "All four appear to be Kreelan warships, destroyer category."

Sato had to commend the Kronstadt coastguardsmen. They had incredible courage to go up against Kreelan destroyers with their lightly armed cutters.

"Request that any surviving Kronstadt coast guard vessels form on us," Sato ordered. "And try to get the merchantmen to all turn toward us. If we can get the Kreelans to head our way, we'll close the range more quickly."

"Assuming they don't jump out," Villiers said through the vidcom terminal on Sato's combat chair.

"They won't," Sato shook his head. "They'll never run from a fight, even when they're completely outmatched." He knew that the actual odds in this battle were against him: four destroyers, competently handled, could take a single heavy cruiser. But not *his* heavy cruiser. Not the *Yura*.

As they watched the display, most of the green icons turned in *Yura's* direction. The merchant captains were desperate for help, and were more than eager to get closer to the only real human warship in the entire system. They weren't fast enough to get far enough from Kronstadt to jump, and were far too slow to run from the enemy ships in normal space. Three of the ones that had sent mayday signals suddenly vanished, destroyed.

"The enemy is just firing indiscriminately, sir," the communications officer said, trying to hold her emotions in check. "Some of the ships are even broadcasting their surrender, but the Kreelans are just ignoring it."

"The Kreelans don't take prisoners," Sato said flatly. "Take my word for it."

***

Riyal-Tiyan tensed as the tactical display showed another human ship jump into the system. As the senior shipmistress of the small squadron of destroyers, her mission had been simple: wreak havoc among the human shipping lanes in this area of space. She was specifically not to attack planets or any orbital complexes, only ships. Her purpose was to test how well the humans had developed their defenses and to rekindle their respect for and fear of the Empire.

This was the second system her squadron had visited. In the first one, they had destroyed six merchant ships and three lightly armed defense vessels before the other merchantmen had jumped away. Some smaller craft, armed only with small kinetic weapons, had risen to challenge her destroyers. She had saluted their courage by allowing them to live as she took her warships on to the next target.

In this system, which the humans had named Kronstadt, her ships had jumped into the midst of a small fleet of merchant vessels, which tried to run away from them like terrified steppe beasts before the claws of a *genoth*. With guns hammering and lasers singing, her ships tore at the fat merchantmen, then turned with equal ferocity on the small human warships that bravely sped into the attack. Like those Riyal-Tiyan had encountered at the first system – Andover, the humans called it – these were only lightly armed and hardly worth calling warships. They put up a spirited fight, however, and succeeded in diverting her attention long enough for the merchant ships to try and race for their jump points.

Now a new ship had appeared, and it immediately began to race directly toward her squadron. Not a merchant vessel, then.

"Ah," she sighed with anticipation as the tactical display showed the targeting systems emanating from the human vessel. "A true warship. Ayan-Kulil," she said to her tactical officer. "Let our ships form in pairs and flank the human warship. Ignore the merchant ships for now."

A moment later the other three destroyers turned from hammering the defenseless merchant ships and sped to their places in the designated formation to greet their new opponent.

***

"They've formed up in pairs, sir, trying to flank us," the tactical officer reported tensely.

Sato eyed the display, silently calculating his options as the range rings showing the maximum effective range of his weapons quickly converged on the charging Kreelan warships. He was under very strict orders not to let *Yura* suffer heavy damage while she was operating solo: the Confederation Navy was still tiny compared to the number of systems they were tasked with defending, and every ship, particularly the new heavy cruisers like *Yura*, were precious. Each captain on solo patrol had discretion on whether to engage the enemy, but they were not to risk destruction of their ships for any reason, even if the Kreelans were mounting an invasion.

In that scenario, a single ship would not be able to make a substantial difference, anyway.

His main problem was preventing the Kreelans from raking him from two sides at once, which could be lethal to *Yura*. "Tactical," he ordered, "prepare torpedo tubes one through five for salvo fire at the left pair of targets on my mark." Sato didn't expect the torpedoes to hit their targets, but he hoped it would distract that pair of destroyers. "Then engage the right pair with kinetics and heavy lasers. Helm," he turned to Bogdanova, "when I give the order, I want you to come forty degrees to starboard. Let's try to keep them from flanking us on both sides as we pass by."

On the tactical display, *Yura* raced toward the two pairs of Kreelan destroyers, the range rings overlapping. Sato let them close, then close further.

"Enemy kinetics, inbound!" called the tactical officer.

"A little closer," Sato whispered to himself. The destroyers were now close enough to be picked up on visual display, their rakish hulls unmistakable. "On my mark, people...stand by...*mark!*"

Yura shuddered as five torpedoes leaped from their launch tubes and streaked toward the farther pair of Kreelan destroyers. In the same instant, two of the main triple-gun turrets volleyed fifteen centimeter projectiles at the nearer pair of enemy ships, while three heavy laser turrets fired, flaying tons of metal from the sides of the nearer destroyers.

At the same time, *Yura* made a sharp turn to starboard, missing all but a few of the projectiles the Kreelan ships had fired. As the ready rounds in the first two gun turrets ran out, Bogdanova skillfully rolled *Yura* to bring the other batteries to bear.

"Cease fire," Sato ordered as the nearer pair of destroyers disappeared in twin balls of flame and debris, struck by a full salvo of heavy shells. One of the other pair of enemy ships disintegrated under the impact of three torpedoes.

The fourth destroyer escaped unscathed.

"Turn and pursue," Sato ordered, setting aside his pleasure at his ship's performance for later.

Bogdanova brought the ship around, even as the crew belowdecks were reloading the guns and torpedo tubes.

***

Riyal-Tiyan was both shocked and pleased. Shocked that the human ship's weapons had been so effective, and pleased that the humans had apparently not been idle in the time since Keran had been taken by the Empire.

She mourned the loss of her ships and their crews, that they could no longer bring glory to the Empress. She and her own crew would have preferred to turn and charge the pursuing human ship, but Tesh-Dar's orders and the will of the Empress had been clear: the squadrons such as Riyan-Tiyal's were not to sacrifice themselves. In such a situation as this, any surviving ships were to return with information on what they had encountered, and how well the humans were fighting back.

"Prepare to jump," she ordered her navigator, failing to mask her disappointment. They would rendezvous with the fleet heading toward the human world of Saint Petersburg.

***

"They jumped, sir!" the tactical officer said incredulously.

For a moment, Sato didn't believe it. He simply couldn't accept that the Kreelans would run away from a fight. But there was no denying that the surviving Kreelan destroyer had escaped. *Could it be a trick?* he wondered.

That didn't fit any better, he decided. While he couldn't deny what the tactical display showed him, he knew deep in his soul that the Kreelan hadn't run because the captain was afraid of challenging his ship. It was something else, some other reason he didn't understand, and it gave him a bad feeling in his gut.

"Very well," he said finally. "Helm, bring us around toward Kronstadt. XO," he told Villiers through the vidcom, "prepare the cutters for launch: let's see if we can't help the coast guard with search and rescue."

"Aye, aye, sir," Villiers said before he disappeared to carry out his orders.

Sato continued to stare at the place on the tactical display where the Kreelan destroyer had disappeared, wondering where she had gone. And why she had run.

***

After helping to rescue the surviving crew members of the merchant ships and turning them over to the Kronstadt coast guard ships, Sato had placed *Yura* in a high defensive orbit over the planet. Before this battle, he would have been sure that the Kreelans would return in force, but the Kreelan destroyer's sudden departure had shaken his confidence in his assessments of their actions. He knew there must have been a reason other than just "running away to fight another day." That would have been a very reasonable action were it a human destroyer facing off against a heavy cruiser, but was totally out of line with all he knew, or thought he knew, about the enemy.

His decision now was whether to proceed on schedule to the next leg of his patrol, or delay here in Kronstadt in case the Kreelans returned. He knew that, unless the enemy returned only with a token force, his single ship would hardly be able to hold off an invasion fleet. Yet showing the Confederation flag to new signatories like Kronstadt was vitally important. *Yura* had already made a lasting impression, but he was worried about leaving the colony if there was a chance the Kreelans might return soon.

He set that matter aside for the moment. They still had seven hours left before they would have to jump out on their next leg to stay on their patrol schedule. Commodore Hanson had built some time into the navigation exercise for her ships to actually patrol, rather than just jumping from system to system. With the other responsibilities, particularly repairs to the light damage the ship had suffered, taken over by the XO for now, Sato had some time to relax.

Sitting on the side of his bunk, he pulled out a shiny black lacquer box that Steph had given him just before they'd parted at Africa Station. She hadn't told him what was in it, and made him promise not to look until after his first jump. He smiled as he opened it.

Letters. She had written him three dozen letters, each lightly scented with perfume. He had only read three so far, and it had almost been enough to make him want to turn the ship around and head for Earth. Neither of them were terribly good at expressing their emotions face to face. They could talk about things, certainly, but there seemed to be a limit to those conversations, something that held them back. Steph's letters broke through that barrier, cast it aside. The words on those slips of stationery were really *her*. He had read the first one at least a dozen times, then sat down and wrote his own. He had grinned to himself at writing his words of love on ship's letterhead, but that was the only real paper (even if it wasn't actually made out of wood pulp) he had aboard ship. In a way, though, it was fitting: his ship, the Navy, was part of him. And even though it kept them apart much of the time, she had made it clear that it was a part of him that she loved.

He had just begun to read the fourth letter when his alert chime sounded. "Yes?" he called, trying to conceal his irritation.

"My apologies, captain," the communications officer said, "but a courier just jumped in, broadcasting a coded message for us."

"What does it say?" he asked, knowing she would have already decoded it.

"It's a recall from headquarters, sir," she said. "The entire squadron is ordered to rendezvous at an assembly point for a possible assault on Saint Petersburg."

"Damn," Sato spat as he carefully folded Steph's letter and put it back in the box. "Have the navigator plot us a least-time course, then ask the department heads, Marine commander, and the senior NCOs to meet in my ready room in five minutes."

If nothing else, he thought grimly, he no longer had to worry about making a decision about extending their stay in Kronstadt.

SEVEN

"You do well, child," Tesh-Dar told Li'ara-Zhurah after they completed their latest sparring match in the ship's arena. Even the smallest ships of the Imperial Fleet had one aboard, for the arena was not just an affectation of their civilization, it was a fundamental institution of their civilization since before the founding of the Empire. As the fleet made its way toward the human world of Saint Petersburg, Tesh-Dar worked each day with Li'ara-Zhurah, trying to ease the pain from her soul and guide her along the path that the priestess so hoped she would choose to take.

Tesh-Dar not only remembered Pan'ne-Sharakh's words of caution about the young warrior, but had used them as a guide to further build her relationship with Li'ara-Zhurah. She had come to believe that there was indeed something the young warrior was shielding in her heart, and had sought to gently sway her into revealing it of her own accord. Tesh-Dar could have simply ordered her to do it, and while that would have revealed the truth of the matter, it would also likely have destroyed the bond between them. That was the one thing Tesh-Dar was loathe to do, for if Li'ara-Zhurah was to follow in her footsteps and become a priestess of the Desh-Ka, her faith and trust had to be complete, without reservation.

"I am honored by your words, my priestess," Li'ara-Zhurah said as she quickly stilled her breathing after their latest round of fierce swordplay. She knew that she would never be a tenth as good as was Tesh-Dar with any weapon, but she found herself proud of her own abilities: she was no warrior priestess, but knew she could defeat any of her peers. Tesh-Dar pushed her beyond the limits she had set for herself, and Li'ara-Zhurah was openly surprised at how much her combat skills had improved, even in the short time since returning from the nursery world. And much as part of her wished to deny it, the gentle spiritual ministrations of the great priestess had allayed the worst of the melancholy that had so distracted her since the battle of Keran. It had not changed her loathing about bearing a male child, or her fears for any fertile female children, but she had set aside the thoughts of sacrificing herself in battle simply to avoid future matings. Early in the voyage, she had gathered her courage enough to speak to one of the other young warriors who had recently suffered through her first mating. Li'ara-Zhurah was surprised to learn that the warrior had felt much the same as she herself had: the warrior had been greatly distraught by the experience and had suffered similar thoughts of casting her life away before another mating could be consummated. Yet, after a time, the warrior told her, these feelings had passed; mating would never be a pleasant experience, but like with all things in the Empire, it was a duty to the Empress that could not be set aside. Honor would not allow it.

"Come, then, child," Tesh-Dar said as she sheathed her sword. "Walk with me."

Li'ara-Zhurah bowed and saluted before following the great priestess from the arena. Walking behind Tesh-Dar as they passed the next group of challengers set on honing their skills before fighting the humans, Li'ara-Zhurah was again amazed, as she had been every time she had witnessed it, that Tesh-Dar left no footprints in the sand behind her. While the priestess possessed a soul in a vessel of flesh and blood as did all of Her Children, there was so much more to her. The powers she possessed, glimpsed here in the grains of sand that were left untouched by her passing, were both frightening and reassuring. Frightening, because Li'ara-Zhurah could not imagine any enemy, no matter how terrible, standing against her, and reassuring for the same reason: as long as Tesh-Dar lived, the Empire and the Empress would endure, would be safe. The other warrior priestesses were great in their own right, yet they could not compare to the high priestess of the Desh-Ka. If the Empress was the body and soul of Her Children, Tesh-Dar was the physical manifestation of their sword and shield. Li'ara-Zhurah had once heard Pan'ne-Sharakh refer to Tesh-Dar as *Legend of the Sword*, and she had come to understand the truth of that name in the time she had spent with the priestess.

Walking in Tesh-Dar's path was truly a humbling experience.

"You could be more than simply a witness to the powers of the Desh-Ka," Tesh-Dar said quietly as Li'ara-Zhurah moved up to walk beside her, once they were clear of the arena. "I would show you the temple where our order has passed on our knowledge from generation to generation, from priestess to priestess."

Li'ara-Zhurah stopped and stared at Tesh-Dar, her eyes wide with surprise. "My priestess..." she began, unsure if she had heard correctly what Tesh-Dar had said. "Did you just say..."

"Yes, I did, child," Tesh-Dar said, turning to face her young disciple. "Your Bloodsong sings to me in a way that very few have over the many cycles of my life," she explained. "You have suffered in a way that few of our warriors have, and you have shown the strength of will to control, and I hope to conquer, your inner fears. At Keran you brought great glory to the Empress in battle, and showed your courage in the face of a worthy enemy." She looked deeply into the young warrior's eyes, into her soul. "One of my greatest honors, one of my greatest responsibilities as high priestess, is to choose a successor, a warrior who shall inherit the powers passed down to me, whom I shall teach all that I know. I have chosen you. You may choose to accept, or not, as it pleases you."

Li'ara-Zhurah closed her eyes and bowed her head. In a shaking voice she said, "Great priestess, I am unworthy of such an honor." She was suddenly stricken with a deep sense of guilt for the thoughts that had clouded her mind earlier, thoughts of casting away her honor even as Tesh-Dar was considering granting her the greatest gift that she could give, a gift nearly as great to one of her kind as life itself.

She suddenly felt Tesh-Dar's hand against her cheek. "Be not ashamed of your earlier thoughts," she said, as if reading Li'ara-Zhurah's mind. "You have endured much in Her name, child. Our Way is never easy, from the moment we emerge from the womb until the instant our spirits pass into the Afterlife to join the Ancient Ones. To honor Her, we each seek perfection in our craft, as warriors or clawless ones. Yet what we aspire to is something we can never achieve; perfection is a state of grace that only the Empress knows."

"I cannot imagine imperfection in you, my priestess," Li'ara-Zhurah noted humbly.

Tesh-Dar gave an ironic *humph*. "Child, I was punished upon the *Kalai-Il* when I was young, before my Seventh Challenge, and wear the scars of my disgrace upon my back, even now."

Li'ara-Zhurah looked up at her, shocked. "You...were punished upon the *Kalai-Il?*" She shook her head. "Then how..." She looked at the great cyan rune on Tesh-Dar's breastplate that was the twin of the one engraved in the oval disk on her collar. The rune of the Desh-Ka, that only priestesses were allowed to display.

"How did I become a priestess after suffering such dishonor?" Tesh-Dar asked as she turned and began walking down the passageway of the ship toward her quarters, Li'ara-Zhurah falling into step beside her. "Because, like you, daughter, I learned what it truly means to bear the burden of Her honor."

***

While her punishment on the *Kalai-Il* was complete absolution of her sin in the eyes of the Empress and the peers, Tesh-Dar was unable to rid herself of a deep sense of guilt. With Sura-Ni'khan's very reluctant blessing, Tesh-Dar left for what was to be a long and lonely sojourn on the frontier. For nineteen cycles she sought out every challenge that her people faced in the deep unknowns of space and the many worlds they sought to conquer. While there were many perils to be found, there were few that truly tested her.

She served on survey vessels that extended the Empire's domain and probed for any threats to Her Children. Along the way, she taught swordcraft in several *kazhas* in the frontier settlements, astounding even the most senior warriors with her mastery of every weapon. She fought in spectacular Challenges, at times taking on five or more highly skilled opponents and never suffering defeat.

She visited worlds that the Empress had left untouched, planets where mere survival was a challenge. She saw and battled amazing beasts that were far more deadly than the *genoth* of the Homeworld, and even learned to survive vegetation that could kill and maim. These worlds were reserves where the more seasoned warriors of the Empire could embark upon the very kind of spiritual quest on which Tesh-Dar found herself. She visited each of the worlds that were thus preserved, hunting and killing the most vicious creatures in the galaxy, sometimes in company with other warriors, but more often hunting on her own.

Over the cycles that passed, the Legend of the Sword indeed became a legend on the frontier, yet this only served to heighten Tesh-Dar's sense of loneliness. As more pendants were added to her collar in recognition of her feats of skill and courage, as she ascended the figurative steps toward the throne that defined her social standing, so did the peers became more reverent, more distant. It gave her some painful insights into how Sura-Ni'khan, who was only five steps from the throne, and the other warrior priestesses and senior mistresses among the clawless ones must feel. It was a great achievement to reach such a lofty height among the peers, yet it brought a kind of social isolation that Tesh-Dar had never suspected as a young *tresh*.

She corresponded regularly with Sura-Ni'khan, as well as Pan'ne-Sharakh, and their words of hope and praise helped to gradually ease the pain Tesh-Dar felt in her heart. The shame and guilt of killing Nayan-Tiral never left her, but eventually she came to terms with it in the great emptiness of the frontier where she planned to spend the rest of her life if the Empress so allowed.

Tesh-Dar's travels eventually took her to Klameth-Gol, a primordial world that had been left by the Empress as a massive game preserve, where some of the most vicious forms of life in all the Empire could be found, from invisible microbes that challenged the skills of the healers to massive sea creatures half a league in length, and predators on land that made a mockery of the most dangerous creatures that had ever walked upon the Homeworld. These great predators were what Tesh-Dar had come for. Yet, as she and her fellow warriors were to discover, on this planet the largest and most fearsome beasts were merely prey themselves.

Tesh-Dar was returning from a solo hunt in the jungle, where she had been tracking a particularly large predator for the last several days, when she heard an eruption of screams from the hunting encampment. Screams of terror. Screams of pain.

Dashing forward along the trail she had earlier hacked through the dense undergrowth, she burst into the encampment's clearing. With a shock, she saw the dismembered bodies of several warriors strewn about the bare, soggy ground, with seven survivors standing back-to-back in the center, swords drawn. They were terrified, which drove a spike of fear into Tesh-Dar's heart. For these were not young *tresh*, inexperienced and untrained. They were seasoned warriors and hunters who had long cycles of experience on worlds much like this. She could not imagine what would frighten them so.

"Tesh-Dar!" one of them warned. "Beware! There is—"

Suddenly, Tesh-Dar sensed something to her left, very close. Her eyes saw nothing, yet she knew with certainty that there was something there: a disturbance in the air that caressed her skin, a strange scent, very faint, wafting toward her. She did not have Sura-Ni'khan's special powers or second sight as a warrior priestess of the Desh-Ka, but her own senses were naturally keen, and had been refined by many years of training and experience.

With a lightning-quick draw, her sword sang from its sheath. Using a powerful two-handed cut, she slashed the air where her senses told her something was approaching, even though her eyes still saw nothing other than the bodies of some of her companions on the blood-soaked ground.

She cringed as her sword found its mark and a demonic shriek pierced the air. Watching in fascination, she saw a wound open in her sword's path, as if the skin and flesh of the air itself had parted and was left exposed and bleeding.

Bringing her sword overhead in a fluid motion, she slashed downward in a move that could cut through stone. The creature shrieked again, but that was its last act as Tesh-Dar's sword cleaved it in two. The thing collapsed to the ground in a heap of bloody meat and bone.

It was not alone. She whirled just in time as she sensed something behind her, and her slashing sword must have caught this beast at the neck. A cross-section of its body, roughly as big around as her thigh and spouting a torrent of blood, was suddenly revealed at her own shoulder's height. She was knocked to the ground as the thing's body continued forward before it collapsed, making a deep indentation in the ground.

Two of the other warriors suddenly screamed, and Tesh-Dar watched in horror as their bodies were plucked from the defensive ring they had formed and were carried into the forest, caught in the jaws of the invisible creatures. The warriors slashed at their attackers with sword and claw, but it was for naught: a maw suddenly opened out of thin air to bite off the head of one of the warriors. The other warrior was simply carried onward into the jungle, still screaming.

Tesh-Dar stood there for several minutes, reaching out with her senses to see if she could detect any more of the creatures in their midst. While she knew she could not be sure, she did not think there were any more. Yet, she had no doubt they would return.

Cautiously, she joined the five remaining warriors. They were even more terrified now, and Tesh-Dar did not blame them: she was only barely able to suppress her own fear. Kreelan warriors were accustomed to being the hunters, not the hunted.

"What are these things?" Tesh-Dar whispered as the group carefully moved toward one of the creatures she had killed. Even now, all that could be seen of it was the bloody wound left by Tesh-Dar's sword; even in death, the creature's body was completely invisible.

"We do not know, Tesh-Dar," one of them said, trying to control the tremor in her voice. "There are no records of such beasts on this world. I have hunted here before several times, from this very encampment."

"Let us see, then, what we face," Tesh-Dar said as she knelt to the ground. Gathering up handfuls of dirt, she sprinkled it over the creature's invisible body. Gradually, an outline of their menace was revealed.

"In Her name," one of the others whispered.

It looked to be a type of saurian creature, with two powerful hind legs and two smaller, yet still powerful arms, that stood a head taller than herself. As Tesh-Dar continued to sprinkle dirt over the body, she saw that it had a long tail and a ridge of long, sharp spines along its back. Its head was oversize, as large as her torso, and after she found its mouth and pried it open, she and the others could see that the creature had a massive jaw filled with an impressive array of razor-sharp teeth and fangs. While it would have been an impressive opponent without its invisibility, it was still nothing compared to an adult *genoth* on the Homeworld, which was far larger and more powerful. In fact, the creature Tesh-Dar had been hunting the last several days was far larger and more dangerous even than a *genoth*.

The *genoth* was adept at the art of camouflage, but it could not make itself invisible. That was what made these beasts, which were also small and agile enough to move about the jungle silently, truly dangerous. And even worse, unlike the *genoth*, they clearly hunted in packs.

There were no warrior priestesses with this hunting party, and of the survivors, Tesh-Dar was now senior; the lives of the others rested in her hands. It did not take her long to decide what to do. While the warriors of the Empire sought challenges of the body and spirit, there was no honor in sacrificing themselves to mindless beasts. "We must leave," she told them. "Now. Gather up water and any weapons you need, and then we leave for the ship." Their ship, a small craft designed for such forays, was in a clearing several leagues from the hunting camp. Tesh-Dar could have summoned it to them, but there was nowhere for it to land, and it had no means to cut through the canopy of trees above them. The path leading there was well-worn and easily followed, but the jungle pressed close along the entire distance, and there were several streams to cross. They could be easily ambushed anywhere along the route.

"Tesh-Dar," one of the warriors said, "it grows dark. Should we not light a fire and wait until morning?"

Tesh-Dar eyed the monster under the thin coating of dirt. "Night or day makes no difference when we cannot see what comes to kill us," she said grimly. "If it is only a small pack of beasts, they may be content with their kill for a time, but I have no doubt they will return." She warily eyed the jungle surrounding them. "Gather your things. I will attend to the last rites of the fallen."

As the five other survivors ran to collect weapons and water, praying to the Empress that the creatures would not ambush them again here, Tesh-Dar quickly moved among the fallen warriors. Muttering a quiet prayer for each, she gathered up their collars and reverently placed them in a leatherite pouch. The Collar of Honor worn by all of Her Children from the time they came of age was made of living metal that did not part from its owner until death. She would return them to the *kazhas* where the warriors had served, assuming she survived to do so.

In a few minutes, they were ready. "I will lead," Tesh-Dar told them, "and try to give warning if I sense any of the creatures around us. Keep careful watch on the trail behind us for footprints appearing in the earth. That should give you warning of their approach."

"What if they attack from the flank?" one of the warriors asked. "We will not be able to see them with the jungle so close to the trail."

Tesh-Dar offered her a grim smile, her white canines glistening in the fading light. "Then hope they choose not to attack that way." With one last look around, she said, "Come, let us go."

After that, they ran, threading their way along the path as quickly as they could. They did not need lights to see in the darkening forest, for the eyes of the *Kreela* are well-adapted to see in near-total darkness. Tesh-Dar had debated the merits of moving quickly versus more slowly and cautiously, but in the end had decided upon speed: not knowing how many more of the creatures might be out there, she felt that moving at a slower pace would simply give their enemy more opportunities to attack. She would slow for the stream crossings, which she felt were the most likely ambush sites, but otherwise she planned to move as quickly as their feet would carry them.

Sword in hand, Tesh-Dar led the others at a fast pace. They were all experienced warriors in prime condition, and had no trouble keeping up. Even though she was well-accustomed to the sounds and smells of the jungle from having spent weeks here, fear clutched at her heart with every grunt and groan from the forest around her, with every rustle of vegetation.

They were nearly halfway to the ship when the first attack came. The trailing warrior called out a warning when she saw tracks suddenly appear in the ground close behind her. Loosing a *shrekka* at the invisible beast, she was rewarded with a gout of blood and a pain-filled cry before the creature crashed into the vegetation beside the path where it fell to the ground.

"*On the right!*" Tesh-Dar shouted as she sensed something moving in the jungle beside them. One of the other warriors slashed outward with her sword, but was not quick enough: long, serrated teeth appeared out of thin air above the foliage to clamp around her face, and with one vicious shake of its massive jaws the creature yanked her head from her body. Tesh-Dar hurled a *shrekka* at the beast, but only wounded it. Hissing in pain, showing a trail of blood down its side that illuminated part of its body in crimson, the creature quickly moved away into the forest with its grisly prize. One of the other warriors paused just long enough to snatch the fallen warrior's collar from the ground before they ran onward.

The warrior directly behind Tesh-Dar cried out as a beast snapped at her from the other side of the trail, but she was quicker than her attacker: with a cry of fear and rage, she stabbed her pike into the creature's flesh. It roared in pain, slashing at her with one of its forelegs. The claw crashed against her chest armor, sending the warrior flying into Tesh-Dar and knocking both of them to the ground. The other warrior screamed as the beast stepped on her legs and opened its jaws wide.

Rolling clear, Tesh-Dar hurled her sword directly into the thing's open mouth, burying the blade in the back of its throat. It fell to the ground, writhing, and the other warriors hacked and stabbed at its invisible body until it lay still in a blood-covered heap.

As suddenly as the attack had begun, it was over: Tesh-Dar could hear several more beasts moving quickly through the forest away from the trail.

Panting heavily, she turned her attention to the warrior who had been pinned by the legs.

"My left leg is broken," she hissed. "Leave me here, I will draw them away from you for a time."

"Nonsense," Tesh-Dar told her as she waved two of the others to help the wounded warrior to her feet. "I will leave none of you behind. Kuirin-Shuril," she told the remaining warrior, "watch our trail. Let us go."

It was a desperate, agonizing trek over the last league and a half to the clearing where the ship lay waiting. The two warriors carrying the one with the broken leg were fighting for every breath as they trotted and stumbled to the ship, their arms and legs burning and exhausted. The nerves of Tesh-Dar and Kuirin-Shuril were worn and raw from watching the jungle around them, expecting an attack to come at any moment.

"In Her name," one of the warriors whispered in relief as they emerged into the clearing.

That was when the second attack came, but in an entirely unexpected way. With an ear-shattering roar, a beast like the one Tesh-Dar had been hunting the last several days suddenly lunged into the clearing. So tall that its spined head crested the lower trees, it was in many ways a much larger cousin of the invisible creatures, except that its thick – and quite visible – hide was dappled in greens, yellows, and browns that helped it blend in with the jungle vegetation. Normally it would silently lay in wait for its prey, which made it difficult to hunt: ambushing a creature that specialized in ambushes was no small feat.

For a moment, the warriors simply stopped and stared at this latest horror that charged across the clearing directly for them, disbelieving their incredible misfortune. That was when Tesh-Dar noticed that the creature was badly wounded, with deep slashes down its flank and thigh.

It suddenly whipped its head to one side and snapped at thin air, but its jaws closed on something more substantial: one of the invisible creatures appeared in a cascade of blood as the leviathan crushed it in its powerful jaws.

The jungle behind the great beast suddenly parted in over a dozen places, and the air was torn by the high-pitched shrieks of more of the invisible hunters.

"*Run!*" Tesh-Dar screamed above the din, pushing the other warriors toward the ship. As Kuirin-Shuril passed her, she said, "Your sword! Give it to me!"

"But..." Kuirin-Shuril stuttered, her eyes wild with fear.

Tesh-Dar reached out and took the sword from her hand before shoving her toward the ship. "Take the others and go!"

Kuirin-Shuril made to say something else, but Tesh-Dar ignored her and began to run toward the massive animal thundering across the clearing, bellowing in agony and rage. The other warriors would need a few seconds to reach the ship, but the great beast would be upon them before they could make it unless Tesh-Dar could somehow slow it – and its pursuers – down. She had no plan, no strategy, other than to become one with her weapons and let the will of the Empress guide her fate. Once the others were safely in the ship, they could bring the small vessel's weapons to bear on the animals.

Yet, in a cold place in her soul, Tesh-Dar hoped they did not. After all that she had been through in these last nineteen cycles, she realized that this would be her true atonement, not for the peers or even the Empress, but for herself. She knew that she would die here, but it would be a death worthy of a warrior, a death worthy to end her own passage in the Books of Time.

For the first time since her sword had taken Nayan-Tiral's life, Tesh-Dar's Bloodsong rang out in a melody of pure joy.

The huge beast charged straight over her, ignoring the puny two-legged creature in its path until Tesh-Dar's swords sliced deep into the flesh of its inner thighs, cutting the muscles and tendons there. With a deafening howl, it stumbled and crashed to the ground.

One of the invisible creatures suddenly crashed straight into her, and she was knocked from her feet and sent flying, one of the swords torn from her grip. She landed heavily in the soft soil, but before she could roll to her feet to defend herself, one of the invisible creatures clamped its teeth onto her sword arm, making her drop the other sword. Grunting in agony as the powerful jaws ground together, tearing her flesh, she gouged the talons of her free hand into its head, hoping to find its eyes.

The creature hissed in pain and released her, its teeth disappearing into its invisible mouth. She sensed others closing in around her, and she was determined not to die on her knees. Regaining her feet, she drew her dagger and was about to stab at the air where she thought the nearest creature might be when she felt an ice-cold wind upon her back.

Turning around in surprise, she saw Sura-Ni'Khan standing behind her.

The great priestess, clad in shimmering black ceremonial armor, stood with her arms outstretched, but with no weapons other than the claws she had been born with. "Kneel, my child," she ordered, "and shield your eyes!"

Tesh-Dar, not understanding, nonetheless did as she was told. She knelt before the priestess and brought her good arm up to protect her eyes, even as she knew half a dozen animals must be rushing toward them for the kill.

Cyan lightning exploded from Sura-Ni'khan's outstretched hands. Tesh-Dar fell to the ground, her skin tingling as if tiny insects were crawling all over her body. Even with her eyes closed and shielded by her arm, she was nearly blinded by the sun-bright bursts of energy that lanced out across the clearing. Through the deafening thunder, she could hear the squeals of terror as the attacking beasts were vaporized, and her nose filled with the stench of burned flesh and hide. She suddenly realized that this was no weapon fashioned by the hands of the armorers, but was among those special gifts Sura-Ni'khan had received when she became the last high priestess of the Desh-Ka.

The lightning storm raged for several minutes, for there were far more of the creatures than Tesh-Dar had suspected: it was not merely a pack, but a herd of predators that had swept through the area like a plague, converging in pursuit of the mammoth beast that Tesh-Dar had brought down.

She dared to look up in the silence that had suddenly descended, just in time to see Sura-Ni'khan slowly fall to her knees.

"My priestess!" Tesh-Dar exclaimed as she moved to Sura-Ni'khan's side, holding her up with her good arm while ignoring the pain of her own injuries. The priestess's skin was burning hot, and the metal of her armor even hotter. Tesh-Dar lay Sura-Ni'khan on her side and slashed the bindings of her armor, pulling the burning hot metal away from her, cringing as wisps of smoke rose from the black cloth garments beneath.

"My priestess," Tesh-Dar repeated worriedly as she held one of Sura-Ni'khan's hands with her own, "answer me!" Tesh-Dar looked up at the sound of approaching footsteps, and was relieved to see Kuirin-Shuril and the two other uninjured warriors, armed now with heavy energy weapons, running toward her.

Sura-Ni'khan's eyes flickered open, and Tesh-Dar felt the priestess's hand squeeze her own. "My time draws near, child," Sura-Ni'khan whispered. "I had almost given up hope of finding a successor, for there could be no other but you. All this time I waited, and at last heard your blood sing with joy. The Empress sent me here to join you, to protect you, for you are my chosen one." She paused for a moment, looking deeply into Tesh-Dar's eyes. "It is time for you to choose, Tesh-Dar, while I yet have enough days to teach you before I join the Ancient Ones: would you accept the way of the Desh-Ka?"

Lowering her gaze, bowing her head, Tesh-Dar knew in her heart that she was ready. She had faced many challenges and stared Death in the face, yet this was the first time she had felt her soul finally break free of its bonds of guilt and shame. Her heart and spirit were whole again. "I accept, my priestess," she said quietly.

As the words escaped her lips, she and the others vanished from the planet, brought home by the will of the Empress.

EIGHT

Despite his best efforts, it had taken three precious days for Sikorsky to set up a meeting with his contact from the train dispatch center, Pyotr Medvedev. After a great deal of wrangling, Sikorsky and Valentina – Scarlet – had agreed to meet him at an underground dance bar in a rundown industrial district of Saint Petersburg city. Accessible through a battered metal door in an equally battered warehouse, it had no sign out front, no parking, no indication of what it was other than the people who trickled in and out. Even in a police state, there were places such as this that were officially outlawed, but unofficially sanctioned. Frequented by dissidents and Party members, men and women, young and old, it was a social relief valve that also served as a venue where needs of every description were satisfied and deals were made. The undergrounds offered a modest amount of protection from the secret police, for the children of senior Party officials were often to be found at such places late at night, and their arrest could prove awkward.

In a back corner booth, vibrating with the deafening beat of the music to which hundreds of young men and women gyrated on the dance floor, they sat with Medvedev. They had tried asking him questions, at first indirect, and then very direct, shouting to be heard above the roaring music.

He had simply waved aside their questions, shouting back that they had plenty of time for business. "Pleasure comes first," he yelled over the music, his eyes firmly fixed on Valentina. Taller than Sikorsky, Medvedev also boasted a lean, muscular body. With slicked-back black hair and deep blue eyes, he would have been considered handsome were it not for the constantly calculating expression he wore. While his official job was as a lowly train dispatcher, his true vocation was making deals in the underground. And dominating women. He considered himself a gift to the opposite sex, and it was clear from the look on his face that he believed that his next conquest was sitting before him: Valentina.

Sikorsky was across the table from Medvedev, knowing quite well what the man was thinking. While he was useful in his own business dealings, Sikorsky had always hated having to deal with him: he was scum. He would make a deal with anyone for anything if it served his purposes. He was also known to be more than a so-called lady's man: he was a beast with a reputation for violence. Sikorsky knew that he himself was no angel, but at heart he was an honest and scrupulous man, and those like Medvedev sickened him. He had told all of this to Valentina, and hoped that she really understood what she was getting herself into by using her body as the currency for this transaction.

Valentina, he thought, inwardly shaking his head, *you have no idea what this man is capable of.* Yet he knew that he was probably underestimating her. He had been shocked at the transformation she had undergone with the aid of some of the clothes and makeup she had brought in the traveling case with her, from wherever she had really come from. Gone was the inconspicuous mouse of a woman who could be mistaken for a thousand others and easily disappear into a crowd. Instead, when she reappeared from the rest room at the back of the restaurant where they had waited until meeting Medvedev, Sikorsky found himself looking at a gorgeous brunette wearing a black leather outfit that looked like it was painted on, hugging her generous curves, with the blouse exposing a generous amount of cleavage.

Clicking across the floor in stiletto heels, he didn't even recognize her until she came right up to him and asked with a wry smile, "What do you think?"

Red-faced with embarrassment, for he had been staring at her open-mouthed, he looked away and muttered, "I think that will work."

Now, sitting between them, he could feel an emotional current running between the two that made him increasingly uncomfortable. He watched as Medvedev stared at Valentina, and wondered who was truly baiting whom as she stared back, shifting in her seat to give him a slightly better look down her blouse. A clear and dangerous invitation.

Sikorsky was just about to get up and announce they were leaving when Valentina suddenly leaned over to Medvedev and shouted something in his ear. Then she got up and disappeared into the writhing mass of people on the dance floor, her hips swaying suggestively.

After a few seconds of staring after her, completely ignoring Sikorsky, Medvedev got up from the booth and followed in her wake.

***

The women's bathroom was about what Valentina had expected: large, ridiculously upscale, as if it were in a luxury hotel, loud – although not nearly as loud as the dance floor – and crowded. While most of the occupants were women, there were plenty of men, too, engaged in everything from polite discussion with their partners, wine glasses in hand, to unabashed sex.

Her most pressing concern was privacy: she could not do what she needed to do out in the open. Several people looked up as she walked in, with a few giving her more than a casual glance. She strutted over to the row of stalls, prepared to yank one of the other women out if she had to. Fortunately, a woman made her exit from the stall at the end, dragging another woman, only half-dressed, behind her, and Valentina moved quickly to take it. She waited, holding the door open until Medvedev walked into the bathroom. Seeing her instantly, he sauntered over, a broad smile on his face.

Without a word, he came into the oversize stall with her, and she closed the door behind him.

After that, things did not go quite as Medvedev probably had expected. When he reached for her, a leering grin on his face, she leaned forward as if she were going to kiss him before viciously slamming a knee into his bulging crotch. As he doubled over, gagging, she slapped a syrette against his neck, then slammed him against the back wall. He slumped down onto the toilet, still gasping for breath as the drugs rushed through his system, carried by his carotid artery. She held his head down between his knees, effectively immobilizing him until he stopped struggling. A moment more and his body clearly relaxed, fully under the influence of the drugs she had given him.

"Now, my friend," she said in a conversational voice that he would be able to hear, but that would not carry beyond the stall over the background of music and the other goings-on in the bathroom, "we're going to play a little game. I'm going to ask you questions, and you're going to give me answers."

"Sure," he said groggily as she lifted his head up and shoved his body against the wall again. The syrette she had injected him with contained a powerful cocktail of muscle relaxants and a psychological uninhibitor that would loosen his tongue about anything he knew.

"Pyotr," she asked him, "where do the special trains, the ones from the big coal-fired power plants, go? What are they carrying?"

"Why do you want to talk about that when you could be–" He tried to clumsily grab for her again.

"Where do the special trains go?" she hissed, grabbing one of his hands and twisting it back in an extremely painful grip.

Medvedev opened his mouth to shriek, but she silenced him with a blow from her free arm, hitting him in the jaw with her elbow. One of the side effects of the drugs she had given him was that they amplified the sensation of pain, and between the wrist lock and the blow to his jaw, he was shivering in agony.

"Tell me what I want to know, and quietly," she said in his ear, "and I'll make the pain stop."

He nodded quickly, desperate for her to make the pain go away. "They just carry waste from the plants, that's all I know," he rasped. "There is a place, a disposal facility, thirty kilometers due north of here. All the special trains go there."

"There's nothing north of the city but forest, Pyotr," she told him, twisting his wrist a bit more. The ship that had dropped her off had also carried a full reconnaissance package. The makeup compact in her tiny purse was in actuality a microcomputer that contained, among other things, a complete download of all the information the ship had recorded, and she had studied it intently before she had landed, and studied it more in the two evenings she had stayed with Sikorsky and his wife. There was nothing north of Saint Petersburg but an endless stretch of forest. Yet it was possible she missed something.

"No, wait!" he said, panting. "The facility is not easy to find. There is no need for people to go there. But it is there. There is a track that leads north from the main ring around the city, near the Chornaya Rechka station. Dmitri will know where it is; he helped to build the station. There is a track from the north that isn't marked, that goes to the main space port. The special trains from the coal plants all take that northern spur. It will take you to the facility."

As Medvedev talked, she took out her makeup case with her free hand and activated the computer it contained. It projected a ghostly overhead image of Saint Petersburg city on the wall, and with a few whispered words the tiny but intelligent computer displayed what she wanted.

"There!" Medvedev panted, pointing at a rail line that went north from the main ring, just as he had said. "That is the one!"

"It only goes a few kilometers north and then ends, Pyotr," she said, her voice holding an edge that made him cringe. The image on the wall showed a rail line that could easily hold a large mag-lev train, but after a short run northward it simply ended in the trees.

"It must be camouflaged," he pleaded. "I *know* it goes north to the facility. It is a priority line, and we control the switches at the facility. It is *there*, I tell you!"

Quickly zooming out to show a larger view of the area, the computer projected where the facility might be and then began a rapid search to find it. In under a minute she found what she was looking for.

"*Chyort voz'mi*," she cursed quietly. "Damn it." Deep in the forest was a set of drab buildings behind a tall concrete wall topped by several guard towers. There were military vehicles, including heavy tanks, inside the compound, with a large landing area for vertical take-off aircraft. And at the base of the mountain against which the compound was sited, a massive concrete apron, carefully painted to make it look like a large forest meadow, lined with cargo vehicles led into a cavernous tunnel that disappeared into the mountain. She had recognized it during her earlier studying of the area as a military facility, of course, but had never suspected that this would be what she was looking for.

The facility was indeed there, and it was underground.

"How do I get in, Pyotr?" she asked him, twisting his wrist again as she slipped the makeup compact back into her purse with her other hand.

"I don't know, I swear!" he whimpered. "It doesn't matter, anyway."

The way he said the last words sent a chill through her. "What do you mean?"

"The secret police are coming for you." He looked up at her, tears in his eyes, "I just wanted to fuck you before they took you away. Such a waste," he sobbed, shaking his head. The drugs were running their full course in his system now. "I tell them things I hear, things they want to know, and they leave me alone. Dmitri told me that he was very interested in the train schedules from the big coal power plants. Not *to* the plants, but *from* the plants. I thought that was interesting, and so did the secret police."

"Is that why you took so long setting up this meeting?" she asked him quickly. "You were waiting for the secret police?"

"Yes," he nodded. "They said they needed some time to arrange things, and that I was to meet you here tonight and have a good time with you. Past that, they did not tell me, and I didn't care. Oh, come here, *dorogaya*, while we still have time!" He suddenly reached for her with his free hand, groping at her breasts.

She was out of time, and so was Medvedev. Letting go of his hand, she put one of her hands on the back of his head and locked the other around his jaw, then gave his head a sharp, vicious twist. His neck broke with a wet *snap* and his body went limp. She carefully propped him up against the wall to make it appear as if he had passed out from too much of a good time. As crowded as this place was, he wouldn't go undiscovered for long, but comatose bodies were commonplace here, and few who weren't comatose were in full control of their faculties. No one would realize that he was dead before she and Dmitri got away.

Her only worry now was how to escape this place without being taken by the secret police.

***

Dmitri was growing increasingly worried. Valentina and Medvedev had been gone what seemed like hours, but he knew from the frequent glances at his watch had only been minutes. He hated this place, and couldn't understand how anyone could find enjoyment here: music so loud that he couldn't hear himself scream, women and men propositioning each other shamelessly. He had gotten half a dozen invitations from both men and women in the few minutes that Valentina had been gone, and he had done his best to not act offended: he already felt completely out of place here, and didn't want to call any more attention to himself than was absolutely necessary. He nursed his drink, trying to give the impression of drinking a lot more than he actually was. And most of all, he forced himself to ignore the overpowering urge to follow after Valentina and find out what was happening. On that, however, she had given him very explicit instructions when they took this booth.

"No matter what happens, Dmitri," she had told him earlier, "do not follow me if I get up to leave and Medvedev follows after me."

"Why not?" he had asked.

She had given him a searching look. "You don't want to know," she had finally said.

He was holding his hands under the table to keep everyone from seeing how he was clenching and unclenching them, a nervous habit since childhood. *If she is not back in another two minutes*, he told himself, *I am going after her*.

A moment later, he saw her emerge from the solid wall of gyrating bodies on the dance floor, heading toward him. Medvedev was nowhere to be seen. She nodded her head in the general direction of the door. It was time to go.

Sikorsky breathed a sigh of relief and tossed back the rest of his vodka. As he stood up, the music suddenly stopped. The crowd instantly howled and jeered, but their voices went silent as the dance lighting, lasers and holographic displays, mostly of nude men and women engaged in lewd acts, disappeared. The entire club was cast into pitch darkness for a moment, which was replaced by the harsh glare of white lights that went on all around the perimeter of the ceiling. If anything, the stark illumination of the club's interior was even more surreal than the light show, exposing the details of the sound and lighting systems, not to mention the deteriorating concrete walls and corroded sheet metal ceiling high above the hushed crowd.

He felt Valentina's hand clamp on his arm.

"This way," she whispered urgently. "Now."

"*Secret police!*" someone suddenly yelled. The effect would have been exactly the same if there had been a fire. The crowd instantly panicked, with nearly five hundred people surging for the single entrance. While there were other doors in the warehouse, most of those now trapped inside didn't know about them, nor did they have the keys to the locks.

Sikorsky fought to follow Valentina through the tide of people stampeding to get out. "We are going the wrong way!" he shouted over the din of screaming voices around them. "The door is back there!"

"Just stay close to me!" she yelled back as she viciously slammed her elbow into the jaw of a wild-eyed man who otherwise would have run right over her, knocking him to the floor. She jumped over him without pausing, dragging Sikorsky behind her.

Finally, they reached the back edge of the crowd. Sikorsky cringed at the screams: they were no longer just of people who were frightened and panicking, they were screams of pain. He knew that dozens were probably being trampled on the floor and crushed to death against the wall near the door.

Valentina ignored the chaos around them. Sikorsky watched as she drew a small case from her tiny purse.

"Makeup?" he asked incredulously. "What..."

His voice died as he saw her flip it open to reveal a miniature computer display.

"Current location," she said into the device. "Emergency exit routes." In a fraction of a second, details of the building they were in and what lay beyond it appeared. She turned the device upside-down, projecting the image on the floor so both of them could see it. Sections of the wall and floor were highlighted in yellow, with dotted paths marked in red from each yellow section into the warehouse district beyond. "This way," she told him after she scanned the map for a few seconds. Then she snapped the device shut and slipped it back into her purse. "Quickly!"

She broke into a run, with Dmitri struggling to keep up with her. She led him to the women's restroom, which was in the right rear corner of the building. Just as they dashed through the door, he heard the doors to the loading docks along the rear wall start to open. As the door to the bathroom swung shut, he looked back just long enough to see men in dark uniforms come pouring through the loading dock doors. They carried clear body shields and wielded electrified truncheons.

"What are we going to do?" he whispered, looking around the room where they were now trapped. "There is no way out of here!"

"Have faith, Dmitri," she said. She stripped off the thin leather jacket, then took out her microcomputer and connected it to a metal tag on the inside of it. With a slight popping sound, the seams of the jacket disintegrated. After quickly pulling the leather apart along the front edges, waist, and the seams of the arms, she was rewarded with several thin ropes of gray material.

"Is that explosive putty?" Dmitri asked, shocked. It looked much like the plastic explosive compound his teams used for blasting out sections of rock or concrete at building sites. It could not be detonated easily, which made it comparatively safe. But he could not imagine wandering around in clothing loaded with it.

"Yes," she said as she pressed the material against the floor, making a dotted circle of small blobs of putty. "Stand back."

There were suddenly shouts outside, very close and clearly audible against the continued screams from the crush of people trying to get away.

"They are coming!" Dmitri warned, pressing his ear against the door to better hear what was going on outside. A simple wooden wedge lay near the corner of the door, a prop to keep the door open when the bathroom was cleaned. He jammed it under the door with his foot, hoping to give them a few extra moments when the men on the other side tried to get in.

Valentina peeled off the small metal plate from her jacket, the one she had temporarily connected the microcomputer to, and put it in the center of the circle of explosives. She ran over to Dmitri, and they both put their faces toward the wall to protect their eyes.

"What are you waiting for?" he hissed as Valentina stood next to him, still holding the microcomputer, which now acted as a detonator.

A shot echoed from outside, then more. The screaming rose even higher, and more shots followed. The voices of the men who had been heading toward them turned to frantic shouts that retreated into the general bedlam beyond the door.

"They're murdering those people!" Dmitri cried.

Valentina said nothing as she pushed him against the wall, then activated the detonator. Behind them, sounding much like the gunshots booming beyond the door, the explosives went off, blowing a ragged hole through the floor into a dark, cramped corridor filled with pipes dripping condensation.

Without another word, she grabbed Dmitri and, now using the tiny microcomputer as a glorified flashlight to illuminate their way, jumped into the darkness below.

NINE

"I know I don't have to say this, but I'm going to say it, anyway," Commodore Hanson said grimly to the ship captains gathered around the conference table in her flagship, the heavy cruiser *CNS Constellation*. "Make sure you review all the nuclear combat protocols with your crews. We've never fought a war in space with nuclear weapons, so the procedures are all theoretical, but they're all we've got."

"Most of the protocols cover weapon handling, launch procedures, and targeting, commodore," Sato said quietly. "They don't have much on what to do if someone is shooting nukes at you, other than to keep the ships spread wide apart and to destroy the incoming weapons before detonation. If possible," he added, with an ironic grin.

His comment drew a few muttered comments from around the table.

"I know, Sato," Hanson said, nodding, "but review the damn things again. All of you. The flag operations officer is working up formation options for us that will be downloaded to your ships, then we'll work on those in simulation exercises before we have to jump in. By then the rest of the task force will be here. I hope."

Needless to say, the orders to prepare for an assault on Saint Petersburg had come as a complete surprise to everyone. Naval couriers had managed to catch up with all the ships of the squadron, directing them to this isolated volume of space that was a day's jump from the target system. Hanson had been gratified and relieved to see that all six ships of her squadron had made the rendezvous, all within twenty-four hours of one another. A flotilla of ten destroyers and a pair of Marine troop carriers were already there when *Constellation*, which was the first of Hanson's ships to arrive, jumped in. The fleet orders said that another heavy cruiser squadron and destroyer flotilla were assigned to the task force, but they hadn't arrived yet. They were to have sailed from Earth with a single patrol stop at Edinburgh, but according to the schedule in the operations orders transmitted by the couriers, they were a full day late. Based on what Sato had reported from Kronstadt about his encounter with the Kreelans there, Hanson suspected that the other ships may have run into trouble at Edinburgh.

"We're also going to set up contingency orders and simulations for an assault with the forces we have on hand," she said. "You've all read the orders we received: I have absolutely no discretion in terms of action. If we receive the go order, we *must* deploy. That one comes straight from the commander-in-chief."

While she didn't show it to her subordinates, Hanson was deeply worried. Not because she was the ranking officer of the naval forces here and would be leading the mission, rather than the two-star admiral who was with the missing cruiser squadron, but because their intelligence information on Saint Petersburg military forces was so sketchy. And that was never a good thing when nuclear weapons were potentially involved. "Intel," she said, turning to a lieutenant commander sitting on her left, "what have you got for us?"

The man grimaced. "Not a hell of a lot, ma'am," he said as he stood up, taking a position next to the briefing room's main screen. Information suddenly flashed into existence, bright text and diagrams showing various types of military vessels and their vital statistics. What few were known. "This is what we have on the Saint Petersburg Navy," he said. "As you can see, a lot of the information is either unavailable, very dated or considered unreliable. I guess after the war, nobody thought we'd have to worry about this particular problem again." That elicited a few grumbles from around the room. Two of the captains at the table had been junior officers during the Saint Petersburg war, and they had been among the few who were not surprised by what was happening. The focus of intelligence gathering after the war was on political and economic concerns; there had been little interest in or resources assigned to monitoring Saint Petersburg's military capabilities. "The main problem is that Saint Petersburg built new naval facilities on their moon after the main demilitarization provisions of the armistice expired. No inspection teams could be sent there, and according to what little I've got, foreigners aren't exactly welcome, anyway. We know that they have shipbuiding facilities there, but have almost no information on what those facilities have been doing. And since they don't conduct any joint exercises with any other navies or invite naval visits, there's been virtually no direct observation of Saint Pete naval units. Just their coast guard vessels, which are about the size you'd expect, but are armed to the teeth." The main screen changed to show an ugly, bulbous vessel that was a quarter the size of the *Constellation*, but that packed a punch roughly equivalent to one of the new Confederation destroyers. "So I think it's highly likely that they have more and better ships than what this," he gestured disgustedly to the sketchy information on ship types and numbers that had replaced the image of the ugly coast guard ship, "is showing."

"That would be a safe assumption," the task force Marine commander said with a slight Russian accent. Colonel Lev Stepanovich Grishin, formerly of the *Légion étrangère* and a veteran of Keran, was in command of the Marine expeditionary force that was made up of four battalions from the new 12th Marine Regiment, and that was deployed aboard the two assault carriers. Grishin was a native of Saint Petersburg, and had fought in the war twenty years before: on the wrong side. He had escaped the final destruction of the Red Army by Coalition forces and the ensuing witch hunt by the winning side, the White Army, to root out any remaining neo-communists. He had eventually found himself in the Legion, where he had risen from a lowly recruit to become the commander of an armored regiment that had been wiped out at Keran.

The irony of the current situation had not escaped him: in the intervening twenty years since the war, the Whites had lost the battle to rebuild the economy. In the resulting social chaos they had been replaced in a quiet and outwardly bloodless revolution by "rehabilitated" communists. Grishin even knew many of the ruling senior Party members, including Chairman Korolev, under whom Grishin had served when Korolev had been a junior political commissar. Over the years since then, Grishin had received subtle entreaties from several of his one-time comrades to return to his former motherland. These, he had studiously ignored, never returning their messages. He had given up his nationality and his past for the Legion, and had willingly given his loyalty to the newly formed Confederation Marine Corps, which now incorporated what little was left of the Legion after the debacle on Keran. The Legion was redesignated as the 12th Marine Regiment, and six battalions had already been formed and trained. While it did not apply to new recruits, one important caveat that had applied to all former legionnaires who transitioned to the new Marine Corps was that they would not be required to take the Confederation service oath. Like most of his surviving comrades, Grishin would never again give his allegiance to any nation or government. His true loyalty was now to the Corps, as it had been to the Legion, and to the men and women who served with him. He knew that many of the officers around the table did not trust him, both because of the side on which he had fought during the war, and because he was from the Legion: the legionnaires, while respected for their sacrifices and combat prowess, were nonetheless the black sheep of the new Confederation military.

"Would you care to elaborate, colonel?" Commodore Hanson asked coolly.

Grishin knew that she had her doubts about his loyalty: she had flat out told him her misgivings when he had first come aboard *Constellation*, but she had no grounds to take any action against him. *Piss on her*, Grishin thought, making sure his face did not betray the inward smile he felt. Her feelings did not anger him. He had endured far worse. "I have no specifics, commodore," he said. "As you well know, I have not been to the planet of my birth since the end of the war. Yet I know some of the men in power there: they are heartless, ruthless bastards. Just like me." He offered up a humorless smile. "Behind their propaganda of equality and brotherhood, they are unapologetic imperialists. They hold Riga under their thumb, and they aspire to claim more worlds as their own. They wish to become a great star nation, superior to the Alliance, and no doubt superior to the Confederation, as well." He glanced around the room, his gaze settling on Sato, whose expression was not clouded or veiled by suspicion: Sato had helped save Grishin's life and those of his legionnaires at Keran, and he owed the young commander a great debt of honor. And Sato was probably one of the few people in this room who did not doubt Grishin's loyalty or question his motivations. "As you all know, the key to becoming a star nation is to have a superior navy. Korolev has been in power now for a number of years, and I am sure has not wasted his time in this arena. While he served as a political commissar during the war and has no naval experience, he well understands what is necessary to build an empire." He turned his gaze back to Hanson. "You have not seen the true face of their navy because they do not wish you to see it. If we have to jump in, however, you will. Even if we bypass Saint Petersburg and sail directly to Riga, they will fight, for they consider Riga their territory; I believe that an image of Korolev's expression when he found out that Riga had applied for Confederation membership would have been priceless." No one smiled at the joke. With a sigh, he went on, "I fear that our naval encounter will not be pleasant, commodore, even under the best of circumstances."

"Don't they realize that the Kreelans are out there?" one of the ship captains asked quietly. "They should be joining forces with us, not fighting us!"

Grishin shook his head sadly. "I am sure that Korolev and his minions believe that the Kreelan threat is merely Confederation propaganda, designed to draw in gullible worlds like Riga," he replied. "The men in power on Saint Petersburg live in fear and suspicion of all that is beyond their control, my friends. They do not see the same reality that we do."

"So what can we do about their navy, *colonel?*" one of the other captains asked hotly.

"Not a damn thing," Hanson interjected before Grishin could say anything more. The last thing she needed was an open conflict among her commanding officers. "Remember, ladies and gentlemen, we have zero leeway in this one. When the mission clock counts down to zero, if we haven't received the order to abort, we jump in, weapons hot. It doesn't matter if they have a hundred heavy cruisers waiting for us: we still go." Turning back to Grishin, she said, "So, colonel, now that we have such a reassuring understanding of their viewpoint, perhaps you'd care to outline the operations plan for the Marine contingent?"

Grishin realized that Hanson probably hadn't intended to come across as being sarcastic, but she certainly sounded that way. He shrugged inwardly. If she wanted to become an expert at sarcasm, she should take lessons from the French officers he had once served under in the Legion. "Certainly, commodore," he said easily as he stood and replaced the intelligence officer at the front of the room. "As you know, our primary mission is to capture or destroy any nuclear weapons Saint Petersburg may possess," he began. "In the task force, we have an entire brigade of

Marines, in addition to the shipboard contingents, which we can call upon to form an additional ad-hoc battalion, if necessary. The basic plan is to conduct a rapid exo-atmospheric assault on their storage site or sites, employing enough Marines and shipboard fire support to achieve overwhelming local superiority. Each Marine assault group will have a technical team whose responsibility will be to assess whether the weapons can be rendered safe and extracted, or whether they need to be destroyed *in situ*. If the latter, the teams have a wealth of demolitions available, and we are also authorized to employ orbital bombardment, if necessary."

"Once the weapons are secured or destroyed," Hanson interjected, facing her ship captains, "we are to take up defensive positions around Riga. We are *not* to engage in battle with Saint Petersburg naval forces unless we have no other choice. I want to make this very clear: we are not here to make war on Saint Petersburg. We are here to take care of the nukes and then defend Riga from any potential punitive action. That's it. Even if the Saint Petes have nothing more serious than a dozen coast guard cutters to throw against us, I don't want a major naval battle. Stick to the job at hand." Turning to Grishin, she said, "Thank you, colonel."

"The real problem," the intel officer said as Grishin took his seat, "is that the entire operation for going after the nukes is based on intelligence information that we're supposed to receive shortly *after* we jump into the system." He rolled his eyes, showing what he thought of that part of the plan, eliciting a few snickers from the others.

"If we don't receive that information," Hanson added, shooting the intel officer a mild glare, "the nuke part of the mission is scrubbed. We can't search the entire system, and we're not going to provoke Korolev by taking up orbit around Saint Petersburg if we don't have anything firm to go on. So, if we don't get the intel we've been promised, our mission is to sail straight to Riga and take up a defensive posture. Any questions?"

Around the table, heads shook to a chorus of "No, ma'am." There would be questions in the next hours before the task force jumped, but right now everyone wanted to get back to their ships.

"That's it, then," Hanson said. The other officers stood to attention as she got up from her chair. "We've got less than twenty-four hours, people. Let's make the most of it."

***

"It's good to see you again, sir," Sato said as he walked beside Grishin on the way to the boat bay to return to their respective ships. The last time Sato had seen Grishin was when he was taken off the *Ticonderoga* after the Battle of Keran: Grishin had been on a gurney headed for the sickbay on Africa Station for the severe injuries he had received.

"It is good to see you, too, Sato," Grishin said warmly. "I also appreciate your...quiet support in there," he nodded back toward the briefing room, "for lack of a better term. It seems that former residents of Saint Petersburg are not in the running to win today's popularity contest."

"I know, sir, and I apologize for that," Sato replied, rather embarrassed. He had felt extremely uncomfortable at the way Grishin had been treated. Sato could sympathize: most of the other ship captains did not want to have anything to do with him, either, "ship thief" that he was in the eyes of some. "Sir," he went on tentatively, "may I ask you something?"

"Of course, Ichiro," Grishin said, smiling. "Asking is always free, but I may not give you an answer."

Sato grinned, but it quickly faded from his face. "Sir, how well do you know First Sergeant Mills?"

"Roland Mills?" Grishin asked. Sato nodded. "I knew of him when we served in the Legion, but he never served under me, and you know of our time on Keran. But I got to know him quite well when the Legion was being merged into the Marine Corps: he was one of the senior transition NCOs and worked for me until you stole him away." He nudged Sato good-naturedly. "He is a good man, and an outstanding legionnaire...and Marine. Why do you ask?"

"Well, sir..." Sato began, then hesitated. He did not want to inadvertently put Mills in a bad light with a senior Marine officer, but he had to ask. "Sir, do you know if Mills ever suffered from chronic nightmares after Keran?"

"We all suffered nightmares after Keran, Ichiro," Grishin said quietly as he came to a stop, turning to face Sato. "I would be concerned about anyone who did not."

"Yes, sir, I agree," Sato told him. "But his nightmares, I believe, are different. They are not just of what happened on Keran, but dreams of him being killed by the big warrior who let us go, of something that did *not* happen. And with a more...spiritual meaning: in the dream she is taking his soul, and it has deeply disturbed him. He was having them with increasing frequency until he finally saw the ship's surgeon because he was on the verge of stim addiction. She prescribed a series of sedatives that initially knocked him out and allowed him to sleep and get some rest." He frowned. "But in the last two days, the nightmares have returned, even through the sedatives, and appear to be even more intense. He woke up screaming before the morning watch. He woke up half the Marine company, sleeping in their bunks. I'm very worried about him." *And I can't have a senior NCO who doesn't have all his wits about him taking men and women into combat,* he didn't add.

Grishin thought a moment. "I cannot recall that he had dreams, exactly, Ichiro," he said slowly. "I know there were times when he clearly had not slept well, but that is not necessarily unusual for soldiers, especially veterans, and I thought nothing of it."

"Do you dream, sir, of her? The big warrior? Or any of the other Kreelans?"

Shaking his head, Grishin answered darkly, "I dream of electric fire, Ichiro, and the smell of burning flesh." He shivered inwardly, remembering how one of the Kreelan warriors had flung a grenade at his command vehicle. The alien grenades did not explode, exactly: they seemed to spawn a confined electric storm that could destroy a heavily armored battle tank, lacing it with electric bolts that were like lightning, and that could burn right through armor plate. His command vehicle was hit by one, and he could clearly recall the screaming of his crew as they were simultaneously burned and electrocuted to death. Grishin only survived because the vehicle hit the edge of a weapon emplacement and flipped over after the driver lost control, sending Grishin flying from his hatch in the top of the vehicle. He had survived, but had been grievously injured. "I do not remember much after that until Africa Station. Why, do you think his dreams are significant, something more than a stress disorder?"

Sato shrugged in frustration. "I don't know, sir. I don't want to make it sound mystical, but...there is just something strange about it, and I wish I understood what it was, what it means."

Grishin snorted, then put a hand on Sato's shoulder. "It means nothing, Ichiro," he told him. "The human mind is a complex thing that often plays tricks on itself. We are victims of our own cruel nature and God's poor sense of humor. And this is made worse by our desire to understand everything, even though some things were made to never be understood. Do not worry yourself about Mills, my friend. He is a tough bastard, as tough as they come. He will be all right, and will do whatever needs to be done."

***

At that moment First Sergeant Roland Mills was inspecting every one of his company's Marines to make sure they were ready for combat, before the detachment commander's formal inspection. He hoped they would be called upon to help the battalions that would be deploying to the surface, because he didn't want to sit out a battle up here in a ship the Saint Petes would want to use for target practice when he could be getting his hands dirty planetside.

He was doubly glad they were so busy now, because the dreams had come back. Even through the knockout drugs the surgeon had given him, the huge warrior had reached through his subconscious to tear out his heart and reach for his soul. Now the dreams were even more real, if that was possible, as if they were a mental signal whose strength was rapidly increasing. He didn't need the stims yet, but had asked the ship's surgeon for some extras, anyway. With her usual warnings of gloom and doom about the risks of addiction, she gave them to him. He was far more terrified of what lay waiting for him when he slept than becoming addicted to stims.

As he expected, there were only a few minor things amiss as he went from Marine to Marine with their respective platoon sergeants and squad leaders. The most important things – weapons, ammunition, armor, and communications – were perfect. Those few things that weren't in order were quickly straightened out. The company had five platoons: four regular platoons and a heavy weapons platoon. Their commander had ordered that they would make ready to support the ground campaign with the four line platoons, while the heavy weapons platoon would remain aboard for ship defense. That had made for some major disappointment among the heavy weapons troops, Mills knew, because everyone doubted that the Saint Petersburg Navy would try any boarding stunts like the Kreelans had. They would likely be stuck in their vacuum combat armor in a battle – if there was one – that would be decided by the guns of heavy cruisers, while their fellow Marines would be down on the surface raising hell. They all hoped.

He grinned inwardly, trying to set aside the dread that had settled over him like a chill mist. *Poor left-behind buggers*, he thought.

***

Sato watched the mission clock steadily wind down toward zero. "Stand by to jump," he ordered. In a task force jump, it was technically unnecessary for a ship's captain to give the jump order, for the sequence of events had already been programmed in to the ship's systems, slaved to the navigation computers aboard the flagship *Constellation*. But tradition demanded it, and Bogdanova had her hand on the manual override controls just in case.

Sato frowned as he thought of the task force's composition. The other cruisers and destroyers that were supposed to join them had never arrived, and the mission orders left no discretion as to the mission profile: they had to jump on time, no matter what. He was distinctly uncomfortable about the lack of intelligence information they had on the Saint Petersburg Navy, particularly in light of what Grishin had said, but there was nothing they could do about it, other than to hope for the best.

"Autolock sequence engaged," the navigation computer announced. "Transpace sequence in five...four...three...two...one...jump initiated."

In the blink of an eye, the ships of Commodore Hanson's task force vanished.

TEN

The fleet was coming. That was the only thing that Valentina could think about. She didn't know the details of how many ships would be coming, but she knew when they would jump in-system, and she had to be ready for them: not just for her own retrieval, but to get them the information she had been sent here for in the first place. She knew that she didn't have all the information she would have liked, but she had found out the main things the Confederation needed to know. Now she just had to get them the data, and hopefully survive.

That was going to be a bit difficult from where she had been imprisoned in the secret police headquarters.

She and Sikorsky had escaped from the underground club, but it had been a near thing. A *very* near thing. They had run for their lives through the filthy sewer and utility service tunnels that snaked under the industrial district, finally emerging through a sewer manhole cover behind a grim, gray apartment complex that was at the edge of the adjacent residential district. They had been able to hear people in the tunnels pursuing them, but none of the tracking devices their pursuers had could function through the stench, moisture, and flowing muck in the tunnels and sewers. The secret police had fired random shots and even thrown a few grenades to try and frighten them and draw them out, but after nearly an hour of running through the tunnels, the sounds of pursuit began to fade: the secret police did not have enough men to sweep the entire tunnel network at once, and fortuitously they headed off in the wrong direction.

While Sikorsky was a strong man, he was not used to such running. Nearing exhaustion by the time they exited the sewer tunnel, she had to help him up the ladder to ground level. Once there, they used water from one of the outdoor faucets protruding from a nearby work shed to rinse the muck from their shoes and the cuffs of Sikorsky's pants.

Then there was the question of what to do next.

"I must return to my wife," Sikorsky argued quietly but forcefully. "She will be worried, and if what you say is true, I need to get her to safety."

Valentina shook her head. "They'll be waiting for you, Dmitri," she explained. "You'll be walking right into their arms."

"Perhaps not," he said. "If Medvedev did not tell them—"

"Dmitri," she hissed, "he told them everything! They know it was you who was asking about the trains. That's why they raided the club: to catch us. It wasn't just a random act. The entire thing was Medvedev's doing." Her voice softened slightly. "The best thing you can do for your wife now is to try and distance yourself from her. Perhaps the secret police will believe she had nothing to do with all this." She couldn't see his expression in the darkness, but she could tell that he was brooding. "Listen, we only have to stay hidden for another eight hours," she told him, revealing more operational information in that one brief sentence than she would have liked. "After that...if you want, I'll try to get you and your wife out."

"What do you mean, *out?*" he asked, curious.

"The Confederation will be willing to grant you asylum for what you've done here," she explained. "You can get a new identity, a new life on a different world. Even Earth, if you want."

"I am a patriot," he said quietly, "not a traitor. I did what I did to bring about changes here, to my homeland. Why would I want to leave? I—"

"Shh," Valentina whispered. She had heard something outside. She had already prepared an act in case they were discovered: she was a prostitute with a client, and the work shed had been a convenient spot for their business transaction.

Such was her surprise, then, when the door flew open and half a dozen men holding automatic weapons burst in, shouting, "*On the ground, now!*"

She had a fraction of a second to decide to fight or surrender. She was confident that she could win a close-in fight with the men who had come into the shed. It was the additional dozen outside that gave her pause.

No way out, she thought. Her first objective had just become survival. Without a word, she got down on the ground, face-down, next to Dmitri.

His face was turned to hers as the secret police cuffed their hands and shackled their feet before roughly hauling them out of the shed.

From his expression, he was not at all surprised.

***

"The Confederation spy and her accomplice have been captured," Vasili Morozov, head of the secret police, announced matter of factly as he put away his secure vidphone. The call had come at a most opportune time: just when the chairman himself was calling into question Morozov's competence in dealing with the situation that had first been brought to light a few days before by the now-dead informant, Medvedev.

"At last," Chairman Iosef Korolev said with just a hint of sarcasm as he leaned back in his plush leather chair, glowering at Morozov. Around the polished antique wooden table that was worth more than ten thousand times the average annual income on Saint Petersburg sat the planet's ruling body, the Supreme Council. It was a loose coalition of vicious predators who ruled a world, and who dreamed of ruling much more. As its leader, and the most powerful man on the planet, Korolev was the most dangerous predator of them all. Yet he only retained his superior position by playing his colleagues and subordinates against one another. It was this skill, more than any other, that had seen him rise from the disgrace of being a "rehabilitated communist" to the position he now held.

Morozov had always been a threat to Korolev, but he was also a key to Korolev's own power: Morozov and the secret police held the military in check and cowed the populace. In turn, Korolev made sure there was constant friction between the military and the secret police to counter Morozov, using the other ministers as necessary to add the perfect amount of weight to each side of the political equation. It was a balancing act in which only true masters of the art could participate. While Korolev periodically derided Morozov in council, he was acutely aware of the man's intelligence and political cunning. Were he not so effective at his job, he would have been "retired" some time ago.

"I would have thought that between the information from your informant and that provided by Sikorsky's wife you would have been able to bring them in far earlier," Korolev said in a voice that was quiet but far from pleasant. "And without the needless deaths of dozens of citizens. That was sloppy, Vasili. Very sloppy."

The others around the room fixed their eyes on Morozov. All of them knew that Korolev cared as little about those who had died in the raid as they themselves did. That is to say, not at all. It was merely an easy and effective way to embarrass Morozov before the council. It was a game, albeit with the highest possible stakes.

The chief of the secret police, however, was unfazed. "Regrettable, but let us be honest, comrades," he said, looking around the table. "Those who died and those who were arrested were clearly engaged in illegal acts. And the shooting only started after a gunman in the crowd opened fire, killing one of my men." He did not add that the gunman had actually been a secret police operative whose specific job was to provoke violence during the raid. He had succeeded quite well, and his reward had been a bullet to the head once the raid was over. Morozov lived, and others died, by the motto that dead men told no tales. "You will also notice that there were no...potentially embarrassing deaths or arrests."

Korolev's expression did not change, but he could feel a rush of heat to his face. His grandson, the only one he had and a young and impudent fool, had been at that underground club. So had the sons and daughters of a number of other powerful Party members. But Korolev was the only member of the council with a family member involved. It was an inexcusable embarrassment, but its resolution would have to wait until later.

Shying away from the bait, he merely grunted. Turning to the defense minister, he said, "And how, comrade, does your expensive space navy fare? Is it ready to protect our world from this so-called *Confederation?*" He said the word as if it were a particularly vicious expletive.

Marshal Issa Antonov nodded. "Yes, comrade chairman," he said in a deep baritone voice. "Our navy is not yet ready to meet their entire fleet head-to-head–" Korolev shot him a frigid glare "–but unless they send the majority of their fleet, we will enjoy a significant advantage. Their newest ships are better in some respects than our own, particularly in targeting and navigation systems, but ours are far more heavily armed." He paused significantly, glancing around the table, making eye contact with everyone except Morozov, before saying, "And all of our heavy cruisers are armed with torpedoes tipped with special weapons."

"Do not be ridiculous," Morozov chided. "Call them what they are: *nuclear* weapons. Everyone in this room knows about them. Everyone in this room gave up resources to fund the program. Stop playing silly word games."

Antonov only glared at him, clenching his fists. "*You—*"

"Enough," Korolev interjected. "We must assume that there are Confederation forces on the way," he went on, "coming to protect those spineless traitors on Riga."

"But when?" Antonov asked. "I do not doubt that we can defeat them, but I cannot keep the fleet at peak readiness indefinitely."

"It must be soon," Morozov said quietly as he studiously examined his fingernails. "We know from Sikorsky's wife that he was very adamant that they should take a holiday by a particular date, something that was very out of character for him. I suspect that may be a clue."

"And when is that supposed to be?" Antonov asked, his hands clenched into fists on the table.

Morozov looked up and smiled. "Why, today, of course," he said pleasantly.

Antonov looked about to explode.

"Vasili," Korolev said carefully, leaning forward, his gaze locked with Morozov's, "when, exactly, did you discover this insignificant bit of information?"

With a shark's smile, Morozov told him, "Only this morning before this meeting, comrade. When we brought in the two fugitives, I thought it prudent to bring in Sikorsky's wife, as well."

"You interrogated her?" Korolev asked, surprised. While Sikorsky's wife, Ludmilla, was not a high-ranking member, she had gained a wide circle of supporters. Her rise to a modest level in the Party had been a marvel of social engineering in the wake of her daughter's arrest and subsequent execution.

"Of course," Morozov said, shrugging. "She is married to a spy. He has not yet divulged anything of interest. She, however, told us what little useful information she knew immediately. The only thing that required any time was...verification."

Torturing her to make sure she was telling the truth, you mean, Korolev thought. *And this is the man who tells us to not play games with words?* "And what of the Confederation spy?"

Morozov frowned. "She has been difficult, I must admit," he said grudgingly. "She *will* break, comrade. I assure you of that. We will know what she knows. She was obviously interested in the nuclear weapons program, and no doubt learned of its location from our now-deceased informant. But it will take time to learn what we wish to know."

"Perhaps that is not the best use of her," Antonov mused.

"You have a momentous thought for us, marshal?" Morozov said with a bored sigh.

Ignoring him, Antonov turned to the chairman. "I suggest we use her as bait," he said. "She clearly came here to learn of our *nuclear*," he glanced sourly in Morozov's direction, "weapons. Perhaps the Confederation fools hope to find them still in their storage bunkers at the Central Facility." The place where the weapons were built and stored, a massive underground labyrinth of nuclear labs and storage bunkers deep in the mountains to the north, had never been given a name, only a bland project number. Yet everyone who knew about its true function simply called it the Central Facility. It was an underground fortress, protected by a full division, over fifteen thousand men, who were stationed inside the facility and in several well-concealed garrisons nearby. If there was an impregnable location on the entire planet, that was it. "I say, let them find the Central Facility. Let them come for the weapons. Let them *try*."

***

Valentina lay naked on the frigid bare concrete of the cell, eyes closed, feigning unconsciousness. She was handcuffed, with the cuffs chained to a ring bolt set in the floor. Her face and body were badly bruised and bloodied from the beatings she had received. Her interrogators had been quite professional about it, and no doubt would have been disappointed had they gotten any information out of her so soon. They had not raped her yet, but she knew that would not be far off. The pain she had endured thus far was hardly trivial, but it was something she had been conditioned to in her training: they would not break her through mere physical torture.

She was surprised that they had not already tried to use drugs on her, although that would also do them little good: she had chemical implants that had been inserted into her body at several key locations, deep in the muscle tissue. Transparent to modern medical imaging technology, they would react to a variety of drugs that were typically used for interrogation purposes, counteracting their effects. It would be up to her acting skills to convince her tormentors that she was under the influence of whatever drugs they chose to use, while keeping her wits about her, prepared to take advantage of any opportunity to escape. If that moment never came, one of the implants was a failsafe device: once the level of certain chemicals in her bloodstream reached a critical threshold, the implant would automatically release a poison that would kill her almost instantly. She would tell her captors nothing other than what she might choose to say to further her own goals.

She assumed they were at the headquarters of the secret police in Saint Petersburg city, but could not be sure, as they had been transported in a box-bodied vehicle that had no windows. Sikorsky had initially been terrified, his eyes bulging with fear as they shoved the two of them into the van. By the time they arrived at their destination, however, his expression reflected only grim resignation. The two of them had been separated after that, although they had probably received their introductory interrogations – and beatings – at the same time: she could hear a man that sounded like Sikorsky screaming somewhere down the dim corridor from where she was being beaten in her own cell by a pair of burly guards and an interrogator.

Sikorsky. For a brief moment, she allowed herself to feel guilty about him. He obviously had his own reasons for being involved, but having to face what would most likely be death by torture was more than most people would be able to deal with. She had the benefit of her training and experience, and being tortured and killed was also an accepted, if not particularly pleasant, risk of her job. *I'll get him out,* she vowed to herself. *I'm not through yet. Not by a long shot.*

Her opportunity arrived only a few minutes later. The same pair of guards, minus the interrogator this time, came into the cell, slamming the door shut behind them. She could sense the change in their breathing, heavy with expectation, rather than exertion, and their pause before they acted tipped her off to their intentions. This would be the rape, she knew. Or might have been, had they brought at least two more men.

One of them stepped forward and delivered a vicious kick to her stomach that sent her limp body sprawling across the floor. His only reward was a grunt from the air expelled from her lungs. For all he could tell, she was completely unconscious. Of course, she knew that they would be much happier with her conscious so that she would understand what was happening to her. These were not the sort of men who would be finicky about such things: raping an unconscious woman was perfectly acceptable, especially since they knew they would be doing it quite a few more times when she was conscious before her suffering – and their entertainment – was ended with a bullet to her brain.

Valentina expected them to take her while she was still handcuffed and chained to the floor, and she stifled an exclamation of amazement when one of them undid the chain to the eye bolt in the floor. Apparently they wanted a bit more freedom to position her the way they pleased than the short chain allowed. After rolling her over on her back, they undid their pants and knelt down on the floor, almost panting now. One took up position between her legs, while the other knelt to one side near her head, clearly intending to gain some oral satisfaction from his unconscious victim.

Sorry, boys, she thought acidly, *not today*. As the guard between her legs was propped up on one arm, using his other hand to guide his manhood to its intended destination, she twisted her body and brought her knee on that side up in a lightning swift strike to his head, shattering his skull and knocking him off of her. She used her momentum to continue rolling in the same direction, which happened to be the same side that her other would-be tormentor was on. Before he could manage a shout of surprise, let alone anything more threatening, she rose to one knee, balancing herself with one hand, and landed a kick to his throat. He fell forward on his face, clutching his smashed larynx and gagging for breath. She pulled the small chain of her handcuffs around his neck and strangled him, finishing the job.

Quickly searching the bodies, she found what the electronic keys to her cuffs and the guards' badges. Unfortunately, she needed one more thing, which forced her to resort to a grisly expedient. The cells used biometric sensors that scanned the guards' thumbprints. Since neither guard had a knife, she had to use her hands and teeth to liberate the guards' thumbs.

Her next problem was clothing. One of the guards was a fairly small man, not much larger than she was. Quickly stripping him, she donned his uniform and boots, doing her best to tuck in the extra material in such a way as to minimize its obviously poor fit. Fortunately, he had small feet for a man, only a size or two larger than her own. She couldn't do anything about the bruises on her face, but she cleaned off the blood with a combination of spit and the tail of her "new" shirt.

Hoping against hope that she could quickly find Sikorsky, and that he was in sufficient shape to mount an escape attempt, she stripped the other guard of his clothes, believing that his uniform might be a close-enough fit for Sikorsky.

Ready now, she placed the thumb of one of the guards – Petrovsky, his name had been – against the biometric scanner and swiped his badge over the magnetic reader. The door instantly opened.

Peering carefully outside, she could see no one else in the dimly-lit hallway. The cell block seemed to be a single corridor with cells on both sides and a monitoring station and a personnel elevator at one end, and a large freight elevator at the other. The monitoring station was presently unattended. Presumably the guards she had just sent on their way to Hell had been manning it before they had taken a few minutes off for a casual bout of rape. Since only the guards had come to her cell, she assumed that their visit hadn't been authorized; otherwise, they would certainly have called for more guards to man the monitoring station. That left her wondering how much time she had before their superiors became alarmed by the guards' absence: certainly more than just a few minutes, but probably not more than half an hour. She would have to move quickly.

Each cell had a small one-way window of armorglass set in the door, and she peered quickly into each one as she went, looking for Dmitri. She saw that all of them held one to three prisoners, most of whom lay in fetal positions in a corner of the cell. Some of the prisoners were sitting dejectedly against a wall, and a few were on their feet, pacing the small perimeter of their cell.

She finally found Dmitri in the second to last cell on the right. Again using the bloody thumb and electronic ID card, she opened the door.

"Dmitri," she said quietly to the bloodied mass of flesh sprawled on the floor. If they had beaten her badly, they had beaten him far worse. For a moment, she thought he was dead. She knew that would have made her mission that much easier, but it was a death that would never have rested easily on her conscience.

"Valentina?" he whispered hoarsely, turning his head to look at her with the eye that wasn't swollen shut. "How...?"

Closing, but not latching, the door behind her, she quickly knelt beside him. "Don't worry about that now, my friend," she said. "We need to get out of here. Can you walk?"

"Help me up," he grunted.

Working together, she got him to his feet. His face was a wreck of cuts and contusions, and he was extremely unsteady on his feet. Just getting the uniform on him would be a struggle, and he would never be able to pose as a guard. Her original plan had been to try and escape by masquerading as a pair of guards and simply walking out of the building, hoping that no one would notice their ill-fitting uniforms. But Dmitri's injuries would call immediate attention from anyone they passed, so she had to come up with something else. After a moment of feverish consideration, she had an idea. She hated herself for it, but there was no time for anything else.

She managed to get the other uniform on Dmitri, who had drawn strength from her presence, and had recovered somewhat by the time he was dressed. She handed him one of the two submachine pistols she had taken from the guards.

"Now what?" he asked.

"Here," she said, handing him the other thumb and ID badge. The thumb he took with undisguised revulsion, but took it nonetheless.

She went to the adjacent cell and showed him how to use the thumb and badge to open the door. "Open all of the cells," she told him. "We're going to stage a breakout."

Dmitri grinned at her, and it was hard for her not to wince at the four bloody stumps where some of his front teeth had been knocked out.

***

"Not bad," said the secret police colonel who, along with several others, had watched the Confederation spy kill the two guards and "rescue" her compatriot from the miniature video sensors in their cells. He regretted somewhat that the guards had not made any progress in their amorous pursuits with her, for she was extremely attractive and it would have made for some enjoyable viewing. But he had to admit to himself that her martial arts performance, though extremely brief, had also been quite exciting in its own way.

"Should we not sound the alarm, comrade colonel?" one of the junior officers asked, his hand hovering above the alarm button.

The colonel said, "No. We are to allow them to escape, then follow them. Those two," he nodded at the naked bodies of the dead guards, "were a necessary sacrifice. We did not want this to appear too easy." He shrugged. "She and her friend will no doubt try to impersonate guards and leave the complex. Our job is to make sure this happens, then follow them."

Nodding dutifully, although with an expression on his face that was clearly intended to conceal his doubts, the junior officer returned his attention to the displays. "Now what is she doing?" he asked quietly.

The colonel leaned closer, a slight chill creeping up his spine. "I am not sure..."

***

Valentina and Dmitri quickly opened all twenty cells in the block and uncuffed the prisoners. Those who weren't catatonic, she herded out into the corridor and toward the freight elevator. She had not bothered trying to tell them that she was trying to save them, because she wasn't: while in her heart she hoped that some might escape, or at least survive, the cold-hearted truth was that they were nothing more than a tool she was using to help her – and Dmitri – escape. For all they knew, she and Dmitri were taking them out to be shot. Which was probably exactly what was going to happen to most of them in the course of the next few minutes. Thousands of lives, perhaps millions, hung in the balance if she failed.

She used her stolen thumb and badge to open the freight elevator, and forced in the nearly thirty terrified inmates at gunpoint. Then she and

Dmitri squeezed themselves in. Pushing the button for what she hoped was the ground level, she noticed that there was a second door to the elevator, in the back, that the indicators showed would be opening at the floor she had chosen.

"Get out when the door opens!" she bellowed menacingly. As the elevator slowly ascended, she tightened her grip on the submachine pistol and worked her way to the new "front" of the elevator.

***

"Dammit!" the colonel hissed as the doors closed on the freight elevator, shutting the escapees away from their view; there was no monitor in the elevator, although the "escapees" would be under the eyes of more monitors when they emerged from the elevator, regardless of which floor they chose. The two spies simply marching out of secret police headquarters was one thing. Staging a major breakout – or using it to mask their own escape – was something else entirely. "That *suka* is going to make this complicated," he muttered.

Unfortunately, he had little discretion in the matter. None, in fact. The chairman himself had sanctioned this operation, which the colonel had thought outrageously risky, although he would never admit it. On top of that, he had received the orders directly from Morozov. In the secret police, such rare face to face orders either meant an opportunity for a major promotion, in the case of a successful operation, or a bullet to the brain for failure. There was no in-between, and no excuses.

"Colonel?" the young officer asked. "What should we do?"

After an agonizing moment, the colonel said, "Nothing, for now. Let us see how this plays out..."

***

When the door of the freight elevator rattled open, retracting upward, Valentina shouted, "*Prisoner escape!*" She had no idea if there was a way to escape on this floor, but they only had one chance at this. She just prayed that there would be a way out.

For a moment, the prisoners just stood there, blinking at each other. They were so terrified, drugged, or simply so far gone mentally that they didn't move.

Then Dmitri loosed a deafening volley from the submachine pistol, blasting holes in the ceiling of the elevator. "*Get the fuckers!*" he bellowed.

That got the message across. With shrieks and screams, the thirty-odd prisoners burst from the elevator and swarmed into what Valentina saw must be the headquarters morgue. Not surprisingly, it was quite large, with at least fifty refrigeration bays for bodies, and a dozen gurneys lined up with their grisly cargo in various stages of post-mortem examination.

There were half a dozen men and women in medical gowns around the bodies, along with two guards. The shocked expressions on their faces would have been priceless had Valentina had the time to appreciate them.

"Watch out!" Valentina shouted to the two stunned guards, "they have weapons!"

She knew that the room was almost certainly monitored, and the words were only for the benefit of anyone who might be listening. She fired her submachine pistol, making it look like she was shooting into the mass of prisoners, with the first two bursts taking the guards in the chest. Then she slaughtered the medical examiners with tightly spaced shots, careful to avoid shooting the panicked prisoners.

One of the examiners managed to reach a double door at the rear of the morgue. The woman was able to scan her thumbprint and swipe her badge in time to avoid being crushed by the prisoners fleeing toward her, but she couldn't avoid the bullets from Sikorsky's weapon. She fell in a bloody heap, the prisoners trampling her lifeless body as they fled outside, Valentina and Sikorsky close behind.

***

"*Chyort voz'mi*," the colonel choked as he saw the catastrophe unfold in the headquarters morgue. The situation became even worse when he saw one of the examiners open the door *to the outside*. The prisoners would still be contained inside the compound, but there was only a single checkpoint at the rear of the facility and four guards. The two spies were supposed to escape, yes, but having the entire staff of medical examiners wiped out had not been part of the plan.

"Colonel," the young officer asked him again, quite urgently, "should we not sound the alarm?"

"No," the colonel said grimly. "Come with me. All of you." Drawing his sidearm, he led the young officer and three guards at a run to the other side of the complex. He doubted he would be able to reach the morgue in time to salvage this disaster.

***

Valentina and Sikorsky herded the prisoners like cattle toward the only visible guard post that sat astride the gate through the wall surrounding the headquarters complex. She could see that Sikorsky was having a difficult time keeping up, and moved over to help him, but he waved her away impatiently. "I am fine," he rasped. "Let us finish this."

Nodding, she moved back over to the side of the screaming mob in time to see the guards at the checkpoint, four of them, raising their weapons. Valentina waved, drawing their attention. "Be careful!" she yelled. "They're armed!"

A rifle barked and one of the prisoners dropped, then the other guards began firing. Every shot tore through Valentina's heart, but she had to get close enough to make sure she could kill all four guards. Sikorsky was falling behind, clutching his ribs, and would be no use in this battle.

Half a dozen of the prisoners had been cut down when she finally judged she was close enough. Pulling far out to one side, she leveled her submachine pistol and held down the trigger, fanning the bullets across the four guards. Two were hit in the head, the others took rounds to the chest. They were wearing body armor, so she put an extra bullet into their heads.

Dead men tell no tales, she thought savagely. Then she fired her weapon into the air, getting the prisoners to flee back the way they had come, away from the check point and past their fallen comrades. Then she went to Sikorsky, wrapping one of his arms around her shoulders and helping him to the small military utility vehicle parked next to the gate. After putting him in the passenger seat, she used her stolen thumb and ID badge one more time to open the gate. Then she hopped in the driver's seat and headed out of the facility, just as the alarm siren went off.

As she was driving out, a platoon of secret police troops ran toward her from their barracks outside the compound walls. She brought her vehicle to a stop and waved their commander, a very young lieutenant, over.

"The prisoners have escaped, and they have weapons!" she said, panicked, as she grabbed him by the lapel of his uniform. "My comrade has been shot," she went on, jerking her head toward Dmitri, who sat beside her, moaning. "Do you have a medical kit in your barracks?"

"Of course," the lieutenant said, as if she were a simpleton. "Get him there and take care of him. We will take care of those scum." He glared in the direction of the gate and the confused screaming beyond it.

"Thank you, comrade lieutenant," she said gratefully.

He nodded once before taking off at a run with his men, weapons at the ready.

Watching them in the rear-view mirror as she turned onto the road that led toward town, ignoring the nearby barracks, Valentina held back her tears as she waited for the massacre to begin.

***

The colonel and his men burst into the courtyard just as the first volley of gunfire *cracked* through the air and bullets whizzed by their heads.

"*Govno!*" one of the men cried as he took a round in the leg. "Shit!"

"Cease fire!" the colonel screamed at the secret police troops he glimpsed beyond the mass of prisoners who were running directly toward him and his men, only a few meters away now, screening them from the view of the other troops. "*Cease–*"

Thirty-four weapons, firing on full automatic, cut down the rest of the prisoners. It was only afterward, as the men of the quick reaction platoon sorted through the bodies, that the colonel and his troops were discovered.

They were the only ones other than Morozov himself who knew of the secret orders regarding the Confederation spies, and the secret died with them. By the time anyone in authority realized the two high-value prisoners were missing and had not been followed, it would be far too late.

***

Valentina drove through the city, using the intrinsic authority of a secret police vehicle to bypass the normal traffic stops and other encumbrances Saint Petersburg drivers normally had to contend with. She was headed toward where she had originally landed a week, a lifetime, ago. Having lost her microcomputer when they were captured, she had to reach the cache of equipment she had left behind: it contained a backup secure transmitter with which she could communicate with the fleet.

"How do you do it?" Sikorsky said. He had been quiet for a long time after their escape. She had thought it was simply from the injuries he had suffered which, while certainly serious, did not appear to be life-threatening. From the tone of his voice, however, it was clear that he had also been doing a great deal of thinking.

"How do I do what, Dmitri?"

He turned his face, now covered with bandages she had applied from the vehicle's medical kit, and gave her a cold, appraising look. "How do you live with yourself, after doing such a thing?" He looked away. "You knew those poor fools would be slaughtered," he went on quietly. "They never stood a chance. You used them. Even Medvedev, pig that he was, was nothing more than a tool to you. And that is all I am, as well."

She bit back her emotions. *Focus on the mission*, she told herself, knowing that there was almost certainly a special spot in Hell waiting for her for all the things she had done. Medvedev certainly did not bother her conscience. And sending those prisoners to be used as cannon fodder was not the worst of her misdeeds, nor – if she survived – would it be the last. What Sikorsky had said about himself, if anything, hurt far worse. Not because it wasn't true, but because it was.

"We had no choice, Dmitri," she told him bluntly. "And what did you think was going to happen to those people, anyway? That the secret police were going to suddenly forgive them and let them go? They were all dead men and women who happened to be still breathing. Every one of them was bound for the grave." She paused a moment, trying to convince herself that it was all true. Even if it was, it would still be a huge burden on her soul. "If there had been any way for me to save them without endangering my mission, Dmitri," she finally said, "I would have. If we had been given more time, and I had more information to make a better plan, things might have been different. But..." She shook her head helplessly.

Sikorsky said nothing, but simply stared out the passenger side window.

Sighing, Valentina glanced up to the clear blue sky. "I only hope we're not too late," she whispered to herself.

ELEVEN

Li'ara-Zhurah stood beside Tesh-Dar, who sat in the command chair of the assault fleet's flagship. Their force, fifty-seven ships headed toward the human planet of Saint Petersburg, was not nearly as large as the one used against Keran, where the Empire's warriors first engaged in battle with the humans. Unlike the attack on Keran, which was intended to frighten the humans, to shock them into action that would make them a more potent and effective enemy, the attacks here and against several other human systems were to be long-term battles of attrition. The Empire would allow the bloodletting here to go on for cycles before the humans were finally extinguished from this world. In this way a great many warriors could be blooded to bring honor to the Empress.

And in that time, or the cycles that would come after, when the Empire attacked yet more human worlds, perhaps Her Children would find the One whose blood could sing, the One who could save them all from extinction.

Throughout the assault fleet, now was a time for contemplation. All the preparations for combat had been made, and the warriors and shipmistresses were ready to open the great battle that lay ahead. Anticipation swirled in their blood like a hungry predator in a deep ocean, but it was yet far from the surface, barely registering on their consciousness. Instead, they turned inward, reflecting on their lives, their sisters, and their bond to the Empress.

Li'ara-Zhurah closed her eyes, seeking to shed the last remains of the melancholy that had plagued her since Keran. It no longer held sway over her heart, but she was determined to expunge it from her soul: she refused to shame Tesh-Dar's legacy by being anything less than completely worthy of the honor that the elder priestess sought to bestow upon her. Relaxing her mind and body, she gave herself up completely to the power of the

Bloodsong. She lost her sense of self in the ethereal chorus from the trillions of her sisters. It was a timeless, infinite melody containing every emotion her race could express, and running through it all was the immortal love of the Empress.

As she felt the great river gently wash away the last of the pain and uncertainty from her soul, she suddenly sensed something that had not been there before, a new voice in the chorus of souls. She gasped at the power of this new voice, at the purity of its song as it joined with the many others of its kind. Opening her eyes wide with wonder, she looked down at her body, gently placing a hand over the armor protecting her abdomen.

There, in her womb, her child's spirit had awakened.

She felt someone touch her arm, and looked up to see Tesh-Dar, smiling at her.

"Her Bloodsong is powerful, child," Tesh-Dar said proudly, "much like her mother's."

Li'ara-Zhurah could only nod her head, still overwhelmed by the sensation of a second spirit singing together with, yet unique from, her own. *A girl child*, she told herself. *Thank you, my Empress*. She knew now that she would bear any male children that might result from future matings, that her earlier misgivings could not deter her honor and duty. Yet she was thankful that this, her first, was a female child. A part of her yet hoped that this child would be sterile, that she would not have to endure the agony of mating. Regardless, Li'ara-Zhurah realized that she would cherish her daughters, of black talons or silver, fertile or sterile. She would bear any male children that fate demanded of her, but in her heart of hearts she would never consider them sons. They were tools necessary to preserve the Empire, but no more. It was part of the heart-rending tragedy that was the Curse, the final act of a heartbroken First Empress.

Beside her, Tesh-Dar's heart swelled with love and pride: Li'ara-Zhurah's Bloodsong was strong and pure, just as that of her newly awoken daughter. Soon, once Li'ara-Zhurah's role in opening the battle at Saint Petersburg had played out, Tesh-Dar would take her to her appointed nursery world to give birth. From there, she would lead Li'ara-Zhurah to the temple of the Desh-Ka, just as Sura-Ni'khan had taken Tesh-Dar many cycles ago. Once she had bequeathed her powers to her young acolyte, Tesh-Dar would spend her remaining days helping Li'ara-Zhurah learn the full extent of her powers.

In one sense, Tesh-Dar was saddened that she would be diminished once she and Li'ara-Zhurah performed the ritual that would make the young warrior high priestess of the Desh-Ka. No longer would Tesh-Dar be able to call upon the powers she had inherited from Sura-Ni'khan; she would still be a force to contend with in the arena and in battle with the humans, but only because of her great strength and skill with weapons. No longer would she be able to walk through walls, or cast herself into the air and float along as she willed, or see far beyond the senses of her body with her second sight. All these things that she had come to treasure, would she lose.

Yet part of her also yearned for release from the crushing sense of responsibility she bore upon her shoulders. For nearly a hundred cycles now had she worn the rune of the Desh-Ka upon her collar as high priestess, and her soul was weary. To spend the remainder of her days teaching Li'ara-Zhurah in the ways of the Desh-Ka and helping the *tresh* at her *kazha* – including, she hoped, Li'ara-Zhurah's daughter, should the Empress bless it – to become warriors were her only ambitions. She had always thought she would die in battle (*And that may yet come to pass*, she thought), but she would welcome a quiet death in a warm bed of animal hides just as well. She was the supreme warrior of a race that lived for battle, but she would not be disappointed if, like Pan'ne-Sharakh, she could live out her remaining days among the arenas of the *kazha*.

Sighing in contentment, her hand on Li'ara-Zhurah's, she watched the ship's displays as her fleet moved inexorably closer to its objective.

***

Sato sat rigidly, strapped in his combat chair on *Yura's* bridge. Beside him, in a special sheath the ship's engineers had fixed to his chair, was his *katana*. Left to him by his grandfather, the weapon had been with him during the most traumatic moments of his life. He knew in his heart that he would die with it in his hands, fighting the Kreelans. *For a warrior*, he thought, *was there any other way to die?*

"Transpace sequence initiated," the navigation computer announced. "Normal space in ten seconds...five...four...three...two...one...now." The main bridge display suddenly resolved into a panorama of stars, with Saint Petersburg's sun a blazing white disk off the port side. "Transpace sequence complete."

They had jumped into the system very close to the planet of Saint Petersburg, barely outside the orbit of its moon. If the task force received the intelligence information they were expecting about the nuclear weapons, they would deploy the Marines or conduct an orbital bombardment. Or both. If they didn't get the information, they would sail directly to Riga, which lay further in-system.

It was just a question of waiting.

"Jump engines off-line and respooling for contingency jump," the bridge engineering officer called out. In case the task force got into too much trouble, the ship would be ready to jump out on thirty seconds notice. "Engineering is ready to answer all bells, captain."

"All ahead, one quarter," Sato ordered. "Keep us in tight formation, helm."

"Inter-ship datalink acquired, captain," the young tactical officer announced, and information on the nearby planets and ships suddenly blossomed into life on the display. The sensors of all the ships in the task force were linked together, with each ship sending what it "saw" to the other ships. The datalink would do the same for targeting information, allowing the task force to fight as a tightly integrated weapons complex, rather than individual ships. It was a wonderful system, but the Kreelans had proven at Keran that it could be disrupted, with devastating effect. Since then, while it was still used on a regular basis, every crew and squadron trained to function effectively without it.

"Any hostiles?" Sato asked, carefully filtering the tension from his voice.

"Negative, sir," the tactical officer reported. Unlike Sato, his voice wavered slightly, betraying how tense he was. Like most of the crewmen aboard *Yura* and the other ships of the task force, this was his first combat patrol. "I see three Saint Petersburg coast guard cutters in low orbit, but that's it for ships in the order of battle database. Everything else is either a freighter or an unknown. None of the vessels has changed course or activated additional sensors. No new emanations from the planet or the moon. There's no reaction at all that we can see."

Sato frowned. Something was wrong. Any planet, particularly now that humanity was at war with the Empire, would react to a fleet of warships appearing in their system. They would be insane not to.

He stared at the display, searching for clues. The ships of the task force appeared as blue icons, while every other ship in the system was painted in yellow: not hostile, but not confirmed as friendly, either. If a ship was later confirmed to be a friendly vessel, it would change to green on the display.

And that's not bloody likely, Sato thought grimly as the Confederation task force moved in closer to the planet.

***

Valentina sped through the forest as fast as she dared. If the fleet had stayed on schedule, they were already in-system, waiting for her signal. She was late.

"Damn it," she muttered venomously as she gunned the vehicle across a small creek, the oversized drive wheels clawing for purchase in the soft soil of the opposite bank. The distance from the road to where she had buried her cache of equipment had seemed much shorter when she had walked into the train station after she arrived. They had made good time getting here, thanks to everyone's fear of anything having to do with the secret police, but these last few kilometers had been nerve-wracking.

Then she saw it. She had buried her equipment container near a dead tree that had been split by a lightning strike. "*Slava Bogu*," she said. "Thank God."

"God has nothing to do with this," Sikorsky said as she pulled the vehicle to a stop.

Ignoring him, she jumped out and ran to the spot, seven paces due south from the trunk of the tree, where she had buried her gear. The vehicle they'd stolen had no utility tools like a shovel, so she simply dropped to her knees and began to claw at the ground. "Help me," she pleaded. "We've got to hurry."

Sikorsky simply stared at her for a moment. Then, with a sigh of resignation, he got down on his knees and began to dig.

In five minutes they pulled a cylindrical container about as long as Valentina's arm and as big around as her leg from the ground. Sikorsky put his hand on the small control panel that was inset into the casing.

"No!" she cried, batting his hand away.

"What?" he asked angrily. "I help you, and this is—"

"It's booby-trapped, Dmitri," she explained quickly as she moved her hands in a peculiar way over the casing, pressing gently at several points. "The access panel you see here is a fake. If you'd tried to open it that way, it would have exploded and killed you. And me."

With a faint popping sound, the cylinder opened. She reached in and extracted a black device that was as thick as her little finger and fit neatly in her palm. Swiping a finger across one edge, the face lit up in a small display.

Sikorsky noticed that the finger she had used to touch the device had come away bloody.

"It's validating that it's my DNA," she breathed as the face of the device suddenly glowed amber. Then she said in English, "The standard four square is hex. Copernicus. Execute." Glancing up at Sikorsky, she explained, "It's a randomly generated code phrase. That, plus my voice print and DNA will enable it."

The face of the device suddenly glowed green. There were no numbers or other data displayed, just a monochrome green.

Closing her eyes in concentration, Valentina began dictating a stream of numbers that would tell the fleet about the hidden nuclear weapons facility and where to find it.

***

"We are taking a tremendous risk, comrade." Korolev's voice was soft, but the threat was clear.

Marshal Antonov nodded. Despite Korolev's implicit threat, he was not nervous. It was not that he doubted what would happen to him if his plan failed, it was simply that he knew his plan could *not* fail. "It will work, comrade chairman," he said confidently. "As long as our friends in the secret police managed to do their job." He shot a sideways glance at Morozov, who sat quietly at his place at the table. "The Confederation ships that just arrived will either surrender or be destroyed."

"What if they try to jump out when your trap is sprung?" one of the other ministers asked.

Antonov shook his head. "If what we know about their naval procedures is true, they will not have time. I believe they will try to engage the force of warships we will soon send to greet them. When they do, they will be within range of the *special*," he glanced sourly at Morozov, "torpedoes. These weapons are very fast, far faster than the Confederation designs: their ships will not have time to cycle their jump engines before they are destroyed."

Korolev nodded, satisfied. Then he turned to Morozov. "And were you, comrade, successful in your part of this grand scheme?"

"Quite, comrade chairman," he said with a carefully controlled expression. He had no doubts that Antonov already knew of the disaster at Morozov's own headquarters, but the defense minister apparently was holding back that bit of news from the chairman to use at a future time when it would prove particularly detrimental. In the end, however, it would do Antonov little good: the goal had been for the two Confederation spies to escape and not be suspicious that their getaway had, in fact, been planned. Morozov had intended for them to be followed so they could be quickly rounded up after they had done whatever they needed to do to contact the Confederation, but that part had not come to fruition. *Obviously*, he thought, cursing the dead colonel who had let things get so out of hand. The fool's family was already on their way to a labor camp in the far south, where they would spend the rest of their miserable lives. "The spies are away, just as we planned," he said in a half-truth. "If what we suspect is true, you should see the result soon enough from the actions of the Confederation ships."

They did not have long to wait.

***

When she had finished dictating the stream of numbers, Valentina quickly set the device down on the ground and grabbed Sikorsky with one hand, holding the cylinder in the other. "Come with me," she said as she quickly walked away. "You don't want to be near it when it transmits."

"Why?" Sikorsky asked, stumbling after her as she quickly pulled him along. He kept glancing over his shoulder at the small device, wondering what could be so—

The forest behind him where she had placed the device suddenly lit up, blindingly bright. He shut his eyes and turned away, only to be knocked to his knees by a powerful blast.

"Does *everything* you brought with you explode?" he demanded as she pulled him back to his feet.

"The ship that dropped me off left some microsats in high orbit to relay any messages to the fleet," she said as she led him back to their stolen vehicle. "With a device as small as that transmitter, the only way to generate the power for a strong enough signal is to create a small explosion and a pulse wave." She looked at him. "Does that make sense?"

"I understand the concept," he grumbled, "but what if you have to tell them something else? You no longer have a way to communicate."

"I have a shorter-range transmitter," she said, showing him the watch she had taken from the cylinder and strapped to her wrist. "It won't reach the fleet, but when my extraction team comes..."

She stopped as they reached the vehicle, and she turned to Sikorsky. "Dmitri," she told him, "you can come back with me. The Confederation will grant you asylum, give you a new life."

He said nothing for a long moment as he stared out at the forest around them. "I cannot leave, Valentina," he said quietly. They had gone over this earlier, but it would have been a lie to say that he had not been thinking about it. The final answer, however, had not changed. "I am disgusted by what our leaders have done to our people, to my family. I helped you in hopes that, in some small way, it might change things for us, make things better, even if not for me." He turned to look at her. "I could not live with myself if I simply walked away. That would make me feel like a traitor, and that is something I am not. And what sort of life would I have somewhere else? I know our world is not listed in many tourist guides of the human sphere, Valentina, but this is where I was born and where I have lived my life. It is my home."

"They'll kill you, Dmitri," she said quietly. "And what about your wife? I doubt she's going to be happy about all this."

"What about her, indeed," he sighed.

***

Commodore Hanson was in her command chair on the *Constellation's* flag bridge, which was a special compartment adjoining the ship's bridge from where her staff could control the actions of the task force.

The door behind her suddenly swished open, and a tall, well-muscled man in civilian clothes stepped quickly to her side. She knew little about him other than his name, Robert Torvald (which she suspected was a pseudonym), and that he was the controller for the Confederation agent whose mission was to get Hanson the information she needed to snatch Saint Petersburg's nuclear weapons. He had arrived in a special courier at the task force's rendezvous point, coming aboard *Constellation* at the last minute, when it had become clear that the rest of the task force and the designated mission commander, a two-star admiral, would not be making the party. Hanson had initially been irked at the man's presence, for he was the only one authorized to make contact with the source, the Navy apparently not being sufficiently trustworthy. He had brought along special communications gear that had been locked away in a small arms locker under the control of two Marine guards. That's where he had been since two hours before the task force's emergence here, crammed into the tiny room with his mysterious equipment.

"Here it is," he told her quietly, handing her a data chip. "I've sanitized the information to a classification level that will allow you to use it in any of the ship's systems."

"And what did you leave out?" she asked sharply.

"Nothing that will affect your mission, commodore," he answered softly, returning her gaze levelly.

She held the tiny chip in her hand, looking at it for just a moment, wondering at the guts of whomever had obtained the data. And how accurate the information was. The lives of her crewmen and the Marines now depended on it. With a scowl, she called over her flag operations officer. "Here," she said, handing him the chip. "This is the data on the nuclear weapons. Get this analyzed and update our operations plans, pronto."

"Aye, aye, ma'am," he said, taking the chip and hurrying back to his station.

"Commodore," the flag communications officer said, "we've got an incoming message from planetside."

Hanson frowned. She had wanted to take the initiative in making contact with the Saint Petersburg government or military, but she had been forced to wait until she had the information on the nuclear weapons. "Put it on the main screen," she ordered tersely, wondering who she would be dealing with.

***

"This is Commodore Margaret Hanson of the Confederation Navy," the woman on the screen said formally. "To whom am I speaking?"

"Commodore, this is Iosef Korolev, Chairman of the Ruling Party Council of Saint Petersburg," he said amicably. "May I ask why the newly formed Confederation has sent a fleet of warships to our peaceful system?"

"Mr. Chairman," the woman said evenly, "I was sent here on the orders of the President of the Confederation to carry out an inspection of several facilities on Saint Petersburg. This inspection is in accordance with article fourteen of the long-term armistice provisions, citing that Saint Petersburg may not develop, construct, or possess weapons of mass destruction. My secondary orders," she went on, "are to conduct a training exercise with the Rigan coast guard and provide supplies and personnel to assist them in forming Territorial Army detachments for common defense. This is required and was agreed to, as stated in the Confederation Constitution, when Riga became a member."

Korolev relaxed back into his chair. "Well, commodore," he said, his Russian accent barely evident in his New Oxford-educated English, "welcome to Saint Petersburg. If you would please have your staff coordinate with our naval personnel, we will be happy to arrange for your inspection parties to land.

"As for your proposed exercise with the Rigan coast guard, however," he went on, wincing slightly, as if the idea gave him indigestion, "I believe your government misunderstands the situation. Riga is a *semi*-autonomous world under our governance. Any claim they may have made to independent status or membership in your interplanetary government is neither legitimate, nor legal. Their defense is well in hand, I assure you, without any involvement by Confederation forces. Please, commodore, I

strongly urge you to seek further counsel from your government —
preferably with clarification from an envoy I would be happy to send with
you — before carrying out those orders. Your ships are welcome in orbit
around Saint Petersburg, but we will consider any deployment of your
vessels further in-system toward Riga to be an...unfriendly provocation."
He smiled, conveying just the right mixture of warmth and menace.

Hanson paused a moment. "Mr. Chairman, I suggest we consider the
two issues separately for now," she finally said. "I'll maintain my task force
in orbit around Saint Petersburg while we conduct our inspections. Once
that is taken care of, we can further discuss the situation with Riga."

"There is not really any more to discuss on that point," Korolev told
her, "but for as long as your ships stay in orbit here, we have no quarrel. If
there is nothing else, commodore, my naval personnel will contact you
with the necessary information to coordinate your inspections."

"Thank you, Mr. Chairman," Hanson said. "You're most gracious."

Korolev nodded, then killed the connection.

"Fools," Marshal Antonov said, aghast. "They cannot believe that we
would just let them walk into our facilities. The armistice conditions
expired years ago!"

"Not entirely true, marshal," Morozov said. "Technically, the
provisions of article fourteen, and article fourteen alone, were to remain in
effect in perpetuity: the good commodore does indeed have legal right to
inspect our facilities if they have reasonable suspicion that weapons of mass
destruction are present or being produced. No doubt she will land her
troops and then stay in close orbit to protect them. Of course, this is
exactly what we wanted." He smiled. "So, you see, even though it caused
us much pain at the end of the war, today the armistice will serve our
purposes nicely, and will allow us to firmly put the Confederation in its
place."

Almost grudgingly, Antonov returned Morozov's smile.

***

"Do not be deceived, commodore," Grishin said with uncharacteristic
vehemence, "This is a trap."

Commodore Hanson had called a final commander's meeting over the
inter-ship vidcom immediately after she got off the link with Korolev. All

of the ship captains were virtually present, their images displayed on the main viewscreen in her ready room. Around the table with her sat her flag staff and the *Constellation's* captain. As the senior Marine commander, Grishin also participated, the vidcom projecting his image from the cramped cockpit of his assault boat. It was ready to be launched with the rest of the boats carrying the Marines from the two assault carriers, as soon as the commodore gave the word.

"Colonel," Hanson's intelligence officer said in a neutral voice, "we're not seeing any indications of a hostile reaction. We've identified every ship in the system as either some sort of transport or a coast guard vessel. There's not a single sign of any warships. We've also not detected any unusual emissions – search or targeting systems – from the planet." He turned to Hanson. "Ma'am, I'm not saying that Korolev may not have a surprise in store for us, but if he is, he's concealing it bloody well."

Grishin shook his head. "*Maskirovka* – deception – is a specialty of theirs. If you review the history of the conflict twenty years ago, you will clearly see this: the Terran and Alliance forces suffered several major defeats and the loss of many troops because of it."

"Colonel," Hanson said, "even if it is a trap, there's very little I can do other than spring it while keeping our eyes wide open. We have confirmation that they have nuclear weapons, and we have details on where they're produced and stored. Our orders are clear on what we have to do next: get down there as quickly as possible to seize them before they can be moved." As she spoke, the task force was taking up position in a series of polar orbits. This would allow Hanson to have at least a few ships passing over the primary target area at any given time in low orbit to provide support to the Marines, while allowing her to also keep an eye on the rest of the planet. "If I knew what their deception was, we could try to disrupt it. Unfortunately, we don't, so we've got to go with what we've got." She paused, looking each of her commanders in the eye. "Let's do it, people."

TWELVE

"You don't have to do this, Valentina," Sikorsky said for the third time as she drove him back into Saint Petersburg city. After she had sent the signal to the fleet, he had wanted to return home, to try and get his wife out of the city before the Confederation Marines came. Before the next war started.

"If you say that one more time, Dmitri," she told him with a wry smile, "I'm going to break your arm. I'm coming with you. So get used to the idea and stop worrying about it."

Sikorsky nodded, an unhappy expression on his face. As he turned to look out the window, however, she saw in the side mirror a small smile form on his lips.

What she was doing was explicitly against her orders. She was supposed to sever any ties with the locals and wait in a secure location for pickup. It was something she had done before, many times. One of those times, she had even been forced to kill her contact, a woman she had worked closely with and befriended over a three month-long mission that had gone bad, literally, at the last minute. Valentina had been known as Consuela then, just one of the many false identities behind which Scarlet had concealed herself. Outwardly, her contact's death did not appear to affect her; she told her controller that it was simply part of the mission, and that the woman had been an asset or, as Dmitri had said, a tool to be used and discarded as necessary.

But she had become so adept at the art of deception that she had deceived herself. It took her several months to realize that part of her soul had died the day that she had turned to this woman, her contact and friend, and wordlessly snapped her neck before she could be captured and interrogated. The two of them had been cornered, trapped, and the woman had simply known too much to fall into the wrong hands. There had been no way for both of them to escape, and so Consuela – Scarlet – had killed her friend. She managed to escape after a vicious fight with her pursuers, but the emotional wound was deep, and had never truly healed. There had been other missions since then, but she had never allowed herself to become close to any of the contacts she had made. Nor to anyone else.

Until Dmitri. He was an anomaly in her experience. There was nothing outwardly special about him. While he certainly was not a homely man, she was not physically or emotionally attracted to him. He didn't play the role of a hero, although he clearly had courage. He wasn't rich or powerful. Had she called him a simple and ordinary man, with simple and ordinary ways, he would no doubt have heartily agreed and poured the two of them some vodka to drink together.

No. Her bond to Dmitri, the sense of loyalty she felt to this human tool, who would be used and discarded as necessary for her mission, was simply because he was a good man, with a good heart. There were few enough of those in the universe, she knew from painful experience, and she had decided that if she could help him, she would. It wouldn't be a full atonement for her past sins, but it was a start.

Now that her primary mission objective had been met and the target information conveyed to the fleet (she hoped, for there was no way for her to know if the fleet had actually received it, or if the Navy had even arrived), the only harm that could come from her helping Dmitri was to herself. She realized that she was an asset to the Confederation in the same way that Dmitri was to her, but the difference was that the Confederation was not here to enforce the rules. What she did now was up to her, and she had chosen to help him.

On the way back to the city, they had stopped at the small town where Valentina had boarded the train to Saint Petersburg only a week earlier. It was risky, but she needed some civilian clothes to do what they had planned. Assuming the arrogant attitude typical of the secret police, she had marched into the shabby local clothing store and bought what she needed using the credit disk of the soldier whose uniform she wore. That caused the clerk to raise her eyebrows, but looking up into Valentina's cold eyes was enough to avert any questions. Valentina knew that there was a chance the woman would report her, but Sikorsky dismissed the notion.

"No one will question you," he said. "You wear a secret police uniform, are driving one of their vehicles, and have a comrade with you, all in plain sight. It does not matter if the name on the credit disk does not match. People do not delve into the affairs of the secret police, because they do not want them knocking on doors, asking questions, and taking people away, never to return. If you look like secret police, to them you *are* secret police."

They had made a second stop, this time at a small deli that was completely empty except for the elderly man behind the counter. Sikorsky bought some questionable looking cold cuts and bread, which actually looked good and smelled delicious, and two bottles of mineral water. In the meantime, Valentina disappeared into the disgustingly dirty rest room to change. She put on her civilian clothes, a pair of black pants and a dark brown blouse that were both shapeless and common, and then put her baggy uniform back on over top. She had also bought a set of sandals that were typical summer casual wear for women here, which she left in the vehicle. So, for all the proprietor of the deli knew, she had simply gone to the bathroom while her comrade had procured lunch.

As they got back on the road and headed toward Saint Petersburg, they saw contrails, high in the sky, spiraling downward.

***

Grishin struggled to keep from gritting his teeth in frustration. *I should not be surprised*, he told himself harshly. *It is exactly what I would do, just before springing the ambush.* The Saint Petersburg government had waited until the Marine boats were away before they had a sudden "unexpected systems failure" that caused all of their planetary defense arrays to activate. Fearing an attack, Hanson had called the boats back and regrouped her ships in higher orbit in a better defensive position, with every vessel poised to repel the as-yet unseen Saint Petersburg Navy.

Not surprisingly – at least to Grishin – no attack had materialized. The whole farce, he knew, had been both to test the Confederation task force's reactions and to gather information on their weapons systems. On top of that, their entire operation had effectively been disrupted. Hanson had been forced to make an agonizing decision: take the time to reposition her ships as she had before, which would have provided optimal support to

IN HER NAME: LEGEND OF THE SWORD   143

the Marines, or send the assault carriers in with minimal protection while keeping the bulk of her ships further from the planet where they had more maneuvering room for combat.

Knowing that the tactic had been nothing more than a play for time, no doubt to move as many weapons and incriminating equipment as possible out of the huge mountain facility, Hanson had sent the carriers in with Sato's ship, *Yura,* and one of her sister heavy cruisers for protection and fire support for the Marines, if they needed it.

After the targeting systems had been shut down, the Russians had been extremely obliging in guiding the boats down and effusive in their apologies. Hanson had accepted their regrets with admirable diplomacy, but Grishin was not fooled: he had planned a small bit of deception of his own.

His original plan, after analyzing the information the Confederation agent had transmitted, had called for a battalion of troops to land at the mountain facility, and two companies each to land at the coal burning facilities (he refused now to call them "power plants"). After the game the Russians had played, however, he knew that the only facility of any true value would be the mountain facility: the locations of the coal burning facilities were known now, and their outward details had been confirmed from orbit. They may be producing uranium, but that was all. The real prize, if there was one, was the massive bunker in the mountains.

Once Hanson finally gave clearance for the landing to recommence, Grishin had his boat pilots follow their original courses, with one small deviation: the boats bound for the coal burning facilities simply did a quick flyover of their targets before turning to join Grishin's main force at the mountain bunker, concentrating the entire Marine brigade at the main objective. The boats dove low, skimming the treetops, to avoid the planetary defense radars as best they could.

***

In a deep underground bunker five kilometers south of Saint Petersburg city that served as the military command center and survival shelter for the planet's leaders, Marshal Antonov grunted in satisfaction.

"All too predictable," he murmured as the Confederation boats that had been heading for the coal plants suddenly disappeared from the defense network displays, no doubt as some sort of ruse. He could have ordered his aerospace fighters up to engage and destroy them, but that would have given away the game. They could only be heading toward one place. "Let them concentrate at the Central Facility where we can apply overwhelming force," he said to Korolev, who stood beside him at the massive map table, whose surface showed the known and projected tracks of the enemy boats as they raced toward the Central Facility, "and we will be done with these fools." The map showed the forces that now awaited the Confederation Marines: in addition to the division that was normally garrisoned in and around the facility, two more divisions had been deployed in concealed positions in a ring around the massive bunker. The Confederation troops would be outnumbered six to one. He glanced at the wall display, which showed the disposition of the Confederation task force's ships, hovering in high orbit not far from the moon. He shook his head in disgust at the sight of the vulnerable carriers, now escorted only by a pair of heavy cruisers. "Then we will formally introduce them to the Saint Petersburg Navy."

Beside him, Korolev could not help but smile as he looked at the icons representing the seventy-three ships of his planet's secretly-built navy, including thirty-eight powerful heavy cruisers, all armed with highly advanced nuclear-tipped torpedoes. Carefully concealed in deep fissures in the small moon's surface, they were perfectly positioned for a surprise attack on the Confederation task force.

***

"Roland, are you all right?"

Mills snapped his eyes open at the sound of Sabourin's voice. She had opened a private channel to him so no one else could hear. Two of the *Yura's* Marine detachment's platoons had been prepared as a quick reaction force to help support the surface operation, with a platoon in each of the two cutters the cruiser carried. The two other platoons, along with the detachment commander, had been ferried to one of the assault carriers, and – if the mission called for it – would be taken down in one of the carrier's assault boats that would soon be returning from the surface after deploying the Marines there. The detachment commander had left Mills in charge of the force waiting aboard *Yura*.

"Yes," he rasped, "I'm bloody fine."

After a brief pause, Sabourin said softly, "You should know better than to lie to me."

Mills looked up at her. "My head has been aching like a bloody bitch," he confessed. "And..." He stopped, shook his head.

"And you're still seeing the Kreelan, as in the dream?" she finished for him.

Unwillingly, he nodded. "It's like it's getting stronger by the fucking minute. Damned if I know why or what it means."

"Could they be coming here?" Sabourin wondered.

Mills laughed mirthlessly, shaking his head. "Now wouldn't that be a capital cockup? As if the Russkies aren't trouble enough."

"I think we should tell the captain, Roland," she said. "Maybe it's nothing, but if—"

"No," he said, cutting her off. "He probably thinks I'm off my fucking nut with this dreaming business. I'm not going to give him cause to pull me off the line now, Emmanuelle."

"But what if it *does* mean something, Roland?" she pressed.

"It doesn't," he snapped. Then, after a moment, he added softly, "Please, just drop it?"

Fearing that he was making a potentially grave mistake, Sabourin nodded and settled back into the combat seat, her worried eyes fixed on her lover.

***

"Okay," Valentina breathed, "let's go."

A secret police vehicle parked on the street during daylight was highly unusual; like cockroaches, the secret police normally came out at night to swarm through the city. Unfortunately, there was no convenient place to park it out of sight and still be close to Sikorsky's apartment building. On the other hand, anyone who saw the vehicle or its two occupants would just as quickly pretend they hadn't.

A few minutes earlier, Sikorsky and Valentina had stopped the vehicle in an alley, where Valentina stripped off her secret police uniform to expose her civilian clothes, and swapped places in the vehicle with Sikorsky, who then drove them to his apartment building.

"Do you think this will work?" he asked quietly as they got out of the vehicle and climbed the worn concrete stairs to the main entrance.

"I don't know," she said, "but we don't have time for anything else." She knew that the Marines must be close to their objectives by now, and was surprised that an orbital bombardment hadn't already begun. Some Marines would be detailed to pick her up: they just had to find her. One of the items in her retrieved cylinder was a special emergency retrieval beacon. She should have activated it as soon as she knew the boats were inbound. She hadn't, because she wasn't going to leave this planet without making sure that Dmitri and his wife were safe.

Valentina led the way, following Sikorsky's quiet instructions to reach his apartment. Her hands were bound by cuffs, although they were loose enough that she could quickly get free if she had to. Sikorsky held his submachine gun trained on her back to round out the image of her being his prisoner.

When they arrived at his door, Sikorsky knocked. "Ludmilla!" he called. He would have let himself in, of course, but his key – along with his clothes and other items he had when they were captured – was still sitting somewhere in secret police headquarters.

After an agonizing moment, the door swung open.

"*Ludmilla*," Sikorsky gasped, horrified.

There stood his wife, her face battered and bruised, with deep cuts in her forehead and on both cheeks, with her lips still bleeding and swollen. Her left arm was in a sling, her wrist and fingers in a poorly-made cast. She stumbled back from the door, trembling in fear of her husband, who now wore a secret police uniform.

Valentina instantly realized that they had made a terrible miscalculation. Neither she nor Sikorsky had thought of the possibility that Ludmilla might have been brought in for questioning. In retrospect, she knew that had been an amateurish mistake. *Of course they would have interrogated her*, she berated herself. And now here the two of them were, Dmitri ready with a story that he had been working undercover for the secret police to bring this Confederation spy to justice, hoping that would fool his devoted Party wife long enough to get her away from the city, and Valentina playing the role of captured villainess.

Worse, now that she was thinking more clearly, she realized that the secret police no doubt had Ludmilla under surveillance on the chance that Sikorsky would return home. They had walked straight into a trap.

Dropping his weapon to hang limply at his side, Sikorsky reached for his wife, but she stumbled backward before collapsing to the floor, a cry of terror on her lips. "No," she begged him, holding up her good arm, trying to ward him off. "*Please, no more...*"

"Ludmilla," he said, kneeling down and reaching for her, "it is me, Dmitri..."

"No," his wife whispered, turning away.

Valentina put a hand on Dmitri's shoulder, drawing him back. "Listen to me," she told him. "Go change into civilian clothes – quickly. I'll look after her."

With a questioning look, but without argument, Dmitri turned and shambled down the short hallway to the bedroom, his own battered face a mask of shocked pain that went far deeper than his physical wounds.

Valentina knelt next to Ludmilla and said softly, "Ludmilla, he's not one of them. He would never, ever hurt you. We didn't know they had taken you in for interrogation."

After a moment, Ludmilla, tears running down her face, whispered, "I have been such a fool. After they took away my daughter, my only child, I was convinced it was something I had done, some terrible wrong for which I was responsible. I tried to be good after that, to do everything the Party wanted. I know...I know that it hurt Dmitri, but I could not help myself. Then...then they came for me, just as they did my daughter. They said terrible things, that Dmitri was a spy, helping you – a Confederation spy – and that I must also be guilty, that I was a traitor to my planet, to my people. They beat me..." She moaned, curling into a fetal position, shivering.

"Your husband is a good man, Ludmilla," Valentina told her fiercely, gently pulling the older woman into her arms. "It is the Party that is twisted and evil. They have used you, just as they have used everyone, torturing and murdering anyone who dares to defy them. People like your daughter and her husband. People like Dmitri. He has been risking his life, trying to change that."

"I don't know what to believe now," Ludmilla said, choking on the words.

"Believe that I love you, and that if I ever catch the fucking bastards who did this to you, I'll kill them with my bare hands," came Dmitri's savage voice from beside her.

Ludmilla turned to see him, now dressed in his customary plain, ordinary clothes. His eyes, staring from his bandaged face, were wet with his own tears. "Dmitri," she cried softly as she finally reached for him, "what are we to do?"

Suddenly there were shouts from down the corridor outside, and the sound of pounding feet, growing louder, nearer.

"What is that?" Ludmilla cried, her face a mask of terror.

Valentina snatched up Dmitri's weapon and handed it back to him. "Don't worry," she said grimly. "Dmitri, take this." She handed him a tiny device with a numeric code lit in red, blinking. "It's an emergency beacon. I've already activated it: help will be coming soon. But in case something happens to me, they'll take you and Ludmilla to safety." He took it and shoved it into his pocket. "Now, take her back to the bedroom and stay there, behind whatever cover you can. If any secret police troops make it past me..." She shrugged. "Just stay alive until help arrives."

"What about you?" he asked as he pulled Ludmilla to her feet and began to move her to the back of the apartment. "Don't you need a weapon?"

"I've got plenty," she said cryptically. "Now get going!"

As he and Ludmilla hurried down the hall to the bedroom, Valentina turned and bolted for the kitchen. Fortunately, Ludmilla was a very good cook and kept her kitchen and its contents, as humble as they might be, in good order and condition.

Especially the knives. The secret police were almost to the door, so she had no time to be choosy. She grabbed a meat cleaver and shoved it into her waistband, then took the two butcher knives protruding from the simple wooden knife block, noting with satisfaction that they had a fresh, sharp edge. She would have preferred to have some knives that she could throw, but there wasn't time. She would have to work close-in.

She darted back into the main room just as the door burst open and the first of seven secret police troops stepped in, weapons raised. In a blur,

Valentina moved toward him from the opposite side of the door, knocking his weapon down toward the floor with one hand as her other slashed one of the knives across his throat. She slammed into him with one shoulder, sending him cartwheeling backward into the others. Blood spurted from his neck, splattering his surprised comrades as his finger spasmed on the trigger of his weapon, sending a hail of bullets into the ceiling.

Then she was among them, spinning, kicking, and slashing, her face frozen into a cold mask of merciless hatred.

***

"Commodore!"

Hanson turned to see Robert Torvald, the Confederation agent's controller, burst onto the flag bridge, the pair of Marines who stood guard on the hatch during battle stations both pointing their weapons at him.

"Bloody hell, man!" she snapped. "We're at general quarters! What the devil are you doing—"

"I've picked up the emergency recall beacon," he said urgently as he came to stand close by her command chair.

"Ma'am?" one of the Marines asked tensely. Few people on the ship had even seen Torvald on this patrol, and the Marines were very uneasy about letting this man stand so close to their senior-most officer.

"It's all right," she said quickly. "Thank you, gentlemen. Return to your posts."

"Aye, aye, ma'am," they said in unison before leaving the flag bridge, but not without a surreptitious glance back at the stranger in civilian clothes.

"The recall beacon," Torvald said again. "You must send a team to retrieve our asset. Now."

Hanson hated it when the spooks talked like that, like there weren't actual people involved. "I'll send a team as soon as Colonel Grishin secures—"

"I'm sorry, commodore, but that won't do," Torvald interrupted her. "If you'll recall the special section of your orders, retrieving our asset becomes your first priority once the beacon is activated. You have no discretion in the matter."

She stared at him a moment, debating in the back of her mind how much trouble she would be in if she recalled the Marines standing guard and had them frog-march this mouth-with-legs to the brig.

"That section of the orders was undersigned by the president herself, commodore," he added.

"I realize that," she told him acidly, grudgingly conceding that she wouldn't be able to throw him in the brig after all. She punched a button on her control console. "Captain Zellars," she called to her flag captain. "We need to get a Marine assault team down to the surface on a...special mission. Right now. Who do we have that's ready to go and in the best position?"

"*Yura* would fit the bill, commodore," Zellars said immediately. "She has two Marine platoons prepped as quick reaction teams, already in the ship's cutters. They just need a frag order to go."

Hanson looked at Torvald. "Give them the coordinates and tell them what they need to know to bring your *asset* back," she said, "then get the hell off my flag bridge."

"I'm sorry, commodore," he shot back, "but that's impossible. I have to go with the Marines on the cutter–"

"That, Mr. Torvald," she interrupted him this time, "is distinctly *not* in my orders. If you want your asset picked up, give my people the information they need to get the mission done. Otherwise, get your ass out of my sight."

Up until then, Torvald had been disquietingly cool. But she could see that she had cracked his armor. She wasn't quite sure what mix of emotions were showing through, but she could tell they didn't include love or joy.

"Here," he said tersely, handing her a data chip. "This has everything they'll need to find..." He paused before finishing, almost reluctantly, "...her."

***

"Mills," Sato said through his bridge vidcom, his face betraying his concern, "we'll be over the horizon and out of support range for ninety minutes. You'll be on your own."

"Understood, skipper," Mills told him as the cutter slipped away from the *Yura*. Outside of her parent ship's gravity field now, he was overtaken by the familiar but queasy sensation of weightlessness. Ahead loomed their destination, the glowing surface of Saint Petersburg. Sato had called him only a few minutes ago to brief him on their new mission, to rescue a Confederation agent in Saint Petersburg city. It was a completely insane mission that fit perfectly with Mills's thrill-seeking personality. *If only the fucking headache would go away*, he cursed to himself, *this might even be fun.* None of the meds he had taken had made a dent in it. He shrugged inwardly. He would have to make do. "Don't worry, sir," he said. "We'll make the grab and be back for more fun before you sail 'round again."

Sato nodded, but did not smile. "Godspeed, Mills," he said before terminating the connection.

"Okay, Faraday," Mills said to the warrant officer who piloted the cutter, "let's get on with this little party, shall we?"

THIRTEEN

Even though everything appeared to be calm and orderly, every hair on the back of Grishin's neck was at stiff attention, screaming that there was something wrong. Here he was with a brigade of troops deployed in a hasty defensive perimeter around a gigantic concrete apron, painted to blend in with the forest, that easily accommodated all of his assault boats at one time, exchanging pleasantries with the man who claimed to be the commandant of the facility. A storage facility, yes, the man, a brigadier, had told him.

"But not for nuclear weapons," the brigadier said, laughing, as if Grishin was mad to even think such a thing.

Grishin had sent the special teams, men and women trained in disarming nuclear weapons, into the gigantic tunnel, accompanied by an entire battalion of Marines. He could have sent a smaller escort, but he had plenty of troops and had no idea how big the complex was. He intended, however, that if they ran into any trouble, they would be able to defend themselves.

He had arranged the rest of his Marines around the inside of the huge wall. He had been sorely tempted to take over the walls and the security positions there, but without any sign of resistance from the "host" military, he under very strict orders to avoid provoking them without cause.

Fuck, he thought savagely. *There is something wrong here, but—*

"Colonel!" one of his men cried, pointing toward the tunnel entrance. The door, a gigantic plug of hardened steel that was easily three meters thick, was closing. The Marines inside would be cut off, trapped.

"Brigadier," he said, turning to the alleged commandant, "what is the meaning of this?"

"My apologies, colonel," the man said calmly as he drew his sidearm with one hand and with the other casually rolled a hand grenade onto the ground in the midst of Grishin's nearby staff. Unbelievably, he made no attempt to escape.

"*Alarm!*" Grishin screamed as he knocked the Russian officer's gun arm to the side, then stabbed his right hand, fingers held rigid like a knife, into the brigadier's throat, crushing his larynx. Grishin grabbed him by the collar and web gear, and with a desperate prayer and a massive heave, threw the gagging Russian to the ground on top of the grenade just before it exploded. His body didn't absorb the full force of the explosion, for two of the staff officers were riddled with shrapnel and killed instantly. But Grishin's quick reflexes had saved the lives of the others. For the moment.

In those few seconds, bedlam erupted around the facility. The formerly peaceful Russian soldiers atop the massive wall turned inward and opened fire on the Marines, who were now caught out in the open with nowhere to hide across hectares of bare concrete. A volley of hypervelocity missiles lanced out, almost too fast to follow with the unaided eye, from points along the wall, obliterating most of the assault boats on the ground in massive fireballs. Two boats actually managed to get airborne, struggling skyward amidst the flames, smoke, and debris from the others that had been destroyed outright. One of them only made it a dozen meters above the concrete before it was skewered by a missile. The other, piloted by either a genius or a maniac, managed to avoid four missiles before it was destroyed. The four boats that Grishin had on patrol overhead were hit simultaneously. Three exploded, while the last plummeted toward the ground, trailing smoke. That boat's pilot guided her stricken craft over the heads of her fellow Marines and straight into the closed gate at the entrance to the facility, blasting a huge hole in it.

That may be our only way out, Grishin thought quickly as he surveyed the carnage around him. The surprise assault on the boats had resulted in a shower of flaming debris that had crushed or burned to death dozens of his Marines, and scores more had already fallen to the murderous fire from the walls.

"Return fire!" he barked over his comm set to his battalion commanders, although most of the Marines had already begun to return fire on their own. He got acknowledgments from all of his commanders except the one who had been swallowed up by the mountain: they didn't have any communications gear that was powerful enough to penetrate the mountain's shielding. They were on their own.

Around the facility, the Marines fought back fiercely, blasting away at their attackers with everything they had.

Grishin knew that it would not be enough. They were totally cut off and surrounded, with the only possible way out being the hole blown in the main gate by the suicidal boat pilot. And judging by the increasing amount of fire coming from the wall, he suspected that there were fresh troops being brought up from some subterranean barracks.

"*Camarón.*" He breathed the name of the famous last stand, from centuries before, of the French *Légion étrangère* that had been his family and country for the last twenty years before the Confederation was founded. He had said it once before during the Battle of Keran when he was sure he was about to die. He had never expected to say it a second time. "Follow me!" he ordered the surviving members of his headquarters staff as he snatched up a rifle from a fallen Marine and headed toward the burning wreckage of one of the assault boats, trying to find some cover from the withering hail of fire from the enemy soldiers on the walls. "And patch me through to Commodore Hanson!"

"Colonel," one of his staff shouted, pointing at the pile of wreckage that was all that was left of their ad-hoc command post, "the FLEETCOM terminal is gone..." Without the terminal or the boats, they had no way to contact the fleet.

"*Merde,*" he said savagely. Grishin knew that their chances of survival had just dropped to near-zero.

***

"We've lost contact with Colonel Grishin, commodore," the flag communications officer reported suddenly. The icons for Grishin's units deployed on the surface suddenly became transparent on the display that showed a map of the underground facility: the real-time feed that updated the information from the sensors the Marines carried was gone.

Hanson took a closer look at the display. Losing all communications with the Marines on the surface should be nearly impossible: even if the FLEETCOM units were destroyed, any of the boats could relay Grishin's transmissions. The bulk of the task force was in a stand-off orbit, far enough from the planet that no planetary defense weapons could reach them without fair warning. The carriers and their two escorting heavy cruisers, including Sato's *Yura*, were in low orbit, now on the far side of the planet. The single small moon was also on the far side of Saint Petersburg, effectively screened from the sensors on the ships with her here, but visible to the carriers.

She suddenly felt a sickening sensation in the pit of her stomach. Losing communications with the Marines was no coincidence. *They were going to hit the carriers first*, she thought, a cold spear of dread lancing up her spine, *from the goddamn moon!* "Contact the carriers and have them get the hell out of there—"

It was too late. A sudden bloom of yellow icons erupted from the moon, echoed by the sensors on board the carriers and their cruiser escorts, and in only a few seconds all of them turned to red: warships, believed to be hostile.

Hanson held her breath as the tactical computer counted the enemy ships and did its best to identify them by class. *Seventy-three warships*, she told herself, shocked. Worse, thirty-eight of them were classed as heavy cruisers. Hanson's entire force amounted to only six heavy cruisers and ten destroyers, plus the two carriers. It would be a slaughter.

"*Radiological alarm!*" her flag tactical officer shouted as the lead Russian ships fired a brace of what could only be torpedoes at Hanson's carriers and their escorts, now frantically trying to escape Saint Petersburg's gravity well so they could jump into hyperspace and escape. "Nuclear warheads, inbound!"

"Extend the fleet formation," Hanson snapped. "Stand by for emergency jump."

"What about the Marines, commodore?" her flag captain asked quietly.

She turned to him, a stony expression on her face. "I said to stand by for emergency jump."

"Aye, aye, ma'am," the flag captain said, turning away to issue the necessary orders.

Hanson stared at the screen, her gut churning at the butcher's bill if they were forced to jump.

On the display, as the carriers accelerated hard away from the inbound torpedoes, *Yura* and her sister turned to fight.

***

"Stand by point defense," Sato ordered. Inside, he was quivering from adrenalin, both from fear and excitement. But his voice only gave away a faint trace of what he was feeling. He was the captain, and his crew would follow his lead. He wanted them calm and level-headed as they charged directly into the teeth of the torpedo salvo, knowing they were fitted with nuclear warheads. *We can do this*, he told himself. "Main batteries, engage on my mark..." The range rings showing the effective range of the ship's main guns intersected the rapidly approaching torpedoes. "Fire!"

With the data-link connecting *Yura* with her sister ship *Myoko*, the two ships became a single virtual weapon, able to more effectively coordinate their targeting and firing. With a measured cadence, their fifteen-centimeter guns began to fire. Unlike the projectiles they normally fired at other ships, which were armor piercing explosive rounds, these shells contained thousands of ball bearings surrounding a large explosive charge. At a distance determined by the targeting computers, the shells detonated, sending a hail of metal into the path of the incoming weapons.

The designers of the torpedoes, however, had anticipated this. The torpedoes were smart weapons, and began individual rapid evasion patterns to confuse the defending targeting systems and dodge around defensive fire.

At a point designated by the targeting computers, *Yura* and *Myoko* did a hard turn-about. Now, instead of heading directly toward the torpedoes as they fired, they were running away from them, continuing to fire astern. The torpedoes were significantly faster, but this maneuver ensured that the two cruisers had the maximum amount of time for defensive fire before the torpedoes caught up to them or, worse, passed them by to strike the nearly helpless carriers.

The Saint Petersburg ships had fired ten torpedoes, and all but two fell to the defending fire of the two cruisers before their basic load of ammunition ran out and the main guns fell silent. The ships' laser batteries thrummed as they fired, but the wildly maneuvering torpedoes were nearly impossible to hit.

"Godspeed, Sato," *Myoko's* captain suddenly said through the vidcom terminal on Sato's combat chair, just before his ship disappeared in a blinding fireball. In space, there was no atmosphere to transmit shock waves that could tear a planet-bound structure or ship to bits. Nor were there thermal effects that could incinerate people or structures, as there was no air for the explosion to heat. There was only a massive blast of neutron and gamma radiation that seared *Myoko* and her crew into oblivion. The blast from the torpedo itself was overshadowed by the detonation of the cruiser's main drives.

"*Sir!*" Sato's tactical officer cried. One torpedo remained, just pulling abreast of *Yura* and clearly locked onto the fleeing carriers.

"Helm, bring us ten degrees to starboard, all ahead flank!" Sato ordered, telling Bogdanova to steer the ship closer to the weapon. "Ready point defense!"

"Point defense, standing by!" the tactical officer reported, his voice tight.

The entire bridge crew waited in tense silence as the next few seconds brought them closer to what they knew was almost certain destruction. The tactical computer had generated an estimated yield of twenty kilotons for the weapon that had just destroyed *Myoko*. The torpedo had managed to penetrate the ship's close-in defenses and detonate at a range of two kilometers, spearing the ship with over ten thousand roentgens of radiation; as few as five hundred were required to incapacitate, and sometimes kill, a human being.

Yura would not be that close, but she would be close enough.

"Stand by..." Sato said. Then: "Point defense, *fire!*"

The lasers and gatling guns of the cruiser's close-in weapons systems spat beams of coherent light and streams of explosive shells at the wildly maneuvering torpedo. The weapon danced across the starfield as it tried to avoid the incoming fire, but with *Yura* sailing on a parallel course, the torpedo had lost its speed advantage. In one brief moment, three laser bolts converged on the weapon.

Sato suddenly saw a blossoming of new ship icons, all of them red, on the tactical display, just before the universe went white.

***

The fleet was just making its transition from hyperspace to the target human system when Tesh-Dar sensed it: the massive spike of energy and radiation that heralded the detonation of an atomic weapon. Such weapons, of course, had been known to the *Kreela* for ages, since long before the First Empire. They were far from the most powerful weapons the Empire had at its disposal, but like its far more destructive cousins, it was a class of weapon that the Empress disdained to use. Were the Empire seriously threatened, She would not hesitate to use everything at Her disposal to protect it. Yet, even the greatest of the Empire's weapons and warships were as nothing compared to the power that dwelt within the Empress Herself.

The *Kreela* had encountered such weapons as these before in the course of the Empire's expansion across the stars: all of the races the Empire had fought and vanquished in the ages-long search for the First Empress had used atomic weapons – very briefly. While the Empress condoned combat with ship-board weapons as long as they were, in essence, controlled by the enemy's warriors, such weapons of mass destruction were an abomination in Her eyes: they took away the opportunity a warrior had to bring Her glory in battle, and to seek the One who might save them all.

Tesh-Dar did not need a sensor suite or computers to tell her what had just happened. She was finely attuned to the space around her, and could in fact pilot a starship by second sight alone.

And what she felt, the Empress felt.

"Prepare yourselves, daughters," she warned the others on the bridge, "for we shall be Her sword hand this day, and shall feel Her power in our flesh."

Then a second nuclear detonation occurred.

"Priestess!" her tactical officer cried as the ship's sensors localized the two detonations and what appeared to be a mortally stricken human ship, and the vaporized remains of a second one, not far from the target planet.

As Tesh-Dar watched, what she assumed was a second volley of torpedoes was fired from a larger human fleet at a smaller one, to which the two ships that had been destroyed apparently belonged.

"They battle one another," she said in confused wonder, shaking her head. Here sailed a battle group of the Imperial Fleet to challenge the humans, and they were destroying one another. She could not understand these creatures.

"The missiles are armed with atomic warheads," the tactical officer announced.

Tesh-Dar only nodded absently: she already knew. And she could feel a sudden strengthening of the Bloodsong, like a massive storm surge through their souls. "Prepare yourselves," she whispered as she gave herself up to the power that soared higher, ever higher, in her veins.

***

"Whose ships are *those?*" Admiral Lavrenti Voroshilov demanded sharply.

"Unidentified!" his flag tactical officer barked. On the main display, fifty-seven ships had just jumped into Saint Petersburg space and were displayed in a glaring crimson: assumed hostile. To the Saint Petersburg fleet, any ship that was not known to be theirs was first considered an enemy. "Configuration unknown. They do not appear to be Confederation vessels." According to the display, the new arrivals were much closer to Voroshilov's fleet than were the Confederation ships.

"Give them a full salvo of torpedoes," Voroshilov ordered.

***

"Holy shit," someone muttered on the *Constellation's* flag bridge in the silence that fell immediately after the new arrivals had been identified by the tactical computers.

A Kreelan battle fleet, Hanson thought acidly. *Could this mission get any more fucked up?* The only good news was that the carriers finally reached their emergency jump points and disappeared safely into hyperspace. At the cost of two of her heavy cruisers.

"Twenty seconds to jump," the fleet navigator announced.

On the flag bridge tactical display, there was now a second – and much larger – salvo of torpedoes heading toward Hanson's ships, and the Russians had just launched yet another salvo at the newly-arrived Kreelans. *How many of those bloody torpedoes do they have?* she wondered.

"Fifteen seconds…"

Her ships would be well away before the torpedoes were close enough to present a danger, but she now desperately wanted to see how the

Kreelans reacted. While she knew that President McKenna was dead-set against using nuclear weapons, if they would help turn the tide against the Kreelans...

***

It took all of Tesh-Dar's will to keep herself from writhing in the agony and ecstasy of the power unleashed by the Empress through her and the senior shipmistresses in the fleet. The other warriors, even those senior among them, felt only the passing tidal wave, but were not chosen to directly channel it: they would not have survived.

For a mere instant that was drawn out into eternity, Tesh-Dar could sense what the Empress sensed, glimpsed all that the Empress knew, sensed all that the Empress was, in mind and spirit, and it drove her to the brink of insanity. As great as her own powers were, Tesh-Dar was reminded of how insignificant they were beside those of the Empress. The most shocking thing was that she knew that what the Empress did now was merely a shadow of Her true power.

Tesh-Dar's body shook and trembled as the Empress reached out through the space around the fleet, to the human ships and missiles, to the planet and its moon, and bent the physical world to Her will.

***

"Jesus!" someone on Hanson's flag bridge shouted as all the ship's systems, even the artificial gravity, suddenly flickered.

"Status report!" Hanson demanded.

"There's no damage to the ship," the flag captain told her quickly after conferring with the ship's captain, "but the emergency jump sequence automatically aborted and had to be restarted."

"Fleet data-links are down," the communications officer reported. "Voice and vidcom backup are on-line."

"So what the devil happened?"

"Some sort of energy spike, commodore," the flag tactical officer reported. "I've never seen or heard of anything like it—"

"Commodore, look!"

Tearing her eyes away from the swarm of torpedoes heading toward her own ships on the tactical display, she saw that the torpedoes fired at the Kreelan warships were almost in range.

***

"Weapons malfunction!" Voroshilov's flag tactical officer reported, confused, as the first torpedo to reach the new set of enemy ships detonated. Or should have. The Saint Petersburg fleet had just recovered from a bizarre mass electrical problem that had affected all shipboard systems, but that apparently had caused no major damage except for taking down the inter-ship data-links. More torpedoes reached their targets. And failed to detonate properly. "Multiple malfunctions!"

On the screen, he watched as one by one the torpedoes detonated under the control of their proximity fuses, which told the weapons when a target was at the optimal range. The fuses then triggered a sort of "gun" that slammed two chunks of uranium-235 together to produce a fission reaction and the desired nuclear explosion. It was a primitive, but quite effective, design. The fleet's sensors told Voroshilov that the weapons were fusing properly and the so-called guns inside the warheads were firing, but there were no nuclear detonations. In fact, there was no further trace of radiological emissions from any of the warheads. Every single torpedo was a dud, and these new enemy ships did not even bother to waste any of their point defense fire on them.

"Comrade admiral," the tactical officer told Voroshilov, "this is simply not possible!"

Voroshilov barely heard. His attention was focused on the other torpedoes that had been streaking toward the Confederation ships, and that now were just coming into range.

***

Hanson stared at the torpedoes bearing down on her task force, thinking about what she had just seen happen to the Kreelans. Or, rather, what had *not* happened to them. *Could it be?* She wondered. *And can I take that kind of risk?* She thought of Grishin and his Marines, and Torvald's precious "asset," all stranded on the planet. Grishin, no doubt, had fallen into a trap similar to the ones the Russians had sprung on her task force. She hated the thought of leaving them behind, and if there was even a chance of getting them back, she wanted to take it. It was a horrible risk, but she didn't get paid to make easy decisions.

"Emergency jump sequence complete! Fifteen seconds to jump, stand by!"

"Belay that!" she shouted over the organized bedlam of the emergency jump sequence. "Terminate jump sequence. Stand by point defense!"

Several of her officers gaped at her for a moment before they scrambled to change the fleet's orders, a process made much more difficult with the data-links out of commission. The jump countdown timer stopped with four seconds left.

Hanson outwardly kept her cool, but rivulets of cold sweat were running down her spine as the tiny icons representing the torpedoes closed with her formation. *Please, God,* she prayed, *let me be right.*

Suddenly the point defense batteries of her ships began to fire, and torpedoes began to die. Several of them got through, and one exploded near enough to the *Constellation* that she could hear fragments of it ping off the ship's armor.

But there was not one single nuclear detonation: all of the torpedoes were either destroyed by the point defense systems or produced very small explosions when their nuclear triggers – which were mere conventional explosives – fired.

"Commodore," her flag tactical officer said, shaking his head, "there's no longer any trace of radiological elements in those torpedoes. If our calculations are right, the uranium-235 in the weapons is now nothing but...lead. We had solid radiological readings on every single one before that energy spike. Then after that – nothing. It's like something just changed the uranium into lead, like magic. It's just...impossible."

"Well," Hanson breathed, enormously relieved to be alive, "thank God for Kreelan alchemy." Then, turning to her communications officer, she said, "See if you can get a channel open to the commander of the Saint Petersburg fleet. If we can convince him to join forces, I think we can knock the Kreelans on their collective asses."

***

Voroshilov stared at Commodore Hanson on his vidcom with undisguised contempt. "Under no circumstances, *commodore,*" he spat, "will we join forces with you, our enemy. This is a trick: those other ships are simply more Confederation vessels. And after we deal with them, we will finish with *you*, if you are foolish enough to remain in our sovereign system. If you want to live, you will depart immediately." He terminated the connection before the woman could respond.

"Comrade admiral," the ship's chief engineer said, a small image of his worried face appearing in Voroshilov's vidcom terminal.

"What is it, Stravinsky?"

"We have checked the remaining nuclear warheads aboard this ship, sir," Stravinsky reported. "All of them have been rendered inert. The uranium cores have been...converted to lead. I believe the other ships will discover the same thing."

"Sabotage?" Voroshilov demanded.

"No, comrade admiral," Stravinsky said, shaking his head. "Such a thing, replacing the uranium cores with lead, could only be done at the Central Facility. I have no explanation for what has happened. It is simply not possible!"

"It was the energy spike," mused the flag captain.

"*Da*," Stravinsky agreed. "I do not understand how, but that must have been the cause. The timing was no coincidence, for we know that the first salvo of weapons worked against the two Confederation cruisers we destroyed."

How could the Confederation have developed such a weapon? Voroshilov wondered, terrified at the possibilities. If they could neutralize Saint Petersburg's arsenal of nuclear weapons so easily, the plans of the Party leadership would come unraveled quickly, indeed.

"Your orders, admiral?" his flag captain asked.

Voroshilov glared at the tactical display, quickly weighing his options. *My fleet does not need nuclear weapons to fight and win its battles*, he thought savagely. "We shall destroy the newcomers," he said. "Then we shall deal with our friend Commodore Hanson."

FOURTEEN

"Son of a bitch!" Warrant Officer John Faraday swore above the roar of superheated air that flamed around the cutter as it dove through Saint Petersburg's atmosphere toward the surface.

"What is it?" Roland Mills asked him over the small ship's intercom. His head was now pounding so fiercely that it was difficult for him to do anything, even speak. The pain had become so intense that he had bitten his tongue to keep from crying out, and his mouth was now awash with the taste of blood.

"We lost contact with the *Yura*," Faraday, the cutter's pilot, told him grimly. He punched a couple of buttons on his console. On the small display that was part of Mills's combat seat, Mills watched the last few moments of the battle in space, transmitted to the cutter over *Yura's* data-link before the signal was lost. There was no mistaking the nuclear detonation that killed the cruiser *Myoko*, and the track Captain Sato had taken toward the remaining torpedo left little to the imagination. "I think she's gone."

"Fuck," Mills hissed. "That just made my bloody day." He was not by nature a sentimental man, but he had to make an enormous effort to keep tears from welling in his eyes. The loss of Sato himself was a huge blow, not to mention the rest of his Marines and the ship's company. *Bloody hell*, he thought. *I'll save that news from the others until we've made our pickup.*

"It's going to get a lot worse," Faraday assured him. The display in front of Mills cleared, then changed to show the planet's surface, below. Angry red circles pulsed all around the city toward which they were heading: radars that were tracking them, that were now locked on. There were also several tell-tale icons of aerospace interceptors streaking toward them. Faraday wasn't too worried about interceptors: the cutter's weapons would be more than a match for them, unless they attacked in large numbers. Heavy ground-based defenses, however, were another story. "Their planetary defense systems are nearly in range. I'm not sure what anybody was really thinking when they ordered us down here, but without the ships upstairs to provide suppressing fire, this is gonna be a really short ride."

Just when Mills thought things couldn't get any worse, his headache seemed to explode in his skull. Crying out in agony, he hammered his fists against his temples, writhing in his combat harness.

"*Mills!*" Sabourin shouted as she began to unbuckle her harness to reach him.

"Stay in your goddamn seat!" Faraday, the pilot, yelled at her. "You'll be killed when we have to maneuver to avoid ground fire!"

With her heart breaking, she watched helplessly as Mills thrashed around in his seat and cried out, his screams carried over the platoon channel for everyone to hear.

"*Fuck!*" Faraday cursed as a sudden energy spike surged through the cutter. Every system flickered for a moment, and he nearly lost control of the ship in the roaring slipstream around them before the attitude control computers came back on-line. The cutter rolled sickeningly on its back and began to yaw, but he managed to wrestle the craft back on course before it went out of control. Looking at the tactical display, he saw that all of the radars had suddenly gone down, and the tracks of the interceptors had also disappeared, as if they had simply vanished. "Thank you, God," he whispered as he pushed the throttle forward as far as he dared, desperate to get into the ground clutter where the ship would be far more difficult to track.

He had no idea where he was going or even why. All that mattered, he had been told – personally – by Commodore Hanson, was to guide on a very peculiar beacon signal and get the Marines on the ground. After that, Hanson had told him cryptically, he would receive further instructions from someone on the ground.

Sabourin had her eyes glued to Mills. At the same instant the ship's systems had flickered, Mills had grunted as if someone had bludgeoned him, then he passed out. He now hung slack in his combat harness, his head lolling from side to side as the atmosphere bounced and jolted the little ship. She normally would have been able to tell from her tactical readout what his vital signs were, for every Marine carried equipment that monitored their physical status, but the energy surge had apparently fried the electronics built into her gear. Everything associated with her weapons and basic communications seemed to be fine, but the technology-based "combat multipliers," the most critical of which was the inter-Marine data-link network, was gone.

Switching over to a private channel that she and Mills used, she said, "Mills, can you hear me?" More urgently, she said, "Roland? Roland, answer me!"

"I...I hear you," he rasped. As he lifted his head up to look at her, she gasped as she saw blood streaming from his nose, with bloody tears in his eyes. It looked as if every capillary in both eyes had ruptured. "Christ, I can't see a fucking thing," was all he managed before he vomited over the front of his uniform.

"Two minutes!" Faraday barked from the flight deck as he suddenly pulled the ship out of its screaming dive, bringing it level just above the massive trees of the endless Saint Petersburg forests.

The copilot, who also doubled as the cutter's weapons controller, stared intently at the ship's defense displays. The ground radars were coming back up, but the cutter was so low now that they couldn't lock on. There was no sign that the interceptors were still on their way, but that could be good news or bad: they had either been destroyed by the energy spike, or were now playing hide and seek at treetop level, just as the cutter was, or running with their active sensors off, so the cutter's sensors couldn't detect them.

The ride was still incredibly rough, and Sabourin ignored the pilot's curses as she finally unstrapped herself and carefully made her way across the aisle to Mills.

"Well," he said, attempting his trademark devil-may-care attitude, "at least my frigging headache is gone." He made an attempt at a cheerful smile, his teeth covered in blood from having bitten his tongue again.

"You are a mess," she told him, ripping open a field dressing and using it to wipe the blood from his eyes. She followed it up with some water from her canteen, half of which she spilled in his lap when the cutter jolted upward, then sharply down again.

"Well, that'll help clear the puke away, then," he muttered, looking at the mess running down the front of his uniform before hissing at the pain as she poured more water into his eyes. "That's enough, luv!" he said, gently batting her hands away. "I'm okay."

She scowled at him as only a Frenchwoman can. "*Imbecile*," she chided, finally putting away her canteen.

Putting a hand over his tiny helmet microphone, he leaned close to her ear. "She's here," he whispered. "Don't ask me how I know, but that huge bitch of a warrior is here, somewhere on the planet or in the system."

Sabourin's eyes flew wide. "An invasion? *Here?*"

He shrugged helplessly. "I don't know. Let's just get this job done and get the hell back to the fleet as quick as we can." Whatever had been plaguing him in his dreams and that had brought on the awful headache was gone now, as if a balloon had suddenly burst, finally relieving the horrible pressure in his skull. Despite the residual pain, he felt much better than he had in days, if not weeks. And as he had told Sabourin, he knew the Kreelans were here somewhere. He was sure of it.

"One minute!" the pilot called out.

"Jaysus!" Mills cursed, shoving aside his thoughts about the Kreelans. There were more pressing matters afoot, and Sabourin should have been getting the platoon ready instead of fussing with him. He would have to talk to her about that later. In bed. Assuming they survived this harebrained operation.

Unstrapping his harness and getting unsteadily to his feet, using one arm to support himself on the forward bulkhead against the cutter's still-violent flight, he boomed, "First Squad, *up!*"

The men and women of First Squad got to their feet in a flurry of clinking buckles and the tell-tale sound of weapons being checked one final time. They shuffled forward toward the two front personnel doors.

"Second Squad, *up!*" Second Squad did the same, taking up position behind the Marines of First Squad.

"Third Squad, *up!*" The remaining squad stood and faced to the rear and the larger cargo door in the cutter's starboard side. Their exit would be a little easier, as the door would drop down to act as a ramp. The first two squads would have to jump a bit over a meter to the ground.

"Thirty seconds!" the pilot called.

"Bloody hell," Mills cursed as he leaned forward into the flight deck to look at the tactical display. But what caught his eye was the view through the forward windscreen. "We're going right fucking downtown, you fool!"

"Hey, Top," Faraday said tightly as he maneuvered the cutter between buildings, the ship's belly a mere two stories above the ground and its sides nearly scraping the buildings on either side. "My orders were to go to the goddamned little bug on this screen, quick like a bunny," he nodded toward the main tactical display and the glowing green icon representing the beacon they were after. "Nobody told me the fucking thing would be in the middle of the capitol city!"

Mills got a glimpse of a street flashing by below. It was crammed with people, all staring up at the passing ship with comic expressions of disbelief on their faces. They were flying that low. "So where is the damned beacon?" he asked as Faraday quickly slowed the ship as they approached their destination. With the Marine data-link out of action, there was no way for the pilot to echo the beacon's location to Mills for him to follow.

"Looks like it's on maybe the sixth floor of this building," the copilot said quickly, pointing to what looked like a run-down apartment complex. "And I think it's moving."

"Disembark!" Faraday shouted as he brought the cutter into a hover above the street. The forward doors slid open and the rear door quickly lowered. The Marines leaped to the ground, forming a defensive perimeter around the ship.

Mills followed Sabourin and the First Squad out the forward doors. "First Squad, on me!" he bellowed above the roar of the cutter's engines as he charged toward the apartment building, with the other two squads and the cutter guarding their backs.

***

Sikorsky felt like a coward, hiding in the bedroom while Valentina fought for their lives and her own. But he was Ludmilla's last defense, and he was determined, more than at any other time in his life, that she would come to no further harm. Keeping his submachine pistol aimed at the doorway, he felt no fear, only rage, and his hands kept the weapon's stubby barrel steady.

He cringed at the sounds coming from the front room: the growls, grunts, and screams of a pitched battle at close quarters. There had been gunfire in the first few seconds, but then only a few sporadic shots after that. He remembered the sounds of combat during the war years ago, and this was little different. Ludmilla whimpered as the wall to the front room shook violently with the impact of a body hurled against it, the wet smacking sound punctuated with the dry snapping of bone. She huddled close to him, shivering in fear.

He heard a noise that he did not recognize, a drone that quickly became a roar just outside the building. The little device Valentina had given him now glowed a solid green.

"Help is here, *dorogaya*," he shouted to Ludmilla over the roar, just as the ferocity of the fighting in the front room suddenly peaked in a flurry of what could only be savage blows and crashes as the combatants flung themselves about the front room in a final killing orgy.

After one last crash, there was only the roar of the engines outside. Sikorsky tightened his grip on the submachine pistol, his finger easing in more pressure on the trigger, preparing to fire.

"Dmitri!" a woman's voice – Valentina's voice – called wearily from the front room. "It's clear! Come on, we have to go!"

"*Slava Bogu*," Sikorsky whispered. *Thank God.* "We are coming!" He gathered up Ludmilla in his arms and helped her into the front room. He was totally unprepared for the sight that greeted him.

The apartment looked as if it had been struck by a bomb. Every piece of furniture was overturned, with the dining chairs reduced to splinters. The bookshelves had been smashed and their contents, most of it Party propaganda and novels by sanctioned authors, spread like confetti across the floor. The kitchen was a disaster, with shattered dishes and glassware everywhere. There were holes punched through the thin drywall by fists and feet, with blood streaked and spattered haphazardly across the walls and floor. He gaped at one of the secret police, whose head had been rammed completely through one of the walls, a spear-tipped leg from one of the demolished dining chairs stabbed through his back. The bodies of half a dozen more secret police were scattered throughout the wreck of their small home, their bodies bloody and broken.

In the middle of it all stood Valentina. She had a deep gash across her right cheek and a bloody welt across her left arm where a bullet had grazed her, but otherwise she seemed unharmed. Sikorsky shook his head in wonderment: she wasn't even breathing hard.

"Let's go," she told them, helping him guide Ludmilla through the mess and around the bodies. She paused only long enough to snatch up one of the submachine pistols, slinging it quickly across her shoulder. "Downstairs."

As they moved down the hall toward the elevator, they heard the sound of heavy footsteps hammering up the stairwell.

"Get behind me," she said grimly as she pointed her weapon toward the stairwell door.

The footfalls suddenly ceased, and the door creaked open slightly. "Confederation Marines!" someone called in a voice with an unmistakable British accent. "I was told to ask if you might be Scarlet," the voice said.

"That's me," she said in Standard, smiling tiredly at the camouflaged face that carefully peered through the door. "We could use a bit of help here. I've got two civilians with me. Friendlies."

With that, a massive man in Marine combat armor, holding an equally massive pistol that he pointed safely toward the ceiling, burst through the door. He held it open as more Marines charged through. Two of them slung their weapons and began to help Ludmilla and Sikorsky, with the rest forming a protective cordon around them and Scarlet.

Up and down the hallway, a few doors cracked open and wide, disbelieving eyes peered out before the doors slammed shut.

"First Sergeant Roland Mills, at your service, miss," the big Marine said, quickly shaking her hand. "Let's get on the road, shall we?"

The young woman offered no objections as the Marines bundled her and the two bewildered civilians down the stairway. Behind them, Mills and Sabourin paused, peering through the door to the apartment.

"Jesus fucking Christ," Mills said, impressed with the devastation.

"Do not piss her off," Sabourin advised with a wry grin as she turned and double-timed after her squad.

"No worries about that," Mills muttered as he quickly followed after her.

They had just pushed through the front doors of the apartment building when a volley of small arms fire cracked down the length of the street toward the cutter, clearly audible through the roar of the ship's hover engines.

"Return fire!" Mills shouted. "But watch for the civilians!" The last thing he wanted on his hands was a bloodbath of innocent people who got caught in the crossfire.

The Marines immediately unleashed a barrage of accurate rifle fire that quickly silenced their attackers, who turned out to be a pair of militiamen who normally directed traffic, but who were armed with pistols and unwisely decided to try and defend their motherland with them.

The Marines got Sikorsky and his wife aboard, and covered Scarlet as she darted up the rear ramp.

"Time to go, Marines," Mills said on the platoon common channel. Instantly, the three squads reversed their deployment order to board the cutter, with the only difference being that they all piled in through the rear ramp. Faraday already had the cutter gliding forward before the hatch hummed closed.

"Well," Mills said to no one in particular, "that was unexpectedly easy."

"Glad you think so, Top," Faraday told him grimly, "because we've got new orders, straight from the commodore."

"Okay, let's have it," Mills said, wanting to kick himself for his comment about the mission having been easy. *Jinxed yourself, you wanker.*

"The fleet's lost contact with Colonel Grishin's force," Faraday told him. "They want us to do a recon to see if we can regain contact. I've got the coordinates, and that's where we're heading now for our first stop."

"Our first stop?" Mills asked, wondering what would top that.

"Yeah, you'll love this," Faraday said as the cutter accelerated hard, shooting down the street as it gained just enough altitude to skim the tops of the buildings. "The Kreelans have just joined the party upstairs–" Mills and Sabourin exchanged a look, "–and the commodore and some civilian guy on the *Constellation* thought it might be a good idea to send us to go talk some sense into the not-so-saintly leadership of this garden planet about working together against the Kreelans."

"The commodore's off her bloody nut!" Mills exclaimed. "What the devil are we supposed to do? Go to their government buildings and hold the chairman and his minions hostage?"

Faraday took a precious moment to turn around and look at him. "How'd you guess?"

From the expression on the pilot's face, Mills knew he wasn't joking. "What a bloody cockup," he moaned as he slid into an open combat seat, strapping himself in as the cutter bucked and jolted through the air, headed toward where Colonel Grishin's Marines had disappeared.

***

At that moment, Grishin was still trying to find a way out of the trap in which he and his Marines were caught. The irony of the boats all having been destroyed was that the wreckage had provided his people some cover from the Russian soldiers on the wall, but there was no way to escape from the massive killing field. Some of his people had taken a run at the main gate that had been blown open by one of the boat pilots, but the Russians had cut them all down. Assaulting the wall itself was out of the question, because they had nothing to scale it with to reach the enemy soldiers along the top. The Marines had at least been able to take out the heavy guns in the towers, using some of their anti-armor weapons to blow the towers to bits. Even with the losses his Marines had inflicted, however, the Russians still enjoyed massive superiority in firepower.

Worse, he knew from imagery the Marine force had received prior to landing that there were armored units garrisoned not far from here. If the Russians sent in tanks, the Marines' only real hope was to knock them out right as they entered through the main gate, blocking the path for other armored vehicles. If even one or two tanks got inside the wall, this battle could be over very quickly.

There was an explosion along the wall near one of the entrances to the underground barracks from where fresh Russian soldiers had been appearing. It was followed by a fierce roar from many voices, punctuated by a massive flurry of firing that, from the distinctive sound, could only be coming from Marine rifles.

Unwilling to believe he could be that lucky, Grishin risked raising up enough to train his field glasses on that part of the wall. *"Merde!"* he exclaimed. "It's the other battalion!"

The battalion of Marines he had originally sent into the massive bunker complex, and that had been trapped when the Russians had closed the massive door and sealed them in, had obviously not given up. Somehow, they had made their way through whatever maze lay in the mountain to find the underground barracks area, and from there had fought their way to the wall surrounding the compound. From what Grishin could see, it was clear that the Russians on the wall had been taken completely by surprise. Charging across the top of the wall, the Marines poured fire into the enemy soldiers. Those Russians who managed to survive the rifle fire were brought down in vicious hand to hand combat.

"Concentrate fire on the center and left flank!" Grishin ordered to his operations officer. The Marines on the wall were to his relative right, and would be vulnerable to fire coming from Russians on other parts of the wall. "We must keep the enemy pinned down so they cannot–"

Grishin's explanation was drowned out by a flight of four Russian aerospace fighters that thundered in low. He watched as the bomb bay doors slid open, the smooth curves of the weapons clearly visible.

It is over, he thought, certain that the weapons were the modern equivalent of the napalm that had once been a popular air to ground weapon on Earth. The walls and the concrete apron would contain the heat, effectively incinerating his entire force.

As the slow-motion movie in his mind continued rolling, he saw streaks of tracer fire from Marine rifles pass by the fighters, and even an anti-armor missile that some industrious Marine had fired. He smiled, proud that his men and women were still fighting, then closed his eyes. He had seen enough death in his time, and had seen the effects of these weapons during the war twenty years ago. He did not want to see them again.

The weapons never fell. Grishin snapped his eyes open again as four explosions shook the ground. Where the four fighters should have been were fireballs that burned through the air to slam into the far wall of the facility, instantly incinerating the Russian soldiers along the top.

That miracle was followed by the appearance of a Confederation warship's cutter, which proceeded to blast the remaining Russian soldiers from the wall. The Russians tried to shoot it down with their hypervelocity missiles, but unlike the assault boats, the cutter carried point defense weapons that were more than adequate to defend it against the non-maneuvering missiles. The ship swept along the wall at low altitude, firing at everything that moved or fired back. Then the cutter's pilot swung the ship outside the wall near the massive entry gate and attacked whatever Saint Petersburg forces were there.

Finally, satisfied that the area was secure for the moment, the pilot brought the ship in to land in the center of the apron, picking a spot that was relatively clear of debris from the hapless assault boats. The rear ramp dropped down and a platoon of Marines charged out, led by someone he instantly recognized.

"First Sergeant Mills," Grishin said as the big Brit rushed over, "I am very, *very* happy to see you!"

"Likewise, sir!" Mills replied with a smile. "Bit of tight spot you were in, sir, it looks like."

"How soon until we can get enough transports to get us back to the fleet?" Grishin asked as he watched Mills's people moving quickly across the apron, gathering up the wounded and moving them to a makeshift aid station close to the cutter where the surviving corpsmen could treat them.

"That's a bit of a problem, sir," Mills said, his smile quickly fading. "We've got orders from the commodore, but they don't include leaving. In fact, she told me that if we found you alive, you're to come with us on our next little joyride."

"And just what might that be?" Grishin asked, sure from Mills's expression that he didn't want to know.

Mills said, "Would you believe we're going to go pay a visit to Chairman Korolev, to see if he would kindly help us with a pesky little Kreelan fleet that's popped into the system?"

FIFTEEN

"Status," Sato breathed, trying to control the nausea that gripped him. *Radiation poisoning.* Every crew member carried a dosimeter, a device that tracked any exposure to radiation. Normally green, his and those of the other bridge crewmen had turned an ominous amber tinged with red. The situation with much of the rest of the crew was far worse. The bridge was located toward the center of the vessel's hull to help protect it against enemy fire. There were many compartments and systems, however, that were closer to the ship's skin, and far more exposed to the blast of radiation from the nuclear torpedo. While the ship was designed to protect its crew and systems from the radiation typically found in space travel, *Yura's* design specifications had not included providing protection against the torrent of ionizing radiation from nuclear weapons. When the torpedo they had been chasing detonated, the electromagnetic pulse had fried half of the ship's electronic systems, while the radiation had devastated the crew. Sickbay could administer a full scope of treatment for radiation poisoning, but the supplies were limited: they were primarily intended to help crewmen in the engine room should there be an accidental radiation leak from the ship's propulsion systems. There was enough medication to treat a dozen cases of moderate radiation poisoning, but Sato was faced with nearly three hundred, many of them severe.

"We've got auxiliary navigation control back on-line, captain," Bogdanova reported weakly. She had already vomited several times and could barely stand without bracing herself against something. Besides Sato, she was in the best shape of those still functioning on the bridge. Most of the ship's crew was worse, totally unable to function, and Sato had ordered the worst ones taken to their quarters. There was no point in taking them to sick bay: half the crew was already there, vomiting and physically too weak to function. "We've patched enough of life support back together to keep us alive for at least the next forty-eight hours, maybe longer."

"Communications?" he asked.

She shook her head. The movement threw her off balance and she almost fell to the deck. Sato grabbed her arm and held her up. The movement left him weak, his head spinning.

"No luck, sir," she said. "Every component we've swapped in has been burned out. We've tried everything, even the Marine radios, but nothing works." She took a labored breath before continuing. "I've got some people in engineering trying to put together a radio that doesn't use solid state electronics. It's all basic theory, it'll work, allowing us to transmit and receive, but I don't know if anyone will pick it up. Scanning the electromagnetic spectrum for analog radio signals is something survey crews do as part of their survey missions, searching for atomic-era civilizations. Fleet communications officers don't normally look for that sort of thing." Exhausted, she suddenly sat down on the deck, leaning back against one of the bridge support pylons.

Kneeling down beside her, Sato patted her gently on the shoulder and said, "Good work, Bogdanova. You keep this up and you'll have your own command pretty soon." He managed a tired smile, which she wanly returned. "Come on," he told her, forcing himself back to his feet. "We've got to get that radio working." Gripping her hands in his, he pulled her upright. She fell against him momentarily, as if they were in a romantic embrace, but Sato could think of few things less romantic than acute radiation poisoning. "Get back with those engineers and get that radio put together. It's the only thing that might save us."

"Yes, sir," she whispered. Then, gathering up her strength, she stood tall and made her way unsteadily off the bridge, heading for engineering.

Sato collapsed into the combat chair at the navigation console. The other four members of the bridge crew who were still functional glanced up at him to make sure he was all right. "Carry on," he told them, and they turned back to their tasks, swapping out electrical components or jury-rigging analog equivalents to get more of the ship's systems back on-line. "Any luck with the sensors, Avril?" he asked one of the men who was half-buried in an access panel.

"Just a minute, sir, I think I've almost got it..." he rasped. Then, "There! Give that a try, skipper."

Sato activated the controls on the navigation console, and was immediately relieved when the main bridge display lit up.

"We don't have anything but visual right now, sir," Avril told him. "We were able to replace some of the external cameras and get some video feeds going. But the main sensor arrays..." He shook his head. "Going to need some time in drydock for those. Every relay, amp, and signal processor between the main arrays and the computer core is fried."

"It will do, Mr. Avril," Sato told him. "It will do quite nicely. Damn fine work."

"Thank you, sir," Avril said with a tight smile, one arm clamping around his stomach. "Jesus, captain," he said through clenched teeth at the nausea that tore at his gut, "make sure the galley doesn't serve any more of those damned burritos, will you?"

Despite his own increasing discomfort, the nausea and a pounding headache, the weakness he felt, Sato couldn't help but chuckle. "I'll do that, Mr. Avril," he promised. "I promise."

In the meantime, using the just-repaired navigation controls, Sato brought the ship to a gentle stop. She had been drifting for the last hour, after the torpedo had detonated. Even with the main navigation systems off-line, he knew roughly where they were from basic spacial astrography using Saint Petersburg and its star as reference points. They weren't too far from the planet in astronomical terms, but he wasn't comfortable with navigating blind. Knowing where they were in the system was only half the problem: he needed to know where the task force was, not to mention the Saint Petersburg fleet. There was also the question of the flurry of red target icons that had appeared on the tactical display just as the torpedo exploded, but he was no longer sure if he had seen them or if he had been imagining things. None of the other members of the bridge crew remembered seeing them.

"Captain, this is Bogdanova." Her tinny voice came from a small speaker in a crude metal box that had been insta-glued to the navigation console. Bodganova had brought it up with her from engineering before she updated Sato on the ship's status. It was another analog contraption they had somehow cobbled together, a crude intercom system.

Sato pressed the switch on the jury-rigged device. "Sato here."

"We're ready, sir," she said. He could tell from the sound of her voice that she must be dead – almost literally – on her feet. That only served to make him more desperate to get his people back to the fleet. He had already lost half a dozen people to extreme radiation poisoning, and he would lose many more if they didn't get medical attention soon. "We don't have a lot of options with this. We can pump in plenty of power, so range isn't an issue, but it'll be voice only and totally unencrypted, so friendly or enemy alike will be able to hear it. We can also only transmit on one frequency at a time, so I picked an old emergency navigation frequency that was standard on Earth and is still used on some other worlds."

"It'll work, Bogdanova," he reassured her, praying that it really would. "Let's do it." He had already decided that if the Saint Petersburg fleet responded first, he would put his crew into lifeboats and then scuttle the ship. There was no point in offering battle: *Yura* would require weeks in the yards before she was combat-ready again.

"Okay, sir," she said after a brief pause, "you're live. Just push the button and speak into the intercom like you have been. Whatever you say will be broadcast. Just make sure you let up on the button or you won't hear any reply."

"Understood," he told her, nausea and anticipation warring for supremacy in his stomach. Taking a deep breath, he said, "Mayday, mayday. This is Captain Ichiro Sato of the *CNS Yura* in the Saint Petersburg system, calling any Confederation vessel. We require immediate assistance. Please come in, over."

He heard nothing at all until he remembered to let up on the transmit button. Feeling foolish, he released it and was rewarded with the hiss of static.

He waited a moment, then began his call again. "Mayday, mayday. This is Captain Ichiro Sato of the *CNS Yura*..."

***

"Bleed the humans and their ships wisely, my sisters," Tesh-Dar counseled the senior shipmistresses of the fleet, most of whom had not been with her at the battle of Keran. "Remember: we come now to do battle over many cycles, not merely to win a swift victory. More ships come behind us, so you need not worry about being overwhelmed. Give the humans advantage where you so choose, that your combat may bring greater glory to the Empress. They are worthy opponents, and will challenge you and your warriors." She looked around at the projected images of the shipmistresses, all of whom knelt on the command decks of their ships, heads bowed. "Go in Her name," Tesh-Dar ordered. The shipmistresses saluted her, bringing their left hands up to crash against the armor of their right breasts before the images faded.

The fleet had been maneuvering against the larger of the two human forces, not quite letting them get into range as Tesh-Dar tested them, seeking to understand these new opponents. It seemed that humans had many clans, at least one per world, and perhaps even more, and this was reflected in the combat style of their ships and warriors. The group her fleet now faced used little finesse, but instead charged forward like a massive bludgeon. Their ships were powerfully armed, moreso than the ships she had faced at Keran, and she would have to inform the builders to upgrade the next crop of ships they were growing. She was willing to confer tactical advantage to the humans, but would not allow her warriors to be needlessly slaughtered in obsolete vessels.

Still, the human who commanded this fleet was clumsy, as if she had never before wielded her – or *his*, she reminded herself, remembering that both female and male humans were sentient – fleet as a unified weapon. The human ships charged forward in a great mass, guns blazing, while her own ships, like a school of gigantic predatory fish, raked the enemy vessels with fire before darting gracefully away.

Turning her attention for a moment to the other, smaller group of human ships, she recognized some of their designs from the battle of Keran. It was incomprehensible to her that the two human groups would have been fighting one another in the face of the Empire's invasion. On the other hand, she consoled herself, they were alien, with alien thoughts and beliefs. Understanding them was not her mission; it was likely she could never understand them, even if she tried. Finding the One whose blood would sing was why she was here, why they brought what would be many cycles of warfare to the humans. And if the One were not found,

Tesh-Dar and her sisters would eventually exterminate the humans from the galaxy, just before the light of the Empire itself was extinguished.

"My priestess," Li'ara-Zhurah spoke suddenly from behind her. "We are picking up a strange signal from one of the human ships, located away from the two main groups."

Tesh-Dar turned in her chair just as a salvo from her command ship thundered, sending a broadside of heavy kinetic rounds toward their human opponents. The starfield in the main display whirled as the shipmistress maneuvered the ship to clear some of the humans' incoming fire. "What type of signal?" she asked, curious. The human communications systems were far more complex than anything the Kreelan ships of a similar technology level had ever used; the Bloodsong communicated far more information between Her Children than any human could ever imagine. Tesh-Dar's ships used mainly voice and a primitive type of holographic display, normally transmitted – in the time when these ships were first designed, over a hundred thousand years ago – by basic electromagnetic waves.

"It is a radio signal," Li'ara-Zhurah said, perplexed. "These ships on which we now sail commonly use such signals, but we have not seen such a basic emanation from a human ship before. It is a human voice that repeats the same message."

Frowning, Tesh-Dar rose from her chair and came to stand beside Li'ara-Zhurah, who looked over the shoulder of the warrior who worked the communications console. "Play it for me," the priestess ordered.

Over the speaker she could hear words spoken in a human language. She could not understand the words, but the lilt of the creature's speech, the timbre of the voice, sounded familiar, and a sense of trepidation mixed with excitement suddenly flooded through her. "I recognize that voice," she whispered. The signal was strong and clear, and while the human male who spoke clearly must be injured or exhausted, to judge from the sound of its voice, she nonetheless knew beyond a shadow of a doubt who it was. "It is the Messenger."

Li'ara-Zhurah snapped her head around to stare at Tesh-Dar for a moment before she realized what she was doing and lowered her eyes in respect. "Fools, they are," she hissed, "to risk him yet again!"

Tesh-Dar *humphed*. "Indeed, daughter," she said. "Is it so surprising? They do not understand the Way." In the Way of their people, from a tradition that was born in the mists of time long before the founding of the First Empire a hundred thousand years earlier, the Messenger was held sacred, sacrosanct in a way that few other things were among Her Children.

Closing her eyes, Tesh-Dar reached out across space with her mind, her second sight taking in the human ships, then speeding beyond them. She could see the signal in her mind like gentle ocean waves. Following them to their source, she found the Messenger's ship. Passing through the hull, she was distraught when she saw the condition of the crew. They were dying, all of them, from the radiation released by one of the nuclear weapons the larger human force had fired upon them before the Empress intervened. Many would live for a few weeks, at most, but all would die unless they were treated, and quickly.

She found him then, sitting at a console on his ship's command deck. He looked so much older now than when she had last seen him, when she had returned him to his people, the sole survivor of his crew and the bearer of tidings of war. She could see and hear him speak into a small, ungainly box, his voice eventually reaching her ears here. She could not understand what he said, but she knew that, like any shipmistress, he would be trying to save his ship, his crew.

With a great sigh, her second sight faded and she opened her eyes to the reality around her. "He is dying," she said with great sadness.

Li'ara-Zhurah, too, was deeply saddened. "Can we do nothing?" she whispered softly.

Tesh-Dar settled her gaze on Li'ara-Zhurah, her heart swelling with pride that her young successor would even consider, let alone say, such a thing. Truly, she had come far in her spiritual journey since the dark days her soul faced after Keran. "I shall give you a ship," Tesh-Dar told her. "Healers are forbidden here, but you may take some of the healing gel we carry with us to care for him." She was not worried about the potential harm to Li'ara-Zhurah or her unborn child from any residual radiation in the Messenger's ship. The Children of the Empress were highly resistant to radiation poisoning, and any ill effects they suffered could be cured by the healers who remained in the support ships that waited well behind the assault fleet.

"Yes, my priestess," Li'ara-Zhurah said, kneeling to the floor. Tesh-Dar had given her a very great honor. Command of a ship for as junior a warrior as she was honor enough. But to protect the Messenger was far, far beyond it.

Tesh-Dar put her hand on Li'ara-Zhurah's shoulder. "Take care, my daughter," she said. "You are not to risk yourself, even for him. For you are not only my chosen successor, but you are with child, and I forbid you to put yourself in danger."

"I understand, Tesh-Dar," the young warrior said, bowing her head deeper, her heart open to her priestess and the Empress, to her entire race, through the Bloodsong. "It shall be as you say."

Tesh-Dar nodded, satisfied. "Go then, my child, in Her name."

Li'ara-Zhurah saluted, then turned to leave the command deck, bound for a boat that would take her to her first command and the greatest honor of her young life.

***

"...Please come in, over." Sato let up on the transmit button for the last time. He had been transmitting over and over for the last half hour with no response. Unable to help himself, he leaned forward, resting his head on the navigation console, exhausted. He had vomited twice since starting his radio vigil, but had kept at it until he simply couldn't utter another word. The other bridge crewmen lay on the deck, resting from their exertions trying to get the bridge functional again.

Just a quick break, Sato told himself. *A short rest. Then you have to start again*. He was terrified that if he stopped for more than a few minutes, he wouldn't have the strength to resume the mayday calls.

After taking in a few deep breaths and forcing himself to ignore the worsening nausea tearing at his insides, Sato looked up at the main bridge display.

"Captain," came Bogdanova's voice from the intercom. "Are you seeing what I'm seeing on the primary display?" She was obviously looking at one of the monitors in engineering that echoed the video feed on the bridge.

"Yes," Sato said, the nausea in his gut quickly overtaken by an even more unpleasant sensation: the cold knife of fear. "I see it." He stared stupidly at the intercom box. "Bogdanova, is there any way I can address the crew on this?"

"No sir," she said apologetically. "It only works from the bridge to here, and to the radio transmitter. We haven't had time to rig anything else yet."

"It's not a problem," he reassured her. "You and the rest of the crew have done a great job." He paused, looking again at the display, his hands clenching in frustration. *As if things weren't bad enough already*, he thought. "We'll just have to do this the old fashioned way," he told her. "Pass the word among the crew: stand by to maneuver."

"Stand by to maneuver, aye," she echoed. "You have maneuvering control from the navigation console there, sir," she reminded him.

"Understood," Sato said, the adrenaline pumping into his system now helping to offset the effects of the radiation poisoning. For a time. "Avril," he called as he began to move the *Yura*, "pass the word along from here to anyone who can hear you down the passageways: the ship is maneuvering." Taking another look at the image on the main display, he added, "And have every crewman who can move get to their battle stations."

Plainly visible now against the velvet black of space and the glowing disk of Saint Petersburg was the unmistakable silhouette of a Kreelan warship, sailing directly toward them.

Sixteen

"Dammit," Commodore Hanson breathed as she watched the Saint Petersburg fleet try to close with the Kreelans. Again. They were inflicting some damage, but the alien ships had an almost uncanny ability to dance out of the way of incoming fire, preventing the Russians from making a decisive engagement. This was totally unlike the Kreelan tactics – if that was the term – used during the battle of Keran, where they simply bored in, all guns blazing (much as the Russians were doing now, she noted). In comparison, this was death by a thousand paper cuts.

The political situation contributed to her frustration. She had already tried twice to assist the Russian fleet, but each time they had fired on her task force as soon as they had come into range. While she was sorely tempted to fire back, to earn some payback for the loss of *Myoko* and *Yura*, if nothing else, she restrained the urge. The lives of millions of people were at stake: she *had* to find a way to make the Saint Petersburg government cooperate. She had tried to convince them peacefully through reason when she had spoken with Chairman Korolev. Now, using the Marines on the planet who had survived the devastating ambush Grishin had reported from *Yura's* cutter, she was trying something that the Russians were perhaps better prepared to understand.

***

"This is nuts," Faraday muttered as he guided his cutter at treetop height through the middle of Saint Petersburg city. The threat display was showing a dozen crimson icons, ground defenses and inbound fighters, that were trying to find them. The only thing saving them thus far was that they were literally lost in the clutter of the buildings of downtown. Navigating through the tight turns necessary to follow the streets, while keeping them alive, also had him in a cold sweat. "If we had an extra coat of paint, colonel, we'd be scraping the sides off these buildings."

"You are doing just fine," Grishin told him calmly, standing in the aisle, leaning against the bulkhead at the rear of the flight deck, seemingly impervious to the sharp turns the cutter was making. "It is not much further."

The threat display chirped for attention. "Standby point defense," the copilot said tensely. A pair of fighters had found them. "Firing!"

The hull was suddenly filled with a deep ripping sound as the point defense lasers fired. The two icons of the inbound fighters suddenly disappeared.

"Targets destroyed," the copilot reported. "We can hold them off as long as they send in their fighters a few at a time and we don't get too close to any ground defenses, but sooner or later somebody's going to figure that out and they'll swarm us."

"We will be finished long before that happens," Grishin assured him.

Faraday glanced at the colonel, turning over in his mind the very different possible meanings of what Grishin had said. He grimaced as he turned his attention back to flying.

In the rear, the Marines were strapped in but anxious to get off of the wildly maneuvering ship. Near the front, next to Grishin, sat Valentina, with Sikorsky and Ludmilla across from her. Both of them were wide-eyed with fear. Valentina had asked them to stay with the larger force of Marines that was now rushing into the city from the base where they had been ambushed, using trucks and armored vehicles they had liberated from the Russian garrison. The two had refused, however, both declaring in no uncertain terms that they felt their best chance of survival was with Valentina.

Looking at the two of them, Valentina felt a deep pang of regret. Despite the tragedies that had rocked their lives, Sikorsky and Ludmilla were still deeply in love. They held on tightly to one another, most of the time with their eyes closed. But when they were open, they were looking at Valentina. And every time they did, a little more of their fear seemed to fall away. She felt unworthy of their trust and confidence, and prayed that she wouldn't fail them.

As if reading her mind, Sikorsky reached across the aisle and took her hands in one of his. Squeezing them tightly, he gave her a brave smile.

Valentina did her best to smile back, but her expression faltered. She was surprised: lying and deceit were second nature to her as part of her profession, but for some reason she was unable to put on one of her many masks for Sikorsky. What he saw now was the unvarnished truth of her, a face that she had shown to precious few people, a face that now betrayed uncertainty.

Standing in the aisle ahead of them, Grishin stared out the cutter's massive windscreen, watching as the ship finally broke free of the last ring of buildings and the city center appeared. Here was the government complex, a poor copy of the old Kremlin in Moscow back on Earth, only uglier, Grishin thought. The original Kremlin and the city in which it had stood had been destroyed in the wars before the Diaspora, but its oppressive architectural ideals, particularly from the time of Josef Stalin, had somehow been preserved. Growing up here, Grishin had loved the monolithic majesty of the massive skyscrapers surrounding the center of government. As a young man, he had happily, almost deliriously, embraced the tenets of the Party and joined the Red Army. His happy delirium had lasted for a brief five years before being transformed into barely suppressed horror at what he had been called upon to do during the war with Earth and the Alliance. Yet he had done his duty, and suffered the consequences in the war's aftermath. One of many accused – with just reason, he thought guiltily – of war crimes, he had managed to escape off-planet, eventually starting a new life in the Alliance Foreign Legion.

Looking out at the monolithic structures that surrounded the faux Kremlin, he felt a wave of hatred wash over him for the men and the ideas that had turned his planet into a war zone twice in as many decades, and had forced him from his home.

As they approached the walled fortress, flying low over the massive square that had hosted gigantic military parades before the last war, and surely before this one, Grishin was surprised that Korolev had not erected a mausoleum in which to entomb himself upon his death and preserve his carcass for the benefit of future generations. Of course, Grishin thought darkly, perhaps Korolev thought himself immortal. If so, that was a delusion that Grishin would be quite happy to dispel.

"Stand by," he told his Marines as the cutter soared over the impressive wall of red brick surrounding the government buildings themselves. The point defense lasers ripped again, sweeping a dozen surprised but heavily armed ceremonial guards from the top of the wall and the entrance to the Central Chamber where the Party Council met.

His plan was absurdly simple: the cutter would put down in the open square in front of the Central Chamber, then Grishin would lead his Marines in, hoping to catch Korolev and the senior members of the Party and bring them to their senses. He knew that the buildings were guarded by a battalion of ceremonial guards who were extremely well-trained and equipped. Normally that would have made odds that were nothing short of suicidal for a single platoon of Marines, but with the fire support from the cutter and the element of surprise on his side, he believed they had a fighting chance. They only had to hold out for thirty minutes: that was how long it would take for the survivors of his brigade to reach them.

Turning around, he looked at Sikorsky and his wife, then at Valentina. "Are you sure about this?" he asked. While he understood the sentiment all too well, he thought the idea of taking the two Sikorskys in with them was utter madness. "I cannot detail any Marines to protect them."

"I'll take care of them, colonel," Valentina replied, meeting his gaze. She understood that he wasn't making it a personal issue; it was simply a tactical reality. "And we'll help watch your back." She held a shortened heavy assault rifle that looked far too large for her hands, and at her feet lay a sniper rifle in a case that, when the weapon was assembled, was a full two meters long.

Any doubts Grishin may have had about her ability to use either weapon had been dispelled by Mills's quiet account of the devastation she had wrought on the secret police squad in the Sikorskys' apartment. He thought her embellishment of his little attack plan was insane, but in a very Russian way. Despite himself, Grishin smiled. He liked this woman. "*Khorosho*," he said before bellowing, "On your feet, Marines!"

As one, the platoon, led by Mills and Sabourin, got to their feet and readied their weapons.

"Stand by!" Faraday said tensely, and the Marines held on tightly to their grab bars as he swung the cutter – a small ship by Navy standards, but huge compared to most aerospace vehicles – in tightly next to the Central Chamber building. "Now!"

The doors hummed open, and the Marines quickly filed out, followed by Valentina and the Sikorskys, with Dmitri clutching a submachine pistol and carrying Valentina's sniper rifle and extra ammunition.

The pilot waited until the last Marine had one foot on the ground before closing the hatches and lifting off into a protective orbit low around the government buildings.

In a break from their normal tactics, the Marines did not bother to form a protective perimeter around the cutter as they debarked, but simply raced inside the building, trying to keep up with Grishin.

Behind them, Valentina led the Sikorskys in the opposite direction, heading for the huge clock tower that rose above the wall's main gate.

**

"Marshal Antonov!" one of the communications technicians called, his voice urgent.

"What is it?" Antonov said, grudgingly turning away from the display of the indecisive battle still raging in space.

"The Ceremonial Guards commander reports that the Central Chamber is under attack."

"Put him on vidcom," Antonov snapped.

Instantly the Red Army colonel in charge of the Ceremonial Guards came on. "Comrade Marshal," he reported breathlessly, "the entire government complex is under attack by Confederation Marines."

"What happened?" Antonov asked.

The colonel hesitated before answering. Antonov could hear a sudden burst of automatic weapons fire, followed by screaming. "We are under attack by Confederation Marines, comrade marshal. We thought at first it was just the Central Chamber," he said. "Then my quick reaction force came under fire from Confederation troops somewhere on the wall. Many of my men are still pinned down, but I have called for reinforcements from the local garrisons."

Korolev had been listening intently. "They think we are there," he thought aloud. "The Confederation fools are trying to capture us!"

Antonov nodded. *They are courageous*, he thought, *if not terribly bright*.

"Kill them," Korolev ordered. "Kill them all, colonel. Do not bother with prisoners. We do not need any."

"Understood, Comrade Chairman," the colonel said, his expression on the vidcom conveying both relief and satisfaction. "It will be my pleasure."

"Carry on," Antonov ordered before closing the connection.

"Sir," a tactical controller called out a moment later, "there is a Confederation ship that is separate from their main group, heading on a bearing toward orbit." He paused a moment, looking at fresh data that was being provided by the orbital sensor stations. "It appears to be one of the ships we had believed destroyed by Admiral Voroshilov's nuclear torpedoes in the first engagement. It is being followed by one of the newcomer ships."

Antonov frowned at the mention of the "newcomer" ships. Korolev was firmly convinced they were nothing more than additional Confederation vessels, but Antonov had been having second thoughts after watching the ongoing space battle and discussing the situation with Voroshilov over vidcom. These newcomers were totally different in design from the known Confederation ships, and their tactics were certainly nothing like what Saint Petersburg's intelligence services had reported. He was not sure what they were, but he was sure what they were not, and they were *not* Confederation ships. He was not ready to challenge Korolev's assessment, however. At least, not yet.

"Voroshilov's forces are fully engaged," Antonov mused. "Do we have anything else available to intercept?"

"There are five orbital defense vessels on patrol, comrade marshal," the controller replied, highlighting the ships on his display. "They are not fast, but are well-armed. Together they may be able to engage both ships." He looked up at Antonov. "The lead enemy vessel, the one that we believe was damaged by one of the nuclear torpedoes, must have taken severe radiation damage, comrade marshal. Unless its hull was specially shielded, the crew is almost certainly suffering from severe radiation poisoning, and many of the electronic components will have been destroyed or damaged. That ship should be an easy prize. The other vessel following it is roughly the same size, but its configuration is unknown."

"Have the defense vessels depart their stations and engage both ships," Antonov ordered without hesitation. "Order them to capture the lead vessel if they can, but they are not to take unnecessary risks."

***

Neither the Russian nor French languages had sufficiently potent curses to express Grishin's sentiments as he burst into the Committee Chamber, weapon drawn and a full squad of Marines behind him.

It was dark and empty.

"*Fuck!*" he hissed, settling on an ancient English expression out of helpless frustration. "Have you found anyone upstairs?" he asked urgently into his comm set.

"Negative, sir," said the squad leader who had taken his Marines upstairs to the main cabinet offices. "This place is a ghost town. None of the leadership is here, no gofers, not even secretaries. We found a few cleaning crews, but that's all." He paused, then said, "Orders, sir?"

"Regroup by the main entrance," Grishin told him, "and prepare for extraction." *Korolev must have a wartime bunker somewhere*, he thought, *something they built since the last war*. Something Grishin knew nothing about.

"Sir?" Mills asked from behind him.

"It is time for us to leave, Mills," Grishin told him. "They are not here." They had fought a brief but intense battle with the Ceremonial Guard troops in the building, losing three Marines in the process. All for nothing. "Let's go."

He followed Mills and Sabourin back toward the main entrance, the other Marines moving watchfully beside them.

"What is the situation outside?" Grishin asked the second squad leader, whose Marines were stationed near the main entrance.

"Scary as hell, sir," the squad leader reported, "at least for the Russkies. Whoever that bitch is with the sniper rifle, she sure knows how to use it. We got tired of counting her kills, and none of my folks have had to fire a shot yet..."

***

Valentina knew their luck would soon run out, but she was determined to give Grishin what he needed more than anything else right now: time. She had nearly two companies of Russian troops pinned down around the open square leading to the Central Chamber building. The massive rifle she now held snugged up tight to her shoulder was a distant descendant of the famous Barrett Model 82A1 that had been widely used by United States military forces through most of the first half of the twenty-first century. Unlike the now-ancient Model 82A1, however, the rifle she now used fired not massive .50 caliber bullets, but tungsten sabot rounds, fired by a powerful liquid propellant. The projectiles were small enough that a single magazine held fifty, yet they were incredibly dense and packed a devastating punch. Combined with an advanced thermo-optic sight and targeting computer, she could kill targets at ranges of nearly five kilometers if she had clear line of sight. The men she had been killing today, however, were much closer: mere hundreds of meters, which was just far enough to put her out of their effective range. She could kill them at will, but they could only hope that one of their bullets would get lucky, if they wanted to risk shooting at her in the first place. Since she had plenty of ammunition – Sikorsky was carrying four additional magazines – she had been able to effectively neutralize the enemy troops who had not been inside the buildings. If one of the soldiers exposed so much as a hand or a foot, she fired, and the resulting damage to the target was generally lethal.

Her only real worry was that enemy troops might try to swarm the clock tower from along the wall, or that an air strike would get past the cutter that patrolled above.

"To the left, behind the fountain," Sikorsky told her. He was looking through the spotting scope that had been in the rifle's case, helping her look for targets.

Behind them, Ludmilla watched the entrance to the clock tower behind them, nervously holding the submachine pistol that Sikorsky had brought. Valentina had booby-trapped the stairwell leading up to their position, but it never hurt to have a set of human eyes watching.

Following Sikorsky's cue, she shifted her aim slightly, the big weapon's electronic sight immediately picking up the thermal signature of the three soldiers who were trying to low-crawl their way toward the Central Chamber building, using a small decorative wall for cover. They had not yet learned that her weapon was powerful enough to shoot through a foot of reinforced concrete and kill a man on the other side.

"Firing," she announced before holding her breath and stroking the trigger. The weapon fired with a deafening boom, the recoil against her shoulder shoving her back a few centimeters.

Sikorsky watched as the three soldiers disappeared in an explosion of stone and flesh. Unlike a standard rifle, which usually simply punched holes through the human body, the rounds from this weapon literally blew them apart. Having been an infantryman during the war against Earth and the Alliance, he could imagine the terror of the men down there in the square, knowing that they would not merely be shot, but blown to bits, if they were not behind solid cover, and if they did not *stay* there. Valentina's aim was supernatural, and her eyesight must also have been exquisite, for she had seen movement and picked out targets that he had barely seen with his more powerful spotting scope. In all, Valentina had killed fifty-six enemy soldiers in the brief time since they had taken up residence in the clock tower, including what he believed must have been virtually all of the enemy battalion's officers and senior NCOs. Leading their men headlong across the square to the Central Chamber building as part of the quick reaction force called in against the Marines, Valentina had massacred them.

The butchery, while gruesome, had reinforced his faith that she was the best chance of survival he and Ludmilla had.

Valentina was scanning for more targets when she heard Grishin's voice in her earphone.

"Scarlet," he said, "they are not here. This was all for nothing."

"Shit," she said in response.

"*Da,*" he said. "Exactly so. I am ordering the rest of the brigade to not bother coming here, but to head to the main spaceport to secure it if they can. They will need to find a ship we can use to get back to the fleet. We will pull out from here using the cutter, and then provide the brigade with fire support as they assault the spaceport." He paused. "With the enemy troops now so close to the building here..."

"Don't worry, colonel," she promised. "I'll cover you as you load up the cutter. We'll be ready to hop on board as you cross over the wall."

"Be careful, *dorogaya,*" he said. "And good hunting."

"Dmitri, Ludmilla!" Valentina called out. "We're pulling out of here. We have to cover the Marines as they move from the Central Chamber building to the cutter, then they'll pick us up on the way out." She turned to look at each of them in turn. "The Ceremonial Guards will do everything they can to stop us. Be prepared."

"We are ready," Sikorsky answered, and Ludmilla nodded before turning back to watching the door behind them.

Above them, the drone of the cutter's engines suddenly became louder, just before its point defense lasers ripped through the sky.

***

Grishin cringed as the sky around the government complex suddenly seemed to explode. The Russians had fired a volley of anti-aircraft missiles at the cutter, trying to saturate its defenses. The point-defense lasers were up to the task, but barely. He could see where the ship's hull was pitted and scored by shrapnel from one of the missile warheads, and he hoped the hull hadn't been penetrated. If it had, the cutter would no longer be spaceworthy until it could be patched.

The ship dove over the wall surrounding the complex, the lasers firing at any enemy troops who were exposed. The pilot managed to maneuver the ship right up next to the Central Chamber building, the ramps already down.

"Get aboard!" Grishin ordered. "Quickly!"

The Marines needed no coaxing. In a fast but orderly manner, they ran up the ramp, diving into their seats inside.

The Russian troops huddling around the fountains, concrete benches, and other bits of cover afforded in the square suddenly came to life. Even with most of their officers gone, they knew that this was their last and probably best chance to kill the Marines. As one, they knelt and stood up and began to pour fire into the cutter, with those who were in throwing distance preparing their grenades.

The cutter's point defense lasers sent a cascade of emerald beams across the square, vaporizing half a dozen men. But the geometry was bad: the weapons simply couldn't be brought to bear against most of the now-berserk Russians, half of whom had gotten to their feet and were charging toward the vulnerable rear of the cutter, their enraged howling nearly as loud as the cutter's hover engines.

Amid the bedlam, two Russian soldiers calmly readied hypervelocity missiles that could obliterate a heavily armored tank.

***

"Firing!" Valentina hissed as she pulled the trigger, blasting a Russian soldier who had been cocking his arm to throw a grenade. The grenade fell to the ground and exploded, sending several other soldiers flying. She selected another target and fired, then again and again. "*Blyad'*," she cursed, "they're rushing the ship!"

She whipped her head to the side as an assault rifle went off right next to her: it was Dmitri, using the rifle she had carried up here, doing what he could to help stop the attacking Russians. He could not fire accurately at this range, but he didn't have to: if a bullet landed almost anywhere in the square down there, it would hit a Russian soldier.

"Keep shooting!" he shouted at her as he fired short bursts into the mass of screaming Russian troops that were now surging toward the cutter.

Putting her eyes to the electronic scope again, Valentina tried to sort out most important targets in the swirling mass of bodies. She caught another soldier about to throw a grenade, blowing his torso to pieces, the tungsten needle continuing on to shred three other soldiers before it stopped. She had to be careful, because if one of those slugs hit the cutter, it would punch right through the hull. *Boom.* Another grenade thrower went down. *Boom.* Four soldiers who had lined up in a perfect row as they ran now lay together in death.

Her first magazine empty, she quickly changed it, keeping her eyes glued to the cutter. She watched in amazement as several small objects arced over the top of the cutter from the far side where the Marines were dashing aboard: grenades they had blindly tossed over the ship into the attacking Russians. They exploded almost simultaneously, wiping away most of the lead rank of attackers, but there were more behind them. Many more.

"Reloading!" Dmitri cried as he popped out his weapon's empty magazine and slammed another home.

Valentina did the same, ramming the massive magazine for her weapon into its slot and pulling the charging handle to chamber a round.

There was a brief hissing sound as a tiny amount of liquid propellant was vaporized in the weapon's breech, and a tiny green ready light glowed.

"Firing!" she announced again, beginning a rapid series of shots that echoed among the government buildings like God's own thunder. Attacking soldiers were blown apart one after another. Just as the first Russians got close enough to the cutter that Valentina dared not fire on them, the attack faltered, her continued hammer blows having literally gutted their advance.

At last, after what had seemed a lifetime but was really less than a minute, the cutter lifted off, the pilot shearing the top from an old oak tree that stood near the Central Chamber building. Free now of the intervening obstacles that had kept them largely silent while the ship was on the ground, the cutter's point defense lasers tore through the Russian troops who now stood in the middle of the square, firing up at the ship's belly as it passed overhead.

"Valentina!" Sikorsky shouted desperately. "*Missile launcher, behind the main fountain!*"

Cursing under her breath, Valentina lowered her muzzle, searching for the target Dmitri had called out. She only saw troops standing, blazing away at the cutter. She didn't see any missile...there! The two soldiers were blocked by several others; she could only see the tip of the missile in its launcher tube, slowly tracking the cutter. As if in slow motion, she saw a plume of white smoke from the ejection charge puff to the rear, boosting the missile out of the launch tube just as she pulled the trigger.

"*No!*" Sikorsky cried as the missile's motor ignited and it raced through the air like lightning toward the cutter.

Valentina had lost sight of the launcher when she fired, her weapon's recoil knocking her back. She lowered the big rifle to stare at the scene: she could see that the launch crew was dead, along with the soldiers in front of them, but she realized that she had been just a fraction of a second too late. "*Nam konets,*" she said, her heart in her throat. "We're fucked."

The missile streaked toward the cutter, blowing off one of its horizontal stabilizers in a cascade of sparks and flying metal shards.

In that instant, Valentina realized that her last round had made a difference: the missile's aim must have been knocked off by just a hair when her shot vaporized the man's torso.

The ship wobbled, but remained steady as it headed directly for them. She knew it would not be spaceworthy, but would get them at least as far as the spaceport. Probably.

"Dmitri!" Ludmilla suddenly cried as a hollow boom echoed from the stairwell behind them: someone had set off Valentina's booby-trap.

"Get behind me!" Valentina cried as she got to her feet. Moving away from the courtyard side of the wall, which was now being hit by a hail of gunfire as the angry Russian mob below fired at the approaching cutter, she knelt next to one of the pillars supporting the huge clock above them, aiming the big rifle at the door. Ludmilla crouched on the other side of the pillar, with Sikorsky standing next to Valentina. "You get her on the boat!" Valentina ordered him.

"We are not leaving without you!" he told her angrily as the cutter swung parallel to the wall, the pilot clearly wrestling with the controls after the loss of the stabilizer.

The door exploded outward with the force of several grenades that had been thrown by the troops coming up the stairwell. Valentina did not even bother to wait for a target: she just began to fire rhythmically into the smoke-filled doorway. Parts of a man flew out of the smoke, then more.

Then one of them low-crawled through the doorway, below her line of sight. He fired his weapon at her on full automatic, and her body flew back against the red brick of the pillar, dancing like a marionette as the bullets slammed into her. She slumped to the ground, leaving wide streaks of blood on the brick pillar.

The soldier's success was cut short by a vicious burst of rifle fire from the cutter: Mills hung out of the open hatch, Sabourin holding onto his utility belt to keep him from falling, smoke swirling from the muzzle of his rifle. One of the other Marines pumped a magazine of rifle-fired grenades down the stairwell, blowing apart the other Russians still inside.

Sabourin let go of Mills as the cutter bounced against the side of the wall, and he jumped to where Dmitri and Ludmilla knelt next to Valentina. He moved to scoop her up, but Dmitri pushed him away.

"I will take her," he said, tears running down his face. "I will carry her."

With Ludmilla weeping beside him, he gathered up Valentina's shattered body in his arms and carried her aboard the cutter, a grim-faced Mills covering his back.

SEVENTEEN

"The Messenger moves away from us," the senior warrior at the tactical station reported, "toward the planet."

"He fears us," Li'ara-Zhurah replied from her position in the ship's command chair. She was in many ways junior to most of the other warriors on the ship, but they acceded to her authority both because she was Tesh-Dar's chosen one, and because the pendants she had earned in battle placed her higher on the steps to the throne. Her own self-confidence had wavered slightly when she had first come aboard the ship, after Tesh-Dar had given her permission to assist the Messenger and heal him. Yet after a few moments in the command chair, her fears of any inadequacy faded away: she was a blood daughter of the Empress, and to this she had been born. "He does not understand the Way, nor his place in it, Ulan-Tyr."

Ulan-Tyr nodded understanding, although the emotions flowing in her Bloodsong betrayed her skepticism. She did not doubt the Messenger's place or importance, only the concept that he could not comprehend it himself.

They continued to pursue the fleeing human ship, gradually closing the range. At first, Li'ara-Zhurah had been surprised that the humans had not fired on their pursuers, but then remembered that nuclear detonations could destroy the primitive electronic components that were critical to the functioning of ships of this technological epoch. The Messenger's ship apparently had some sensors remaining that could detect other ships, but no functioning weapons with which to engage them. This made Li'arah-Zhurah's mission much, much easier: otherwise, the human ship would have been able to fire on her with impunity, for she could not return fire without fear of harming the Messenger whom she had come to save. The nature of her mission also required her to board the other ship, to take the healing gel to the Messenger. She suspected that the ship's crew would be largely incapacitated from radiation poisoning, but she knew enough about humans after fighting them on Keran not to underestimate them. Her mission of mercy would not be bloodless.

"Mistress!" Ulan-Tyr suddenly called for her. "Five human vessels are breaking from low orbit and moving to intercept the Messenger's ship!"

Li'arah-Zhurah got up from the command chair and moved closer to the tactical display. "Are these ships native to this world, of the fleet that launched the nuclear weapons?"

"They were not part of the main body, mistress," Ulan-Tyr said as she analyzed the information the ship's computer provided, "but they appear to be of this world, not of the Messenger's fleet."

"All ahead flank!" Li'arah-Zhurah ordered. She had been closing on the Messenger's ship gradually, in hopes he might understand that she meant him no harm. Had any of her warriors been able to speak his language, she would even have attempted to communicate with him. As it was, there was no point: each of them would only hear gibberish from the other. This was clearly a case where action would speak far louder than words; she hoped he would understand her intentions.

***

"Captain! *Captain!*"

Sato heard a familiar voice as if he were at the bottom of a deep well and they were shouting down at him from the opening far above. Unwillingly, he forced his eyes open. He was still on the bridge, slumped in his command chair, the combat straps holding him in place. He turned to see Bogdanova, now sitting at the navigation console. She looked terrible, just like he felt. "What is it, Bogdanova?" he asked, nearly choking on the taste of blood in his mouth. Only through a supreme effort of will was he able to keep himself from throwing up.

"The Kreelan ship following us must have gone to flank speed, sir," she rasped. On the main display, the enemy ship was quickly closing the gap between them.

"Are they in firing range?" Sato asked, confused.

"Sir, they've been in range of our weapons – if they were working – for at least ten minutes, maybe more. So I assume they could have hit us, too."

She suddenly doubled over, groaning, as a wave of nausea hit her. Sato empathized with her, but there was nothing he could do. There was nothing any of them could do. Every one of them was a dead man or woman walking. Even if they could get to a major planetside hospital, he doubted that most of his crew could be saved.

"I wonder why they suddenly accelerated," Sato mused as Bogdanova pushed herself back upright, panting.

"Because of these...I think, captain," she managed. On the main screen two bright objects, clearly ships, were heading straight for them, the glowing disk of Saint Petersburg behind them. "There are ships coming up from Saint Petersburg, sir," Bogdanova rasped. "It's hard to tell without the main sensors, but I think they may be some of the coast guard vessels. I can only find two, but it's possible there may be more. Coming right for us."

"Is this radio still rigged up?" Sato asked suddenly.

"Yes, sir," she said, nodding.

Sato pushed the radio transmit button. "Saint Petersburg vessels approaching CNS *Yura*, be advised that we surrender. Repeat: we surrender! Our crew is suffering from acute radiation poisoning and needs medical attention–" He broke off as he saw flashes winking from the two ships visible on the screen, and then flashes from three more ships that were in the planet's shadow, hidden in the darkness. "Damn them!" he hissed. "All hands, brace for impact," he shouted. "Pass the word!" As the crewmen relayed his warning to the rest of the ship, he ordered, "Helm, bring us to two-three-six mark one-six-five. Can we get any more speed out of engineering?"

"We're at redline now, sir," Bogdanova reported as the ship began to turn sluggishly to port, her bow raising up over Saint Petersburg's north pole.

Sato gritted his teeth in frustration as he watched the scene on the display move all too slowly.

"Engineering could only get one fusion core operating and stable," she explained, "so we're only at twenty percent of full power."

Sato had known that, of course, but something didn't add up. *The Kreelan ship*, he suddenly realized. *We were a sitting duck. Why hadn't they closed the range and finished us off,* he wondered, *instead of creeping up behind them until the Saint Petersburg ships showed up?*

"Estimated time to impact?" Sato asked. The Russian ships had continued to fire, pouring a steady stream of shells in their direction. Sato had no doubt that no matter how he maneuvered, *Yura* would be heading into a solid wall of steel, and there wasn't a damn thing he could do about it.

Bogdanova and the other handful of bridge crewmen turned to him with pained expressions on their faces.

"Without the sensors, or at least some way of gauging the range to the enemy ships, we have no way of knowing, sir," Avril said quietly. "But probably soon."

"Look!" Bogdanova cried as the main display suddenly filled with the bulk of the sleek Kreelan warship as it pulled alongside *Yura*, matching her course and speed with uncanny precision. "What are they doing?"

Sato clenched his hands on the arm rests of his combat chair, waiting for a cloud of warriors to spring forth from the enemy vessel, warriors they would be powerless to repel with most of the ship's combat systems inoperative and its crew, including the Marines who had remained aboard, largely incapacitated.

He waited, but they didn't come. Then, in a moment of utter clarity, he understood that the Kreelan ship had placed itself between *Yura* and the Saint Petersburg ships. "Good, God," he breathed. "They're shielding us!"

As he spoke, the Kreelan ship was surrounded with a halo of crimson and emerald fireworks as the weapons on her far side began to fire at the incoming Russian shells and the ships that had fired them.

***

Tesh-Dar gasped as she saw what Li'ara-Zhurah was doing on the tactical display. "No, my daughter," she breathed as tiny icons representing the inbound human shells fell like rain upon Li'ara-Zhurah's ship. Many were stopped by the ship's point defense weapons, yet it was inevitable that some would get through. Li'ara-Zhurah was furiously returning fire at the attacking human vessels, which had immediately begun evasive maneuvers. While there were more of them, and they were clearly heavily armed, they were small and could not take much damage. Torpedoes arced out from Li'ara-Zhurah's ship, vaporizing first one, then another of the attackers. Then the remaining three closed in, firing non-stop as they came. "Maneuver," she whispered, willing Li'ara-Zhurah to get out of the way of the incoming bombardment. "You must move clear!"

Li'ara-Zhurah's ship did not move, but stayed abeam of the Messenger's ship, shielding it from the rain of fire from the other human vessels. Tesh-Dar did not have to reach out with her second sight to see the battle: she could feel it all in the Bloodsong of Li'ara-Zhurah and the others on her ship. She did not have to know exactly what they thought, for she could sense their fear or trepidation. There was none. Only fierce pride and joy that they would bring great glory to the Empress.

In that moment, Tesh-Dar realized that Li'ara-Zhurah would not hesitate to give her life and that of her unborn child for the Messenger. It was an epiphany bound in pride for the young warrior whom she had chosen as her successor, and fear that Fate would somehow snatch her away.

For one of the very few times in her life, Tesh-Dar, high priestess of the Desh-Ka and the Empire's most-feared warrior, was captured by indecision. She considered sending other ships to assist Li'ara-Zhurah, but the senior shipmistresses were fully engaged with the large human force here. Moreover, it would not do to coddle Li'ara-Zhurah: if she were to become what Tesh-Dar hoped, she must be able to face and survive the challenges placed before her; she must find her own Way. She would also resent Tesh-Dar's interference, and rightly so.

At last, doing her best to force aside her mounting anxiety for Li'ara-Zhurah and the child she carried, the child that Tesh-Dar had allowed to be carried into battle instead of being safely sequestered on a nursery world, Tesh-Dar decided to simply watch the situation closely, content in the knowledge that she could yet intervene, if necessary.

Having decided that internal struggle for the moment, she decided that the next phase of the battle for this planet was to begin. Perhaps it would draw the attention from the three ships clawing at Li'ara-Zhurah as she sought to defend the Messenger. Closing her eyes, she sought out the thread in the Bloodsong of one of the other warrior priestesses who waited nearby with a special fleet. The streams of their spirits touched and briefly entwined, and in that moment Tesh-Dar's emotions conveyed a simple message: *It is time.*

***

"My Marines are marching on the main spaceport now," Grishin said through the vidcom. "We hope to find a ship that can transport us back to the fleet."

"We could send our cutters down to ferry you back," Hanson told him.

Grishin shook his head. "We will not last long," he explained. "We no longer have the element of surprise, we are low on ammunition, and our cutter is badly damaged. Korolev's troops will finish us long before we could get everyone ferried back. We will either find a ground to orbit freighter with which we can link up with you, or a ship with jump drive. If the latter, we will need additional crewmen to man it, assuming the cutter pilots can get it off the ground."

"You'll have them," Hanson promised. "Just get your butts into space, colonel."

"New contacts!" cried the flag tactical officer on *Constellation's* flag bridge. "Eight...ten...no, shit..." He paused, a look of disbelief on his face as he stared into his console display. Turning to Commodore Hanson, he said, "*One hundred and seventeen* new contacts just jumped in-system, ma'am. So far."

"Are you sure...?" Hanson's voice died away as she studied the tactical display. The count spiraled upward until it finally stopped: two hundred and forty-three ships. She looked at the data displays next to each of them, almost unreadable because there were so many ships. Half of them appeared to be warships in the heavy cruiser class. The others were huge. "My God," she exclaimed. "Two kilometers long, massing half a million tons? Those numbers can't be right!"

"I think they are, commodore," the flag captain interjected. "Look." The ship's main telescope was now focused on the mass of ships that had jumped in, dangerously close to Saint Petersburg's gravity well. Their markings, large cyan runes over a brilliant green on the sleek hulls, left no doubt as to whose ships they were.

"The small one there," the flag captain highlighted a vessel that was perhaps an eighth the size of the larger ones around it, "is about the size of a heavy cruiser. If I had to guess, I'd say these are troop transports. Massive ones."

"Colonel, did you catch all that?" she said urgently to Grishin.

"Yes, commodore," he told her. "It appears that a Kreelan invasion force has just joined our quaint little party. Do not worry about us. Fight your ships, and we will contact you when we are on our way." He paused. "I truly hope to not have to fight them on the ground again. Not now."

"I understand, colonel," Hanson told him. "Good luck."

"Godspeed, commodore," Grishin said just before his image faded to black on her console.

Hanson sat back, stunned at the size of the enemy fleet. She watched, speechless, as the armada moved in, taking up orbit around Saint Petersburg.

"Orders, ma'am?" the flag captain asked quietly.

Hanson heard his voice as if in a dream. She had kept the task force at arm's length from both the original Kreelan fleet and the Russians, firing at the former when she could while trying to avoid being fired upon by the latter. It was like sparring in a boxing match, but with three boxers in the ring, all fighting one another. *Saint Petersburg is lost*, she thought. *There's no way we could help them, even if they let us. Even if every warship from Earth and the Alliance were here, they still wouldn't be enough.*

"You can't run now," a vaguely familiar voice said quietly. "You have a duty to the men and women on that planet who need you to get them out of this, to bring them home."

She turned to find Torvald, her resident spymaster, standing beside her combat chair, staring at her. His words snapped her out of her dark reverie. "I don't get paid to *run*, mister," she told him angrily, "but I'll also be damned if I'm going to lose my entire goddamn task force! In case you can't add, we're slightly outnumbered here."

The flag bridge became utterly silent, with every member of her staff, even the flag captain, studiously looking anywhere but toward her and Torvald.

"I'll do everything I can to get my people – including your agent – off the planet," Hanson went on in a quieter voice, forcing the words through gritted teeth as she jabbed a finger into Torvald's chest, "but I don't need the likes of you to remind me of my duty. Now, if there's nothing else, get the hell off my bridge before I have the Marines throw you in the brig."

Torvald looked at her impassively, then quietly turned and left the flag bridge.

Orders, she thought, pushing Torvald from her mind. *What orders can I give in a situation like this?*

Before she could say anything, the flag tactical officer said, "The Saint Petersburg fleet is trying to disengage with the first Kreelan force, commodore. It looks like they're trying to come about to intercept the invasion fleet."

Hanson nodded. That gave her something to work with. "Communications," she ordered, "try to raise Admiral Voroshilov from the Saint Petersburg fleet again. Let's see if he might like our help *now.*"

***

"The sensors cannot be correct. This must be some sort of electronic *maskirovka*, a deception by the Confederation fleet," Korolev's image said decisively.

"Comrade chairman," Admiral Voroshilov said, fighting to restrain his anger, "the sensor readings you see are correct. We have verified the size of these massive vessels with every type of sensor, including optical measurement. *There is no doubt.* And from their design and markings, they are clearly nothing like the Confederation ships. The Kreelan threat is real, and they are here. I believe these ships to be troop transports. You must have Marshal Antonov activate the military reserves immediately, and bring the remaining orbital and planetary defense sites to full readiness. We should also activate Riga's defense forces—"

"Limit yourself to things you understand, admiral," Korolev said, the threat in his voice plain. "Marshal Antonov shall handle the planetary defenses as he sees fit. *You* will concern yourself with dealing with this new *Confederation* threat."

The vidcom suddenly went blank.

Voroshilov sat in his command chair, seething. Even now, with the enemy at the gates, Korolev was in complete denial. He looked up at the tactical display and the icons of the massive enemy ships encircling his planet like a string of bloody pearls. He was a Party man and always had been, but he was also a patriot who had devoted his life to the military and fervently believed in the oath he took to defend his people. These aliens, whatever they were and wherever they were from, had come to destroy his motherland and his people. They, not the Confederation, were the enemy. The path of his duty was crystal clear, even if it would cost him his life in front of a firing squad. Korolev did not look favorably upon those who committed treason.

"Is the Confederation flagship still hailing us?" he asked his communications officer.

"Yes, sir, continuously." the officer said. "I have ignored them as you instructed."

"Tell them that I wish to speak to Commodore Hanson at once," Voroshilov ordered.

The officer gaped at him for a moment before turning his attention back to his console, quickly obeying his orders.

In seconds, Hanson's face appeared on the secondary viewscreen. "Admiral Voroshilov," she said formally.

"Commodore, let us dispense with any formalities," he said bluntly. "I am committing treason merely by speaking with you, but I have no choice if I am to have any chance of saving my homeworld...if it can be saved. I would like to accept your offer of assistance against the aliens, if it still stands."

Hanson frowned. "Admiral, your fleet has repeatedly fired on us when we tried to assist you earlier. What assurance do I have that you're not pulling us into a trap?"

"Commodore, I give you my personal word of honor," Voroshilov said earnestly. "There is nothing else of substance that I can provide."

Hanson nodded. "I'll accept that, admiral, but I want assurances that your ground forces will not launch any further attacks on our Marines on the planet, and will let them depart peacefully."

"I can give you no such assurance, commodore," Voroshilov said grimly. "Our leaders believe the invaders are Confederation ships in disguise, bringing yet more of your Marines, and I have not been able to convince them otherwise. Your people will have to fight their way to safety if they are to survive." He paused. "Commodore, I have not informed the chairman that I am asking for your assistance. Assuming I survive the rest of this battle, I will most likely be shot for my troubles. In that way," he glanced around the flag bridge at his officers, who were watching the discussion with expressions ranging from utter surprise to quiet resignation, "my subordinates may be spared the same fate."

After a brief moment's consideration, Hanson said, "Very well, admiral, I agree. If I may, I suggest that we attempt to break contact with the first group of Kreelan ships you have been fighting and focus our efforts on disrupting the invasion force. Our sensors indicate that they're already deploying smaller vessels to the surface. We don't have much time..."

Eighteen

Li'ara-Zhurah held on to her combat chair, the restraints digging into her shoulders and waist as the ship shuddered violently beneath her. The command deck was wreathed in smoke from a fire in the electrical system, the acrid stench of burning metal and plastic still burning in her nose.

"We are heavily damaged, mistress," the tactical controller reported, fighting to keep her voice level. Her hands had been badly burned when her console had exploded from a short-circuit of the electrical system that had started the fire. Li'ara-Zhurah had pulled her away from the burning console, while others had put out the flames. The controller had refused to leave her post, and had managed to reroute the controls to another station on the bridge. "We cannot long survive unless we destroy the human ship." To retreat, she well knew, to abandon the Messenger, was unthinkable.

The human ships, while small, had been most worthy adversaries. Armed to the teeth and far more resilient than Li'ara-Zhurah had given them credit for, the five human ships had crippled her own vessel. The cost had been high: four of them had been destroyed, and the fifth was damaged. Li'ara-Zhurah was impressed with the fortitude of its commander: even though the ship had clearly suffered grievous damage in the fight, she – or he – had not given up. Apparently grasping that Li'ara-Zhurah's ship was protecting the Messenger's vessel, he had changed his tactics, maneuvering to use it as a shield from Li'ara-Zhurah's guns. They were at knife-fighting range in space, the three vessels locked in a deadly orbit around one another at a range of no more now than a few ship lengths.

"Send forth the warriors," Li'ara-Zhurah ordered. Over a hundred of the ship's crew had been preparing for boarding operations as the human ship had drawn closer. It did not appear to have the deadly close-in defense weapons that ships such as the Messenger's vessel mounted, and that had proven so devastating in the battle for Keran. She only hoped that the Messenger understood what her warriors were doing, and did not fire on them himself.

At a word from the tactical controller, airlocks in the ship's flank cycled open and warriors in space armor poured into the utter silence of the raging battle, their thruster packs propelling them toward the remaining human attacker.

***

"Captain!" Bogdanova cried. "Warriors!"

Sato looked up at the visual display and his blood ran cold at what he saw. "No..." he breathed. A cloud of Kreelans in space combat armor left the alien ship, speeding toward them across the few hundred meters of empty space that was all that separated the badly wounded vessels.

Yura rocked again as the Russian ship pounded her with another broadside, even as the Kreelan ship swept over, trying to protect Sato's command. He didn't understand what was happening, but he could only be thankful for the Kreelan's intervention.

"Preparing close-in defense mortars," Bogdanova said, her hands now flying over the console's controls, the effects of radiation sickness be damned. The weapons were a cheap but incredibly effective innovation that had saved the then-Terran ships from the menace of Kreelan boarders during the battle for Keran. Nothing more than large-bore mortars, they fired projectiles up to a few hundred meters from the ship. The mortar bombs then exploded in a cloud of shrapnel that would tear any warrior, even wearing space armor, to shreds, but not cause any significant damage to any ships, even at very close range. While none of the weapons that required more sophisticated sensors were working, the mortars, which were "dumb" weapons, were still functional.

"Standing by to fire, sir," she said, her voice shaking. She had been aboard Sato's first command, the destroyer *Owen D. McClaren*, when it had been badly damaged and boarded by Kreelan raiders. It was an experience she did not wish to relive. "Firing..."

"Belay that!" Sato snapped, looking carefully at the warriors as they swarmed across their field of view. "They're not coming for us," he said. "They're going after the Russian ship!"

Bogdanova's hand didn't move from the firing console. "Captain," she asked, her voice quavering, "are you sure?"

"Yes," he reassured her. "Look at them! They're sweeping right past us!"

On the screen, they watched as the warriors jetted past *Yura's* torn hull, some of them coming to land on the ship for an instant before pushing off again, using *Yura* to adjust their trajectory.

The Russian ship began to fire at them, but it was too little, too late. Unlike larger warships, she had no close-in defense weapons, and the Kreelan warriors attacked her hull like black-clad locusts. Sato saw the flare of the boarding charges the Kreelans used to blow entry holes in the hull of the target ship. But they weren't content with making one hole: they made dozens. The ship's outer hull was being flayed from her keel, with chunks of hull being blown outward by the air pressure within, with everything – including the crewmen – being blasted out into space. Then the warriors crawled inside, and Sato could well imagine the carnage that followed. Even though the Russians had tried to kill him and his ship, he didn't wish on anyone what he knew was happening to them now.

He closed his eyes as the Kreelan ship that had been protecting them slid beside *Yura*, blocking their view just as the captain of the Russian vessel detonated his ship's self-destruct charges.

***

Dmitri Sikorsky sat in the rear of the cutter, still cradling Valentina's body. Ludmilla was next to him, leaning on his shoulder, her eyes firmly closed against the horrors around her. The Marines were crammed into the ship, sitting in the combat chairs or standing in the aisle, their uniforms blackened and dirty, many of them wounded. Their bodies swayed in time with the sickening roll of the badly damaged cutter as if they were on a ship at sea. Their faces, streaked with camouflage paint and sweat, betrayed nothing but numbed exhaustion.

He stared at Valentina's face, haunted by the last image he had of his own daughter when she was hauled away by the secret police. Proud.

Defiant. How much Valentina reminded him of her. He had already cried all the tears his body had to give, but he felt a crushing burden of grief and guilt. It should have been him who died, he thought over and over again. It should have been him the secret police had taken, not his daughter. And would it not have been better for him, who had lived a long and full life, to have died, rather than Valentina?

He squeezed his eyes shut, trying to force away the bitter waste of his life. Ludmilla was his only comfort now, but he feared they were both among the walking dead. Either the secret police or the Red Army would kill them, or the Kreelans would. Were it not for his determination to get Ludmilla to safety, he would have welcomed death.

He felt a hand touch his face, and a soft voice spoke, barely audible over the rumble of the cutter's engines.

"Dmitri..."

He opened his eyes and his heart leaped into his throat as he saw Valentina looking up at him, her mouth curled up in a gentle blood-smeared smile.

"Valentina!" he cried. "You...you were dead! They checked you!"

Ludmilla sat up at his exclamation, her eyes wide with shock.

"*Pomogitye!*" Sikorsky shouted. The colonel, Grishin, snapped his head around, but then Sikorsky remembered that the others probably did not understand Russian. "Help!" he cried in Standard. "Help me! She is alive!"

The female sergeant, Sabourin, was at his side instantly. With one look at Valentina, she shouted, "*Medic!*"

"How is this possible?" Dmitri asked hoarsely, looking again at Valentina's body. She had been hit by at least half a dozen rounds in her chest and abdomen. "You were dead, *dorogaya.*"

"What the fuck?" the medic cursed as she knelt next to Valentina, already checking the readouts on her field medical scanner. Addressing Sabourin, she said, "I checked her out carefully when she was brought on board, staff sergeant. But she must have some sort of implants that activated: I'm reading a ton of stimulants in her bloodstream." Turning to Valentina, she asked pointedly, "Were you augmented?"

Valentina offered a weak smile. "Let us just say that I'm not like other girls," she whispered before passing out.

Quickly moving to where Grishin stood, Sabourin told him, "The agent, that Valentina woman. She is alive."

"How is that possible?" Grishin asked, shocked.

"Some sort of augmentation, according to the medic," Sabourin said, shaking her head. "She does not know how, but the woman is very much alive."

"Unbelievable," Grishin whispered, looking again at where the Sikorskys and the medic hovered over Valentina. "Thank you for letting me know, staff sergeant."

With a nod, he dismissed her before turning his focus on other matters: directly ahead lay the spaceport.

"Fighters inbound!" the copilot reported. "Firing..." The point defense weapons again blasted coherent light at the attacking aircraft, wiping them from the sky. The copilot shook his head. "Let's hope they keep playing the game that way," he said. "Aerospace fighters are dead meat against our lasers."

"As long as we can pick them up at a distance," Faraday reminded him. "If they can get in close enough with enough weapons, we're toast."

"Surface-to-air defenses?" Grishin asked, his eyes scanning the console displays.

"Several heavy missile emplacements, sir," the copilot reported, "but I don't think they can hit us. We're too low. Looks like the defenses were designed more to fend off a large-scale exo-atmospheric attack."

"There's the field!" Faraday exclaimed as the cutter roared over the outer barriers and the massive earthen berm that had been put in place as part of the port's security features. Several dozen ships squatted on the enormous landing apron, with men and equipment – ant-like against the bulk of the big ships – busily at work next to most of them. "Let's go shopping."

He flew down the orderly rows of ships, scattering the ground crews below and ignoring the frantic calls from the control tower. "I don't recognize most of these types," he said. "A bunch of them must be locally built. I'd really rather not have to try our hand at figuring out controls in cyrillic..."

"Wait!" the copilot said. He had been scanning the ships with his sensors, trying to find matches in the cutter's ship recognition database.

"There's a La Seyne-built light freighter in the next row to the right. According to this, she should have jump capability and only needs a flight crew of four." He turned to Grishin and said, "They're designed for a hundred passengers and five thousand tons of cargo. It'll be a little tight for the Marines, but should work to get us off this rock." Shaking his head as he looked at the other ships, most of which were far too large to get into space with only two pilots. "It's really the only option out of all this other space junk."

"Let us check it out, then," Grishin said, nodding. "Mills," he went on, "how much time until the rest of the brigade arrives?"

"One moment, sir," Mills told him. After a brief conversation over the vidcom with the acting commander of the Marine forces now speeding through Saint Petersburg city toward the spaceport, he reported, "Major Justin estimates another thirty minutes, sir. The Russkies must have figured out what our game is and have started trying to put up blocking forces in the city, and the Major's had to make few side trips."

Grishin frowned, momentarily considering getting on the vidcom and reiterating to Justin the vital importance of the brigade getting here as quickly as possible. Then he set it aside. Justin, his senior surviving officer, was a competent leader and knew what he was supposed to do. "Give the major my compliments, Mills, and tell him we'll have a ship ready and waiting by the time he gets here."

"Yes, sir," Mills said before passing the word along.

"There she is," Faraday said as he hauled the cutter around into the next row and headed for the French-built ship. "*Mauritania*," he read from the rust-streaked letters of the ship's name painted on the hull. "What the hell kind of a name is that?"

"She's in the ship registry database," the copilot said after a moment. "She's La Seyne-flagged, and according to this was impounded four months ago for alleged smuggling."

"That's not good," Faraday said as he nosed the cutter toward the tarmac in front of the much larger ship. "If she's been sitting here for four months without maintenance, we may be screwed."

"What other options do we have?" Grishin asked.

"None, sir," the copilot answered as he checked his threat display again. "This is the smallest ship here that can carry the whole brigade. The rest of them are too big for us to even have a chance of getting off the ground by ourselves."

"Then let us hope the Saint Petersburg government was kind enough to keep it in running condition for us," Grishin told them. "Mills!"

"Sir!" Mills barked.

"We'll need a team to clear the ship," Grishin told him, "with the rest of the platoon in a defensive perimeter."

"Yes, sir!" Mills replied before turning around and barking orders to the platoon's team leaders.

As Faraday was setting the cutter down, it yawed unexpectedly to port as the damaged stabilizer finally failed completely, sending the cutter's stern swinging dangerously close to the bow of the *Mauritania*. "Shit!" he cried as he and the copilot struggled with the controls. "Hang on!" Terrified of damaging their only possible way off the planet, he cut the hover engines and dropped the cutter the last few meters to the tarmac. They missed smashing the *Mauritania's* bow by centimeters before it slammed into the ground, collapsing the nose gear.

The cutter was filled with screams of fear and surprise as everyone not strapped down suddenly found themselves weightless, then were smashed to the deck when the cutter hit the unyielding reinforced concrete of the tarmac.

***

Tesh-Dar felt an electric jolt pass through her as the Bloodsong of the warriors Li'ara-Zhurah had sent forth to attack the human ship bedeviling the Messenger were snuffed out of existence when the vessel exploded. She knew Li'ara-Zhurah remained alive, but her ship had been close – very close – to the human vessel, again shielding the Messenger's ship from harm. Both ships likely suffered even more severe damage.

"Can you reach Li'ara-Zhurah?" she asked her communications controller, fighting to keep the fear from her voice. She could tell much from the Bloodsong, but needed the reassurance of hearing Li'ara-Zhurah's voice.

"Yes, my priestess," the warrior answered instantly, and Tesh-Dar was rewarded with Li'ara-Zhurah's image on the secondary view screen.

The bridge behind her was a shambles, looking much like that of Tesh-Dar's ship before it crashed during the battle of Keran. Li'ara-Zhurah was wreathed in smoke, with fire flickering from half the consoles in Tesh-Dar's view. Several of the bridge crew lay on the deck, quite still, and she knew that they, and many others aboard, were dead.

"My priestess," Li'ara-Zhurah said, bowing her head. She had a deep gash in her left cheek and blood was seeping from beneath the armor of her right arm, but other than that she appeared to be uninjured. "We have grappled with the Messenger's ship. Our vessels are now joined. I was just about to take a party across and give him the healing gel and whatever other aid that we may."

Tesh-Dar had been about to tell her that she was to leave the Messenger, and that she was sending other ships to retrieve her, but Li'ara-Zhurah's words gave her pause. She was so close now to her objective, and despite the terrible risks she was taking, Tesh-Dar could not force from her own lips the words she had intended to speak, words that would keep her young disciple from the glory she and the warriors aboard her ship had already sacrificed much to earn.

Running in the current of the Bloodsong, too, were the deep notes of the melody of the Empress, and Tesh-Dar could tell that she was watching her blood daughter closely, and approved of her actions.

Gritting her teeth as she clenched her fists so tightly that her talons drew blood from her palms, she told Li'ara-Zhurah, "Do what you must, child, but I am sending ships to watch over you and retrieve you when the Messenger is safe." She looked deeply into the younger warrior's eyes. "I will not lose you, child, you or your daughter-to-be."

"In Her name," Li'ara-Zhurah said, "it shall be so." She looked a moment longer at Tesh-Dar before saying, "Thank you for believing in me, my priestess."

Her words touched Tesh-Dar's heart. Yet the rush of warmth the great priestess felt only partly offset the lingering chill of fear as she nodded one last time and closed the communications channel between them.

Aboard her crippled ship, Li'ara-Zhurah waited until Tesh-Dar's image faded before she allowed herself to succumb to the coughing fit that had taken monumental control to suppress.

"Mistress," the senior surviving bridge controller told her, "you are bleeding."

Li'ara-Zhurah put her fingers to her lips; they came away bloody. She had been hit in the chest by a flying piece of debris from the bridge support structure when the human vessel had exploded. If she had not been wearing her armor, she – and her child – would have been killed. "It is a trifle," she said, forcing her body back under control. At the look the other warrior gave her, she explained, "A rib has pierced my lung, nothing more. I have experienced worse." She stood up, ignoring the lancing pain in her chest. "Come. We must take those who are left and cross over to the Messenger's ship. We must render him what aid we might to satisfy Her honor, and await the ships the priestess is sending to take us back to the fleet."

***

"Are you sure about this, admiral?" Hanson asked tensely as *Constellation's* guns fired another salvo at the pursuing Kreelan fleet. She had agreed to use her task force to try and help Voroshilov's ships break contact with the first group of Kreelans, so the Russians could try to attack the invasion force now in low orbit over Saint Petersburg.

The problem was that the Kreelans were having none of it. While they still seemed to be sparring, rather than seeking a decisive victory, the human ships needed to somehow escape and regroup. The Kreelans, however, stayed close on their heels, their ships at least as fast as the human vessels. As they had been doing with Voroshilov's fleet, they played with Hanson's forces, charging into range to fire a salvo or two before retreating beyond effective range. Hanson liked to think that her handling of her task force was far more polished than Voroshilov's had been, but the end result had been the same: a stalemate, which was something Voroshilov and Hanson could not afford.

"*Da*, commodore," Voroshilov answered. "We have practiced this many times during in-system exercises as a tactic to defeat Confederation ships attempting to defend Riga." He gave her a mirthless smile. "It will work."

"But the proximity to the system's gravity wells..." Hanson cringed inwardly. Voroshilov had proposed that they use what was often referred to as a micro-jump, a very, *very* brief trip through hyperspace. While such jumps had been demonstrated in the past in deep space, no one had ever done so in a planetary system. If a ship came out into normal space within a certain threshold in the gravity well of a body like a star or planet, it would be torn apart.

"We have extremely refined calculations for many jump point pairs," Voroshilov reassured her. "I know it is much that I ask of you to trust in me this way, commodore, but this is the only path that offers some hope of retrieving your people from the surface, and of trying to stop the alien invasion force."

Her mouth pressed into a thin, worried line, Hanson nodded. "Very well, sir. We'll jump on your mark." Turning to her flag captain, she asked, "Have all of our ships verified their calculations and reported readiness to jump?"

"Aye, ma'am," he said, equally worried. "The ship captains aren't too thrilled with this, but everyone's ready."

"I'm not thrilled with it, either, believe me," she told him. Turning back to Voroshilov, she said, "We're ready, sir. Our jump systems have been advanced through the interlock stage, bypassing the normal jump cycle procedure. Once you give the order, we'll be jumping out immediately."

"Very well. Stand by, commodore," he told her. "We approach one of our pre-plotted jump positions. Stand by...three...two...one...now!"

As one, the ships of the Saint Petersburg and Confederation fleets vanished.

NINETEEN

Grishin came to at the sound of Emmanuelle Sabourin's voice as she desperately sought to wake him.

"*Mon colonel!*" he heard her say. "Colonel Grishin! Can you hear me?"

"*Da*," he managed. Remembering that Sabourin was French, he added, "*Oui.* I am fine." He opened his eyes, but suddenly wished he hadn't. He was staring up at the deck of the cutter, and was taken by a sudden bout of vertigo until he realized that the ship must have rolled onto its back when the pilot brought it down and the landing gear collapsed. The troop compartment was dark, lit only by the red emergency lights, and filled with smoke and the stench of burning electrical components. He heard moans of pain from both fore and aft, and saw that three Marines still hung from their combat chairs, unconscious or killed by heavy equipment and weapons as the craft tumbled over. Other Marines were trying to cut them down. "*Bozhe moi,*" he breathed as Sabourin helped him up. "Casualties?"

"Four dead, sir," she reported wearily. "Three more seriously injured – broken bones – and several with minor injuries. Mills is trying to get one of the hatches open. Right now we are trapped in here."

"Watch your eyes!" Mills called from the rear hatch. A moment later a dazzling light lit the compartment as Mills, wearing a protective mask, turned an electric arc cutter on the hatch's hinges and lock. Sparks flew through the dark compartment, tiny fireworks in the smoky gloom. In the eerie light, Grishin caught a glimpse of the three civilians and the platoon's medic, all of whom appeared to have survived.

He wondered why the compartment was so dark: it should still be daylight outside, and there should be light streaming in through the flight deck windscreen. When he turned around, he understood why: the flight deck had been crushed when the ship rolled over. With a sickening sensation in the pit of his stomach, he asked Sabourin, "Did either of the pilots make it?"

She glanced at the mangled wreckage of the flight deck, then looked at one of the figures nearby, lying back against the curve of the hull, moaning. "The pilot got out, sir," she answered quietly. "He is shaken up, but will be all right. The copilot is dead. We could not even get to his body." The copilot's side of the flight deck was nothing more than gnarled wreckage. He hadn't stood a chance.

"*Merde*," he cursed.

"Bloody..." they looked up as Mills cursed, kicking at the jammed hatch with all his might. "...fucking..." Another kick, and a tiny sliver of light shone through. "...*hell!*" With one final kick and a rush by several other Marines throwing their weight against it, the big hatch groaned open, letting in both light and fresh air. "First and second squads," Mills called, "form a perimeter around the freighter! Third squad, board and search her. Do *not* shoot anyone unless they shoot at you first. Maybe we'll get a bit of luck and some old sod on board can help us get that bucket off the ground. *Move!*"

The Marines piled out of the overturned cutter and immediately ran to carry out Mills's orders.

"Do we have contact with the rest of the brigade?" Grishin asked Sabourin.

She shook her head. "*Non, mon colonel*," she said. "The cutter's systems are out, and I have not been able to raise anyone outside of our own troops on our gear. The equipment seems to be working properly, but I cannot raise anyone. I suspect we are being jammed."

"Better and better," he grumbled. "Do we have any anti-air weapons aboard?"

"Yes, sir," she told him, nodding toward several crates that still remained tightly strapped down to the deck above them, all the way aft. "Six Viper missiles."

"Put together an anti-air team and have them set up on the top hull of the freighter," he ordered. "Our Russian friends will not leave us be for long, and they will certainly not be happy when we try to take off." He looked again at the pilot, Faraday, who seemed to be recovering his wits. "If we take off."

"Yes, sir," she said, immediately moving aft toward the missile crates as she called Mills to let him know.

"Pilot," Grishin said, kneeling next to the man, "how do you feel?"

"Like I got flattened by a goddamn bus, colonel," Faraday rasped, grimacing. He was holding his right arm protectively against his chest. "Think I broke a rib or two."

"Can you still fly?"

Faraday grinned. "Are you giving me a choice, sir?"

"No," Grishin said, offering a smile in return. "I wish I could, but it appears that you are not going to get out of work so easily."

"In that case," Faraday said quietly, looking at the crushed remains of the flight deck and the blood that was the only trace of the copilot, "I can fly, sir. I just hope that tub out there is spaceworthy."

"As do I," Grishin agreed, fervently wishing that the rest of the brigade arrived soon.

***

Tesh-Dar did not know what to make of the disappearance of the human fleet. From what she had learned of the humans since first contact, she suspected they would be back, and soon. Tactically, it was a good move, and the same that she would have made had she been in their position: jump away, regroup, and then reenter the fight. Depending on the timing, it would work out well, for the invasion force would only be in orbit just long enough to drop the warriors and their supplies. After that, the great ships would return to the Empire, while Tesh-Dar's ships would remain here to do battle with the humans.

The temporary lull afforded her an opportunity to go planetside, and she took one of the ship's shuttles – like the ships themselves, very primitive affairs compared to the Empire's modern starships, but necessary to allow a fair fight with the humans – and docked with one of the many assault craft that had been disgorged by the gigantic transports. With another check on Li'ara-Zhurah through her spiritual second sight, Tesh-Dar noted that she was well, if injured, and was continuing on her quest to save the Messenger, Tesh-Dar boarded the assault craft that would take her to the planet.

Not content to join the many warriors dropping into the unpopulated areas to establish the roots of a wartime colony, she ordered her pilot to join in the assaults against the planet's population centers, choosing to participate in the attack against the largest city.

Flexing her massive hands in anticipation, she looked forward to again facing human warriors in battle. Humans, even many at a time, were not a challenge in combat against a warrior priestess such as she. Her powers, greater than any other living warrior priestess, were not understood among her own people; to the humans they were nothing less than magic.

***

"We must sound the invasion alert, comrade chairman!" Marshal Antonov stated flatly to a stunned Chairman Korolev. The display screens in the underground command center were painted with red icons, showing the massive enemy fleet that was now sending forth a torrent of landing craft.

"I do not believe these are aliens!" Korolev grated. "It is simply a ruse!"

"It does not matter, sir," Antonov persisted, "if they are aliens or Confederation troops. We are being invaded by *someone*, and we must prepare!"

With that, Korolev could not argue. "Very well," he said. "Initiate the invasion protocols. And find out where that bastard Voroshilov and his expensive fleet disappeared to!"

"Yes, sir," Antonov said before moving over to the control center's communications section. "Sound the invasion alert," he told them. "All Red Army units are to report to their invasion defense positions, and recall all reserve personnel immediately." Every able-bodied man, along with women who had no young children, were part of the reserve, from age fifteen on up. If they could stand and hold a weapon of any kind, they met the necessary qualifications. "Notify all commands that they have full authority to engage enemy forces at will: weapons free. The Air Force and surface-to-air elements are to engage the landing craft."

"What about the Confederation Marines at the spaceport and the others trying to join them?"

With a sideways glance in Korolev's direction, Antonov lowered his voice and said, "Let them be. Call off the pursuit. If the invaders are who and what I think they are, every human being who can hold a weapon may be of use. Let them spill their blood for our cause."

"Sir, what should we do if they are successful in stealing a ship?"

"Do nothing. Conserve our weapons," Antonov answered, gesturing toward the display and the mass of red icons for enemy ships. "Where could they go? Which brings us to the next question: have you had contact with Admiral Voroshilov?"

"No sir," one of the other controllers answered. "We have had no contact since the fleet jumped. But we do know that they jumped from a pre-designated jump point that corresponds to one of the positions near Riga."

Antonov nodded, considering. "Very well. Notify me immediately when you regain contact. And update the tactical display as our forces come to full readiness."

"Yes, sir!" they chorused in response.

With that, he turned and headed back to join Korolev, thinking, *Voroshilov, you old bastard, I hope you know what you are doing.*

***

"*Collision alarm!*" Hanson heard someone shout as the *Constellation's* klaxons bleated their warning tones through the ship. In the tactical display, just moments after emerging from the micro-jump, she saw that the combined human fleet had indeed emerged on the far side of Riga, but their formation – or, rather, the Confederation ships' formation, she thought bitterly – was a deadly mess. Untrained in the peculiarities of this type of jump, there had been small inconsistencies in their formation and velocity that had been magnified tremendously during the micro-jump, putting some of the ships in dangerously close proximity.

"Task force base direction zero-nine-zero mark zero!" she shouted at her flag captain, ordering her ships to turn to the same heading to help avoid colliding with one another. "All ships reduce speed to station-keeping until we get this sorted out! Communications," she barked to the flag communications officer, "get me Admiral Voroshilov!"

"Aye, commodore!"

On the main display, her ships quickly wheeled around to their new heading and reduced speed, and in a few moments were starting to slide back into their assigned positions in the formation.

"Damage report?" Hanson asked.

"None, commodore," her flag captain reported, relieved. "Some close calls, but not so much as any scraped paint. We made it."

Hanson nodded, greatly relieved. It could easily have been a disaster, but certainly no worse than going up against a vastly superior Kreelan fleet. *On the other hand*, she thought acidly, *Voroshilov could have given us some warning as to the dangers.*

"Commodore," Admiral Voroshilov's image suddenly appeared on her vidcom, "welcome to Riga, an autonomous republic under Saint Petersburg's beneficent protection." He gave her another one of his mirthless smiles. "I congratulate you on your successful jump, commodore, and my compliments to your crews. On our first task force micro-jump during an exercise, we lost two ships to interpenetration. You did very well."

Hanson choked down the hot remarks she had been about to give the admiral. The Russians had made it look easy, their ships still in perfect formation. But many had obviously died in the perfection of their technique. *Maybe we didn't do so badly, after all*, she consoled herself. Instead of biting his head off, she said, "Thank you, sir, I'll do that. What do we do now?"

"We must regroup quickly, before we move out of Riga's shadow and again come under direct observation of the enemy," he told her. The jump point had left them on the far side of Riga from Saint Petersburg, temporarily shielding them. "I believe that the large transports will stay only long enough to deploy their troops, then they will leave. After that, we may stand a fighting chance against the remaining covering forces. In the meantime," he went on, "I must make contact with the Rigan government: they must prepare as best they can." While the Party had decreed that the Kreelan menace was nothing more than Confederation propaganda, Voroshilov had seen more than enough to convince him the alien threat was real.

"What about Chairman Korolev?" she asked him.

Voroshilov shrugged. "I am already a dead man in his eyes, I am sure. Giving him one more reason to have me shot is a worthwhile trade for saving human lives." He paused. "My wife is from Riga. Something tells me she would not be happy if I did not warn them of what is coming. While I am doing that, get your ships in order and prepare to reengage the enemy, commodore."

"Aye, aye, sir," she said. "We're with you."

***

After closing the connection with Hanson, Voroshilov told his communications officer, "Get me President Roze." The officer merely gaped at him. "Did you hear me, comrade?"

"Yes...yes, comrade admiral," the man answered uneasily, turning away to his console, his face bearing a fearful expression.

"Sir," his flag captain asked quietly, "may I ask what you are doing? Some of the officers are not..." He paused and looked around quickly before whispering, "Some of the men are beginning to be concerned over your actions, comrade admiral. You have so much as declared that you are committing mutiny by allying us with the Confederation fleet. And now contacting Roze directly?" He looked at Voroshilov with undisguised concern. "The crews in the fleet know your wife is Rigan, sir, and they will think you are doing this only for her sake. You know this is a political decision that must be made by the Party leadership, comrade admiral. Please, I beg you to reconsider!"

Voroshilov looked at him. "Yuri Denisovich, my friend," he answered quietly, "I am doing what I feel I must. Yes, my wife is Rigan, but that is not why I must speak with Roze. It is because Riga is part of our small star nation that is under attack. It will not help our cause to leave Riga blind and deaf when the invaders turn their attention to them: if Riga is prepared, they will be able to kill far more of the enemy than if they are not. Chairman Korolev does not see this, any more than he believes the invaders are aliens. Tell me, Yuri, do you still believe the invaders come from the Confederation after seeing their ships?"

Captain Yuri Denisovich Borichevsky had known Voroshilov most of his adult life, and had served under him his entire career. More than anyone beyond his immediate family, he trusted Voroshilov. "No, comrade admiral, I do not believe they are from the Confederation," he said. "That does not help with the crews, however. They are losing faith in you."

Voroshilov turned again to his communications officer. "Open a channel to the fleet," he ordered tersely.

"Including the Confederationships?" the man asked.

"*Nyet*," Voroshilov told him. "Only our own."

"Yes, comrade admiral," the man answered quietly. "Channel open."

"Comrades of the Red Navy, men of the fleet!" Voroshilov said. "Some of you no doubt are wondering at the course of the actions we have taken, why we have joined forces with the Confederation ships that we initially fought, and why now we have jumped to Riga while enemy forces surround Saint Petersburg, the motherland to most of us." The "most of us" was for the benefit of the fleet's crewmen − mostly officers − who were Rigan. "Many of you have no doubt heard that I took these actions without the consent of the Party leadership, that I acted on my own authority. This is true."

Around him, every man in sight turned to stare at him. In the last twenty years, since shortly after the war with Earth and the Alliance had ended, such a thing would have been considered unthinkable. The Party had been everything, particularly to the younger officers.

"I assure you, comrades," he went on, steadily meeting the stares of those around him, "these are not actions that I have taken lightly. Comrade Chairman Korolev and Marshal Antonov are fully occupied with organizing the ground and air defenses of our motherland. I know the chairman still believes that the ships attacking our world are humans from the Confederation. However, I cannot accept this in light of what we have seen with our own eyes and sensors: these ships that have come to our system are not of human design. With our world under attack, we cannot blind ourselves by what we want to see, ignoring what truly is. Our families, our people, are depending on us to save them, and the only way we can hope to do that is to understand what we are up against. In the past, the Party has often tried to shield us from unpleasant truths; in this hour, we cannot afford such a luxury.

"For those who are concerned about why we are now above Riga, it is not because it is the world of my wife's birth." Some of the faces around him looked away with embarrassment. Like Flag Captain Borichevsky, they had all served with Voroshilov most of their careers, and had come to know him well. When faced with such a blunt statement, their unvoiced thoughts about him acting purely out of personal desires were shown to be hollow and untrue, yet another manifestation of the negative side of human nature. "We are here because Riga is part of our *kollektiv*, and we have an obligation under the constitution to protect her. This is indisputable, even by the Party. I cannot now spare any ships to stand guard over her people, but I will provide them with information and what encouragement I can by speaking with President Roze.

"Once that is done and we are again fully prepared for battle," he continued, "we will mount another attack against the invaders. And *this* time," he promised, "they will not simply dance away from our guns like ballerinas!

"Comrades," he concluded, "do your duty to protect the motherland and the Party. Our world depends on it."

With that, he snapped the connection closed. *And if that does not mollify them*, he told himself, *they can all go to hell*.

"Comrade President Roze is on the vidcom, comrade admiral," the communications officer informed him.

Voroshilov glanced at the man and noticed that there was indeed a change in his expression. He was perhaps yet unsure of this strange path they were taking, as in a way was Voroshilov himself, but he was no longer acting like a dog afraid of being whipped. "Thank you, comrade lieutenant," he said. Then, turning to the face that had appeared on his vidcom, he said, "Hello, Valdis." Voroshilov had known Valdis Roze for many years: the man's sister was the admiral's wife.

"Lavrenti," the president of Riga answered cautiously. "This contact is a bit...unusual, is it not?"

"It is," Voroshilov told him bluntly. "Valdis, have your military people been monitoring what has been going on in-system?"

Roze hesitated a moment, clearly wondering if Voroshilov was trying to entrap him. Then, thinking better of it only because he knew that Voroshilov was a man of honor, even if the Party he served held such a quality as a vice, he said, "Our astronomers noted that there were two energy spikes that conform with nuclear detonations in space. Other than that, we have little to go on: we were totally cut off from the datasphere a few hours ago. And, as you know, we have little in the way of sensors that can see in-system."

Voroshilov frowned. He had repeatedly argued with Marshal Antonov to upgrade Riga's defenses, but he had steadfastly refused, even with the suggestion of keeping Saint Petersburg military personnel in charge. Now it was too late. "Valdis, we are being invaded," he told his brother-in-law. "The Confederation reports of an alien attack on Keran were true; now they have come here. Over two hundred enemy ships are dropping troops all over Saint Petersburg, and it is only a matter of time before they come to you."

"And what are we to do?" Roze asked hotly. "The only military forces here are yours, and are intended to keep us in our place, not to defend from invasion. We are helpless."

"No," Voroshilov corrected him. "I know that you have an extensive underground militia, a resistance. I recommend that you have them and as many of your people as possible evacuate the cities. From the account of the battle of Keran, the enemy seems to concentrate on the cities. I will give orders to the garrison commander that he is to place himself under your command."

Roze scoffed. "He is a Party lapdog, Lavrenti. I know you are doing this without Korolev's permission, and so will he. He will spit in your eye."

"Indeed." Turning to Borichevsky, Voroshilov said, "You will detach the destroyer *Komsomolskaya Pravda* to provide early warning coverage for Riga, on my direct orders. The ship's captain is to place himself under the direct command of President Roze. He is also to send a party to the garrison commander and deliver my orders that he do the same. Let them understand that if the commander refuses, they are to shoot him on the spot. If the garrison resists, the *Komosomolskaya Pravda* is to destroy it from orbit." The ships of the Saint Petersburg fleet were equipped with weapons that were designed for orbital bombardments, for occasions just such as this. "Is that clear, flag captain?"

"Perfectly, comrade admiral!"

Voroshilov nodded, and Borichevsky began barking orders to the fleet controllers. "I know that is a token effort, Valdis," he said, "but it is all I can do for now. We have Confederation ships with us, and I will ask their commander to ensure that one of them is sent back to their government to request that supplies and, if possible, troops be sent as quickly as possible. I would detach more ships to defend Riga, but I fear we already do not have enough ships to defeat the force that faces us."

"I...I appreciate what you've done," Roze said. "You are a good man. I can imagine what it will cost you in the end."

Voroshilov gave him a wry smile. "I have much to survive before Korolev can shoot me," he said. "Good luck, Valdis."

"You, too, Lavrenti."

TWENTY

The two ships, joined now by the grapples Li'ara-Zhurah's crew had fastened to the human vessel, turned slowly together in space like dreaming lovers. In her armored space suit, she led her surviving warriors to the Messenger's ship. She ignored the spectacular scenery around her: the millions of stars, the brightly colored disk of the human planet below, and the shimmering spears of flame that were the hundreds of assault craft penetrating the planet's atmosphere. She had seen things like these before at Keran, and shut them from her mind: they brought her only unpleasant memories.

The crossing between ships was merely a matter of jumping across the few body lengths of space separating the vessels where the hatch opened. The hulls would have been even more closely bound were it not for the profusion of unsightly antenna arrays, turrets, and various other protrusions with which the humans chose to encumber their ships.

Had they been making a combat boarding, she would have simply found a patch of hull and burned a hole through it to the interior compartments, but that was not an option in this case. She had no idea where the Messenger might be inside the ship, and thus had to exercise caution.

Instead, they moved across the hull of the Messenger's ship toward one of the holes that had been blown in it by the attacking human vessels. The damage there was already done. She led her warriors inside the blasted compartment, noting that it had contained the force of this particular shell's explosion: there were no major breaches in the interior bulkheads or the hatch. She approached the latter, carefully placing a boarding airlock – essentially a double membrane with sealable flaps down the middle – around the scorched hatch coaming. The edges stuck to the metal with a molecular glue that fused the membrane material to the steel.

Once that was accomplished, she stepped inside the airlock, sealed the membranes behind her, and then carefully cut a small hole in the hatch with a small cutting torch. The membrane suddenly inflated with a loud pop as air from the other side of the hatch flowed through the hole she had cut, pressurizing her side of the airlock. She used the torch to cut the hatch's jammed lock, then swung it open to reveal a red-lit corridor beyond.

Darting her head through the hatch to check in both directions, she saw that the way was deserted. "Come," she told her accompanying warriors, "we must move quickly now."

After gratefully shedding her armored suit, she stood guard while her warriors entered through the double airlock in pairs. In a few minutes, all had entered the ship.

"Which way, mistress?" one of the warriors asked. Li'ara-Zhurah was the only one among them who had ever been on a human ship, another of her experiences during the battle of Keran.

Li'ara-Zhurah considered: they had entered the hull roughly two-thirds of the way aft. If this ship was anything like the ship she had boarded at Keran, they were near the engineering section. The command deck, which is where she assumed the messenger would be, should be somewhere forward of that. The corridor they were in ran fore-and aft. "This way," she said, leading them in the direction of the bow, the front of the ship.

At the first turn, they came upon several humans who lay slumped against the walls and sprawled on the floor. All had vomited profusely, and had blood streaming from their mouths. She did not have to see their faces to know that the Messenger was not among them: she had never seen his face, and had only heard his voice the one time over the radio. Yet she knew instinctively that she would recognize him when she saw him. It was a paradox that she did not understand, nor did she try to: it was as elemental to her as breathing.

One of her warriors raised her sword to kill the humans, but Li'ara-Zhurah signaled with her hand to leave them be. "Leave them," she said as she moved onward. "We must find the Messenger."

They moved forward as fast as they dared in the eerie red lighting, skirting around the many damaged areas of the ship. The passageways were filled with swirling smoke and the bitter reek of burned metal and plastic, along with the stench of bodies that had lost control of their digestive systems. Li'ara-Zhurah momentarily regretted leaving her vacuum suit behind, for her species had an extremely acute sense of smell, and the stink was nearly overwhelming.

They came upon more humans, unconscious or dead in the passageways. She surmised that those whose stations were out here, close to the outer hull, must have absorbed a great deal more radiation than those further in toward the ship's central core. She prayed to the Empress that the Messenger had been deep in the ship, protected as much as possible.

Descending a ladder, she suddenly came face to face with two humans who, if not healthy, were nonetheless able to move about. They stared at Li'ara-Zhurah, and she stared back as her warriors quickly formed up behind her. The humans began to edge backward, eyes wide with fear.

Suddenly, they turned and began to run away, screaming in their native tongue. Three of her warriors instantly had *shrekkas*, deadly throwing weapons, in their hands ready to throw, but she said, "No! Follow them, for they may lead us to the Messenger. Let any humans alone unless they resist or interfere."

Her warriors obeyed, putting away their weapons as Li'ara-Zhurah led them quickly along the path taken by the screaming humans, who shuffled down the passageway, their bodies too weak to carry them faster.

As they passed an open doorway, an unexpected *boom* filled the passageway and one of her warriors was flung against the opposite wall, a massive hole punched in her chest armor. Three of her other warriors pounced on the human, one of their warriors in vacuum armor, and slashed him to pieces before he could fire another shot.

They encountered more humans in what Li'ara-Zhurah could only think of as a bizarre situation: here they were, warriors of the Empire, marching by the humans in the haze-filled passageways, holding their swords toward the aliens to ward them off, but otherwise offering to do them no harm. Except for one more of the armored warriors, who was killed before he could attack, the humans shrank back and offered no resistance. Li'ara-Zhurah knew this was not because they lacked the warrior spirit, but because their bodies were so weakened from radiation poisoning that most of them could barely move.

At last they reached what she hoped was the command deck. Forcing the door open, she surveyed the humans within. Four of them were conscious, all of them staring at her in amazement; the rest were unconscious or dead, sprawled on the deck. Of the four, one held a weapon, a pistol, pointed at her chest.

The Messenger.

She knelt to the deck before him and saluted, bringing her left fist against her right breast. Normally to salute one not of the Way was forbidden, but a Messenger was an exception. Her warriors in the passageway did the same.

As they did, the Messenger spoke in words that she could not understand.

***

"Bogdanova," Sato croaked, "are you seeing what I'm seeing?" Sato was afraid he was having a hallucination.

"If you mean a bunch of Kreelan warriors, sir," she replied, shivering from the pain in her abdomen and the fear of seeing Death kneeling a few meters away, "then yes, sir, I am."

"None of you move a muscle," Sato ordered. He held his sidearm, unsteadily pointing it at the lead warrior. It felt incredibly heavy, and he was sure that if he tried to fire it the recoil would send it flying from his hand.

The Kreelan simply knelt there, head bowed, and made no move to attack. *I'm either incredibly blessed or incredibly cursed*, Sato thought tiredly. He almost wished the warrior would kill him with the sword and get it over with. It would be better than the agonizing death he faced from radiation poisoning. He lowered his weapon and let it fall to the deck. He simply had no energy left to fight. All he wanted was to try and save his crew, but knew that virtually all of them were going to die, no matter what happened. The ship's surgeon had analyzed the radiation absorption data, and they had all absorbed far more radiation than he had initially believed. More than any of the anti-radiation medicines carried by the fleet could deal with. That was before the surgeon himself had collapsed into a coma.

"What do you want?" he asked the warrior. He knew she would probably not understand him, but it was all he could think of to say.

She tentatively raised her eyes, as if she was in awe of him, and then gracefully came to her feet. The other warriors behind her remained on their knees. Approaching him slowly, her head again bowed down, she knelt before him in his command chair. Then she removed a smooth black tube, about as long as her forearm and as big around, from her belt. It looked much like the black scabbard for his sword, and Sato imagined it was some sort of weapon, something special just for him. He nodded, relieved. *It will be over soon*, he thought. He tried to focus his last thoughts on Steph, calling up an image of her in his mind, but even that much effort was too much. He simply sat there, staring at her as she opened the tube.

What he saw inside was not at all what he expected.

***

Li'ara-Zhurah had to concentrate on holding her hands steady as she opened the special vessel containing the healing gel. She wished that she could speak with the Messenger, to reassure him that she meant him no harm. She hoped he would remember the healing gel, for she knew from Tesh-Dar's recounting of their first contact with the humans that all of them had been treated with it. Normally it was physically bound to a healer until just before it was used, but this was an unusual circumstance, and a vessel such as this could preserve it for a period of days before the gel, a living symbiont, perished.

As she opened the top, revealing the swirling pink and purple mass inside, she glanced up at the Messenger. Even without understanding human body language, she could tell that he was repulsed by it, feared it. She paused, unsure of what to do.

***

When he saw what was in the tube, Sato instinctively pushed back in his command chair, his eyes wide with revulsion. He would have tried to turn and run, anywhere, but his body was far past that now. He doubled over, his abdomen a writhing mass of pain as he vomited again. The only thing that came up was blood, and the pain was excruciating. Clasping his arms around his stomach, gasping in agony, he passed out, collapsing into the Kreelan's outstretched arms.

***

Li'ara-Zhurah gently caught the Messenger as he fell, writhing in great pain, and she gently laid him onto the deck. "Alar-Chumah, Kai-Ehran!" she called. "Assist me!"

The two warriors dashed forward, followed quickly by the others, who formed a tight defensive ring around the Messenger and the others trying to save him. The watched the conscious humans on the bridge, who stared open-mouthed at what was happening, but there was no sign of any threats from them or down the passageway leading to the command deck.

"Hold him down and help me remove his clothing," Li'ara-Zhurah ordered. "Be gentle, and beware your talons against his skin; they do not wear armor as we do."

In but a moment, using their razor sharp talons, they had stripped his clothing from his body, discarding it to the side. Li'ara-Zhurah upended the vessel with one hand, catching the oozing mass of the healing gel in the other. It shimmered and writhed with life, and she noted absently that the three other humans who were still conscious were clearly repelled by its appearance. She did not understand their aversion, nor did she care. With her heart hammering with the importance of what she was doing, and the glory it brought the Empress, she began to knead and thin the healing gel on the deck, trying to expand its area to cover as much of the Messenger's body as possible. It was difficult, both because she had no experience doing this, and because she had talons, unlike the clawless healers.

After a few moments of effort, she decided that she would never be able to duplicate what the clawless ones did, covering the entire body with a single thin film of gel. Instead, she carefully cut it into sections, flattened them out, and then draped them over different parts of the Messenger's body. It was not perfect, but it did not have to be: half a million cycles of evolution and – in the early ages of her civilization's recorded history – genetic engineering ensured that the gel would itself know what to do, even without a healer to guide it. She watched as the pulsating mass penetrated the Messenger's skin, completely disappearing into his body after only a few moments.

Normally, the healing gel worked very quickly on nearly any injury, but the healers had warned her that this would take longer, for the gel had to repair every cell that had been damaged or destroyed by radiation. The gel was also not fully attuned yet to human DNA, and she hoped that no unforeseen complications arose: only a healer could interact with the gel to guide it in what to do.

With the other three humans looking on in frightened awe, she waited silently next to the unconscious Messenger as the healing gel did its work.

TWENTY-ONE

"No one was aboard her, colonel," Mills reported to Grishin after getting the information from the squad that had boarded the light freighter they planned to steal. "The ship has power from the field umbilicals," he glanced at the massive cables that snaked from a terminal on the tarmac near the ship's forward landing gear and were plugged into various power receptacles, "and looks like she's had at least some maintenance work done."

"So what's the bad news?" Faraday asked. He hurriedly walked between Grishin and Mills, ignoring the pain in his left leg and back from the crash.

"Nothing," Mills told him matter-of-factly, "except that the sodding buggers physically removed the navigation core."

Faraday stopped in his tracks. "They pulled the whole core, not just the memory cells?"

"Yes," Mills confirmed grimly. "There's nothing but a fucking hole where the core should be. That's how my chaps found it, not being too clever about such things normally. Whoever pulled it didn't even bother to seal the socket to keep out the dust."

"Fuck," Faraday exclaimed, balling his fists in anger. "*Fuck!* Well, colonel, even if everything else on this ship is hunky-dory, we've just made this trip out here for absolutely nothing."

"Why?" Grishin asked. He realized that this was a serious problem, but was smart enough to understand that he didn't know everything. "Can you not still take off and make orbit without it? Our ships may be able to pick us up if we can make it that far."

"I might, if they'd only taken the memory cells, which contain all the star charts." He shook his head. "The navigation core itself, though, that's the brain behind the operation, the processing unit that translates the information we give it through the controls into machine-level language that the ship's systems understand. Without it..." He shrugged. "Trying to fly without it would be like trying to drive a skimmer on manual without a steering wheel or any other controls. If we had a full crew, we might be able to manage on full manual, although that would be dangerous as hell. But with just me...I'm sorry, sir, but it just can't be done. It's just not physically possible."

"Brilliant," Grishin muttered.

"Sir?" Mills asked.

"It is a perfect way to ground a ship," Grishin told him. "It does not matter if you can fire up the engines or other systems manually. If you cannot control them, it makes no difference." He sighed.

"What now, sir?" Mills asked quietly as Faraday wandered over to the pile of equipment that had been salvaged from the cutter and flopped down, dejected. "We can't let the troops give up hope."

"No, Mills, we can't," Grishin told him. "Yet I do not have any bright ideas. This ship was our only hope of getting off-planet unless more Confederation ships arrive, which is most unlikely. Even then, I doubt they would be able to fight their way to the surface to retrieve us. We're going to have to think of something else."

"Yes, sir," Mills said, pressing his mouth into a thin line. *Dammit,* he thought, *we came so bloody close!*

He and Grishin both looked up at the sound of distant gunfire from near the spaceport's entrance.

"Well," said Grishin, "there is some good news, at least. It appears that Major Justin has arrived with the rest of the brigade."

"And not a moment too soon," Mills told him, pointing skyward. "We have visitors, I'd say."

Grishin looked up to where Mills was pointing and his heart sank even further, if that was possible. He saw the tell-tale streaks of inbound assault craft in the high atmosphere, hundreds of them, swarming toward the surface.

Missiles suddenly rose from the ground on pillars of fire and smoke, streaking away toward their targets. They only made it a few kilometers into the air before they were vaporized by defensive fire from the incoming enemy boats. More missiles fired, then more. Saint Petersburg was ringed with dozens of surface-to-air missile emplacements that were now belching missiles into the sky. A few of them actually got through the torrent of defensive fire from the boats, blasting a few of them into fiery shards, but not enough to make any difference.

As the boats came closer, ground-based defense lasers began to fire. Similar to the point defense lasers carried on Confederation warships, these had roughly the same amount of power, but their range was far more limited because of the interference from the atmosphere. But where the missiles had failed miserably, the lasers achieved some success: there was no defense against them except armor or reflective coatings, neither of which the attacking craft had. In ones and twos they began to die. Some exploded in huge fireballs, while others simply spun out of control.

Yet the Kreelans were not content to let the defenders have things their own way. Grishin watched in awe as several waves of what looked like shooting stars blazed through the sky from space, kinetic weapons that passed straight through the weaving cloud of assault boats toward the ground. While most of them impacted on the defense positions on the far side of the city, one group hit a site only a few kilometers from the spaceport: thunder boomed across the landing field, so loud that the men and women who stood outside had to cover their ears. As the alien-made thunder died away, giant clouds of smoke and debris rose above the targets.

"Good God, colonel, what was that?" Major Justin had to shout for Grishin to hear him.

Grishin turned to him, not having heard the final approach of the column of vehicles as he watched the fireworks display unfold. "That, major," he shouted back, "was the Kreelans suggesting that we find a way off this planet."

***

Inside the ship, Valentina lay quietly in one of the beds in the small but well-equipped sick bay, Dmitri and Ludmilla by her side. The medic tended to her and the seriously injured Marines, thankful that the stocks of plasma and blood expanders had not gone bad. The ship's autodoc had managed to improve on her field dressings, fully sealing the wounds and even extracting the bullets. It had also managed to isolate and cauterize the arteries and veins that were the most serious contributors to her internal bleeding.

"I'll be damned if I know how," the medic said, "but I think she'll actually live if we can get her to a real surgeon fairly soon."

"She is yet in danger?" Sikorsky asked worriedly just before Valentina woke up from the surgery.

"Yes," the medic said, "but I'd say her chances are good. The autodoc fixed the worst of the trauma, and we've got plenty of plasma and even whole blood for more transfusions if she needs it. She definitely needs a real surgeon, but..." She shrugged. "It's a freakin' miracle, my friend. That's all I can say."

A miracle, Sikorsky thought, just as Valentina opened her eyes.

"Don't look so sad," she whispered.

"I am not sad," he told her, wiping his eyes. "I am so happy you aren't..." He refused to say the word that threatened to come to his lips. "That you are still with us." He ran a hand over her forehead, brushing her hair back, and the gesture gave him a sudden sense of déjà vu: he had done the same for his daughter many years ago. Ludmilla held one of Valentina's hands, squeezing it gently.

Sikorsky glanced up as someone else entered the sick bay: the cutter's pilot. He limped in and slumped into an unoccupied chair. Closing his eyes, he leaned his head back against the wall as if to sleep. Sikorsky noticed that the medic and a couple of the injured Marines give the pilot a long look, then they turned away, stony expressions on their faces.

"Why are you not preparing the ship to leave?" Sikorsky asked.

Faraday sighed in resignation before opening his eyes and turning his head toward him. "Because we're not going anywhere in this tub," he said flatly, his usual flippant attitude having evaporated.

"What does that mean?" Sikorsky demanded. "Why not?"

"Because the Russkies took the fucking navigation computer core," Faraday snapped. "The nav system is nothing but an empty goddamn box. Without it, I can't control the ship. We're stuck here."

"Those explosions we heard outside," Ludmilla said, her Standard thickly laced with her Russian accent. "Are Red Army troops coming for us?"

Faraday gave her a death's head grin. "No, nothing that easy. The Kreelans are invading. What you heard were the city's air defenses being blasted to bits by a huge wave of Kreelan assault boats. We're probably next on the menu. They won't pass up a nice, juicy spaceport for long."

"Did you inspect the nav core?"

Sikorsky was shocked to hear Valentina's voice, and saw that she was looking intently at Faraday.

"What's to inspect, lady?" the pilot snapped. "The damn thing is gone. They pulled it."

"No," she said tiredly, "not the module they removed, but the housing itself."

"Of course I did, for what that was worth." He looked at her more closely, noting that she was obviously intent on something he wasn't picking up on yet. "What difference does it make?"

"Does it have an RP-911 interface?" she asked, ignoring his question.

"Sure," he said, curiosity and irritation both evident in his voice. "That's a standard connector for uploading data and doing system troubleshooting using an external terminal. Why the hell are you asking about it?"

"Because," she told him in an unsteady voice, as if she had suddenly been chilled by a bone-deep dread, "I can help you fly the ship."

***

"There," Tesh-Dar said, pointing out the assault craft's forward window at what could only be a spaceport. "We shall land there and disable the ships."

"Could we not simply destroy them from the air, my priestess?"

Tesh-Dar shook her great head. "And what challenge would that be?" she chided gently. "What glory to the Empress would it bring? No, destroying ships is the work of the fleet. Ours is to meet the enemy in close combat when we may. With the ships disabled, the humans cannot use them to flee, and there shall be more for us to fight, and more glory to bring to the Empress."

The young warrior bowed her head in submission.

"It is not a violation of the Way to enjoy great explosions," Tesh-Dar consoled her with a gently touch on the shoulder, "but we have other work this day."

As they approached the spaceport, with a dozen other assault craft flying a loose formation around them, Tesh-Dar sensed something else, an odd stirring in her soul that she did not immediately recognize. It was as if she were looking at a face she had not seen in years, and now was unable to recognize its owner.

Closing her eyes, she reached out with her mind, her second sight taking her spirit ahead of the ship her body rode. Slowing time to a standstill, she searched the spaceport, seeing the humans frozen as they were in that instant. Through the buildings, across the great expanse of the landing apron, through the ships, she searched.

Suddenly, she found him. A face that she recognized. He stood before one of the smaller ships, near a craft much like an assault boat that had crash-landed. Larger and, she knew, fiercer than his fellow warriors, he stood a head taller than most of the camouflage-dressed humans around him. She did not know or care to know his name, nor did he have any special standing as did the Messenger. Yet she knew more of him than most of his human companions, for she had fought him in ritual combat on Keran. She had let him live then, for he had fought bravely and well, and it would do the Empress no service to cull from among the greatest of the warriors the humans had. Tesh-Dar knew that his blood did not sing, and he was not the One they sought. Yet she relished the thought of fighting him again, to see if he had learned anything new.

Drawing her spirit back to her body, time resumed its normal course, and she clenched her fists in anticipation of the combat that was to come.

***

"You can't be serious," Faraday said, clearly dismayed. "Colonel, this is nuts!"

Colonel Grishin heard the pilot, but his attention was focused on Valentina. She still lay in the bed in sick bay, her haunted eyes staring back at him. "Valentina," he said, figuring that was as good a name to use as Scarlet, "is this even truly possible?"

"Yes, colonel," she told him, "it is. I was specially augmented for black operations, and one of the...modifications was an organic RP-911 interface."

"There's nothing odd that showed up on the autodoc scan," the medic interjected, not sure to believe what the young woman was saying, wondering if she was suffering from some sort of dementia. "There would have to be connectors, something..."

"There are," Valentina breathed. "Believe me, there are. But that's why the interface is organic: so it doesn't show up on medical scans."

"Then how do you use it?" Faraday asked, looking at Grishin like she was nuts.

"You have to apply a small electrical current to a specific location at the base of my skull," she explained in a small voice. "There is a matrix of special material there that will realign to form the interface. Then I just...plug in." She closed her eyes and shivered.

"What are you not telling us, Valentina?" Sikorsky demanded, his eyes full of concern. "Why are you frightened of this so?"

"Because..." she whispered, looking up at him. "Because the machines are so cold, so inhuman. I had to do it once before. I don't remember much..." She lied, shaking her head, trying to force away the horrible memories. "We have to get out of here, and without the nav core we have no choice."

"Let's see this interface," the medic demanded. She dug through the medical equipment, coming back with an electrical cauterizing unit. "What sort of current do you need to make this work?"

"Thirty-seven volts at two point five milliamperes, alternating at one hundred and five kilohertz," Valentina whispered, her eyes fixed on the cauterizing unit as if it were a dreadful monster.

The medic looked at her, then at Grishin. The pilot shook his head, circling an index finger around his temple: *she's nuts.* Grishin shrugged.

"That's, um, a bit of an odd setting, don't you think?" the medic said as she dialed in the settings. Surprisingly, the instrument accepted them.

"It was intended to be," Valentina explained quietly. "You wouldn't want an interrogator to torture you with electrical current and accidentally discover the interface, now would you?"

Sikorsky looked up at Grishin and said, "Colonel, stop this! Valentina, I do not doubt that you have this...thing in your body. But this is madness! It is—"

"It is our only chance, Dmitri," Valentina pleaded, squeezing his hand tightly. Turning to the medic, she said, "You will find a small mole on the nape of my neck. Apply the current there and you will see."

"Well, the current certainly won't hurt her much," the medic muttered as she stepped up to the bed and gently turned Valentina's head. She touched the tip of the cauterizing probe to the designated spot and pressed the button on the instrument. It began to hum. "Nothing's happen...ing. Oh, *Jesus!*"

Before her eyes, a small patch of Valentina's skin began to reshape itself into the form of a non-metallic electrical interface: instead of metal, it was moist organic tissue, but quite hard and shaped just like a standard jack interface. Looking up at the autodoc's display of Valentina's real-time body scan, she could see it taking form. It was not simply an interface, however: tendrils quickly formed from the external connector that led to various areas in Valentina's brain like a dark, malignant spider.

"*Bozhe moi*," Grishin breathed. He had never had any idea that such things were even possible.

"Does it hurt?" Sikorsky whispered as he watched the awful thing take shape.

"No," Valentina said, "not really."

He could tell she was lying.

"Do we have to keep this current applied?" the medic asked, still unable to believe what she was seeing.

"Only until the jack is inserted," Valentina told her. "After that, the auxiliary power lead in the jack will provide enough power to hold the matrix in place. It will remain until the jack is removed."

"No," Sikorsky said angrily, standing up to face Grishin. "This is monstrous, colonel! I will not allow it!"

Grishin faced him calmly. In Russian, he said, "My friend, she is our only hope. If she does not do this, we will all die. Every one of us, including her. The Kreelans take no prisoners, and this planet will soon be a graveyard: there were no survivors left on Keran after the aliens finished with them. They have come here to exterminate us. You do not wish that for her, do you?"

"No," Sikorsky breathed, feeling utterly helpless. "No, I do not."

In English, Grishin said to the others, "Let us get her up to the flight deck and—"

"Colonel!" Mills's voice suddenly burst over Grishin's helmet comm unit, "We've got Kreelan assault boats coming in over the spaceport perimeter!"

"Understood!" Grishin told him. "Get going!" he ordered the others in the sickbay. "We are out of time!"

He ran down the passageway toward the loading ramp, just as the anti-air team perched on top of the freighter began to fire their missiles at the inbound enemy boats.

***

Tesh-Dar hissed as three assault boats in her formation disappeared in fiery explosions, victims of hypervelocity missiles fired from the ship where she knew her human opponent waited. "Land!" she ordered the pilot tersely.

The boat instantly plunged toward the ground, followed instantly by the others. The pilot flared her landing at the last moment, bringing the nose up just in time while the jump doors along the boat's flanks slid open. Warriors leaped to the ground even as the pilot set the ship down on its thick landing claws. The boat's pilot would not be staying with her craft, but would go with the other warriors: fighting face to face brought greater glory to the Empress.

Tesh-Dar led the others across the flat landscape of the landing field. The warriors took cover where they could behind the massive landing struts of the ships that now stood between them and their objective. They moved as quickly as possible over the flat, open landing apron to avoid the torrent of weapons fire now pouring from the humans surrounding the ship that was their goal. Tesh-Dar did not bother trying to shield her body, for she had no need to: the projectiles from the human weapons simply passed through her without leaving a trace. She strode toward the humans, her mind's eye fixed on the one that she wanted, the one she had come for.

***

"Mills!" Sabourin gasped. "Is that her?"

Next to her, crouching behind the relative safety of the cutter's wreckage, Mills felt his insides turn to ice. The huge warrior, the one he had fought on Keran and who had let him live, the one who had been the focus of his nightmares, was walking straight toward him.

"She knew," he murmured into the cacophony around him as hundreds of Marines fired at the advancing Kreelans. "She bloody *knew!*" And so had he, he realized. When his headache had abruptly stopped, it was because she had entered the system. He suddenly wondered if the headache itself had been caused by her being in hyperspace, aboard whatever ship that had brought her here. He pushed the thought aside: it was nothing more than idle, useless speculation for a man who had been living on borrowed time. He knew that the sand had just run out of his life's hourglass.

"Knew what?" Sabourin asked, her eyes filled with fright. She grabbed him by the arm and pulled him to her, breaking him away from the advancing alien horror. "Knew what, Roland?"

"She knew I'd be here," he told her. "Somehow, she knew. She came for me." He tried to put on his famous devil-may-care smile for her, the smile she had always thought made him look so young, but it faltered, failed. Pulling her close and putting his lips to her ear, he told her, "I love you, Emmanuelle." He held her for a moment, kissing her with a passion he had only ever shown during their lovemaking.

Then he was gone, sprinting across the tarmac toward his destiny.

"Roland, no!" Sabourin screamed after him, feeling as if her heart had been ripped from her chest. "*Come back!*"

***

From his vantage point behind the main forward landing gear of the ship, Grishin saw Mills suddenly break cover and dash straight for the Kreelans. Or, rather, straight for the huge warrior who stalked across the tarmac toward the human positions, totally impervious to their weapons.

"*Chyort voz'mi*," he whispered, instantly recognizing her. She had killed one of his crewmen on Keran, snatching him out of his command vehicle's rear hatch with an alien version of the cat-o-nine tails, a dreadful multi-barbed whip. Grishin could still hear the wet smacking sound the legionnaire's body had made when it hit the metal coaming of the vehicle's open hatch, smashing the skull and leg bones, just before Grishin's driver had panicked and driven away.

"Colonel," Major Justin shouted over the firing, "look!"

The Kreelans had stopped, taking cover as best they could behind the landing gear and ground equipment of the nearest ships. Only the huge warrior was out in the open now, standing. Waiting.

"Cease fire!" Grishin called through the brigade command net.

"Cease fire!" His command was repeated by his surviving subordinate commanders and NCOs, and in only a few seconds there was a sudden silence as the Marines stopped firing.

Grishin felt more than heard a deep rumble behind him. The Mauritania's engines were spooling up. He switched over to another channel, linked to Faraday in the ship. "How long?" he asked tersely.

"Jesus, colonel," the pilot said, "I don't know! Five, maybe ten minutes if we're lucky."

"I hope it's closer to five than to ten," Grishin told him grimly as he watched Mills warily approach the huge alien warrior. "We may not have that long."

***

"I'm doing my best, sir," Faraday told him. He was panting from having run back and forth twice between the bridge and engineering on his injured leg. "Your Marines are trying to be helpful, but they don't know shit about running a ship, and I'm having to figure all this crap out on my own." *And it's a fucking good thing I know some French*, he told himself. *Otherwise I wouldn't be able to understand what the hell anything was.* Since she was a ship out of La Seyne, all of *Mauritania's* instrumentation was in French. Slipping into the flight command chair, he frantically typed in a series of commands into the main control console, and was rewarded with a series of green indicator lights on the ship's main status panel. "All right! We've got the main drives up, jump drives check out, and thrusters are green. Sir, if you can get someone to disconnect the umbilicals, that'd be a big help."

"Consider it done," Grishin's voice informed him.

"All we need now is navigation," Faraday said quietly as the medic and the Sikorsky's appeared, carefully carrying Valentina. They strapped her down in the navigator's chair, leaning it back as far as it would go. She was white as a sheet, and shivering as if she were freezing. "Are you going to be okay?" he asked her. He had never claimed to have much emotional depth, but his heart ached when he looked at her. *Talk about having guts*, he thought.

"Just get us out of here," she rasped. Turning to the medic and the Sikorskys, she grabbed Dmitri's arm. "Whatever happens to me after the medic plugs in the jack," she told him in Russian through teeth that were now chattering with fear, "*do not unplug it*. No matter how badly you may want to. Do you understand me?"

Dmitri glanced at Ludmilla, with both of them wearing terrified expressions. They were not afraid of death so much as what was about to happen to Valentina. They could tell she was petrified.

"Promise me!"

"We promise," he whispered.

Satisfied, Valentina relaxed her grip, sliding her hand down to hold onto his. "Let's get this over with," she told the medic, turning her head to the side, toward Dmitri, to expose the back of her neck. "Please hold my hand," she whispered to him as she felt the tingle of electricity from the cauterizer begin to tease the interface into existence, "and don't let go."

"Okay," the medic said, simultaneously fascinated and repelled by the interface as it formed in Valentina's skin, "here we go." She took the slender cable and gently inserted it into the receptacle, then took away the cauterizer.

Valentina suddenly stiffened as if she'd been hit with a massive electric shock. Just as suddenly, her body relaxed and stopped shivering. The fearful expression fell from her face, replaced by limp placidity.

Sikorsky took a deep breath, leaning against Ludmilla. *That was not so bad as I had feared*, he thought, just before Valentina began to scream.

TWENTY-TWO

Mills stood facing the warrior of his nightmares, the warrior he had faced on Keran a lifetime ago. The firing around him had stopped, but he barely noticed. She was his universe now, and he knew they had now come full circle, and she would be the end of him. Part of him was bitter at the thought, not just because he hated the thought of dying, but he had actually found someone he truly loved, a love born in the most unlikely of circumstances. *I'll miss you, Emmanuelle*, he thought. But he dared not look back at her. It was too late for that.

"Well," he said casually, "let's get to it, shall we?" She had beaten him to a bloody pulp the last time he had faced her, and he doubted today would be any different. For some reason, that thought eased much of the tension out of his body. Facing one's destiny was sometimes easier when the outcome was crystal clear.

Without another word, he launched himself at her.

***

Tesh-Dar was pleased with the human animal, that he had lost none of his fighting spirit since she had last seen him. He had also learned from their last encounter: he was much better at feinting, trying to conceal his true intentions from her as he attacked.

She began sparring with him, careful not to injure him severely, again enjoying the thrill of single combat. She did not use any weapons other than her body, for she had no need. Nor did she wish the combat to be over too soon. She did not yet know if she would allow him to live as she had last time: much would depend on how well he fought.

So focused was she on the human that she failed to sense what was taking place far above, in space.

***

"They're leaving!" the flag tactical officer reported excitedly. On the flag bridge display aboard Constellation, the swarm of red icons orbiting Saint Petersburg suddenly thinned.

"Recall the cutter!" Hanson ordered. The ship had deployed its cutter to the limb of Riga, allowing its sensors to peer past the planet at Saint Petersburg while the human warships sheltered behind the planet, waiting for the right moment to strike.

"Aye, ma'am!" the communications officer reported. "The cutter is on its way. ETA three minutes."

"Commodore," Voroshilov's image said on Hanson's vidcom terminal, "you see the change in the enemy fleet's disposition, *da?*"

"Yes, admiral," she said. "It looks like our time has arrived. My ships are ready to jump on your command, sir, once our cutter is back aboard."

"Do you have any questions about our strategy, commodore?" he asked.

"No, sir," she said. "We make a micro-jump back to Saint Petersburg," she continued, quickly recapping his instructions, "make a slashing pass against the enemy fleet, and then micro-jump away again before we can become decisively engaged."

Voroshilov nodded. "Yes, commodore. Just so. Our opponents are not foolish, however," he told her. "Do not be surprised if they attempt to follow us, for our exit point for the second jump will leave us in a position visible to them. I do not expect them to let us have a 'free ride,' as you might call it, again."

"If they do, admiral," she told him gravely, "we'll be in serious trouble. The Kreelans have incredible navigation capabilities." She remembered the reports of the return of the Aurora, the ship that had made first contact with the Kreelans. It had emerged from hyperspace within meters of Africa Station in orbit over Earth after the ship had been traveling in hyperspace for months. It should have been impossible, but it happened. "Even without having carefully mapped the space in this system for any perturbations as you have, if they want to jump after us, they will."

"I am counting on it," Voroshilov said with a cunning smile. "Our comrades on Saint Petersburg's moon have not been idle in our absence, commodore. They have been launching a steady stream of mines to saturate the space surrounding the emergence point for our second jump."

"Will our ships be safe?" Hanson asked. The last thing she needed was to jump into a mine field and have half her ships blown apart – by human-made mines.

"Yes, commodore," Voroshilov reassured her. "The mines have been programmed to ignore your ships as well as ours. The Kreelan ships may get an unpleasant surprise, however. It is a trick we may use only once, but once might just be enough."

"Very well, sir," she told him. She glanced over at the flag captain, who gave her the thumbs-up sign as the status board indicated the cutter had been brought aboard and was secured. "We're ready on your mark."

"Stand by..." Voroshilov said tensely from the vidcom terminal. "In three...two...one...mark!"

As they had once before, the ships of the joint Confderation-Saint Petersburg fleet disappeared into hyperspace.

***

For a moment, no one on *Mauritania's* flight deck could move as Valentina's screams pierced their ears. Her eyes were open, her face completely slack except for her lips, which were parted wide as she screamed.

"Valentina!" Sikorsky cried, panic-stricken. "*Valentina!*" He reached for the interface cable, intent on pulling it away from her.

"Dmitri, no!" Ludmilla told him, grabbing his hands. "You must not!"

"I cannot let this happen," he shouted, tears in his eyes. "I will not..."

"You promised her, Dmitri," she told him, her face etched in anguish at the young woman's torment. "You promised!"

"Nav systems are coming up!" Faraday suddenly shouted. "We don't have any star charts, but we can get this fucker off the ground." He tapped a few buttons on the console. "I've got control."

Just then Valentina's screams stopped, as if the last button Faraday had pushed turned them off. She simply lay slumped in the navigator's seat, her eyes vacant, her body completely limp. Her mouth still hung open, as if she were still screaming.

"Is she dead?" Sikorsky asked.

The medic shook her head. "No," she managed, her skin still crawling from seeing Valentina's vacant expression as she'd screamed. "Her pulse and respiration are fast, but she's alive. I don't know how much of this she can take, though. I had no idea there would be this kind of psychological trauma."

"She tried to warn us," Sikorsky whispered, desperately holding Valentina's hand. "May God forgive us."

"Colonel!" Faraday called over the comm link. "We're up! Get your asses on board and let's get this tub off the ground!"

***

"Understood!" Grishin told Faraday, not daring to take his eyes off the drama that was playing out before him between Mills and the alien warrior. "Major Justin!" he called.

"Sir!"

"Start loading everyone aboard, as quickly as you can. Have Bravo Company of Third Battalion provide cover until the rest are aboard." That company was actually more like a reinforced platoon in strength after it had been decimated by the Russian ambush when they'd landed, but it was in better shape than the other companies were. He hoped that the distraction Mills was providing would be enough to get most of his Marines aboard before the Kreelans started shooting again.

"What about Mills, sir?" Justin asked.

Grishin gave him a hard look. "Carry out your orders, major."

"Yes, sir!" Justin nodded his understanding, then moved along the line of Marines, getting them moving toward the ship's massive loading ramp.

***

She hasn't lost her touch, Mills conceded as the Kreelan warrior landed another blow. He had fought his fair share of men in both combat and in barroom brawls, and it amazed him how bloody *hard* she was. He expected that of her metal armor, of course, but the few blows he'd managed to land on her face or the parts of her body that were not protected by metal felt like he was hitting a granite boulder. And, when she hit him, it felt like he was being hit by one.

He had his combat knife, but was hesitant to use it. To this point, she seemed content to play by the same rules as their little engagement on Keran: fists and feet only, with her essentially toying with him for her alien pleasure. He was afraid that if he pulled out his knife, she might do the same. And the smallest bladed weapon he saw on her was nearly as long as his arm, which would put him at more than a slight disadvantage.

He ducked and just managed to avoid another open-handed strike she made to his face, then darted in and landed a hard right jab to her gut, just below her breastplate. *Bloody hell*, he thought, *how does someone get abs that hard?* She grunted from the blow, however, so he gave himself a brief mental pat on the back for at least hitting her hard enough for her to notice him, just before she brought a huge fist down on his shoulder, knocking him flat on the concrete tarmac. His head slammed into the unyielding surface, and he lay there, momentarily dazed.

He didn't see Sabourin sprint from cover toward them, her knife drawn and a look of cold hatred on her face.

***

"Enemy ships, close aboard!" the flag tactical officer shouted as *Constellation* emerged into normal space from the fleet's first micro-jump.

"All ships, commence firing!" Hanson ordered, her spine tingling with a dreadful mixture of excitement and fear as she checked the tactical display. All her ships had made it, and their formation, while not as good as the Russians, at least had all of her vessels pointing in the same direction. They had landed on top of the bulk of Kreelan ships that remained in Saint Petersburg space, and that now circled the planet in low orbit. The huge transports and most of their smaller consorts had left, although the human fleet was still considerably outgunned.

Jesus, admiral, you cut it close, she thought as a Kreelan warship – *Constellation's* current target – showed on the view screen. Even with no magnification, the sleek shark-like shape nearly filled it. Her flagship's main batteries went to continuous fire mode, pouring shells into the Kreelan warship at point-blank range. She heard the ship's captain order the secondary and point defense weapons to fire, as well: it was a knife fight.

She watched as the lasers etched the enemy ship's hull, vaporizing armor plate, just before the shells from the main guns hit. The *Constellation's* gunners were spot on: a dozen flashes lit the enemy ship's flank as the shells hit home, all of them concentrated amidships. In a spectacular flash, the enemy ship's midsection exploded, her back broken, sending the remaining bow and stern sections tumbling in opposite directions, both of them streaming air and bodies behind.

The Kreelan ship had not fired a single shot in return.

A cheer went up from the ship's bridge crew even as the captain called for a shift in targets, and the *Constellation* poured fire into yet another Kreelan warship that was only slightly further away.

"Prepare for jump!" Hanson ordered. This first part of their plan was only to get the Kreelans' attention, to poke them with a sharp stick in hopes of getting them to follow after the humans as they fled. If they stayed here any longer, her ships would be gutted.

"Coordination signal from the flag!" her navigation officer called out. Voroshilov's flag navigation officer was coordination with his counterpart on Constellation directly, while Voroshilov and Hanson concentrated on keeping their ships alive. Their level of trust had matured at least this far, their officers were cooperating directly as fellow professionals. It was difficult for Hanson to believe that she had originally been sent here to blow the Russians out of space.

"All ships, secure for jump!" she ordered in the din of *Constellation's* continued firing. The ship rocked from several shells that hit almost simultaneously. The lights dimmed ominously for a moment and several electrical panels overloaded, sending sparks flying across the flag bridge.

"Jump execution..." the navigation officer called as the center of the human formation tracked exactly over the pre-designated jump point, "...*now!*"

The *Constellation* disappeared along with the rest of the human fleet as a hail of heavy shells passed through the space where she had just been.

***

Li'ara-Zhurah knelt quietly, her eyes fixed on the Messenger, her warriors formed around her in a protective circle. Perhaps they need not have done so, for there was certainly no threat from the human crew: they were all but finished. Only one of the handful on the command deck who had still been conscious when she had arrived remained so, a female warrior who was clearly near death. The others had already slumped lifelessly to the deck.

She did not envy them the death that they faced. While they may have been soulless creatures in the eyes of the Empress and Her Children, Li'ara-Zhurah knew better than most of her sisters that the humans were worthy of respect. They had certainly earned hers during the attack against Keran. She would never understand their species or the peculiar things they did, like fighting among one another here in this system, even as Her warships descended upon them, but understanding was not required. In the end, there was only duty to serve Her honor and glory, for nothing else truly mattered. It had taken her a great deal of pain and much help from Tesh-Dar to fully understand that, but now it was a source of deep contentment.

She thought about the child she now carried in her womb, the song of its spirit strengthening hour by hour. Its melody was simple, yet strong: she would be a great warrior or clawless mistress one day, she knew, placing a hand reverently over her abdomen where she knew the child's tiny heart had begun to beat. In time, the child's song would grow as rich and complex as that of the countless others that flowed in the river of the Bloodsong of her race.

The Messenger's body suddenly began to twitch, and she knew that the healing gel had run its course. Being treated with it was sometimes not a pleasant process, but her race had not suffered from disease for millenia, and virtually any injury short of destruction of the brain could be repaired, if She so willed it. His body suddenly convulsed, and the gel flowed from his mouth, out of his lungs. It had penetrated the various layers of his body, repairing the damage left behind by the radiation, or so she hoped, and at last had gathered in his lungs before exiting through the mouth.

She reverently took the gel, now laced with sickly yellow streaks, and placed it back in the tube, where it pulsed weakly. It could normally could be reused after it had bonded with a healer, but this symbiont would never again know such a bonding. She would take it back with her, but it would perish long before they could return it to the Empire: treating radiation sickness was a terribly rare thing, and one of the few applications that for some reason sickened the symbionts. It was a great loss, for the healing gel was one of the most valued things in their civilization, but its sacrifice was for a worthy cause.

The Messenger lay back on the deck, his eyes fluttering open. He looked at her, his strangely-shaped eyes, narrower than most of the other humans she had seen, as if he were born squinting, then sat up to face her. She bowed her head low to honor him.

***

As Sato woke up, he felt wonderful. It was not simply that he was still living and breathing, but he felt truly alive, his body completely refreshed.

Opening his eyes, he saw that there was a Kreelan kneeling in front of him, head bowed, and with sudden clarity he remembered what had happened. She had used the awful goo that the Kreelans he had encountered on first contact had used to heal him, to eliminate the radiation poisoning. It would also have "fixed" anything else that was wrong with his body, something that was far, far beyond the dreams of modern human medical science.

He sat up, and she raised her eyes to meet his. He had not come across this warrior at Keran, but she obviously knew him. They all seemed to. It had been maddening during the battle of Keran, when he faced a group of warriors aboard his now-dead destroyer, and they had simply knelt before him as this warrior was now. He had been so enraged that he had wanted to kill them all, and they would have let him. In fact, it had almost seemed as if they wanted him to kill them. In the end, despite all that he had gone through, all the Kreelans had done, he couldn't. He simply was not capable of killing in cold blood, even the aliens who had invaded the human sphere.

"Captain," he heard a voice rasp weakly.

With a shock, he saw Bogdanova on the deck, looking up at him with glassy eyes.

"No," he moaned, suddenly noticing the state of the bridge crew, which he knew would be reflected in the rest of his people. They were dead or dying. All of them. "Bogdanova!" He got up and made his way toward her, and the Kreelans parted to let him pass, the group of surrounding warriors melting and flowing to reform around him where he knelt next to Bogdanova. "I'm going to get you out of here," he promised her fervently, holding her hand and brushing the hair from her eyes. Her skin was cool, far too cool, to his touch. She had seemed to be faring better than many of the others, but the radiation poisoning had clearly caught up with her. She was dying, as was the rest of his crew. "I'm going to get you out of here, all of you. You're going to be okay."

Turning to the warrior, he pointed to the slowly pulsating mass of goo in the tube next to her, then at Bogdanova, then the other members of the bridge crew. "Please," he pleaded with her, "help them. Save my crew."

The warrior gestured toward him, then the goo, holding it up for him to inspect more closely. It wasn't the grotesque purple and pink color he remembered from the first time he had been subjected to it. This specimen was clearly damaged or diseased, leprous in appearance.

"Can't you get more?" he demanded, pointing at the goo, then at Bogdanova again. "Goddammit," he shouted angrily, "you saved me, why can't you save them?"

The Kreelan simply stared at him, her silver-flecked feline eyes fixed on his. He had no idea if there was no more of the healing substance to be had, if she refused to get more, or if she simply had no idea what he was asking.

He suddenly felt a fiery rage building inside, a manifestation of his complete helplessness and his fear that, as on his first voyage when humanity had made contact with the Kreelans, he would again be left alone, the sole survivor of his crew. It was a possibility that he could not, would not accept. *Not again*, he thought bitterly. *Please, not again.*

His attention was brought back to Bogdanova as she squeezed his hand, her grip little stronger than an infant's.

"They saved you, Ichiro," she whispered. He and Bogdanova had been together since before the battle of Keran, and while they had never been anything more than friends and shipmates, it tore his heart out to see her like this. Tears welled up in his eyes as he watched the life slip away from her. She smiled one last time. "I'm glad they did..."

Then she was gone.

Ignoring the Kreelans, Sato picked her up and held her in his arms, tears flowing freely. "No," he moaned. "God, why do you hate me so much?"

He was still weeping when the ship was suddenly torn apart.

***

"Direct hit!" cried the tactical officer aboard the *CNS Southampton* as her shells slammed into the Kreelan warship at point blank range. About twice the size of a heavy cruiser and already badly damaged, it was an easy mark for their first target upon emergence in the Saint Petersburg system. It had an extremely odd configuration, but no one noticed in the heat of the moment: if it was Kreelan, you shot first and didn't bother to ask questions.

Too goddamn bad for you, Captain Moshe Braverman, the *Southampton's* captain, thought savagely as the ship's engines exploded, sending what was left of the forward hull spinning away. He turned his attention to the other three Kreelan warships that were close aboard. It had been only blind luck – whether it was good or bad depended on your point of view – that had put their task force's emergence point right on top of the Kreelans. *Southampton* was assigned to the second flotilla of cruisers that was supposed to have rendezvoused with Hanson's force before jumping into the system to take the nuclear weapons away from Saint Petersburg and to defend Riga. Unfortunately, they and their escorting squadron of destroyers had been ambushed at Edinburgh by Kreelan raiders, who had put up enough of a fight to delay the task force's arrival until now. Braverman certainly hadn't expected to find Kreelans here, as well, but he had made sure that everyone had been fully prepared for the unexpected.

After blowing *Southampton's* first target into pieces, Braverman ordered his tactical officer to shift fire to one of the other Kreelan warships that were furiously fighting back. All three of them were making full speed toward the one that *Southampton* had just finished off, which put them right in line with Braverman's guns.

"Fire!" he ordered, and the ship thundered as the main batteries blasted another salvo of twenty-centimeter shells at their next target. "Anti-boarding, units, stand by," he ordered as the enemy ships drew closer. He had been at Keran and had seen the devastation Kreelan boarding parties could wreak upon a ship, and he had no intention of letting that happen to *Southampton*. Just as another Kreelan cruiser exploded, he said, "Continue firing. Let's show these Kreelan bitches how it's done."

Blazing away at the remaining pair of Kreelan ships, *Southampton* and her sisters sailed by the remains of *CNS Yura* and the Kreelan warship that had been bound to her.

TWENTY-THREE

Tesh-Dar was enjoying the challenge posed by the human warrior. While she could easily have killed him, giving him a chance such as this to fight brought greater glory to the Empress, and also served as a useful lesson for her warriors, who watched the combat with rapt attention.

She had noticed the second human warrior approaching, of course, but was unconcerned: two of them would pose a more interesting contest, especially since the second human had drawn a knife. Tesh-Dar had no intention of drawing a weapon other than those her body possessed, but she might consider indulging herself in the use of her talons. Her warriors did not interfere, for they knew that two humans, a dozen, could not harm a priestess of the Desh-Ka.

After blocking a blow to her face by the human male, she was just preparing to make a counter-strike when there was a terrible surge in the Bloodsong, one of pain and fear from a dozen among the billions of spiritual melodies.

"Li'ara-Zhurah," she gasped, feeling as though a bolt of lightning had pierced her heart. She staggered with shock, nearly falling to her knees. The human warrior wasted no time, throwing himself upon her, but she brutally shoved him away.

Then she was seared by white hot pain as the second human warrior, about whom she had completely forgotten as she considered Li'ara-Zhurah's plight, plunged her knife into Tesh-Dar's back, just below her armored backplate.

***

"Emmanuelle," Mills shouted, "no!"

It was too late. He had seen her rush from the cover of the downed cutter toward him, but had been unable to wave her back as he staggered back to his feet after the Kreelan had knocked him to the ground. And now, just as the enemy warrior mysteriously stumbled, temporarily losing her focus on the fight, Sabourin had dashed forward the last few meters, her combat knife held at ther eady.

Mills threw himself at the warrior, trying to hold her and keep her from turning on Sabourin. Even as addled as she clearly was, however, she was still far too strong for him. With an angry growl, she flung him half a dozen meters across the tarmac, where he landed hard, breaking his right arm and scraping his face on the rough concrete. "Emmanuelle," he cried desperately. "*Get back!*"

***

The Messenger's ship suddenly exploded around them, the force flinging warriors and humans alike across the bridge as the hull was torn apart. The lights flickered, then went out, plunging the command deck into total darkness. The artificial gravity failed, leaving the living and the dead flying through the compartment like ricocheting bullets before they were sucked into the screaming torrent of the ship's air as it vented into space through the shattered hull.

Sato flailed his arms and legs, trying desperately to find something to cling to as he was sucked toward the bridge hatchway, but in the total and utter darkness it was impossible. His lungs felt like they were about to burst, and he forced himself to exhale to relieve the pressure. It wouldn't matter in another few moments, he knew, but that is what he had been trained to do, and that is what he did.

His leg slammed into something hard, making him gasp with pain, his lungs venting what little air they had left. For just an instant while he tumbled, he could see down the passageway from the bridge: ten meters down the passageway, *Yura's* hull was simply gone. There was nothing left of the rest of the ship, and he could see the stars whirling outside as the chunk of her that he was on spun out of control.

Steph, he thought. *I'm sorry. I'm so sorry I won't be coming home...*

A clawed hand suddenly grabbed his arm like a vice, and he felt himself being pulled against the quickly subsiding rush of air. Before he could react, he was forcibly stuffed head-first into something that felt like a bag made of metallic cloth. He struggled, his lungs totally out of oxygen now, but the owner of the clawed hands had both strength and leverage.

The Kreelan, whichever it was, finished cramming his body in and sealed his malleable sarcophagus shut.

***

Li'ara-Zhurah was in agony. Her punctured lung had collapsed and one of her legs had shattered when she had been flung across the compartment when the ship's aft section exploded. She realized that more human ships must have come, and had fired on her abandoned ship, not realizing that it was tied up to one of their own.

Yet in defeat, she could still find victory. Even though her warriors had perished, sucked into the vacuum of space, the Empress had graced her one last time, for she had found a spot to anchor herself near the hatch leading from the command compartment. As the air howled into space, taking everything in the compartment with it that was not locked down, the human ship had automatically released what she knew must be survival devices, cloth-like bags that probably had emergency air supplies and more inside them. Even without the ship's lighting, she could see quite well by the starlight that entered the compartment from the torn hull behind them. She had snatched one of the survival devices as it sailed past her, careful not to puncture the device with her talons. Holding it between her thighs, ignoring the pain in her broken leg, she pulled the Messenger from the airflow as he passed her. She had to wait a moment until the air was nearly gone before she could stuff his struggling body into the safety device, hoping it was smart enough to function automatically.

With one final effort, she forced his feet through the opening in the bag, then sealed the flap shut behind him.

***

It's a beachball, Sato thought. *I'm in a beachball.* They were life preservers in space, cheap but effective devices that were stored in every compartment of the ship in case the hull was breached. While they had a long-winded official designation, the spherical survival bags were traditionally called "beachballs" because of their shape.

As soon as the Kreelan sealed him in, a small tank filled the beachball with life-giving air, its shape snapping from a formless bag into a tight sphere. An emergency beacon began to transmit, and a set of small lights came on, providing him with gentle illumination of the ball's interior, along with bright lights on the exterior to help rescuers see it. A section of the ball was transparent, allowing him to see out.

And there, in the beachball's external lights, was the face of the warrior, looking in at him. She placed a hand against the transparency, and he raised his hand to meet hers.

"Why?" he asked. "Why me?"

But there was no answer. She took her hand away and reached around the back of her neck, releasing her collar. She attached it to one of the handholds on the outside of the beachball, and with one final look at him, she let him go.

***

The living metal of Li'ara-Zhurah's collar would normally never have unclasped until she was dead, but the collar knew in its own way that she had reached the end of her Way in this life; all that remained was for the spirits of her and her unborn child to leave the dying vessel that had carried them. She watched as the ship's last remaining breath of air carried the Messenger into space.

May thy way be long and glorious, she thought one last time before closing her eyes.

Willing her body to relax, she focused on the Bloodsong of her child, calming it. For even the unborn had a place in the Afterlife, and together the two of them crossed the infinite bridge from the darkness to the light.

***

Tesh-Dar shuddered, then fell to her knees as she felt Li'ara-Zhurah and her unborn child pass on to join the Ancient Ones.

"No," she whispered, her eyes wide with pain and disbelief. "No!" A warrior's death in battle was something in which her people normally rejoiced, for that was their Way. A part of her understood this, but only a part. The rest of her was overcome with anguish so great that it sent a shock wave through the river of souls that sang the infinite melody of the Bloodsong, echoing her pain throughout the Empire. The young warrior she had come to love like a daughter was gone, along with her unborn child. The child that Tesh-Dar had looked forward to training after she had passed on the honor of the Desh-Ka to Li'ara-Zhurah, in a time that would leave behind the crushing responsibilities of being who and what she was now.

Her mind stared into the future, realizing that it was now empty, her entire existence pointless. She was far older than all but one other among her race, and she knew that Death would come for her, if not today, then soon. It must. And she would have no successor, no legacy. All that she had accomplished, all for which she had suffered, had been for nothing. "My Empress," she whispered in prayer, "please let it not be so."

And yet it was. For even the Empress, with all Her powers, could not bring the dead back to life. Only Keel-Tath, the First Empress, had such power in the times of legend, but She had been lost to Her people for a hundred millenia.

Tesh-Dar, Legend of the Sword and greatest warrior of the Empire, knelt on the field of battle, her heart broken by Fate.

***

The warrior suddenly fell to her knees as if she had been struck a great blow, and stayed there, gasping and clearly in distress.

Sabourin wasted no time. Rushing up behind the warrior, she put the force of her own body behind her attack, plunging her knife up to the handle into the Kreelan's back, just beneath her armor near where a human's kidney might be. The warrior made no reaction at all, as if she had not even noticed.

Furious, Sabourin yanked out the knife, covered now with alien blood, deftly changed to an overhand grip, and plunged the blade through the gap at the top of her chest armor, deep into the Kreelan's flesh where her shoulder met her neck.

As if suddenly coming to life again, the Kreelan roared in pain and rage. She grabbed Sabourin's hand, still clinging to the handle of her knife, and yanked her over her shoulder so hard that Sabourin's arm popped out of its socket. The alien stood fully upright now, holding Sabourin in the air, gasping in pain, their faces mere centimeters apart.

Sabourin spat in the alien's face. "*Nique ta mere!*" she shouted defiantly as she slammed her free fist into the warrior's mouth, then brought a foot up and slammed it into the alien's stomach.

Having managed to get back on his feet, Mills watched helplessly as the huge warrior plunged her free hand into Sabourin's chest, right through her armor and ribs, and ripped out her heart.

***

Tesh-Dar let the dead human's body slip from her grip to fall to the ground. Then she crushed the creature's still-beating heart in her fist before flinging it away. The other warrior, the large male, made to charge at her, but he was tackled to the ground by yet another human.

She ignored them, ignored the warriors who stared at her in shocked disbelief as they felt the depth and intensity of her loss. Ignored the pain from her wounds and the blood that poured from them. She simply stood there, the torn body of the human at her feet, feeling nothing, caring for nothing.

In the Bloodsong, she felt the empathy of the Empress pour into the great river as if a dam had broken, but it washed against Tesh-Dar as a wave might break against a mountain. She sensed it, yet she was not moved by it. She could have blamed the Empress for not saving Li'ara-Zhurah, for certainly that might have been within Her power, but that was not their Way, nor was it entirely true: Li'ara-Zhurah had given herself for a higher purpose, bringing great glory to the Empress and Her Children through her sacrifice. Had it been any other warrior in the Empire, Tesh-Dar's heart would now be singing praise and joy at such a feat as saving not just a Messenger, but a Messenger-warrior, a thing never documented in all the Books of Time.

But there was no joy to be found in Tesh-Dar's heart now, and part of her wondered if there ever would be again.

Instead, she felt the stirrings of a primal rage at Fate, at the humans, at the Universe around her.

***

"No, Mills!" Grishin shouted as the *Mauritania's* engines roared to life. "She's gone!"

Mills struggled against his commander, determined to get to Sabourin's lifeless body. "I'm not going to leave her!"

"If you do not, her sacrifice was for nothing," Grishin yelled at him. "Nothing!"

"Emmanuelle!" Mills cried, reaching for her even as he realized that Grishin had spoken the truth. She had bought him his life, paying for it with her own. "I love you," he whispered as he let Grishin help him to the ship.

The Kreelans made no move to stop them as two other Marines ran down and carried Mills up the massive loading ramp, which slowly closed behind them.

"We've only got one little problem," Faraday said as Grishin made it to the flight deck. "This tub doesn't have any armor. If those Kreelans fire at us..."

"They will soon have other things to worry about," the colonel told him, fighting to keep the emotional exhaustion out of his voice. "There is a Saint Petersburg combat regiment coming right toward them." He had seen a stream of armored vehicles and personnel carriers pour through the spaceport entrance and head across the massive landing field while Mills was sparring with the alien. He suspected the troops had originally been sent to kill him and his Marines. *Even that fool Korolev must have realized by now that the invaders were not human*, he thought. In any case, it did not matter: either the *Mauritania* would make her way to safety, or she would not. Grishin was almost too tired to care anymore which it would be.

He looked at Valentina, then quickly looked away. He had seen enough death for one day, and there was certainly nothing to be gained by looking at the inhumanly empty expression she wore.

"Here we go," Faraday muttered tensely as he manipulated the controls, ordering *Mauritania* to lift off, the commands mysteriously translated by Valentina's human-machine interface.

The ship rumbled and shook, then slowly began to lift. A cheer went up from the hundreds of exhausted Marines on the passenger deck and in the cargo hold as they heard the whine of the ship's landing gear cycle into flight mode.

As *Mauritania* took flight, Grishin caught a last glimpse of the huge alien warrior, standing still as a statue over Sabourin's body even as the approaching Russian troops opened fire on her and the other warriors.

Then they were gone as Faraday flew away from Saint Petersburg toward the surrounding forests, trying to get away from any Kreelan ground defenses before they made their climb toward the relative safety of space.

***

Tesh-Dar was not sure how long she had been standing there. It was as if she had fallen into the deepest level of meditation that she had been taught to achieve in the many cycles she had spent at the Desh-Ka temple, cycles that had passed in but a few hours of time to the rest of the Empire.

She knew that her injuries were severe, and that she should seek the attention of a healer, but she no longer cared. She felt nothing, save a cold fire that had taken root in her now-empty soul.

As if in a dream, she saw the warriors around her fighting, firing their weapons at the enemy. At humans. She could sense the bullets the humans fired streaking past her, others striking her armor and flesh. Some had actually hit her, for the power that let her walk through solid objects and let other objects pass through her was a conscious one. She glanced down at her feet, her gaze passing over the human warrior she had killed, to see a pool of blood, her own, spreading at her feet.

The humans, she suddenly seethed. Within her, a power began to build, one that she had never had cause to use. Until now.

Fully aware now, using the powers she had inherited and trained to use over many long cycles, she turned toward the humans. She saw that many of her warriors were dead, others wounded, as the humans fired their primitive rifles and larger weapons from their war machines. One of the latter had its massive cannon aimed directly at Tesh-Dar. Firing with a great gout of flame and smoke, she instantly slowed the flow of time, examining the dart-like projectile that was pointed at her. Letting time begin to flow again, but slowly, she waited until the projectile was just in front of her before she batted it away as if it were an offending insect. Then she let time speed up to its normal rate, and watched with satisfaction as a number of the humans gaped at what she had just done.

"You have seen nothing yet, animals," she snarled to herself.

The humans began to focus more of their fire on her, and she let the projectiles pass through her. Inside, she felt the surge of power begin to peak, a wave of heat rushing through her body, her soul, like the core of a long-dormant volcano about to erupt.

All around her, the surviving warriors threw themselves to the ground. They did not know what was about to happen, but they could feel Tesh-Dar's power in the Bloodsong rising higher, a tide the power of which none had ever felt since the time of Sura-Ni'khan, Tesh-Dar's predecessor as high priestess of the Desh-Ka.

Tesh-Dar spread her arms wide, fists closed, and opened her soul and her body to the energy that eagerly sought release. Had anyone been close enough, they would have seen electric sparks dancing in her cold eyes. At last judging the moment to be right, she opened her hands, her palms facing the enemy.

The warriors around her cried out in fear and shock as bolts of lightning suddenly exploded from Tesh-Dar's hands, accompanied by a deafening barrage of thunder. Hotter than the surface of a star, the bolts lanced through the humans and their machines, melting, burning, and vaporizing all that they touched. The electric storm danced along the human line, blasting the animals to cinders, leaving nothing behind of the individual warriors but ash and black scars on the landing field. As the bolts touched the war machines, the metal turned white hot and began to flow, baking alive the creatures within who were not already dead from electric shock.

The humans stopped firing at her and tried to flee, but none would escape her wrath. There were nearly a thousand of them that had come to die here, and she disappointed none of them. By the tens, then the hundreds did she kill them. All of them. Using her second sight, she knew that there were other humans on the landing field, some in the ships, some in the buildings near the ships, and others caught out in the open, running between the two.

Her own warriors fled from the field as her lightning struck the ships containing humans, the electrical surge electrocuting those who were not insulated from the hull. Some yet survived, but not for long: her rage now a rampaging beast in her soul, she poured electrical fire into the ships around her, probing to their power cores, overloading them. One by one they blew up, exploding in tremendous fireballs that could be seen by Her warships in orbit. Their fire and debris washed over her, passed through her, and she let the winds of the storm she created lift her from the ground and carry her toward the large human city nearby. She did not need wings to fly, for she could control the fall of her body above the ground, another of the powers she had inherited. As the roiling clouds from the explosions carried her higher and higher, she looked out over the human domain, her second sight sensing the thousands, millions of souls below.

She would kill them. All of them.

TWENTY-FOUR

"Damage report!" Hanson snapped after the fleet emerged on the near side of Saint Petersburg's moon, the same one that Voroshilov's fleet had originally launched their ambush from. *It seems like a lifetime ago*, she told herself wonderingly.

"One moment, commodore," the communications officer told her. Then: "All ships are combat-ready, with none reporting anything more than minor damage."

"We got a lucky break, admiral," she said to Voroshilov's image in her vidcom terminal.

"Yes, commodore," he said. "And I am hoping for another one, although that is perhaps too much to hope for. By my estimate, we destroyed at least six ships outright and damaged eighteen more. The Kreelans will not be happy with us. I hope." He paused, looking at something off-screen. "Ensure your ships are radiating as much as possible, commodore," he told her. "We want the Kreelans to know exactly where we are."

"I don't think you have to worry about that, admiral," she told him. "If they want us, they'll find us."

"New contacts!" her flag tactical officer reported. "Eight new contacts, classify as Confederation heavy cruisers, and twelve destroyers just jumped in!" On the tactical display, a group of yellow icons flashed into existence, then quickly turned blue as the ships were identified by their transponder signatures. "They're right on top of a group of three Kreelan cruisers, commodore..."

Hanson nodded absently as she used her console controls to zoom in on the section of the tactical display that showed the new arrivals. *It's about goddamn time*, she told herself, seeing the *Southampton* and the other ships that should have been with her since the beginning.

"One Kreelan cruiser's been destroyed!" the tactical officer cried.

"That didn't take long," her flag captain murmured.

"It shouldn't," Hanson said quietly. "Southampton has the best gunnery scores in the entire fleet." She often thought that Captain Braverman, the Southampton's captain, could be a real asshole, but no one could argue about his ship's combat capabilities.

A few moments later and that fight was finished. "Scratch a total of four Kreelan ships," the tactical officer reported.

"Commodore," the flag communications officer said, "we have an incoming hail from Southampton."

"Let's have it," Hanson said.

Braverman's image appeared on the secondary display screen on the flag bridge. "Commodore Hanson," he said formally, "my apologies for not making our rendezvous sooner, but we were attacked during our patrol stop at Edinburgh."

Hanson frowned. "With all due respect, Captain Braverman," she said, "where's Rear Admiral Assad?" He had been designated the overall force commander when the mission had been put together, and should be taking over command of the Confederation forces here.

"Dead, ma'am," Braverman said bluntly. "He went down with the Bayern. There were only seven Kreelan ships, but they concentrated their fire on her. She was lost with all hands. As the senior officer, I took command of our task force and got here as quickly as we could."

Assad's death left Hanson in charge. "Very well, captain," she told him, sensing that Braverman was being overly defensive about how long it had taken him to arrive. "Moshe," she said, trying to reassure him, "you and your people did well to get here as quickly as you did. And that was damn fine work on those enemy ships you killed on arrival."

"Thank you, commodore," he said, relaxing slightly. "May I inquire as to the tactical situation, ma'am? I see from your proximity to what I assume are Saint Petersburg ships that things have changed somewhat since the operations plan was drawn up."

Hanson offered him a wry smile. "Indeed they have, captain," she said. "The planetary government still seems to think we're the invaders, but Admiral Voroshilov, who commands the fleet, has—"

"*Multiple contacts, close aboard!*" the flag tactical officer suddenly shouted. "Enemy ships!"

"Execute plan alpha!" Hanson ordered. Then, turning back to Braverman, she said hurriedly, "Captain, we'll try to form up as soon as possible. For now, you're in charge of your ships. Take the fight to the enemy as you see fit, but do not – repeat, *do not* – become decisively engaged or sacrifice your command. Give them hell, Moshe."

"Aye, aye, ma'am," Braverman said gravely before he signed off.

Turning to her vidcom terminal and Voroshilov's seemingly ever-present image, she said, "It looks like your plan worked, admiral."

"*Da*," he replied stonily. "Perhaps too well. Most of their ships emerged inside our safe area." The Saint Petersburg Navy forces on the moon that had launched the mines had created a spherical minefield centered around one of the pre-designated jump points. At the very center was a cleared area where the human ships could jump in without fear of emerging right on top of a mine, which would be fatal to a ship. Their assumption had been that the Kreelans would jump in close by, but not quite *this* close. Some of them had appeared within a hundred meters of one or more of the human ships.

Red icons ringed the blue icons of her and Voroshilov's ships at what was, for space combat, stone-throwing distance. Her ships and those under Voroshilov's command were already firing, but the Kreelans weren't firing back. They were closing in.

"Dammit," Hanson hissed. "Admiral! They're going to try and send boarding parties across to our ships! We've got to maneuver away from them!" Her ships had Marines and effective anti-boarding weapons. Voroshilov's ships did not.

He gaped at her for only a moment, the universal reaction of commanders who had been told that the Kreelans actually boarded starships, and preferred that over simply firing at them. "Scatter your ships, commodore," he ordered. "Lead the enemy through the minefield in as many directions as you can. We shall do the same." Turning to someone off-screen, he barked a rapid series of commands in Russian. "We will rendezvous with you once this is over." He paused. "It has been an honor, Commodore Hanson. *Udachi.* Good luck."

"You, too, sir," she said. Scattering their ships into the minefield was a desperate move. While the mines had been programmed to recognize their ships, that was something that no ship commander who wished to live very long would ever trust. The fact that mines were inherently dangerous to any ships near them, not just their designated targets, added to the adrenaline surge in her system. Turning to the fleet communications officer just as a cloud of tiny icons – warriors in armored vacuum suits – erupted from the enemy ships, she ordered, "All ships: scatter! Repeat, scatter, and prepare to repel boarders!"

Clenching the arms of her combat chair, she kept her eyes riveted to the main display screen as *Constellation* wheeled to a random bearing and surged forward into the minefield and away from the approaching warriors at flank speed, every weapon aboard blasting at the enemy ships that turned to pursue her and her sisters.

***

"Captain," *Southampton's* tactical controller called out. "Sir, you need to see this."

Scowling, Braverman got up from his combat chair and went to stand next to the controller, looking at her console. "What the hell?" he muttered. "Is that right?"

"Yes, sir," she said. "I confirmed it. It's a survival beacon from the *Yura*."

The blue icon on her display flashed, calling for urgent attention. It was well astern now, but was directly along the bearing where they had engaged the Kreelan cruisers.

"Recall the data from the engagement," he ordered.

The woman quickly called up the ship's logs of the sensor and weapons data, starting at their emergence point. In just a few seconds, she had forwarded it to where they had opened fire on the first Kreelan warship.

Braverman studied the information, which now displayed on three separate screens: non-visual sensors, visual data from the ship's external video arrays, and weapon pointing and ammunition expenditure.

"Son of a *bitch!*" he cursed. He had thought something was peculiar about the first target, but there had been no time to think or ask questions. That, however, did nothing to lessen the burden of guilt and responsibility he felt. Now, looking at the data again, he could clearly see what they had really been firing at: the Kreelan warship that was their intended target was grappled to what was clearly a Confederation cruiser. While none of the sensor data he had could tell him which one, other than that it was the newest class that had been launched, he could add two and two. The emergency transponder was coded for the *Yura*. Ichiro Sato's ship. He had never cared for Sato, and thought he had been brought up to command level far too quickly. *But he wasn't the one who fucked up and fired on a friendly ship, now was he?* Braverman told himself harshly. He could have made excuses for himself about the fog of war or the heat of battle, any one of a dozen valid reasons why he fired on that ship. But Braverman would never have tolerated such an excuse from one of his crew, and he certainly would never tolerate it from himself. That simply was not the kind of man he was. As soon as this battle was over, he promised himself, he would report himself to Commodore Hanson and await the inevitable court-martial.

"Are there any enemy vessels behind us?" he asked, clearing the past from his mind so he could focus on the mission at hand.

"Negative, sir," the tactical officer replied. "We have multiple targets rising from orbit to engage us, but nothing astern."

Braverman punched the button to activate the vidcom link at her console. "XO," he barked.

"Yes, sir?" the ship's executive officer immediately responded from the ship's alternate bridge.

"I want you to take the ship's cutter and a team of Marines on a SAR mission," Braverman said. SAR was short for Search And Rescue. "The first ship we fired on wasn't one ship, it was two: a Kreelan and the *Yura*, Sato's command, grappled together. We've got an emergency locator beacon, probably a beachball, that lit up astern. Go recover it."

"On my way, sir," the XO replied and instantly signed off.

On the tactical display, eleven enemy ships were rising to meet him, while the rest of the Kreelan fleet in the system was after Hanson and Voroshilov.

"Come on, then," he growled at the approaching enemy ships. "We'll kick your asses, too."

***

Pan'ne-Sharakh hurried through the antechambers of the Great Palace to the throne room, moving as fast as her ancient legs could carry her. Normally she would have *chuffed* with good humor at her pace, so slow that a sleeping warrior could move faster. There was no humor in her soul now, however. Only pain, fear, and dread.

More than any other, save the Empress, Pan'ne-Sharakh was attuned to the Bloodsong. It was a random gift of birth that she had honed over her many cycles into a tool that had served her uncommon wisdom. And none of the threads of the great song that echoed in her veins had ever been stronger than that of Tesh-Dar. Savage and primal it had always been, for that was at the core of the great priestess's soul. But it had changed with the death of Li'ara-Zhurah, and Pan'ne-Sharakh feared that Tesh-Dar might stray from the Way, that she might fall into the Darkness that consumed those who fell from grace. While she trusted in the might and wisdom of the Empress, she had to be sure. Not only because she loved Tesh-Dar as a daughter, but because she was sure that the Empire's greatest warrior had a greater role to play in the Way that lay ahead of Her Children than merely slaughtering humans. But to play that part, she had to keep her soul.

As Pan'ne-Sharakh entered the throne room, she paused. Even in this hour of need, the sheer grandeur of what her forebears had worked in this place was breathtaking. Located at the apex of a huge pyramid, the largest single construct their race had ever conceived, the throne room stood above the city-world of the Empress Moon. Made of transparent crystal, one could see the stars and the glowing disk of the Homeworld, above. The soaring walls, inlaid with precious jewels and metals, were decorated with tapestries that told of the birth of the Empire and the fall of Keel-Tath, the First Empress. While Her Children were born first for war, they also understood the concept of beauty, and nowhere in all the Empire was there a better example than this.

High above her, on a great dais atop a sweeping staircase of hundreds of steps, was the throne. Even with her aging eyes, she could see the Empress sitting upon it, her white hair shining in the glow of the light that shone from the Homeworld and the sun. It was a trek she had made many times in her life, but the last time had been many cycles ago.

Looking at the steps before her, for once she wished for a return to her youth or a mechanical conveyance to whisk her to her destination. She had not the time to waste, but her body was not what it once was, and fantasizing that she could wish herself to the top would not get her there any faster.

The Empress, of course, knew she was here, and no doubt also knew why. And while she on rare occasion would use Her will to move one of Her Children through space and time, Pan'ne-Sharakh knew that this would not be one of those times. Like everything else that was of the Way, this was a trial, a test of self, a test of her love for the Empress.

Her face creased with grim determination, she shuffled across the enormous fresco-covered floor that led to the great steps, hoping she would survive the climb to the top.

And praying that she would not be too late.

***

Tesh-Dar floated free above the human world, carried now by her will and momentum more than the roiling clouds of smoke and flame that were all that was left of the human ships at the spaceport.

While she still sensed the Bloodsong, it was like a painting devoid of color, lifeless and faded. Powerless over her. She had given in to her rage, embracing it, letting it fill her heart and mind. Her strength, her true strength, was drawn from a core of animal passion that she had always had to rigidly control. But no longer. She knew that her rage, her anger, surged from her through the Bloodsong, overwhelming many of Her Children with its power, but she no longer cared. All she wanted was to kill.

She had seen several human aircraft and a few small ships rise from the surface, trying to escape the onslaught of Her Children: she had destroyed them all with the power that boiled within her soul, blasting them with lightning, tearing them from the sky.

The city lay before her, and her mind's eye knew where every human was. She could sense the beating of their alien hearts, almost as if she could hear them, and was eager to silence every single one. By the powers that had been passed down to her, by the sword or by claw, it did not matter. She was Death, coming for all of them.

Her wounds still bled, and a distant part of her mind realized that she would soon die if she did not seek out a healer. The rest of her, the animal that had taken over her soul, did not care.

As she came lower to the ground, she noticed a group of warriors battling against a mass of humans in a large compound not far from the edge of the city. The place was strange: it was little more than a great open field, surrounded by several sets of fences with strange coiled wire along the top, with watchtowers along the fence line. In the center, next to a large landing pad strewn with destroyed aircraft, stood a squat, ugly structure of concrete. Not large enough in itself to house anything substantial, her second sight told her the truth: like a burrowing *kailekh*, a rare serpent on the Homeworld, the thing above ground was merely a portal to tunnels the humans had dug beneath the ground.

She paused, considering. The fraction of her mind that remained rational managed to convince her animal consciousness that she would likely bleed to death before she could destroy the inhabitants of the city. She decided to expend her remaining wrath on these humans.

Landing gracefully ahead of the young warriors who surrounded the place, all of whom hugged the ground in fear of her, she marched toward the line of humans behind their defensive barriers. They fired their weapons at her, and she snarled as their bullets and rockets passed through her, as if she were no more than shadow and smoke.

Drawing her sword, she charged their line. With a deafening howl of rage she slaughtered the humans at a pace almost too fast for her terrified sisters to see. It was a gruesome spectacle that none of them had ever seen, or would ever see again.

When it was over, the human defensive positions were awash with blood. Tesh-Dar herself was painted in crimson, and the coppery smell was lodged so deeply in her senses that she doubted she would ever be rid of it. Yet she was not finished.

Trembling now, her great body on the verge of succumbing to her wounds and the strain for using her powers so intensely, she moved toward the mound of concrete. A short tunnel led her to a massive metal blast door that, she knew from her second sight, was nearly as thick as she was tall.

Baring her fangs in contempt, she brought up her sword, holding it ready as she stepped forward into the door, her body merging with the metal as she crossed through it toward the other side.

***

Constellation's hull shook as her main batteries fired off yet another salvo at a nearby target that had already been severely damaged by a mine. The Kreelan warships that had jumped into the minefield after them had not fired on the human ships at first, apparently hoping that their boarding parties would be successful in attacking their targets. Fortunately, Voroshilov had accepted Commodore Hanson at her word when she warned him about boarding attacks, and the Saint Petersburg ships joined their Confederation counterparts in diving into the minefield before the Kreelans could close the range.

Looking at the tactical display, Hanson smiled grimly at their conundrum, temporary though it might be: the Kreelan ships either had to pause and pick up their warriors, which would put them at a severe tactical disadvantage, or pursue the human ships with only a skeleton crew aboard, which also worked in the humans' favor.

For once, she knew, the Kreelans had made a major tactical blunder: some ships stopped to recover their warriors, and others didn't. It was as if they had suddenly become confused or preoccupied with something she could not even guess at.

Whatever works, she thought as the Kreelan ship that was *Constellation's* target exploded. A few seconds later she could hear the debris rattling against her flagship's hull like metal rain.

"I'm not sure I believe this," her flag captain said tensely.

"We're clobbering them," she said, hoping the words would not jinx the battle. The tactical display, however, told the story: between the mines, her ships, and Voroshilov's fleet, the Kreelans were being pounded. They had already lost twenty ships with as many more damaged, for the price of only three destroyers and two cruisers of what she had come to think of as the Combined Fleet.

"Captain Braverman reports that he's engaging enemy ships coming up from Saint Petersburg orbit," the flag tactical officer told her.

"Show me," she ordered, and a secondary display lit up with a depiction of Braverman's fight. The Kreelans had a slight advantage in tonnage – all of their eleven ships were heavy cruisers, whereas Braverman had only seven pre-war cruisers and ten destroyers – but her money was on Braverman.

She watched as he split his destroyer escort into a ring forward of the conical formation of his cruisers, pointed right at the center of the enemy formation. The cruisers began to fire their main batteries on a continuous cycle, and at just the right moment the destroyers ripple-fired their torpedoes so they would reach the Kreelan formation at the same time as the first wave of shells from the cruisers. It was a masterful display of precision gunnery.

It was a massacre. The Kreelan formation's point defense weapons were saturated with far too many targets at once, the rain of shells allowing more than half of the far more powerful torpedoes to get through to their targets. In less than a minute, all eleven Kreelan ships had either been totally destroyed or were nothing more than flaming hulks that were finished off by the destroyers.

A cheer went up among her staff as *Constellation* fired her own salute, finishing off yet another Kreelan ship.

"Damn," her flag captain said.

"I wish every engagement could be like that," Hanson told him, opening a channel to Braverman. "Captain Braverman," she said as his image appeared in her vidcom terminal, "that was absolutely superb. My compliments to your captains and crews."

"Thank you, ma'am," he told her. "I'll do that. And commodore..." He paused, and Hanson prepared herself for bad news. "Commodore, I've sent a cutter to our emergence point where we destroyed several Kreelan ships. I regret to inform you that..." He grimaced before going on, "...that I believe *Yura* was grappled to one of them, and we destroyed her. I'll submit myself for court-martial as soon as conditions permit."

Hanson sat up in her chair amid the thunder of another salvo fired from Constellation. "What? Captain, *Yura* was destroyed by a russian nuke when we first arrived," she told him. "What you fired on was nothing more than a lifeless hulk. In fact, if a Kreelan warship was grappled to her, I would have ordered you to destroy her anyway, to keep her from falling into enemy hands." She paused to let those words sink in. "There will be no court-martial, captain."

"That's...that's good to know, ma'am," he said, an expression of relief washing over his face. "But she wasn't a completely lifeless hulk: there was at least one survivor. We picked up an emergency transponder beacon, we think from a beachball, and I sent the ship's cutter to retrieve whoever it is."

Hanson thought of the radiation the ship must have received, what it must have done to the crew. She doubted the cutter would find anyone alive. "Very well, captain," she said. "Let me know immediately about any survivors. And now that you've cleared out the enemy ships from orbit, how would you like to come up here and join our little party in the minefield?"

"With pleasure, commodore," he answered with a cold smile.

***

Pan'ne-Sharakh was in agony by the time she reached her designated place on the great stairway, the fourth step from the throne. She paused for a moment, turning her mind inward to calm her racing heart and burning lungs. Even more than the warriors, the clawless ones such as she were trained in deep meditation techniques, for control of their minds was essential to carrying out the tasks assigned to their caste, and control of the mind extended to control of the body. It would not keep her ancient muscles from being terribly sore come the morning, but the task at hand made such concerns nothing more than trivialities.

"Pan'ne-Sharakh," the Empress called to her softly.

She opened her eyes to see her sovereign standing on the step above her. Kneeling down in reverence, saluting just as did the warriors, she said, "My Empress, to thee I come for Tesh-Dar's sake."

"This I know, my child," She said. "I have tried to reach out to her, but she does not hear Me." Her voice lowered. "I fear forcing My will upon her in her present state, for if she raised her hand against Me, I would have no choice but to cast her away her soul."

The mere thought sent a tremor of fear through Pan'ne-Sharakh. The Empress loved and commanded both the living and the dead. Those who fell from Her grace and were cast into Darkness lived in eternal agony, lost to Her love and light. Tesh-Dar could not be allowed to suffer such a fate.

The Empress took Pan'ne-Sharak's hands. "Together, perhaps," She said, "we may bring her back to the Way. She is too important to the future of the Empire to risk her falling into Darkness. I cannot see into the future, yet I know to the depths of My soul that she yet has a great role to play in what time our race has left. But we have not much time: powerful as she is, her body, badly wounded, grows weaker by the moment."

"Then let us begin, my Empress," Pan'ne-Sharakh said, firmly clasping her hands, intent on bringing home the daughter of her heart.

TWENTY-FIVE

"Okay," Faraday said nervously, glancing back at Valentina, who still lay comatose in the navigator's chair, "this is where it might get interesting." He had flown *Mauritania* away from the spaceport, staying as low as he dared in hopes of avoiding any Kreelan forces that might be lurking in the area before climbing toward orbit. No one had fired on them, but they had seen the destruction of the ships back at the spaceport through the electronic eyes of the ship's sensors, and he had no wish to have his ship experience a similar fate. He had gotten intermittent locks on ships in orbit, but the Mauritania did not have military grade tactical sensors, and could tell him nothing about whether they were enemy or friendly. "It's time to head upstairs."

"Take us up, Faraday," Grishin told him, now sitting in the copilot's seat. He avoided looking at Valentina: the sight of her gave him what he knew Mills would have called the heebie-jeebies. The Marines were settled in as well as they could be, with the wounded in the passenger cabins and the rest in the otherwise empty main cargo hold. He hadn't given Mills any choice about taking over the job of assisting Major Justin in getting things organized: having no idea of where they might wind up at the end of this lunatic caper, Grishin wanted his Marines ready to fight again if need be. What was left of the brigade had to be reorganized, weapons and ammunition redistributed, and the available food and water inventoried. The *Mauritania* could carry them through space, but its food processing capability was far too small to support all of his people. They had to find a refuge, and without any star charts to plot hyperspace jumps – even assuming that Valentina could stand such a strain – there was really only one option: Riga.

Looking out the flight deck's massive windscreen, Grishin saw the horizon fall away as Faraday brought the ship's nose up, climbing toward the clouds.

After only a few seconds, the ship's sensors displayed two groups of ships in near space above them, heading directly toward one another.

"I don't like the looks of this," Faraday muttered as he watched the game play out between the two sets of amber icons on the screen.

Suddenly the ships of one group, the one higher in space, began to change to blue, with ship data displayed next to each one.

"Hot damn!" Faraday cried. "Those are ours!"

He and Grishin stared as the two groups closed the range, gasping in surprise as the yellow icons representing the eleven Kreelan ships were wiped out.

"Holy shit," Faraday said, looking at the colonel. "We certainly kicked their asses that time."

"Indeed," Grishin said, impressed. "Can you raise them on vidcom?"

"Should be able to," Faraday said. "They should still be monitoring the merchant GUARD frequency." He glanced around the ship's console, finally finding the communications controls. Putting on the headset, he tapped in the frequency he wanted and began calling. "Any Confederation vessel, this is the merchant vessel *Mauritania*, please respond." He paused, waiting.

He was just about to repeat his call when a clipped voice answered. "*Mauritania*, this is CNS *Southampton*. You are in an active combat zone. Clear this area immediately."

"Let me talk to them," Grishin said, and Faraday handed him a headset. "*Southampton*, this is Colonel Grishin, Confederation Marines. I would like to speak to your commanding officer, please."

There was a pause before another voice came on. "This is Captain Braverman, commanding *Southampton*," a male voice said. "I take it that you're aboard the merchant vessel rising toward our formation?"

"Yes, captain," Grishin replied. "All of our assault boats were destroyed by the Russians, and then the Kreelans tried to finish the job. We had to...borrow an impounded ship to get into space. Unfortunately, we do not have enough provisions aboard to make a hyperlight jump, and our navigation system is, shall we say," he looked at Valentina's limp form, "not fully functional. I would be greatly obliged if you could provide an escort to guide us to Riga."

"I appreciate your situation, colonel," Braverman said grimly, "but I can't detach any of my ships right now to provide an escort. We're moving at flank speed to join Commodore Hanson near Saint Petersburg's moon to see if we can finish off the Kreelan fleet here."

"I understand that, captain," Grishin said, "but I have five hundred and seventy-three men and women aboard. Over one hundred of them are seriously injured. We have no star charts or navigation aids aboard; we are flying blind." While Riga was in the same system, the ship's sensors were not designed for survey work: finding a planet in a star system was much easier said than done.

Aboard *Southampton*, Braverman paused, scowling. He could not in good conscience leave Grishin and his people to fend for themselves, but the Kreelans – while taking a serious beating at the hands of Hanson and Voroshilov – were far from finished. He simply could not part with even a single destroyer.

Then the solution struck him. "Colonel," he said, "we detached a cutter a short while ago on a SAR mission. I'll order them to rendezvous with you and guide you to Riga. I'm sorry, but that's the best I can do right now."

"Thank you, captain," Grishin said, relieved, "that would be most appreciated."

"I'll give the orders immediately," Braverman told him. "Continue to climb toward our formation and stay on this vector. Your instruments should pick up the cutter soon."

"Understood, and thank you. Grishin, out." Taking off the headset, Grishin sat back in his seat, thanking God that Braverman had been able to help them. He had not relished the thought of Mauritania wandering about the system looking for Riga. At least fifteen of his Marines were wounded badly enough that they would die in a day, maybe less, if they did not receive proper medical attention. The ship's autodoc had helped stabilize them, but that was all it could do. And for those with burn injuries, it could do little more than temporarily deaden the pain.

As Braverman's ships sailed away at top speed, Faraday and Grishin kept their eyes glued to the navigation console, looking for the promised cutter.

***

Ichiro Sato looked through the transparent pane of the cramped survival beachball that imprisoned him, staring at the stars and the world of Saint Petersburg as he slowly tumbled through space, utterly and completely alone. More than once he had reached for the tab that would open the beachball and vent the air it contained into space. The only thing that stayed his hand was the thought of Steph. Yet even that, as much as he loved her, was only barely enough.

His emotions, were a confused kaleidoscope of guilt, anguish, and helpless rage. Twice, now, he had been the sole survivor of a ship aboard which he served. The first time, when humans had first encountered the Kreelans, the aliens had slaughtered his fellow crewmen and sent him, alone, back to Earth to bring word of the coming war. This time, fellow humans had killed his ship and his crew, but the "enemy" – the Kreelans – had saved his life, sacrificing themselves, an entire ship and its crew, for him.

He thought, too, of the warrior who had saved him as he was being swept from the *Yura's* shattered bridge and into space, saw her hand against the beachball, feeling his own pressed up against it as he looked into her eyes. He wept for her as he watched the wreckage containing her body spin away into the darkness, thanking and cursing her in the same breath. He had endured a crushing sense of survivor's guilt after the Kreelans had sent him back to Earth after killing the rest of the crew of the *Aurora*, but that had been nothing compared to this. Then, he had only been a midshipman, the youngest member of the crew, on his first interstellar mission. This time, *Yura* had been *his* ship, *his* command. He had been responsible for her and every man and woman aboard, and he felt as if he had failed them all. As much as he wanted to see Steph again, he would have gladly traded the his life and the miracle of Kreelan healing for any one of his crew, Bogdanova most of all. Her loss, more than any other single person aboard, tore at his heart. The part of his mind that clung to logic knew that he had done the best he could, had done his duty, and that fate and the enemy – humans and Kreelans alike – had dictated the rest. Yet that was little consolation in light of a destroyed ship and a dead crew.

As he stared into the void, he caught glimpses of bright flashes, orange and crimson against the black of space near the limb of Saint Petersburg's moon. *No doubt they're Kreelan warships*, he thought gloomily, *hammering our own into scrap.*

He let such dark thoughts take him as the fireworks continued, then intensified into a non-stop chain of brilliant, if distant, flashes. There was no way for him to know who might be winning, human (Confederation or Russian) or Kreelan, but he felt a sudden flush of pride. Even if the human fleet was losing, it was obviously fighting back hard. That thought penetrated to the heart of the warrior that lay inside of him. He couldn't help them, but the least he could do, he realized, was to cheer them on, even if his only audience was himself.

"Come on," he growled angrily, clenching his fists as he leaned forward, wishing the beachball would stop spinning so he could see better. "*Fight, damn you!*" he shouted as a pair of explosions, larger than the others, lit the dark side of Saint Petersburg's moon.

And that was how the crew of *Southampton's* cutter found him, yelling at the top of his lungs as if he were watching the game-deciding play of an Army-Navy game, damning the enemy and cheering for his own kind.

***

Colonel Yuri Rusov, the commander of the bunker's internal security detachment, stared in unabashed awe and disbelief as the alien warrior systematically killed every one of the troops defending the bunker's entrance on the surface. He had never seen anyone or anything move as fast as she had, her sword nothing more than a brilliant disk as it cut down the men outside. Their weapons had no effect on her at all, as if they were nothing more than movie props that gave one the impression of being lethal, but that only produced a loud bang and a satisfying flash.

When she was finished with the men outside, she approached the blast door at the entrance, and Rusov breathed a sigh of relief. *She cannot get through that with her sword*, he thought. He watched the security monitor as she looked at the door. Then, with barely a pause, she stepped into it, her body disappearing into the two-meter thick metal.

"*Tvoyu mat'!*" one of the men on the security monitoring team choked, his eyes wide with disbelief. "That is impossible!"

"Get the reserve company to the main entrance!" the colonel snapped. "And sound the intrusion alarm!"

One of the other controllers flipped open a clear plastic cover over a large red button and slammed down on it with his fist. Throughout the massive underground complex, a klaxon began to bleat it's warning. Another controller spoke urgently into his headset, ordering the commander of the reserve company of troops to double-time to the entrance.

"What is going on?"

Rusov turned to find Marshal Antonov standing at the threshold of the darkened security room, glaring at him.

"Comrade marshal," Rusov reported quickly, "I believe an alien has somehow penetrated the facility."

"Don't be ridiculous, colonel," Antonov told him, stepping toward the large bank of security monitors. "That door and the entrance tunnel can hold against a nuclear strike. What did the alien do, walk right through it?"

"Yes, sir," Rusov answered, holding his ground, "she did." He gestured for one of his men to play back the video of the alien stepping into the door, her body eerily disappearing into the thick steel, as if she had stepped through a wall of liquid.

Antonov said, "It is a trick, comrade colonel. *Maskirovka.* This..." he gestured at the video monitor, "this is a charade."

The both turned suddenly as they heard a sound like a string of firecrackers going off, but heavily muffled by distance and many tons of reinforced concrete. Gunfire.

"Sir!" one of the controllers cried, as he quickly changed to a different video feed. "The guard detachment at the main door reports they are under attack!"

The camera view switched just in time to see the alien warrior finishing off the last of the eight men assigned to guard the inside of the blast door. She then turned and moved on down the massive entrance tunnel, her sword at the ready.

"The reserve company is moving to block her," Rusov informed Antonov, "although I doubt they will fare no better than the troops outside."

"I will not tolerate defeatism, colonel," Antonov warned sharply.

"It is not defeatism, comrade marshal," Rusov told him, looking him squarely in the eyes. "It is the simple truth." He played back part of the battle on the surface, again watching as the alien butchered his men.

Antonov visibly paled. "You must stop that creature, colonel," he ordered. "Use every man you have, including yourself."

"Yes, sir," Rusov said quietly, trying to keep the resignation out of his voice. He had faced his share of danger during his service in the military, and had even been in situations where he had faced the possibility of dying. But this was the first time that he knew with complete and utter certainty that he would not survive. "Men, get your weapons and come with me," he told the controllers as he headed for the door, drawing his sidearm from its holster.

They quickly followed him out, each of them taking a last fearful glance at the alien apparition on the security monitors as it tracked her movements.

***

Tesh-Dar was breathing heavily now, her heart racing to keep enough blood pumping through her system. She was still bleeding heavily from the wounds the human warrior had given her at the spaceport, but her own blood would have been indistinguishable from that of the humans she had killed, covering her from head to toe in wet crimson. Her muscles burned, weakened to the point where her entire body was vibrating like a taut string that was being repeatedly plucked.

Inside the human hive, she continued to slaughter the soulless creatures, but the passionate fire to kill that had burned so brightly only a brief time before was guttering, dying. As was she. Yet this last thing – killing the humans here in this underground warren – would she accomplish before her life ended. The rest she had killed in murderous rage; these she killed to honor the Empress and, in a small way, pay for her lack of obedience. A sliver of her mind, the rational part that was slowly reasserting its dominance as she grew weaker, was cloaked in the fearful certainty that her soul would rot in the Darkness for all eternity: she had stepped from the Way, essentially defying Her will and falling from grace.

More of the human warriors charged at her, a large group this time, and she began to kill them, but not as before, when the fire in her was at its peak. Then she had been a raging *genoth*, a great dragon and the most-feared creature that dwelled on the Homeworld. Now, her powers drained, she was only an extraordinarily powerful warrior. Even her ability to pass through objects, and let objects pass through her, was waning. Their bullets stung as they passed through her, and soon they would pierce flesh and shatter bone.

Baring her fangs in rage, at herself as much as the humans, she swept her sword through their ranks. They closed with her, throwing themselves upon her, until her sword was useless. Dropping the weapon, she resorted to the weapons she had been born with, and reached for them with her talons.

***

Voroshilov stared, disbelieving, at the vidcom and its projection of Chairman Korolev's panicked image. "Comrade chairman," he said, "what you ask is impossible. Our ships – all of them – are engaged in battle near lunar orbit. Even if I could detach a destroyer and with a microjump closer to you, it could not possibly reach you–"

"Stop making excuses, comrade admiral," Korolev hissed at him. "*You* will come here, right now, or you will face the most severe repercussions! We have been monitoring your communications, even as you ignored our calls, and know that you have been in collusion with the Confederation enemy that even now comes to kill us!" He paused in his tirade, before suddenly shouting, "*I will have your family shot!*"

Voroshilov turned away to look at the tactical display, an uncharacteristically stony expression on his face. There were very few red icons left now, the combined human fleet and the minefield having done their work. He was deeply surprised that the enemy ships chose to stay and fight to the death, rather than jump to safety, where they could live to fight another day. It was as if they simply did not care, or perhaps is was a point of honor that they fight to the bitter end.

A point of honor, he thought coldly, *was something that the likes of Korolev would never understand.*

Turning back to his so-called superior, he said quietly under his flagship's still-thundering guns, "Your threat is an empty one, comrade chairman. As I am sure you and that *chekist* in charge of the secret police know, my wife and children are on Riga, visiting her brother's family. I doubt that President Roze will let any harm come to her." Glaring at Korolev, he told him, "The Confederation commander has some ships that are not yet engaged with the enemy. I will ask that she send one to your aid, with the understanding that if you fire on them, they should fire back with everything they have and leave you to rot. If you survive, you can have me shot, should you wish. Yet even you should see now that your time is over." He paused, a scowl deeply etched on his face. "I do this not because you threaten me, comrade, but because saving some of our planetary leadership may allow us to better repel the many aliens that now roam free on our world. Remember that."

Korolev, his face contorted in cold rage, was just opening his mouth to speak when someone off-camera screamed, followed by a sudden eruption of gunfire close by. The chairman looked up at what was happening, then turned back to the vidcom, his face a mask of terror. "The alien is here!" he screamed.

Voroshilov watched silently as the last few seconds of Korolev's life played out before him.

***

Korolev turned away from his argument with Voroshilov as someone screamed. He turned to see the giant alien drop what was left of one of the communications technicians, blood pouring from his throat where she had ripped it out with her huge claws. She had not come through the door, which was locked and guarded: she had come right through one of the reinforced concrete walls!

Standing behind Korolev, who was now frozen with fear in front of the vidcom terminal, Marshal Antonov calmly drew his sidearm and fired at the alien, which focused her attention on him. Every round hit her, but she simply shrugged them off and kept coming.

Terrified, Korolev turned back to the vidcom and Voroshilov, screaming, "The alien is here!"

***

Tesh-Dar was running now on nothing more than force of will. She had finally dug her way out of the mass of humans who had tried to overwhelm her, stabbing and slashing them to death with her talons, biting them with her fangs, ignoring the revolting taste of their blood.

This room, the last in this warren that she was able to find with her rapidly failing mind's eye that contained living humans, was her last challenge. She knew the door was guarded, so she chose to penetrate the wall. She almost did not make it: the power within her that made such things possible was now little more than a flickering spark. She was halfway through the thick wall when she nearly lost control. Had that happened, she would have been entombed there, dead, the molecules of her body interspersed with that of the concrete.

Yet with one last agonizing push, she emerged into a large room, brightly lit with many screens and consoles, with a small number of humans. The closest to her was the first to die as she snatched the surprised human from his chair and slashed his throat before tossing him aside.

Another drew a gun and began shooting at her while the handful of others panicked. For the first time, her powers failed completely and the bullets slammed into her. Slowed and deformed by the strength of her armor, they still had enough energy to penetrate her skin and rend her flesh. She ignored the pain as bullet after bullet found its mark in her chest and abdomen, struggling forward the last few lengths to reach the human shooting at her.

With a roar of fury, she grabbed his gun hand as he was trying to reload and ferociously yanked it up and back toward her, tearing the arm from its socket. She slammed her other fist with all her remaining might into the human's skull, crushing it and driving his body to the floor.

The human next to him, who might have been able to get away had he not clearly been paralyzed with fear, babbled at her in one of the incomprehensible human tongues. She stood there for a moment, observing with disgust what she thought must be a form of supplication, perhaps begging for mercy.

"No mercy shall you be shown, animal," she hissed before driving the talons of her right hand into the creature's rib cage, piercing its heart. She hurled the still-writhing body against one of the nearby control consoles. She was rewarded with a cascade of sparks as his body smashed into the console, shorting out the circuits within and starting a fire that began to blaze fiercely.

Such is my funeral pyre, she thought sadly, knowing that it was the closest to the death ritual she would receive now. When her spirit passed from her body into the Darkness, there would be no one to take her collar. She felt the love of the Empress crashing upon her through the Bloodsong, but Tesh-Dar turned away from Her call, shame filling her heart for having lost sight of the Way, of losing control of her rage after the death of Li'ara-Zhurah. She could not bear the thought of again facing her sovereign.

Taking one last look around the room, now quickly filling with smoke and flames, she saw that the remaining handful of humans had escaped. *No matter,* she thought. *It is done.* She wanted now only to die, for her life to be finished.

As her eyes closed and she collapsed to the floor, Tesh-Dar opened her spirit to the cold of the Darkness that she knew awaited her.

***

"*Now,*" the Empress whispered.

Pan'ne-Sharakh held her eyes firmly closed. This was not the first time she had been whisked across the stars by Her will, but it was a mode of transport that she had never been entirely comfortable with. She much preferred the feel of her sandaled feet against the earth.

She sensed infinite cold and dark around her for an instant that seemed to stretch forever, yet was only a tiny stitch in the fabric of time. She felt the air change around her, and when she breathed in her sensitive nose was assaulted with the vileness of smoke from burning plastics and metal, intermixed with the unmistakable scent of blood, Kreelan and – she surmised – human.

Opening her eyes, she saw that Tesh-Dar lay deathly still upon the cold floor, her body laying in a pool of blood that glittered with reflections of the flames that roared from the strange bank of devices next to her.

Rushing to her side, Pan'ne-Sharakh knelt beside her. She was aghast at the damage that had been done to Tesh-Dar's body, the many holes piercing her armor and her flesh. Pan'ne-Sharakh still sensed Tesh-Dar's Bloodsong, but it was fading quickly. Lifting the great priestess's head, holding it to her breast, Tesh-Dar opened her eyes. Pan'ne-Sharakh could clearly see the dark streaks of the mourning marks under Tesh-Dar's eyes in the flickering light of the flames.

"Pan'ne-Sharakh," the priestess whispered, her voice nearly lost to the crackling of the fire burning around them. "This is...no place for you, ancient one."

"I come in Her name," Pan'ne-Sharakh said urgently in her ancient dialect of the Old Tongue, lovingly stroking Tesh-Dar's battered and blood-smeared face, "for She feared forcing you to come home, that you would spite Her and truly fall from grace. Neither of us could let that happen, child. Too important are you."

Tesh-Dar groaned, both in physical and spiritual agony. "I have already fallen from Her grace...I am...lost."

"No, child," the ancient armorer said, gazing deep into Tesh-Dar's eyes. "Do you believe that the Empress would forsake you, among all of Her children? That She would send me here to you if She did not want you to return home? There will be penance for what you have done, priestess of the Desh-Ka, but only to prepare you for the future. For on you shall our race someday depend, Tesh-Dar."

Tesh-Dar said nothing, her face twisted in indecision and pain as she fought for breath, a trickle of blood spilling from her mouth from her pierced lungs.

"Let Her take us home," Pan'ne-Sharakh begged, taking one of Tesh-Dar's hands. "I will not leave you here, alone to die."

"Will She forgive me?" Tesh-Dar whispered.

"She has already forgiven you, child," Pan'ne-Sharakh said. The fire was now so hot that it was scorching her ancient skin, but she would not move from Tesh-Dar's side, even if the flames took her and she burned alive. "Surrender to Her love."

Tesh-Dar finally nodded, opening her spirit to the power of the Bloodsong.

Her heart stopped beating just as the two of them disappeared in a swirl of smoke and flame as the Empress brought them home.

EPILOGUE

Former Commander, now Captain, Ichiro Sato came down the gangway of the CNS *Oktyabr'skaya Revolyutsiya* where she had tied up to Africa Station in Earth orbit. Six months had passed since he had taken *Yura* to Saint Petersburg, months in which a great deal had happened.

With the decapitation of the planet's government, Voroshilov had taken command of the Russian military forces in an effort to exterminate the tens of thousands of Kreelans who had been seeded across Saint Petersburg by the alien invasion force. He was, however, unwilling to accept the role of leader of the government. "I was a Party man because I had to be to serve as I wished in the military," he had explained to Commodore – now promoted to rear admiral – Hanson after the last Kreelan ships in the initial attack had been destroyed. "I am not suited for it. But I know someone who may have some interest in the job, and would certainly be well qualified."

That is how his brother-in-law, Valdis Roze, President of Riga, found himself elevated from leading a planet struggling for political survival, to leading a star system that was immediately accepted into the Confederation under a hastily drawn-up charter as the Pan-Slavic Alliance. Riga, formerly Saint Petersburg's dumping ground, suddenly became both a safe haven for Russian refugees fleeing their parent world, and a base for the Confederation's efforts to eradicate the Kreelans. Roze had managed to masterfully set the formerly at-odds populations working together toward a common goal: survival.

The long-term outlook for Saint Petersburg was uncertain. Despite the generous terms of the Confederation charter for supporting member worlds with training, weapons, and equipment, the bureaucracies and industries to support those terms were still being put into place. For now, aside from shipments of smaller weapons and light equipment, of which there were plenty in stock and more quickly made, the Russians and Rigans in the system largely had to make do with what they had. This was the only silver lining to Korolev's despotic rule: Saint Petersburg had built and stockpiled a tremendous quantity of weapons over the years. These were now being put to good use.

While the Confederation fleet, which now incorporated Voroshilov's forces, had retained control of the system, the Kreelans continued to make what Sato considered probing attacks. Unlike the attack on Keran, where they came and quickly subdued the system and eliminated the human populace in a matter of months, with Saint Petersburg they seemed content to play cat and mouse. Kreelan squadrons would appear in the system, drop more warriors to the surface, and then brawl with the human ships. But each attack seemed to be slightly stronger, and Sato wondered if there would come a tipping point when the Kreelans would finally put enough into their attacks to drive the human fleet out.

A further oddity was that they had left Riga completely alone. Not a single Kreelan ship had ventured there. It was as if they wanted to give the humans a safe base to operate from, and were using Saint Petersburg as the designated battleground.

"It's nothing more than a gigantic arena where they can fight us," he had told Hanson before he left the system to return to Earth. It was like a massively upscaled version of the arena aboard the first Kreelan ship humanity encountered, where Sato's shipmates from the *Aurora* had died.

They had received news from courier ships that six other systems had been attacked in a similar fashion, although none of them had suffered the spectacular damage that had been inflicted on Saint Petersburg's primary spaceport. There had also been no reports of any incredible feats by the Kreelans like the tale told by Voroshilov about Korolev's death. The senior officers and civilian leadership listened to him intently, but quietly dismissed what they heard. It was simply too fantastic.

On Riga, Sato had not had any time to get depressed over the loss of *Yura*. With the blessing of Admiral Phillip Tiernan, Chief of Naval Staff, Hanson had promoted Sato to captain, and Voroshilov had promptly given him a ship to command: the *Oktyabr'skaya Revolyutsiya (October Revolution)*. Voroshilov had been forced to remove a number of ship captains who were

Party hard-liners and had refused to accept the "new order" after Korolev's death. That had left a number of slots open with too few officers to fill them. *October Revolution's* captain was both highly competent and loyal to his people above the Party, and Voroshilov had promoted him to take a squadron command. The ship needed a new captain, and Vorishilov had felt that Sato would be an excellent choice.

"You commanded your ship, *Yura*, bravely against my fleet," Voroshilov had told him, "and your commodore speaks very highly of you. I cannot bring back your dead, but I can give you a new ship to command."

Sato had misgivings about the crew accepting him, but as it turned out, he need not have worried. Despite the information control exerted by Korolev's government, many Russians – and virtually every Rigan – knew of him as the only survivor from first contact with the Kreelans. His handling of *Yura* during the battle that led to her destruction had also earned the Saint Petersburg Navy's respect. The worst he had to contend with was learning as much Russian as quickly as he could.

He still felt the ghosts of his dead shipmates with him, especially Bogdanova, but he had never spiraled into depression as he had feared he would. "You can rest when you're dead, Sato," Hanson had told him once. "Until then, I've got too much work for you to do."

Sato smiled at the memory. He liked Hanson.

Pushing those thoughts aside, he began to quicken his pace down the gangway. He had brought his ship here for a weapons upgrade, but that would be mostly in the hands of the shipyards, and his XO had shooed him off the ship. He had free time now, at least for a while.

At the threshold there was a gaggle of civilians, mostly reporters, and military personnel waiting to catch a glimpse of him. But there was only one he cared about. Standing there in the red dress she had been wearing when he had first met her was Steph, his wife. While they had been in touch as often as possible, President McKenna had been keeping her press secretary – Steph – as busy as Hanson had been keeping him, and Steph hadn't been able to come see him for those long months.

But that was all in the past now. Running to him, her face streaked with tears of joy, she leaped into his arms. As he twirled her around, his own heart rejoicing in the feel of her warm body against him, her scent, in the sound of her tearful laughter, their lips met in a passionate kiss.

Captain Ichiro Sato was finally home.

***

Dmitri and Ludmilla Sikorsky were living a life that they could not even have dreamed of on Saint Petersburg. For the service that Dmitri, in particular, had rendered to the Confederation, the Confederation Intelligence Service had offered them a chance at a new life. They owned a small horse farm in what had once been the state of Virginia, with Ludmilla working from their new home as a consultant for relations with the Pan-Slavic Alliance, while Dmitri tended the farm. It had been a bittersweet decision for the Sikorskys: on the one hand, both of them were patriots, and wanted to do what they could to help Saint Petersburg repel the alien invaders. On the other hand was a very personal consideration for both of them: Valentina.

After Faraday had landed *Mauritania* on Riga, they had disconnected her from the ship's computer interface, but she had never regained consciousness. Her eyes and mouth had closed, as if she were asleep, but that was all. The Rigans had taken her to a local hospital, but before any doctors could evaluate her, President Roze himself had called and, obviously with great unwillingness, told them she was to be given what she needed for her body to stay alive, but otherwise was not to be examined or treated.

Dmitri had been furious, but there was nothing any of them could do. A day later, a man named Robert Torvald came for her, giving orders to the hospital staff that they were to prepare for transport back to Earth aboard a special courier ship.

"What is to become of her?" Dmitri, standing over her like a sentinel, asked him pointedly.

"That, Mr. Sikorsky," Torvald said with cold detachment, "is none of your business. She is a Confederation Intelligence Service asset, and that's all you need to know."

Unlike Valentina, Torvald had never been a special operative, only a field handler, and had no special self-defense training. He was totally unprepared for Dmitri's work-hardened fist slamming into his mouth, followed by a powerful uppercut that lifted Torvald from the ground and slammed him against the wall of Valentina's hospital room.

"Listen, *svoloch'*," Dmitri growled as he grabbed Torvald by the neck and hauled him up from the floor, slamming him against the wall again as the hospital staff looked on in stunned silence. "She is not a machine! She did all she was sent to do, saved all of our lives, and was shot for her trouble. Then she suffered the horror of whatever that thing is that you put in her head to get us here. And you treat her – and us – like we are cattle? I do not know or care who you are, but if you want to walk out of this room alive, you will do as I tell you."

"I think you might want to seriously consider it, Mr. Torvald," Colonel Grishin said casually from the doorway. Many of his wounded Marines were on the same floor, and he had come to see what the commotion was about. "She is a very special young lady," he said sadly.

Mills stood behind him, his face an expressionless mask as he glared at Torvald. His hand rested on the pistol that was strapped to his hip.

Eyes darting from the two Marines and back to Dmitri, Torvald said through bleeding lips, "Just what is it that you want, Sikorsky?"

And Dmitri had told him.

Even now, there were days when Dmitri was unable to believe that he had gotten his wish. But thanks to the intervention of Grishin with Commodore Hanson and Admiral Voroshilov, Dmitri's "request" had been granted on Hanson's authority as the senior Confederation representative in the system.

Torvald had been livid, but there was absolutely nothing he could do about it until he returned to Earth. He had the political clout to browbeat President Roze into not having any doctors poke and prod at Valentina, but he had no leverage over the military chain.

Dmitri's request had been simple: he wanted to take care of Valentina. Torvald had finally explained that she would probably never come out of her coma. The cerebral implant she carried was a one-of-a-kind prototype that had only been tested once before. Valentina – Scarlet – had suffered so much neurological trauma that she had been hospitalized for weeks afterward. After a thorough and quite secret review, the program had been abandoned as a failure. The implant had never been removed, Torvald had confessed, because it couldn't be done without causing her irreparable brain damage.

"As long as the implant was dormant," he had explained, "there was no danger to her. But as soon as you plugged her into the ship's navigation system..."

Torvald had wanted to take her home by himself to try and keep the implant's existence as secret as possible. He had quickly learned from Grishin while Sikorsky held Torvald pinned to the wall that there was no longer any point: every soul aboard *Mauritania* knew, and they had passed on the tale to the hospital staff, who in turn had gotten a copy of the *Mauritania's* autodoc scans.

Dmitri forgot all about Torvald as he headed back to the house after feeding their three horses, two mares and a young colt. He had always enjoyed stories and movies involving horses when he was a boy, and it just so happened that CIS's suggested relocation plan for Ludmilla and himself was here. He could not have planned it better.

Washing his hands of the dust and grime of the stables, he went to see Valentina. The CIS would not tell him her real name, and he did not feel right calling her Scarlet. So she was Valentina until she told him otherwise.

His spirits fell at the thought, because she would probably never say another word as long as she lived. *I will not give up hope*, he admonished himself. At least three times a day, every day, for the last six months he had come to spend time with her. They had a live-in nurse, a pleasant older woman who cared for all of the medical necessities, but she could not tend to the young woman's mind and soul. Dmitri knew beyond a shadow of a doubt that Valentina was still there, trying to escape the damage done by the implant. He hoped that every day would be *the* day, the day she came back. He would not stop trying to guide her and comfort her. Never.

He came in and nodded at the nurse, who smiled and left to give them some privacy. Dmitri gently brushed Valentina's hair and fluffed up her pillow, then sat down and took her hand in his. Sometimes he would read to her, sometimes tell her about the latest antics of the horses, or just chat about anything that came to mind. He grinned at himself, knowing that he probably spoke more to Valentina than he did to Ludmilla.

There were other times, like this one, when he simply came to be with her, to hold her hand and let her know that someone was there for her. He gazed out the window at the horses (he had made sure that her room had a good view of the corral), thinking only idle thoughts as time passed. As he sometimes did, he sat back in his chair, still holding her hand, and fell asleep.

When he opened his eyes again, he was still holding her hand, except that something was different: her other hand was gently stroking the back of his. Holding his breath, not daring to hope, he shifted his gaze to her face to see her eyes open, looking at him. She was smiling.

"Dmitri," she said, the sound of her voice filling him with joy, "I knew you wouldn't leave me..."

***

Roland Mills stood on the spot where Emmanuelle had died. Beneath his boots, the scorched and blackened concrete of the landing field was a reflection of his soul. This was the only monument, the only remembrance of her death other than some electronic forms filed by the Corps. There was no monument, no headstone or other marker that others might know that she had died here.

While the Marines had taken back the spaceport months ago, there had not been enough engineers available to clear the wreckage from the field until an engineering regiment had been sent from La Seyne. This was the first time he had been able to come here. There was no marker, nothing special about this patch of concrete, but he knew it was the place where she had given herself up to save him. As hardened to the horrors of war as he had become in the last six months, as dead as he had thought his heart to be, he found himself kneeling down. Just this once, he didn't try to fight it, but let the tears come. She deserved at least that much.

Still serving under Grishin, Mills had been one of the first Marines to return to Saint Petersburg, and had been fighting there ever since. The battles had ebbed and flowed as they rooted out the Kreelans who had been dropped across the planet. But he held out little hope that they would ever succeed in fully driving back the enemy: it seemed that every time they cleared out one area, more Kreelan ships would arrive to drop in more warriors somewhere else.

That was fine with him. It gave him more of them to kill. He knew that even if he killed every single one of them, it would not bring Emmanuelle back to him. But it was all he had left.

"I love you," he whispered, placing his palm on the ground where she had fallen.

Then, wiping the tears from his face, he stood up and silently walked away.

***

President McKenna set down the stylus pad and the electronic copies of the reports she had retrieved earlier. Of necessity, her staff controlled every minute of her day, ensuring that she met the right people and made the necessary decisions to keep the Confederation running. One thing that she had insisted on, however, was at least a full hour each evening that she could spend doing the one thing she had little time for during the rest of the day: thinking.

She rubbed her eyes and then rose from her desk, stretching out the stiff muscles of her legs and back. Another casualty of the war, she thought ruefully as she massaged her aching neck, was her daily exercise routine. Moving over to stand before the windows that looked out on the gleaming lights of New York City, she silently pondered the information she had just reviewed.

Let's review the bad news first, she told herself. A total of fifteen human colonies had been attacked in the six months since the Kreelans reopened their offensive against humanity with the invasions of Saint Petersburg and six other worlds. The number of casualties was uncertain, but Penkovsky's intelligence analysts put the figure at roughly half a million dead. That was a horrible figure, but still paled in comparison to the millions who had died on Keran in the first attack.

Unfortunately, the enemy seemed bent on a long-term war of attrition, committing just enough warriors and ships to keep the humans fully engaged in a multi-front war, but without delivering any knockout blows. As Ichiro Sato had told his commanding officer in a report that had eventually reached McKenna's desk, it seemed as if the Kreelans intended to make the entire human sphere a collection of arenas in which they could satisfy their alien bloodlust.

McKenna wanted to push the enemy back, to give them a brutal kick of strategic proportions, beyond simply defending the worlds under attack. But there had not been enough ships or trained personnel available to do anything more than to throw them into desperate local defensive actions. Under enormous pressure from Joshua Sabine, her defense minister, she had grudgingly authorized the use of nuclear weapons in the hope that what had happened at Saint Petersburg had been a design flaw in the Russian weapons. But in three separate engagements where Confederation ships had used them, the Kreelans had somehow disabled the warheads. Forensic examination of six recovered warheads confirmed the unbelievable findings reported by Admiral Voroshilov: the fissile material had somehow been changed into ordinary lead. It was impossible, yet it had happened. Once those reports reached her, she decided to recall the remaining weapons from the fleet and had them returned to storage. If they were no threat to the Kreelans, she wanted to at least make them protected from potential loss or even theft by some of the colonies that steadfastly refused to join the Confederation.

In the meantime, the military high command had been working out the details for a strategic offensive. She had been impatient for them to finalize their plans, but they had needed time to build the infrastructure necessary to provide the Confederation with the weapons and ships it needed, and time to train the men and women who would use them.

And that brought her to the good news: the military and the industrialists who had been charged with putting the Confederation on a war footing had used those intervening months well. Beginning with Earth and the Alliance worlds, they had transformed the peacetime industrial base, and now several dozen worlds were churning out enough weapons to fully arm the Territorial Army units that were being formed on the Confederation's one hundred and thirty-seven member planets. The Marine Corps was growing at a rapid pace, with a massive new training facility established on a previously unsettled world that was now called Quantico, named in honor one of the training facilities used by the old United States Marine Corps.

Best of all, she thought, were the ships. Just two weeks before, the first of a new class of warship had been launched from the orbital shipyards annexed to Africa Station. The *Lefevre* class battlecruisers were twice as large as the latest heavy cruisers like the one Ichiro Sato had commanded at Saint Petersburg, and had nearly four times as much firepower, plus berthing for a full battalion of Marines. Twenty three more battlecruisers were under construction in various shipyards across the Confederation, and would be launched within the next two weeks. Over one hundred smaller warships, from frigates to heavy cruisers, were being built at the same time, and the shipyards were still being expanded.

Two more months, Admiral Tiernan, her Chief of Naval Staff, had promised her, and the Confederation would be ready to launch its first major strategic offensive campaign against the Empire. McKenna knew that throwing the aliens out of human space would not be easy, nor would it be done quickly.

But by God, she promised herself, *we'll do it. However long and whatever it takes, we'll do it.*

***

Tesh-Dar rode silently on her *magthep*, a two-legged beast that had been used as common transportation by her people since before the first Books of Time had been written. Save for her mount and two others of its kind that carried provisions, she was alone on this trek, as alone as any of her kind could truly be. For the Bloodsong in her veins was a link to her sisters across the Empire. And to the Empress.

Making the decision to return to the Empire had been the most difficult thing Tesh-Dar had ever done in her long life. The wounds to her body, while grievous, were yet trivial for the healers to mend. The injury she had done to her honor was far worse, or so she had thought.

When she regained consciousness, wrapped in a cocoon of soft and warm animal skins in the *kazha* in which she had grown up, Pan'ne-Sharakh had been at her side. As was someone else.

"My Empress," Tesh-Dar whispered, averting her eyes. "Please...forgive me."

The woman who had once been her blood sister gently stroked her face and held her hand. "All is forgiven you, priestess of the Desh-Ka," She said softly. "The powers within you are great, Tesh-Dar, greater, perhaps, than any of your forebears, yet you have never had cause to tap them to the full. You could not have known what would happen; you were not prepared to control it."

"I did not want to," Tesh-Dar told her. "I *chose* not to."

"This, too, I know," She said. "Obedience and duty, even to the Way, may sometimes waver when one's heart is broken."

Her spoken reminder of Li'ara-Zhurah's death sent a fresh wave of anguish through Tesh-Dar's heart. "You could have saved her," she whispered.

"With great honor did she die," the Empress told her. "It would have been a disservice to Li'ara-Zhurah to deny her sacrifice. You know this."

Unwillingly, Tesh-Dar nodded, realizing that her thoughts had become so clouded by her own emotions that she had completely lost sight of the path, of the Way. "I am lost, my Empress," she said.

"No, my child," the Empress told her, "you have merely come to a part of the Way that you have never before traveled, where the path is *not* clear. Children can follow the Way as a path of stones laid out in a line, but they could not find their way in a dark forest. It is this forest that you must enter now, Tesh-Dar, a place where your wisdom and faith will be tested. Few have reached so far as you; even Sura-Ni'khan, powerful as she was, had not come this far."

"What must I do, my Empress?" Tesh-Dar asked.

"You must return to your roots," She told her, "to the temple of your order. There shall you learn how to follow the Way, not as would a child in spirit, but as the great warrior that you are."

"How long?" Tesh-Dar asked.

"You will know," She said, "when my heart calls to thee." With one last caress of Tesh-Dar's face before She turned to leave, the Empress said softly, "May thy way be long and glorious, Legend of the Sword."

Throughout the exchange with the Empress, Pan'ne-Sharakh had stood in reverent silence. Now, she said, "A gift for you, I have," she said proudly as she reached down from where she knelt next to Tesh-Dar. In her hands, as she raised it up where Tesh-Dar could see it, was a sword.

"Oh, mistress," Tesh-Dar breathed. The black scabbard gleamed like a dark mirror. The handle, wrapped in matte black leather, was studded with diamonds that spelled out Tesh-Dar's name in the Old Tongue. Tesh-Dar felt a deep pang of guilt, suddenly remembering that she had lost her sword, the one Pan'ne-Sharakh had made for her earlier, on the human planet.

Knowing exactly what Tesh-Dar was thinking, the old armorer told her, "The other sword was but a toy compared to *this*." With a smile, Pan'ne-Sharakh drew the blade partway out of the scabbard, exposing the living metal into which she had poured her soul since Tesh-Dar's return. It did not simply gleam in the light, it shimmered, as if the metal reflected the water of a pond, its surface driven by the wind. "This is the greatest level of my craft," she said, "the finest that any of us, in all the ages, has ever done. This, to you, is my gift, that it may see you through the challenges you will face where you now are bound..."

The sword hung as a welcome weight on her back as she rode, with the ancient short sword of the Desh-Ka in its scabbard at her side.

She brought the *magthep* to a halt for a moment, letting it and its companions catch their breath from the climb up the mountains. It was a long trek from the *kazha*, over thirty days' travel, to reach this place. Above her, on a massive overhang that jutted out beneath the peak of the mountain, stood the temple of the Desh-Ka. She had last been here when Sura-Ni'khan passed on the stewardship of the order to Tesh-Dar, and the site of it sent a tingle of anticipation down her spine as she urged her *magthep* onward.

The temple was a collection of massive structures built from green stone that once had boasted carvings depicting warriors in battle, telling the tale of the ancients who had first formed the order. The temple had been erected so long ago that the carvings in the hard stone were worn nearly smooth from the work of wind and rain, and most of the structures had fallen into ruin.

Yet the stone was merely a façade, for the true temple was formed by the spirits of her forebears that yet dwelt here. When she had first come with Sura-Ni'khan, many cycles ago, she could feel a presence in the place, could hear the quiet murmur of the Ancient Ones in the Bloodsong.

Now, she could sense them clearly. Among them, she heard the melody of her own priestess, Sura-Ni'khan, beckoning to her.

Guiding her animals to the entrance to the only part of the temple that had not succumbed to time, a great domed arena, the largest of the structures in this ancient place, she dismounted. After quickly removing the packs she had brought, she freed the animals of their bridles and harnesses.

"Go where you would," she told them, gently slapping the rump of her mount, sending it trotting off, its companions close behind. She had no need of them here, and she suspected she would be here for quite some time before the Empress called for her.

Time, she thought, *in this place has no meaning.* Pushing open the massive door to the ancient enclosed arena, she stepped into the darkness and the embrace of the spirits that awaited her.

Discover Other Books By Michael R. Hicks

The *In Her Name* Series

First Contact
Legend Of The Sword
Dead Soul
Empire
Confederation
Final Battle
From Chaos Born

"Boxed Set" *In Her Name* Collections

In Her Name (Omnibus)
In Her Name: The Last War

Thrillers

Season Of The Harvest

Visit **AuthorMichaelHicks.com** for the latest updates!

AFTERWORD

I would like to personally thank you for purchasing and reading this book. Writing the story of the Human-Kreelan war has been – and continues to be – a great deal of fun for me, and I sincerely hope that you enjoyed reading it as much as I enjoyed writing it!

Please consider taking a little extra time to help others find this book by leaving feedback where you purchased it. Your opinion does truly matter, both to myself and to other readers.

If you have any questions, comments, or suggestions, please don't hesitate to contact me through my web site at AuthorMichaelHicks.com.

- Michael R. Hicks

About the Author

Born in 1963, Michael Hicks grew up in the age of the Apollo program and spent his youth glued to the television watching the original Star Trek series and other science fiction movies, which continues to be a source of entertainment and inspiration. Having spent the majority of his life as a voracious reader, he has been heavily influenced by writers ranging from Robert Heinlein to Jerry Pournelle and Larry Niven, and David Weber to S.M. Stirling. Living in Maryland with his beautiful wife, two wonderful stepsons and two mischievous Siberian cats, he continues to work full-time while dreaming and writing.

CPSIA information can be obtained at www.ICGtesting.com
Printed in the USA
BVOW02s1151211113

336954BV00001B/32/P